UNRAVELING
ARVA

NICOLE LUNDRIGAN

UNRAVELING
ARVA

NICOLE LUNDRIGAN

jesperson
publishing

100 Water Street
P. O. Box 2188
St. John's, NL
A1C 6E6

National Library of Canada Cataloguing in Publication Data

Lundrigan, Nicole
   Unraveling Arva / Nicole Lundrigan.

ISBN 1-894377-05-2
I. Title.
PS8573.U5436U67 2003   C813'.6
C2003-905281-8

Design/Layout: Freak Design   afreake@roadrunner.nf.net

Photography: Stephen Tizzard
Editor: Jocelyne Thomas

Although Upper Island Cove is an actual community on the East Coast of Newfoundland, its portrayal in Unraveling Arva contains several fictitious elements necessary for the progression of the story. Names are fictitious, and any similarity to real persons either living or dead is coincidental and not intended by the author.

Printed in Canada.

For my mother, Nancy Lundrigan

1

The water sang to me, you know. Of course that sounds just crazy, but it's absolutely true.

Once upon a time I was just like you, only hearing the clatter of a wave. I would listen to its salty tongue, how it frothed over a million rounded stones. Years earlier I suspected a message was disguised in those sudsy fingers, but I could not decipher it, and never thought to try.

Yes, yes, that was me. Everything was a mystery, the gurgles and the gulps. Until one afternoon I caught the whisper, a coded rumour trapped inside the ocean's spray. It was a melody, a soothing stream of poems, its ebb and flow a perfect rhyme.

Someone was there, you think. At first I thought so too. I glanced up to the edge of the cliff. My gaze roamed the jagged rocks, and I checked every inch of the path down to the water. Not a soul to be seen. There was only a mossy brush of lichens and those bitter black berries you often tried to eat, and they were both without a word to say. Then I heard a second sigh. Stronger now. It tickled my ears like the tufts of cotton I stuff in during thunder.

At first, I was fearful. I marched right up to Bette Mackay's biscuit box on the hill and rapped at her door. I knocked so hard, burgundy paint came away and clung to my knuckles like flecks of dried blood. While I waited, a naughty gust teased through my hair, fluttered my dress. Then that wind stole a peep at my slip. I knew instantly what it wanted. There were hints everywhere.

Without hesitation, I asked Bette if it was natural for a

woman. The sheer force of it all, to have your mind filled with wonder. But the mound between her eyebrows only grew and several silver hairs sprouted out from her mousy mop. "Ave ye bin drinkin'?" she said. "Or else yer near gone mad. Don't go'round tellin' no one dat, woman, or ye'll be shipped to the Waterford so fast yer shadow'll crack off." Poor Bette. What to expect from a woman who can't hold onto the beginning long enough to grasp the end?

Water called me back day after day. Whenever I could, I went. There was much to know now, and with so many voices, concentrating was an honest hardship.

But tide was patient. It told me how to move. And I listened to every word.

Hooking her fingers between damp boards stained with fish guts and gull splatter, Arva House was able to lean out over a wharf in Upper Island Cove. She stared at her reflection in the sea. Calm water in the darkness always made her cringe, but she did not look away. She was certain her mirror image was obscuring a whole world of murky dealings just underneath the polished surface. Before her eyes, smooth-edged shadows coursed through the depths, slivers of bottle green flickered and dissolved. Then a burst of gassy bubbles rumbled up and boiled her watery face.

From somewhere well beyond the wharf, Arva heard the sound of her mother's voice spitting hasty instructions into the evening air. "If it budges, Arva, don't bawl out. Fetch me instead."

Arva remembered that night, how she fixed her sleepy eyes on the overflowing slop bucket. Within it, a damp coppery mass remained motionless, the attached baggage limp on the grass. The only movement came from copious pockets of air sliding up behind the ears, popping to release a stench of fermented sugar. The hair fluttered, but everything else was still. So Arva had stood, chilled by pervasive dampness, and waited for her mother to appear at the edge of the cliff.

As the voice withered back into memory, Arva watched the sea. For a moment, she expected to see a flash of ghostly skin rolling like a playful seal in the moonlight. But there was noth-

_ing. She was alone. Everything was restful, except for the thin ropes of fog drifting out from beneath the wharf and tangling around her ankles.

The very next evening, the wind was still dormant, though it had not left the cove. Resting just beyond a rocky ledge, it was rolling itself into a gust, building strength, drawing up salt from the sea. And for the time being, it would stay there, waiting to tease knitted hats, sneak in around doorframes, tug at coattails, and tempt tears from dry eyes. Earlier that night, Lolly Young had prayed to God for calm, no wind to muss her hair.

Halfway up Main Road, jigs and reels could be heard, sweet-talking their way out of the worn building and into the warm air. The local Legion, seated conveniently at the foot of the mountain, was within walking distance for most. With paint flaking on the outside, graying everywhere else, it had become a meeting place for old fishermen. When they were not out on the waters jigging freckled-skinned cod or eating a supper in their steamy kitchens, the men were found here, ample rumps planked on worn wooden stools, drinks at the tips of their fishy fingers, mouths talking all kinds of talk.

Though tonight there was not a tired-eyed fisherman in sight. Both doors were swung wide so the young ones could have a time.

Inside, young men decorated the walls, shirtsleeves sharp, their hair locked in greasy combat with their scalps. Hard-soled shoes tapped the linoleum and women's dresses swished like stunned moths. There was a needy smell, clinging to the clothes in the way fried-out fatback permeates a woolen coat hung on the handle of a pantry door.

Wearing a watery-blue buttoned dress, Arva felt neither particularly confident nor particularly ill at ease as she walked down the decline and stepped through those double doors. She had never been to a dance before, had no expectations, and therefore no reason to feel much in the way of excitement or anxiety. Though Lolly knew this, she kept her arm slung loosely around Arva's waist, coaxing her forward like a reluctant child.

"We don't bite 'round here, me dear," Lolly said just loudly enough to prick up a few ears. "Ye needn't be nervous 'bout this crowd."

People shuffled aside slightly, letting Arva and Lolly through. "What're ye gawkin' at?" Lolly said to one woman, whose mouth was gaping wide, her eyes on Arva without a blink. Then to Arva, "Ye'd think I was cartin' in the Queen herself."

Arva knew the reaction well, so it was little surprise. People often stared at her, turning as she strode past, speaking words in a whisper. She simply stood out, although she never really made a genuine attempt to blend in. "You're no raving beauty," her mother had once said when she found Arva, hair piled atop her head, gazing into a mirror, "and you're not rock-cod ugly. So you should let well enough alone and be satisfied with that."

Her mother had spoken the truth, Arva was somewhere in between, but not regular or ordinary by any means. Her hair, like a slash, was too black, and her skin just a few shades too brown, especially after a summer of sunshine. But it was her eyes that often made people divert their glances. She had a stare that could cause indigestion, a look that was too close to that of a damaged animal's, an old dog gone silent, its story swallowed down with its growl.

Most people Arva had seen in the harbour and beyond were under-a-stone pale, reddish almost. They had eyes that were a pleasing assortment of seafoam green, honeyed brown, clean wintry blue. If their hair were dark, the sun would waste no time and flicker out light tinges. Strip-of-lawn sideburns, down the sides of most men's faces, were almost always smattered with brown, gray, and telltale red whiskers. At one glance, it was an easy guess: Irish through and through.

"Hey Lolly Dolly," Frank Smith called out when they were well into the Legion, smoke thick like the worst kind of fog.

"Hey Frankie Spankie," Lolly replied, hand plumping her pin curls. Frank reached for her wrist, but with a quick twist, skirt fanning, she dodged his hand. "Jeez Frankie," she said, smirk over her shoulder, "can't ye do any better than that?" Then to Arva, "C'mon, me love, let's snag a nip."

Lolly took Arva by the arm, and used a firm grip to guide her to the back of the room. There, the bar was not much more than painted lengths of wood nailed firmly in place, the boards smoothed from ever-present elbows and being slapped so often with laughter. Lolly ordered a gin and lime, no, two. One for

Arva, here.

"Who's yer pal?" Frank asked as he sidled up next to Lolly.

"Don't even think about it, Frankie," Lolly said, taking a generous swallow. "She's nowhere near that desperate to be after the likes of a Smith."

"Ye got more lip than a flatfish," Frank said as he was towed to the dance floor, waist hooked, reeled in, quick nod of his head to Arva.

Lolly leaned back, forearms behind her on the bar, dark crease of cleavage catching eyes. "Like I says," she whispered. "Everyone's askin' 'bout ye. Sure as Hell don't look nothin' like the crowd 'round here." She clicked pink fingernails against the glass in her hand. "Ye've been here for near three months now, me love. Cooped up at Old Man Crane's. Not much of a man to have in yer life." Lolly laughed, displaying her small stubby teeth. "Time the real men had a go at ye."

Lolly Young had lived in Upper Island Cove since she first cried for attention some twenty-two years ago. Her father was a fisherman who, like most fishermen in the bay, never swam a length in his life. He was inhaling his last mouthfuls of water round about the time when Lolly was inhaling her first mouthfuls of air. Tossed overboard when a whitecap pitched his dory, Lyle Young was brought back to shore, drenched, bitter cold, and completely lifeless on the floor of his best friend's boat. Lolly's mother Rose remained faithful to Lyle's ghost, and never did crave the doting gaze of another. Though, in all honesty, this was more than likely due to the lack of doting gazes available.

"'Tis all 'bout Lolly now," she had said to Alf Jones shortly after the funeral. "And that's the extent of it. She's his only daughter."

"Seems so," he had answered, speech slurring from the liberal amounts of whiskey served to take the edge off the grief. "Don't say he'll be havin' no more where he's goin'. Though ye never knows."

Arva had met Lolly when she moved into Old Man Crane's house. Lolly and her mother lived next door in an identical three-bedroom clapboard bungalow, theirs sunshine yellow, the Cranes' dried-blood red. Arva had been in the kitchen not more than an hour when the porch door opened, a young woman strolled in, lipstick first, cheerful face next, loaf of bread under her broad arm last.

"Anythin' ye needs, me love, Mother and me are right next door," Lolly had said, getting comfortable on the daybed. "Though don't go askin' Mother for too much, mind yerself, she's as crooked as sin today. And, oh yes, she sent this over for ye." Lolly handed Arva the double-mounded brown loaf. "Figured ye mighten'd of had time to bake up a batch yet."

Both the Young and Crane homes were literally carved into the mountain, embedded down deep in solid rock. From the living room window, they could tell at a glance if the day was calm or windy by the caps on the waves. Never a question about the temperature, it was almost always cold. Looking out over the kitchen sink at the back of the house, there was a clear view of the mountain, shady dimples of a cave or two, a wayward sheep nuzzling at the grass.

Alice Stone, Old Man Crane's daughter, had happily left the cove, and moved to Holyrood when she married Ron Stone, son of Morton, the largest homebuilder in Conception Bay South. Shortly after Arva's mother had passed on, she took a room with Alice to help her care for her three, soon to be four, young sons. "All I ever wanted for meself was a daughter," Alice had said when she first met Arva. "Teach her how to knit, how to crochet. And see what I got, a trio of little men. And I reckons this one'll make it a quartet." She rubbed her pregnant lump. "Ron is right pleased."

On the weekends, Alice had to travel with the baby to Upper Island Cove and care for her father. His lungs, grown weary of breathing, were quickly filling with smut like a moldy sponge. She would make enough loaves to last him, throw a few handfuls of lime down the outhouse hole, and irritate her skin washing his bed sheets with near boiling water and lye in her dead mother's galvanized bucket. Arva stayed behind with three of the boys, cooked meals on an electric stove, scrubbed the indoor bathroom, and twisted load after load of wet laundry through the wringer of Alice's brand new washer. It was the first opportunity Arva ever had to take a warm bath.

When Old Man Crane became too ill to take care of himself, he was too obstinate to move to Holyrood, though Alice never actually asked. She invited Arva to spend some time in the cove. There the air was so clean, according to Alice, Arva would not recognize the smell. Would she have the heart to go, enjoy the company of a few of the young people, and bide her time till he passed?

"'Tis a lovely little town," she had said. "Neighbours are right friendly and helpful, ye probably won't spend a minute alone with Father. His back door's never locked."

Alice began to fold laundry, snapping out a pair of clean jeans hardened from the clothesline. "Ethel Drover looks in on him in the mornin'," she continued, "and Clarice Lynch checks in at night. But, he needs full-time care, Arva. I means Mother's been dead near twenty years, now. God only knows if he ever cooked a meal for hisself since I left him." Alice laid the jeans on the kitchen table, pulled a second crisp pair from the basket. "He needs more than a visit or two from those old women, God bless them both, ye hears me, but I can't dig up me life here. I've worked too long to get where I is. I won't do it."

Arva agreed, really having little choice. She was used to moving, it was the way she had lived all those years with her mother. She stepped past Alice, went to her room just off the kitchen, and began to arrange the contents in her steel blue trunk.

"He's right like a baby, now," she heard Alice say. "No, not even. A baby I can take. More like a stubborn old boot." Then she stopped talking, no doubt for fear that Arva might change her mind.

Arva arrived by taxi in the afternoon to find Old Man Crane tucked into his marriage bed, his body no more than a wrinkle in the fabric. Behind his discolored pillow towered a sturdy wooden headboard with two panels. Carved was a man and woman, in modest farmer clothes, each holding a sheaf of wheat in hand. He rested underneath the man panel, and below the woman's side, the soft mattress still bore a lonely well-worn sag.

Arva noticed a large metal chair with a pale blue plastic seat and catcher bucket next to his bed.

"'Tis for me business," he said, his voice surprisingly strong. "That's 'bout as fancy as it gets. Ye won't be findin' stuff from Alice's house 'round here. Ye too good for a outhouse?"

"No, Mr. Crane," Arva replied. "I'm quite accustomed to it actually."

The air was fatigued and unresponsive, stale from being over-breathed. Drawing back the heavy green curtains, Arva noticed startled dust scattering in the light. The window had been painted shut; she would have to take a knife to it.

"Now then," he said. "Ye needn't be thinkin' to yerself yer goin' to oust this ol' man." His 's' sounds were a muffled whistle, quivering lips no longer supported by teeth.

"I have no such intention, Mr. Crane."

"I's got a right to die in me own home."

"I think so."

"Wha?" he replied, tilting his head closer.

"I said, I think so," she answered, a little louder.

"Now, then. Let's get on with it. S'pose ye wants to take a gander at me."

"Nothing I'd like better," Arva replied and saw his watery eyes soften.

"Go on with ye, then."

When Arva lifted the cotton sheets, she smelled the odour of a long forgotten library book, damp, musty, and full of knowledge. His skin, parchment paper thin, looked wrapped in a blue and white roadmap of veins. Hands and feet were pastry flaky, his thickened nails ridged and deeply jaundiced. But it was his night-gown that had caught her eye, diluted of colour, coming barely to his knee. Even though it had been washed in lye so often, the pale flower print was still detectable. It had belonged to a woman.

"I's not queer in the head yet, Arva," he said as she pulled a fresh blanket up to his chin, propping his head with a pair of pillows. "Keeps me close to her, is all. Know what I means?"

"I do," she said, her hand, mind of its own, reaching up to touch the dull silvery dragonfly at the base of her neck.

"How old are ye anyways? Yer no more than eleven, twelve, I'd say."

"Not quite. Just turned eighteen."

"Well, now then. I's close enough. House, hey? Yer not from 'round here with a name like that."

"No. From Bonavista, and the like. Trinity Bay, too. We moved around some." Arva took a chair next to his bed, its seat a rose embroidered from thick wool thread.

"Yer father fish?"

"No, never fished. Didn't like the water." She folded her hands in her lap.

"Never could trust..." his words cut by a hack into his handkerchief, stiffened with phlegm, his chest rippling. "... a Newfie who didn't love the water. Not much else to love, really."

"Yes. Although I remember he'd go out for a run after he took a drink or two."

"Wha?" he said, eyes squinty.

"He would take a run after a drink," she raised her voice further, spoke slowly.

"Well, then. That's somethin'." He rattled again, a chained ghost in his chest. "Yer mother, could she put on a decent meal?"

"Oh, yes. She'd cook pea soup, or fish and brewis. Boiled rice pudding. That's what I recall most."

His eyes opened wide, tongue to his bottom lip. "Good Lord, I's already dead and gone to heaven. Finally, Alice has done me right, sendin' ye out here." He curled his lips, revealing receded pink gums, and made a snapping sound as he clamped them together. "Don't go usin' too much ol' spice though, and keep me away from that whiskey bottle, for Jesus' sake, or ye won't get me clear of me potty."

"I'll keep that in mind," Arva said. "Cup of tea? Slice of porridge bread? I brought a fresh loaf with me. Baked it in Holyrood at Alice's house this morning. And there's also bread from the lady next door, if you'd prefer that."

"From Rose? That loaf is likely tough as a gad. Couldn't get me teeth through it if I tried." Another snap of the gums. "I'll give yers a go. And a drop of tea. Yes, a bit of both. Bring 'em on, maid."

Arva went into his dimly lit kitchen, overshadowed by a rocky ledge, and returned a few moments later with a warm teapot, flowery cup and saucer, and a hefty slice of light brown sweet bread. She poured some of the rich orange brew into his cup, an escaped tealeaf floating near the surface. He lifted the cup and slopped hot tea into his saucer.

"Cools it," he said as Arva watched him. "Don't want me burnin' me lips off, now, do ye? I'd be some sight then, nar tooth in me head, nar lip on me face." He gummed at the bread, making little squelching noises. "Jesus, 'tis uncanny. Just like me Peggy's. Yer mother must've been some fine cook."

"She was. Yes. And she taught me."

"Good woman," he said, snapping his gums again. "And I loves to eat. Ye can tell by the size of me."

Arva gazed into his face, a dried apple on stick shoulders, his eyes opaque, slushy. She had been this close to death before, had been there often, in fact. Death seemed to follow her, or maybe, she followed it, she could not be sure. But, as often as she had watched it, saw it lingering close by before it took hold, dying never quite seemed this pleasant.

"I can see ye sizin' me up, missus, and I knows what yer thinkin'. Ye wouldn't guess it, that a weary old trout like meself used to be a real looker when he was yer age." A sunken grin. "Maid, if I was a bit younger and could move these old legs, ye'd have somethin' to worry 'bout. Ye can be sure of that."

"Yes, Mr. Crane. I have no doubt." She smiled.

Arva picked up the baby-soft brush from the dusty nightstand and began to detangle the determined hairs that refused to release from his scalp, his skin loose and spotted like the backside of a toad.

"Jesus. Wait 'til I's finished with me bit of bread before ye starts pickin' at me."

"Pardon me," Arva said.

He chewed down another bite, a slurp from his saucer, louder than it needed to be.

"Wha?"

"I said 'pardon me.'" Louder.

He put down his bread, leaned back, closed his eyes. "Alright now, get on with it. Don't forget me comb-over," he said as Arva began. "Oh, Lord. I loves a set of hands on me scalp. Use a spot of cream from that tube in the drawer, maid. I can't have the ladies comin' in here thinkin' I's losin' me last bit of hair."

"Yes. We can't have that."

"Wha?"

"We can't have that," said Arva, her voice high, straining.

"Ah, Jesus," he said, eyes wide open, a choked-up chuckle. "I heard ye the first time, me love. I can heed a pin drop, if I cares to."

Arva thought to take his dry hand in hers, but hesitated, never did. He slurped his tea, snapped his gums as hard as he could right onto the porridge bread, and winked at her. She found it difficult to believe that someone edging close to death was still completely alive, his spirit not faded, not yet beginning the lengthy transition. She knew from those last years with her mother that people could be dead, dreams dried up, souls withered, just knocking about inside empty barrels waiting to be lifted up, loaded on, and moved out. But that was not the case for Old Man Crane. His presence filled an entire room, spilled out into the hallway. It took her breath away.

"What a wild time," Lolly said when she returned, tripping in shoes too small. She lit a cigarette, inhaled deeply, and then smoothed the back of her full skirt, hair rumpled, cheeks like hot coals.

"I should be getting back, Lolly," Arva said, rising from a wooden bench. "Mrs. Drover doesn't want to be there too late. She told me she's got to finish getting ready for tomorrow."

"Ah, Jesus. The Lord loves Ethel. Yes He does," Lolly said. "Ethel on a Sunday. Ye'd think she was a minister's wife, the way she gets on."

Ethel Drover had told Arva earlier that night she was a good Anglican, brought up in strict religious fashion. She knew it was sinful to lift a hand on any given Sunday not like the young people today, leaving everything to the last minute, sinning left and right. Her potatoes and carrots were already peeled, sitting in a dish of water on the porch floor. Her wood was piled by the woodstove, linoleum clean, chicken stuffed with dried bread, drop of butter, pinch of savory. All she would have to do was pull pins from her rollers, dress, put splits on the fire, bring a pot of water to a boil, and open the oven door for the meal. "Nar sin there, surely, me dear," Ethel had said.

"Arva, I was only gone twenty minutes," Lolly continued, sipping a fresh gin and lime soda. "The fun's just beginnin'. And, look, here comes the Lord Almighty hisself. The mighty Clive Mercer."

Arva glanced up to see a man swimming through the smoke, his body obscure, face vague until he was only a few feet away. But she had already recognized his shape, like a catch rising up through murky waters revealing itself just before it breaks the surface.

"Well, well, Miss Lolly," he spoke. "Who's yer friend?"

She strung her sweaty arm through Arva's and leaned in hard. "Clive, this here's Arva House," she said. "The angel who's been changin' Old Man Crane's dirty diapers. I finally hauled her out, brought her down here meself."

"Hello Arva House," he said. "Clive Mercer."

"Steer clear of he," Lolly said, tightening her grip around Arva's arm. "He's a born actor."

"Don't be talkin', Lolly," he muttered, arms crossed, eyes hard. "No one's listenin' to what ye got to say."

Lolly let out a puff of air like a breaching whale, and said, "Oh, dry up, Clive." She flounced off, skirt bouncing around her backside, a splash of gin and lime slopping down onto her shoe.

"Seems like ye don't know too many people," he said. "Lolly's not much of a friend to leave ye standin' here."

Arva wondered for a moment if Lolly was a friend. Lolly sauntered into the kitchen nearly everyday, early mornings on the weekends, afternoons during the weekdays. When Arva was with Old Man Crane, she would hear a rattle, cupboards opening, kettle lifted from the stove. "I'll just make meself at home," she would always call out. To which Old Man Crane would invariably reply, "That one's back to wag her tongue again for an hour. I don't how 'tis yer ears are still hinged on, me dear." Arva imagined that Lolly had told her, in full breathy voice, every single thing about herself from earliest memory onward. Then, after a spill of stories, Lolly's mouth would close, she would hold her breath, hesitating for only a moment to encourage Arva's own narrative to drift out naturally. When she met with silence, Lolly seemed obliged to carry on, her meandering tale continuing to overflow from a bottomless culvert.

"She lives next door to Mr. Crane," Arva said finally.

"Yes, I knows right where Lolly lives. Half the men in the harbour do." A light chuckle. "Will ye be stayin' in the cove long?" he said, then cleared his throat.

"I'll be here until Mr. Crane is back on his feet," she said.

"It'll be a while before Skipper is back on his feet, from what I've been hearin'."

"You may be right," she said. "He doesn't seem to be getting much better."

"I'll stop up and pay a visit," he said.

"You're more than welcome," she said. "He loves company."

Arva considered this man who now stood so close to her, his body not too tall, not too skinny. He had one foot up on a wooden chair near Arva, but kept his eyes turned away, feigning interest in the opposite wall, though it was barely visible through the choking smoke. Yes, he was handsome in a way, well laid-out like a rowed vegetable garden or a pegged hardwood floor. His smile was practiced, easy, a penny in the hand of a child. Brown hair tousled, thinning but still there, his eyes, toast burnt black.

"Would ye like to take a walk?" he asked, turning his gaze towards her.

A simple request, Arva thought. One that gets asked every day of young children, single women, lifelong men friends needing to discuss something necessary away from the crowd. Yet she had never been asked to take a walk. She had often walked with her mother, actually, walked, no. She kept up, close behind, with a steady run, followed by a quick paced step, soon to lag behind, a steady run again. Her mother never walked, never placed one foot in front of the other in that relaxed way people do when strolling for pleasure. "Too slow, Arva, you're too slow," she had always said. Her gait had the swiftness of purpose, direction, a subconscious need. But they never seemed to go anywhere, up to the top of a cliff or hill, her mother would stop to stare at the ocean, breathing slowing, shawl tugged tightly around her shoulders. Always she would whisper into the wind. Sometimes she would weep, more often not. After a few moments of standing, another wrinkle etched into her drained face, she would say, "Let's get back to the house, my love. I've got a chill coming on."

"I'd love to," she said to Clive. Then she added, "A walk. Yes, a walk," just in case he had forgotten his question.

He reached out his hand to her, a secure grip, and together they left the Legion. As he led her to the wharf, she slipped out of her shoes and felt the dried smooth boards warm beneath her feet. The wharf was littered with coils of wet rope, mounds of netting, a wall of handmade lobster pots. Other couples passed by, a man winked at Clive, one said, 'Nice night,' another, 'Good to see ye.' The women, eyes arrow-straight ahead, never uttered a word.

Clive removed his shoes as well and rolled up his pant legs.

They sat, shoulders almost touching, on the edge of the wharf. Water lapped, but the licks never stroked their toes, never cooled their ankles. She leaned over to see ancient barnacles crusting onto the support posts, seaweed, relaxed like a drunk, rising and falling with each slap of the tide.

"Are ye feelin' sick?" he asked.

"No, no," she replied. "Just looking."

"Not much to see, I doubts."

"Oh, I think so. Life finding a way, no matter where."

"I don't see no charm to it. Told Father the day he died he won't be catchin' me out on the water when he's lookin' down from above. Told him I'd never touch a raw fish again. Can't stand the smell of fish guts on me hands." He lit a cigarette, inhaled deeply, the wind shoving smoke back into his sturdy face. "Me father lived out on that water. Thought I'd do the same. No ma'am."

"Oh God," said Arva. "Tell me I'm not a 'ma'am' already."

His head still facing the water, he caught a glimpse of her through one shiny eye, a cod scanning for supper. "Hardly. Yer no more than a maid, a young maid, me dear." He nudged her shoulder, taking another drag of the cigarette, the reddened butt a beacon to his mouth. "As soon as I gets a bit more money, I's goin' to haul me ass out of here," he continued.

"I've been here just three months. I'm still enjoying it."

"Enjoying it? Ye must be cracked. Rocks in yer head. I can barely breathe here. Ye can't blow yer nose without someone else hearin' 'bout it."

"I guess that's what a small town is like. You have to try and give them nothing worth discussing."

"They'll find somethin', and if they don't, someone'll make somethin' up."

Arva could think of no response. Talk often spun around her as she stood silent, trying to avoid the woozy feeling that descended upon her when people's mouths rushed with reports, tongues pounded out intelligence, flared nostrils sucked in air so that lips need not brake. And so, instead she said, "Mr. Crane is wonderful. A real joy. No trouble for an old man. Not what I'd expected, really."

"Must of come on with the age. He was always into somethin'

when he was younger. Some kind of trouble." Clive leaned his head in close to Arva's. "Old Man Crane was right bent on makin' moonshine. Liked a drop, but never drank much, mind ye. Must've made a mint in sales, though he rarely spent a cent."

"Well, he's not into much now, except for a good game of cribbage and a few yarns."

"Really. What sorts of stuff is he on 'bout?"

"Oh, he's got a story or two about everyone. Nothing too off-colour, though."

"Don't listen to a word he got to say, maid," Clive said, clapping his hands together. "He's soft in the head."

Clive had seen Arva two months earlier, striding up the gravel lane at a good pace with a brown paper bag in her arms, wind whipping her black hair in every direction. He thought to stop, take her bag, carry it up the hill, but figured she would find that childish, high-schoolish. Nothing a man would do.

Since that day, he thought of her constantly, her image nagging somewhat uncomfortably at his mind during the strangest moments, when he was relieving himself, when he looked at his mother cutting meat for stew, when Alek stuck his ugly mug in his and bugged him to confess, confess, confess. "I's not bloody Catholic," he had said, and smacked Alek in the gob. "Now, now, b'ys," his mother had said. "If only yer father was here. Ye wouldn't be getting' on with the likes of that." Then, a memory of his father, catching him by the collar, dragging him from his cozy bed, Alek asleep, drooling like a swine, and there she was, Arva's sway, her thin hips, sharp nose, olive skin, tanned and freckled.

Now, she was arm's length, even closer.

"Mother says yer mother drowned in the harbour 'cross the way," Clive said. The bay was shaped like a horseshoe, Arva and Clive sitting on a wharf on one side, her mother's body having floated up by a wharf on the other.

She never spoke for a moment, but stared out across the water, trying to locate the very spot, impossible though, as it was miles away. "Yes," she said. "Yes, she did."

"Sorry to hear it," he said. "Real sorry."

Her fingers knotting together in her lap. "Thank-you."

She had a way, Clive thought, of thinking before she spoke, or not speaking at all. He made a note to watch his accent, hold more tightly to his h's and let a few of the extras go. Laziness, was all it was, he knew how to talk right. He was a schoolteacher, for God's sake. Who to set the example if not he? She made him want to talk proper, be proper, not like the rest of them. Most of the girls in the bay had bodies like bread dough, just starting to rise. He could see the baked loaf in their mothers and was interested in neither heel nor slice. They drank too, those girls. Nothing more tasteless than a drinking woman, slipping in her shoes, ready. His mother never let a drop come across her lips. Of course he liked the drink every bit as much as the next man, always had a taste for it, even as a child when he'd steal the last sip of beer, loved it. But it wasn't the same on a woman. It was a man's smell. Mixed in with a pack of smokes. Then there was that ignorant way some women breathed through their mouths. He couldn't stand it. They were good enough to have, of course, wouldn't any man feel the same? But he'd never want to spend an hour with one in any type of conversation. No b'y. When he was with one, if he closed his eyes he'd start thinking about his brother. And that's saying something he didn't want to hear.

But Arva, no, she was different. God, yes, right different. Something to put under his tongue, savour in his mouth. She could pull him up and out of this cove. She'd never belong here, never fit in. Like himself, he always thought. The only place they could go together would be somewhere far from here. Away from Alek, a bag of stones on his back. His bloody mother, a constant rattle in the kitchen. Yes, a good distance away. And wherever that was was exactly where he wanted to be.

"I don't want to stay here, Arva, without seein' the world, without at least seein' somethin'," he said, coughing lightly, taken aback by his openness.

"I'm sure you won't, Clive," she said. Arva started to reach out her hand, but brought it back to her lap. "I'm sure you won't."

Behind them, the evening air tore with a crackle of haughty laughter. Patty Lynch, standing just steps away with Frank Smith, had been as absorbed in the conversation as they were. "Good luck, Clive," she said, with a grin, wet mouth shining. "Good luck to ye, me son."

Clive leaned back towards her, his top lip curled. "Go home to yer mother Patty. No one wants ye here." He pushed in closer to Arva. "Lobsters, they is, the whole lot of 'em. Bloody lobsters. We're all boilin' in this pot together, heaven forbid one tries to climb out. The others, they's on ye like flies to garbage, haulin' ye back in."

He rested his elbow on his knee, thumbnail stuck in the space between his front teeth, and gazed out. Silence coiled in like a tress of fog. After moments, he turned his head and looked at her squarely, cod's eye replaced with full striking face. "Yer really lovely," he said. "Really lovely."

Arva thought of how to respond. 'I'm glad you think so,' came to mind, but it seemed too ridiculous an answer. How could she share that, yes, at this very moment, she did feel lovely, absolutely lovely. An unfamiliar lightness had entered her, and if a word escaped, she might collapse, shrink down right there on the wharf, get rinsed away again. So, she kept her still tongue behind her front teeth, and instead intently watched the waves swallow and burp, swallow and burp. She hoped the night sky did not divulge her flushed cheeks, her glassy eyes.

Clive leaned over, his sweet breath on her neck, then up to her mouth. He kissed her, lips and tongue tingled, alert, gratified. Time slowed to a deliciously frustrating pace, like the last drip of sweet molasses on a cold, cold day.

He stood up, slipped into his shoes. "Let me walk ye home," he said as he reached for her hand, pulled her to her feet, weightless as she was.

2

I don't know why I did it. Convention, I guess. Some strand of me still trusted in it, thought it was a solid choice when I was fast becoming disillusioned with my watery companion. There. You have it. That's mostly why I married.

The asking part was simple enough. Arm in arm, Henry and I strolled out to the flat rocks behind Clarence Hiscock's. With a chisel, he chipped out a handful of foolsgold and dropped the pieces one by one into my pocket. The poor man's dowry, he called it. And I laughed light-heartedly because I knew he was ashamed when he said, "Someday I'll be droppin' real treasure in yer pocket. If ye'll stay with me, that is." He told me I was lovely, and I absorbed his words.

What did Bette Mackay think? The only decent friend I had. "He's a fine catch," she said. "Gettin' married will knock all that ol' garbage out o' yer head."

Perhaps she would be right. I was already exhausted from the constant din, the ceaseless chatter, the persuasive suggestions. So I agreed.

But as I was leaving for the church, head to toe in eggshell white, a gentleman's black umbrella slipped from the corner and tumbled across my doorway. I knew it was telling me to stay put. But I didn't heed the warning. I just didn't.

Arva felt the history of this town was so close, if she cupped her hands together, it would pour in, spill over. Upper Island

Cove, a settlement clinging to a mountain like snails to the bottom of a boat, was dense, isolated, and character heavy. Starting as a small fishing village in the 1600s, it had prospered and grown, with the ocean always as its core. Most of the bold fishermen, souls baptized in icy salt water, came from Devon and Dartmouth, Wales and Ireland.

Once settled, they sent for their wives and children, willing to fashion a life, grueling as it was. Chipping away from the mountainside, they scraped away High Road and Main Road. Then they constructed crannies for their homes and built nooks for their pleasures. They used rock to erect stunted walls as property dividers, each family having a plot of land to farm potatoes, carrots, the scattered head of cabbage. From meager beginnings, the "Walled City" rose up from those looking to the sea for existence, those knowing how to be an honest neighbour, those that readily accepted the limitations of a two-foot stone fence.

The people were sturdy, firmly entrenched, weather-beaten, but stronger for it. Men would rise early on, bleary-eyed, and check the conditions of the water by sitting up in bed, gape at the ocean. If it were fit, they would be in their dories, hauling up codfish, not even a flinch when their hands dipped into the frigid seas. The women were waiting at the shoreline to split the catch, slide a sturdy thumb along the backbone, remove the workings, a coat of coarse salt and then onto the flakes, flat to dry. In the drizzly afternoons, they cooked lunch upon lunch, stoked the woodstove with logs, knit thick woolen socks for their men, and made bulging loaves of bread, never a recipe, but with a learned hand.

Young men mostly followed close behind their fathers, drinking more and brushing up against the law, trivial scrapes that time and a wife would surely settle. The young women were pleasant enough, sit and talk, cup of tea, and would kindly offer their opinion, asked for or not, on anything that tickled their tongue.

Because everyone knew everyone and then some, it was only a matter of time that the news of Arva's arrival had passed from door to door. Dot Jones pitched dirty dishwater out her back door and heard all about it from Amanda Adams while she pinned laundry to the line strung between house and shed. Junior Lynch stopped in for cigarettes at Mercer's general shop and heard it from Alek Mercer who warmed a chair there. And because Arva was different, there was talk.

"Not much Irish in her. No, b'y."

"She might be part darkie. Brown as a beaver. Hair like an Indian's."

"Her mother walked right off a wharf. Drowned herself. Yes, she did. Lord above."

A blue morning had rolled in off the water, carrying a fresh breeze with just enough energy to flutter the sheers. Arva was making a cup of tea for Old Man Crane when she recognized Lolly's legs walking across the smooth rock path outside the kitchen window, nightdress lifted by calm August air. Lolly crouched down to peer in, wave her hand, announce herself. Never a knock, the backdoor opened, feet padding on the linoleum. She came into the kitchen, face still awash in last night's make-up, hair and skin steeped in stale tobacco.

"Christ," she said smacking at her leg. "I just run through a patch of stinger nettles." Lolly took a seat on the daybed. "Me ankle's red like a beet. That's all I needs."

"Give it a few minutes. The redness will work itself out," Arva said. "Cup of tea?"

"God, no, Arva," she said.

"A bit of bread, then."

"No, no. Thanks, though. Can't take nothing down this mornin'. Mother's right sour at me, puss on her like ye wouldn't believe. She's tryin' to get me to eat before Church. I'd rather have me head in the slop bucket, if truth be told." She pulled her nightdress to her knee, rubbed a hand up and down her solid calf. "Not much choice though, got to go to Church, or there'll be talk, Mother says."

"I've never been much for Church myself, Lolly."

Arva had not set foot in a church since her father was buried. He had drowned during a spring night in early June, her mother had told her, after taking a night-run in his boat, mind and body brave with moonshine. "Not much sense to church going," her mother said in the years to follow. "It's just about talk, talk, talk. Never doing, taking action." Her father was laid out in a pine box, edges sanded smooth, resting like a pauper in God's house. Arva remembered the Samson sisters tut-tutting, clicking their tongues. "What kind of wife who has a few dollars to her name doesn't put out for a decent coffin?" The sisters had never missed a funeral, kept black dresses pressed for the unexpected occasion, and knew well the kind of coffins that were available.

"Yes," Lolly said. "They've noticed. There's already talk yer some kind of heathen. Where on earth did Alice dig ye up? But I don't heed a word of it. They got nothin' better to do than chew their gums." She wiped stale mascara from under her eye with a stout finger. "Mother wanted me to come by and tell ye she'll be sendin' over a plate of cold supper, salads and the like. So ye don't need to put nothin' on."

"Tell her not to go to any trouble."

"No trouble, Arva, for God's sakes, she's already got a chicken goin' for dinner. Too much for the two of us, she never stopped cooking for Lyle. Lyle'd love a feed of this chicken, she says. Lyle'd love a drop of this gravy. Acts like he croaked yesterday." Lolly put a thin strand of hair in her mouth. "By the way," she continued, "Patty Lynch stopped by this mornin'."

"Oh?" Arva said, and her previous evening began to leak back in, a trickle of memories, her mouth suddenly dry, thirsty.

"Said that Clive's talkin' 'bout leavin' town. Is that right?"

Arva paused to choose her words carefully, knowing that whatever she said would flow into Lolly's ears, then dribble out from her mouth. "He mentioned his desire to leave town, but I don't believe he's any plan."

"No doubt," Lolly said. "He'll never leave his mother. Or Alek, for that matter. His brother. Queer as a stick. Stolen by the fairies, the old folks say. More to that story if ye asks me." She yawned, mouth open like a gate. "But I don't like to talk, Arva. Never was much for that, ye knows."

"Yes, I can believe that," Arva replied, her eyes watching a dirty sheep wander over the rocky ledge just outside the window. Lolly nodded agreeably.

"Mother tells me to steer clear of Clive Mercer, nothin' but trouble, that man. And I'd advise ye to do the same. Make up yer mind for yerself, though, of course."

"Thank-you, Lolly, I'll do that," Arva replied.

"Mother says all we needs is a man with a bit of land and a

few chickens. That'll do us. And last time I checked, Clive Mercer had neither."

Arva's mother had never told her what kind of man to find, or even how to look. No substantial advice about chickens or land, just a breezy answer that he would appear, sent down to cross your path. "You'll know one when he's right," she had said. "One day you'll turn your head around, and he'll be standing there. Take you into his lungs with one breath, and hold tight. You'll feel like you can't take a step without him. At least until the love wears off, anyway."

"I wouldn't know anything about what he has, Lolly," Arva said. "I only spoke with him on the wharf."

"Nothin' else?" Lolly asked, eyes staring at Arva from tilted head.

"No, Lolly. Nothing else."

"That's not what Patty's sayin'. She's says he was half on top of ye down by the water, then ye two took off. Made a real show of yerselves, she's told me."

Arva lifted a cup towel from over top of Peggy Crane's widest ceramic bowl and drove her fingers deep into the warm sticky bread dough. "Believe what you will, Lolly." Cracking sounds, sweet yeasty smell released. "Nothing I say will make it otherwise."

"God, Arva," she said, rising from the daybed. "Yer some serious. Don't tell me Clive's under yer skin, because I knows he won't stay there long. And ye needn't worry about Patty, though. Even I knows ye can't trust a thin' that falls out of her big trap. I don't listen to a word she says."

Old Man Crane's voice splintered out from the bedroom, down the hall, and into the kitchen. "Arva, where's me drop of tea. I's chilled right down to the bone."

"Won't be a minute," she called back. "Lolly is just leaving."

"Ye can mark my words, lovey," she said on her way through the door. "Clive ain't goin' nowhere. This town's in his blood, if the water ain't. He always flappin' his jaw 'bout leavin', but the only way Clive Mercer's goin' to move is if his own mother gives he the boots herself." Door slammed shut, and Arva could see Lolly's heels through the kitchen window, nightdress lifted to her knee, bare feet darting across hot rock, the startled sheep scuttling off.

Arva quickly pinched out three loaves, clenched fist pressing them into their pans. She brushed the flour and bits of dried dough from her fingers. The water in the kettle was near boiling, she could tell by the gentle rattle of a loose lid. Maybe Lolly was right, she thought. Clive was as fixed in this cove as the homes were into the mountain. It seemed plain to her, though he said he wanted to leave. He taught at the school here, had a family here, good friends, the makings of a life. Arva knew for certain from his sullen eyes that he was angry. And she believed there was nothing as reliable as anger to fasten a person to the ground, render them immobile. He could weigh her down, keep her from washing away again, or worse still, drifting up on just any shore. And anger, Arva supposed, was a better anchor than no anchor at all.

She had first seen those eyes when she had been walking home from Mercer's, flour, sugar, tea in a heavy brown paper bag. A Chev slowed, she had looked up. Normally she would not have, she never looked up, made a point of it actually. Over the years, she had learned to walk like her mother, with a purpose, head tucked down to keep the stinging wind away from her neck. But she had looked up, caught his gaze, and click, key in lock.

With a single glimpse, Arva felt energized, freshened, eyes wide open. Juvenile, she knew, but still, it was there. She had the urge to stop, rub her hands in gravel, plant something, but instead she picked up the pace, needing to move. For the rest of the walk up the lane, she kept her head held high, her whole body listening carefully for a second spin of crushed stone. When she reached the back door, damp porch, tidy kitchen, his face was still lucid, framed in her mind. When did she, Arva House, all of a sudden become a woman who wanted?

Then a voice sounded in her head to betray her, filming over her clear thoughts, completing the picture. Arva could not resist it, like a canker sore, tongue darting even though it irritates. "Never think too much about any man, Arva," her mother had said, finger wagging, "for you're bound to make him greater than he is."

Arva folded the brown paper bag, slipped it under the crocheted cushion on the kitchen rocker, and tried to quiet her mind.

"God love ye, Arva," Old Man Crane said. "Yer too good to me."
She had rolled the wooden bed table so it fit snuggly over his lap. Junior Lynch made it himself, nailed and sanded, bottom rollers and all, so that Old Man Crane could have a warm drink

in bed, without having to make his way to the kitchen. He sat now, fresh pillows behind him and clean striped pajamas, the material thinning dangerously close to disintegration. He admitted to Arva when she arrived that he was in his wife's nightgown to keep her close, but it was more than that. He was also putting a decent piece of fabric to use.

"Why waste a good nightdress?" he had said. "Like I minds if it got flowers all over it."

"How about ordering up something new from the catalogue?" Arva asked.

"The catalogue? Jesus, Arva. Catch hold to yer tongue. That'll be the end of the people in this harbour. That and the telephone. They'll be spendin' half their money on the call, the other half orderin' up crap they don't even need. Not like me Peggy. She'd sew up a coat for Alice from a pair of me ol' trousers, save elastic from a bit of ol' underwear, and never once did she buy a button, kept a tin of ol' ones slid under the couch." He stopped, closed his eyes, took a burdened breath. "God, I loved her, Arva. She was yer size when we married, but she got some fat. Fattest woman in the harbour, maid. So fat on the end of it she had no need to carry a purse, just tucked her few dollars in a roll down under her chin." A phlegmy chuckle. "Jesus, I loved every inch of that woman. And, mind ye, there was plenty of inches to love."

Arva tipped the cup for him, tea slopping out into the saucer. Old Man Crane picked it up and took a deep slurp, the hot drink heavily laden with tinned milk. He dunked a dry lemon cream biscuit into the steaming cup, fished out the broken melting bits with his spoon. With flattened thumb, he pressed in the fallen crumbs and brought them to his tongue.

"If I dies now, I'd be a happy man," he said.

"That's good to hear, Mr. Crane. But, let's hope that doesn't happen."

"Why not, me dear? I've had eighty-one years to have a go of it. Never should've had Alice so late, took the good right out of me. Though I guess there wasn't no choice 'bout it. She came when she wanted. No surprise there."

"From what I know of your daughter, she couldn't have been too much trouble."

"No, she wasn't a terror, kicking up Hell or the likes of that. Just she was born hand-first, Peggy told me, and that should've been a sign to us. Always wantin' somethin', and whatever we gave her was never good enough. Well, that's not the way I was raised. Ye makes do. Yes, with whatever ye got. Never could make that child happy, though she was a wonderful baby, sweet as a sugar cookie. Though that was before she started talkin'. Jesus, how she'd bawl if we took the catalogue out to the outhouse. 'All the pretty things' she used to say. I did me best with her once Peggy passed on, but I got no ideas 'bout raisin' a daughter." He rubbed his rough hand over the table. "Now, what odds 'bout Alice. How's 'bout a game of crib, me dear. We're all set up."

Arva pulled out the cribbage board, and with a flick of her wrist, dealt out the cards, a pile for the kitty. Old Man Crane shuffled through his with skilled fingers, then laid down a seven, hard knuckle knocking wood as the card spun across the table.

"Tell me, Arva, what's Lolly chewin' her cud 'bout this mornin'? I couldn't make it out."

"Oh, last night, I guess. Nothing too serious."

"Could've guessed. She's always exercisin' her tongue 'bout somethin'. Just like her mother. Tough to get that woman to shut up. Always was. Tryin' to talk at me over the wall whenever she spotted me in the yard through her damn kitchen window. She'd waste no time gettin' her arse out back. Haulin' the ears off me with some story or another, me there, arms stretchin' down with junks of wood." He took another loud slurp of the tea, wiped a dribble away with the back of his hand. "So, now, tell me. What kind of time did ye have?"

Arva rifled her cards, dropped an eight. "Fifteen for two, Mr. Crane," she said, then pegged her points. "I met some nice people."

"Nothin' worth talkin' to me 'bout there. Got to be somethin' more by the sounds of the young girl. Don't be holdin' back on me now, maid. I needs a bit of excitement in me ol' life. Anyone grab yer interest?"

"Yes, I would say so." A faint heat rising to her cheeks. She suddenly felt like an elderly woman, mind slogging, needing to explain herself to someone, have her memories out into a room with more than two ears, making them real.

"I s'pose ye did, the hour ye came in. I'd a hoped ye weren't wanderin' 'round all night by yerself," he winked. He knocked down an eight, arthritic clunk resounding, "Twenty-three for two," he said, one-sided smile. "Go on."

Arva offered up another eight. "Thirty-one for six, plus two more for eight."

"Ah Arva," he said, pulling his cards to his chest, half-smile withdrawn. "Ye plays crib like the Devil."

"It was Clive Mercer," she said, the name coming forth involuntarily as her fingers were occupied counting points.

"Good God, Arva. I could've guessed it. He's a real charmer, gets that from his mother's side. She's a sweet one, that Doris Mercer."

"What about his father's side?" she asked.

"Oh, Clive's father was a real son-of-a-bitch, God love him. Tried to steal me Peggy from me, though I never had her at the time, mind ye. Said he'd rip the drawers right off her and have his way if she dared come back down the lane with that dress on. Summer dress, light blue, real airy," he grinned, leaned back against the pillows. "Peggy never did go in for that kind of banter. Of course, she was only thirteen at the time. Took a shine to me, though, runnin' 'round with me sister's shoes on, not a copper to spare for a decent set. I had to clout Tom Mercer right in the gob."

"Well, well."

"She never forgot it. Valiant, she called me. Valiant. Can ye imagine? Valiant in a pair of girl's shoes. I never forgot that word. She must've read it in a book somewhere, and saved it up for me."

"Yes, I can imagine," Arva said and touched him on the shoulder. "Lolly tells me that Clive has a brother. He never mentioned it." Arva could hear her own words, the questions muffled in her ear.

"No, he wouldn't," Old Man Crane said, his cards motionless, a story coming on. "Can't miss him, Alek Mercer. He's down at Mercer's shop everyday on that stool. Probably leers at ye, tongue hangin' out. Got to forgive him though, he's right soft in the head, like a spoon of bread puddin'."

He put the saucer to his lips, but never drank. "Put in another drop, Arva. With all me yammerin', 'tis gone cold." He took a slow slurp, closed his eyes for a moment. "Where was I? We all says he must've been one of those Catholics once, always on 'bout Confession. Doris and Tom Mercer haven't been right since Alek was born."

"Is that so," Arva said, her shoulders off the back of the chair, fixed.

"Yes, maid. Everyone figured he was a bit queer early on, cryin' all the time. I remembers it clear as yesterday. Alice was 'bout the same age and never made a peep. Then you got Alek. Could be heard halfway down the lane. His bawl could flatten a cake, Peggy used to say. 'Twas a real job to comfort him."

"Then Doris took the boy with her one afternoon to pick a quart of berries, get him a bit of fresh air. To settle him, ye knows. Dusk came on quicker than she'd expected, and she says she just bent at a good patch, had her back turned for no more than a second, the boy was gone, blanket still warm. The fairies got him."

He poured the last drop of his tea out into the saucer, hand wobbly, peering up at Arva through wiry eyebrows, an armor of hair above soggy eyes.

"Yes, the fairies got him. There was no other explanation. Blueberry pickin' at dusk like that. She should've known better. But no point to talk 'bout that now." He paused to bark, spit into his hankie, breath wheezing like a squeezebox.

"What fairies? I've never heard of such a thing."

"Well, 'bout time someone told ye. Ye've been here all summer. Yer not to be pickin' berries or out in the woods when night falls. If yer young enough, the fairies might steal ye away. Who knows when someone'll lay eyes on ye next. And if yer too old, they'll twist ye right round and ye won't know yer ass from yer elbow. Ye'll have a devil of a time makin' it home."

"Is that right. I can't believe it." Arva said as she laid her cards on the table, face down.

"Young Doris came runnin' out of the woods like her backside was on fire, we heard her hollerin', 'the fairies got him, the fairies got the b'y.' I allows they heard she in Harbour Grace. The woman was beside herself. Near gone mad. Ran home to get Tom, and there she found the boy wrapped up on the back porch, a fresh blanket from her own line. Not a scratch on him. Tom was sleepin' so sound in the kitchen, no one could wake him. Hasn't touched a drop since. Blamed hisself, I s'pose, for not bein' there. Alek never bawled much after that, 'til he opened his gob to talk 'bout confession. Them fairies must've done somethin' powerful to him. He got a real odd way 'bout him."

"That can't be true, Mr. Crane. Someone must have made that up."

"Yes, 'tis then. And ye can bet he don't go a day without his underwear on inside-out. Keeps the fairies away. Underwear or socks. Inside-out. Don't matter. Guaranteed."

"I must say, that's close to the strangest thing I've ever heard," Arva said.

Old Man Crane sighed and closed his eyes. "Oh, I could tell ye stranger, no doubt. But not today. 'Tis good to talk, though. Have someone close by. Not many young people wants to lend their earholes to an old man these days." His breath arduous, lungs sopping. "I's goin' to rest for a spell, Arva. Just a short spell."

"You don't want to finish the game?" Arva said, pulling back the table and re-arranging his pillows.

"I could tell by the way we started, ye was goin' to take it, so no. I'll play again when I gets a better hand."

Arva lifted the lid from the woodstove with the removable handle and dropped in a handful of splits that Alf Jones had brought over. The dry wood crackled, giving off a soothing heat that guarded against the mild evening chill, slinking in off the water. Days were shorter, the air teased by smoke from smoldering potato stalks, burning until darkness solidified. She could hear a rattle of a laden cart pushed along the high road.

Seated in the rickety wooden rocker next to the stove, her foot pushed the linoleum, creak of the floorboard, creak of the floorboard. She picked up a needle and began to thread a long strand of white thread. Old Man Crane asked that the loose buttons be tightened on his best shirt, his good pants taken in.

"I wants me Sunday suit lookin' as fine as the day I bought it," he had said one afternoon. "Sewed up nice, fit me like when I was married. Pressed nice and crisp."

"Now, now, Mr. Crane," Arva replied. "I don't think you're quite up for a Church service yet. But if you've got it in your mind to go, I can talk to Junior Lynch."

"Church service? Have ye gone right round the bend, me dear?" he said. "I'll be there soon enough whether I likes it or not. And I wants to be lookin' me finest when I is. Haven't seen me Peggy in near twenty years."

"You listen to me," Arva said. "I don't want to hear that kind of talk when you're still alive and well. You can tell me all about it when you're dead and gone." Though she had smiled, lightened the air, here she sat, ripping out old seams and sewing in new.

There was a knock at the porch door, strange, door pulled open, hard soles, men's shoes clicking across the floor. Creak of the rocker stopped. Arva's heart stood up, and her thoughts, well trained, shifted to her dilapidated trunk, cold brass edging, sitting at the base of her quilted bed. "Peep out the window, Arva," her mother had always said when there was a rap to the door. Most often it would be a woman, shirt or pair of pants in hand needing mending. Sometimes a lady with a mound of fabric over her shoulder, her mind on a new dress. But if it were a stranger, empty handed, shuffling feet, then there was some other reason for the visit, a reason her mother could not stand to consider. "It's time to move on," she would say. "Now, pack up your few things. People are calling on us."

"Is anyone 'round?" A voice from the porch. "Clive here."

Arva's grip on the needle loosened. She had not heard his truck pull up, he must have walked down the lane. "Come on through," she said. Then added, "Clive."

And then he was in the kitchen, face shaven clean, his presence changing the feeling of the air. "Just came by to pay me respects to the Skipper. See how he's feeling."

"Ah," Arva replied, her voice sounding like someone else's. "He's sleeping now. Doing okay, though not much change since I came here. Won't be going to a dance anytime soon, but he sits for a bit."

"Wouldn't be shocked if he outlives the lot of us. How's his spirits?"

"Pretty good," she said, putting aside the shirt and pants. "If he's talking, then he's content. He loves to talk."

"Always did. Even during a Sunday service, he'd be interruptin' Reverend Parsons. When he got somethin' to say, now's as good a time as any."

Clive sat down on the daybed, elbows on his knees, closed hands under his chin, Sunday jacket on. Arva was reminded of the wharf.

"A lovely night out, maid," he said. "How's 'bout a walk? I can show ye 'round the cove a bit."

Another walk. Arva felt as if she could take walks forever, slow and easy, an effortless indulgence. She could stroll to the corner of the world as long she came back around to the exact same place where she began, not moving, not shifting, steady, ever steady.

"I'd enjoy that," she answered. "Just give me a minute."

Arva went to her bedroom, slipped out of her dress, pulled on a pair of navy jeans, knit ribbed turtleneck, and laced saddle shoes. Running a brush through her hair, she twisted a plait, released it like a thick black rope suspended from the base of her skull. In the mirror above the dresser, glass distorted, top layer flaking, she could not recognize herself, body thin, face flushed, an eager girl.

They walked down Main Road, gravel scrunching under their feet. Even though the summer lingered, the evening was heavy, clammy on her skin. Shades of near-ripe berries and ginger spice were drawn across the horizon as the sun began to settle down. A sailor's delight. He reached behind, caught her hand. She noticed tonight the sides of his hair were neatly combed into a ducktail.

At the base of Main Road, Clive led her to a footpath, shoe-worn, dizzyingly close to the edge of the cliff. They continued one by one along the trail, salt water spraying up, waves thunderous in her ears, neither saying a word, though any word spoken would have been instantly devoured by the sea. There was a clearing, a few smooth rocks placed just so, natural chairs.

"Lovely night."

"Yes, lovely."

"Have a beech nut," he said, handing her a flattened black lozenge, and one for his own mouth. "I really enjoyed meself up to the Legion," he continued, foot up on one of the rocks. "Although I've never been much for dances and the like."

Arva let the drop suction onto her cheek. Anise, razor sharp. "Yes, me as well. Enjoyed myself, that is." She sat down on the flattened rock near Clive. Her seat sloped on one side until it came to a much smaller rock, snuggled in so tightly it looked as though the two were joined. It reminded her of a tiny child, hiding in the grass, head tucked in, eyes covered and counting to ten.

"Arva," he said, her name travelling out over the water.

"Clive," she said quietly, his name following hers.

"Yes, by God, 'tis a lovely night."

Clive pulled a flask from an inside pocket, uncapped it, and tipped his head back as he drank the last inch. Holding up the empty bottle, he said to her, "I've had this in me jacket since the dance. Just as well to finish it."

"Right," she agreed, even though she imagined he was lying.

Tossing the bottle out, he grinned, not at her, but to himself. Glass tinkered against the rocks, a throaty chortle from the ocean foamed up to tidy the mess. His face, skin pink, looked spirited from the sunset and more. Leaning down, he began picking up fragments of glass near the head of Arva's child-rock, pitching them beyond the cliff.

"Bloody kids," he said. "Bustin' glass all over the path. Someone could cut themselves." Then, when he had finished throwing the largest shards, he said, "Mother was askin' 'bout ye."

Tongue to the drop, Arva waited for him to continue.

"She heard from Lorna Lynch, Junior's wife, that I met ye at the Legion. Lorna told her it looked like I took a fancy to ye, to use her words. Mother was just wonderin' what ye was all 'bout. Not much to talk about this week for them, I guess."

"What did you tell her?"

"No need for me to say nothin', me dear. Rose Young's already been tellin' her what a fine job yer doin' with Skipper. Says ye got the patience of Job, takin' care of that old man. Mother's surprised Peggy wasn't driven to the drink, livin' with Skipper all those years."

"You make him sound pretty intolerable. He can barely get out of his own bed."

"Oh, he may be bed-ridden now, but his tongue hasn't stopped clickin', sure as I's standin' here. Used to be a rumour goin' 'round when I was in school that his tongue was forked right down the middle. I 'llows he got a tail like that too. Though you'd know that better than meself, these days." He nudged her with his elbow. "I believes he started that rumour hisself, scare us kids off his land, in case we wanted to pinch a bottle of his moonshine. I imagine that'll be the last thin' to die on he, the rest of him'll pass over, save for his tongue."

A faint giggle. It came from Arva's mouth, and the sound of it surprised her, causing a warm throbbing to move up to her cheeks.

Clive laughed himself. "There's no one quite like ye 'round here," he said, fortified.

"I'm not sure how to take that," she responded. "As a compliment?"

"Oh yes, indeedy," he said. "That's how 'twas meant."

Arva followed the ocean waves with her eyes, distant water like wrinkled skin on a cold pudding. Using her tongue, she lifted the drop from her cheek, a roughened licorice patch where it had been fixed. Focussed on the glorious night sky, she watched how it tiptoed in and was choking out the twilight.

"Let's keep movin'," he said, grabbing her hand. "There's more to see."

They ambled for an hour, walking along winding narrow pathways, and edging their way up the side of the mountain. Care taken with each step, he told her precisely where to position her foot, proud to have the route stamped on his mind. Ankles swollen, her shoes had bitten into her skin, but the pain would wait until another time.

"I knows a spot," he said. Arva silently followed as he led her to a grassy stoop. Someone had been here recently, flattened grass, an empty rum bottle cast aside.

Yards away a clump of blueberry bushes waved in the wind, glistening leaves clutched moonlight. Clive crawled over, pushing green into the heels of his hands and fabric of his pants, and tore a branch from the bush. With practiced fingers, he plucked the berries and fed them to Arva. Though she did not want them, she squished each one by one against the roof of her mouth. Still seeming to possess the warmth of summer, they tasted of wild sweetness, salt washed.

After casting the barren branch aside, Clive held Arva by the shoulders and she felt four fingers left and right, two determined thumbs. She tried to roll on her side, but his grip was firm, decided, and she followed its direction. He fumbled with his belt and then unzipped his crumpled beige pants. Then he hauled her dark jeans below her knees, never took the moment to unlace her shoes.

Arva strained her neck, her eyes searching for the ocean, but she was heavy on her braid and her view was concentrated in Clive's damp armpit. Two sheep lying down, a stones throw away, tore grass idly, the ruminating chew echoing in her ears.

As she was being pushed deeper and deeper into the grassy knoll, his full weight crushing her lungs, she watched her hands gripping the dewy grass. She was reminded of them as a child, skin drawn tight from plumpness, wrists still slightly creased with baby fat. Arva's eyelids lowered, mind drawn back, her mother coming into view.

Fingers, points on a starfish, clutched at a kitchen wash-pail, icy salt water sloshing out and over. "Hurry Arva," her mother was saying. "Hurry, my love. You have to take a hand in this." Arva dumped the water into the white enamel slop bucket on the back step, the very one she used for her business during the dark hours and rinsed out in the sea during the morning light.

A solitary crow, blackened bead for an eye, sat on the corner post of the porch and was watching Arva. "I can see what you are doing," it had cawed, as the bucket emptied. Her mother, feet firmly planted, her mind and body weighty with strength, picked up the potato spade and flung it at the bird. "One's for sorrow," she said with gaiety, her tone more unnatural than the crooked twist in the bird's neck. Then the woman grabbed at Arva, hands encircling her slender hips, leaning her wide face down, breath, alive. "And, my sweet Arva." Her words straight into the child's ear. "Two is for joy."

A new moon, bold-faced and shimmering, bobbed in the sky with increasing vigor. Arva braced her body against the earth. There was a promise hovering.

"Are you going to marry me?" she asked, sitting in her own impression, knees bent, hands gripping the toes of her shoes.

Clive thought she was terrifically naive. But because she was so unusual, he said yes without a moment's hesitation.

Eight days later, Arva was lying in bed when the air swelled with an overpowering scent of wild roses. She put her hand on her lower abdomen, felt the prickly twinge, and thought of her mother. "When that smell comes on," she had once said to Arva, "and there's not a single rose in sight, make way, for a soul has entered the room."

3

With all my expectations, can you imagine my surprise when I discovered whom I had really married? Oh, the realization was not immediate, mind you, but when it simmered to the surface, it polluted my entire shoreline.

Clive and Arva married on a Thursday afternoon in late September at St. Peter's Anglican Church. Uninvited snowflakes flirted in the sky, while the wind itself was acrid with backyard fires, smoky smell of oil hitting a hot pan. Reverend Parsons had agreed to join the couple, even though Arva's religious commitment was in question, and he was given a generous helping of good amber whiskey for his troubles.

Old Man Crane had wanted to attend, but was too ill, so Ethel Drover sat with him for the afternoon of the wedding. "I don't play no cribbage now, Skipper," she had said, long needles clacking through the blur of her hands. "But yer welcome to tell me a story 'bout Peggy while I knits on Arthur's sweater."

Lolly was there first, leaning against the painted doors of the wooden church, her body impossibly squeezed into a burgundy dress, snake belt, peter pan collar. Cheeks burnished with too much rouge, and her smile was tapped from depths eternal. Arva had asked her to be a witness, stand up at the church, write her signature across the marriage certificate. Lolly prepared for the role by practicing her earnest expression, and dubbed herself 'Arva's best girl' to all who were listening.

Doris Mercer soon established her place in the front left

pew. She wore a pale pink skirt and jacket, pillbox hat atop her head, a respectable touch of lace. Thrifty to the bone, and a consummate planner, she had purchased her outfit nearly seven years ago from a Simpson's catalogue sale, assured one day Clive would marry, and praying one day Alek would as well. Finally, then, she would be alone - what she had always wanted.

Tucked in next to Doris was Aunt Helen, the late Tom Mercer's sister-in-law. Side by side, the two were paired hens nestled down on their eggs, securing heat in the drafty church. Aunt Helen was murmuring to Doris, guppy mouthed, her hurried inhale echoing off the grand walls.

"I can tell by one look at her, she's in the family way," Helen said, a subtle nod towards Arva. "She got a green glow 'bout her, she do. Take a gander at her feet, almost swoll right out of her shoes."

"Last thing I wants to be doin' is starin' at her feet, Helen. Ye knows, now."

"She got some face, is all. Comin' in here like that."

Doris squirmed on the hard pew, like an earthworm halved by a shovel. "Well," she said, with a stream of air through her nostrils. "There's only so much a mother can do. I told him to watch his bobber."

"Lot of good that did, Doris," Helen said, her generous tongue snap, snapping.

Doris inched away from Aunt Helen, pushed in a little closer to Lorna Lynch.

Doris and Lorna had already discussed Clive's need to tie the knot within a month of meeting that girl. It certainly did not bother Doris, she was personally familiar with the predicament, but having Helen's hot breath drying up the wax in her ears was the last thing she wanted. And Doris and Lorna were certain Helen would be talking up a storm before she even stepped a foot out of her car.

"Shotgun for sure," Lorna had said to Doris shortly after Clive's announcement. "I can hear Helen already."

"Yes, her gums are apt to be flappin' all over town," Doris said.

"The good Lord never scrimped on Helen's gob," Lorna said. "No, me dear."

"All good and well for Helen, heavin' stones hither and yon in her big glass house," Doris said. "She thinks we's that dunce, we don't remember."

"That's right," Lorna said, hot potato passed. "Daughter-in-law, six months married, havin' an eight-and-a-half-pound baby, hear me. Pre-term, she says, and not a bit of trouble with his latch. Can you imagine the size, she says, if he was in for the whole nine months?"

"She, now," Doris said, "married to Harry. That man never worked a day in his life, if ye asks me. Pushes 'round papers in that bank, makin' all kinds of dollars buyin' his house in the city, keepin' his house on the bay. And Helen there with her 'help,' hands smooth on her like a baby's arse. God, I've spent me life cookin' for Tom and the b'ys, fryin' a breakfast, makin' a mornin' lunch, dinner at noon, early afternoon lunch, late afternoon lunch, a supper, and then a lunch before bed. Ye knows what I's sayin'. I's worn with it all, Lorna, right worn down. If I never prepares another lunch, I won't miss it, I swears to God. And I 'llows Helen's dress'll be fresh from the shops in St. John's. I bet her shoes'll be just out of the box."

With that thought, Doris stole a sideways look at her brother-in-law's wife. Helen's back was ramrod straight against the pew. Crossing her legs at the ankle, Doris pushed her feet neatly underneath the seat.

"What did ye expect, Helen," Doris said, voice a little firmer, one pink glove over the other. "I can't live his life for him. Watch his every step. He's a grown man."

"I's not sayin' nothin' about ye. Heavens, no. Just thought he'd find hisself a nice girl. Local girl. 'Tis a real sin, is all, Doris. A real sin."

"For God's sake, Helen," she said, her throat tight, lips white. "Yer actin' like we all went 'round with a pill between our knees before we took our vows."

"Don't get me wrong, me dear. Just we don't know a thin' 'bout her. She's don't belong to nobody. Who knows? She could've come from a brood of murderers."

"God help us, Helen. Ye always did go in for a bit of drama," Doris said. Aunt Helen pursed her peach-coloured lips, turkey jowl jarred, fingers knotted together in her lap. "She's soon to be me daughter and yer niece," Doris continued, resolute, "and I don't want to be hearin' another mean word 'bout her come 'cross yer tongue."

Men weighed down the opposite front pew; Junior Lynch's substantial rear end planked in the middle. Alf Jones, adorned all in drizzly gray but for a canary yellow shirt, was leaning hard against Junior, head too heavy to keep upright. A fake rose dangling from his lapel looked as though it had been round the wash bucket more than once. Doris could spy the gin blossoms on his puffed nose from the other side of the church. "That's some disgustin' display," she muttered to Lorna, gloved hand across her mouth. "Some'll use any excuse for a drink."

Doris glanced over at Alek, seated on the opposite side of Junior, his body slender, caplin next to cod. That morning, she helped Alek dress in Tom's suit. He was clothed in chocolate brown pants and jacket, muddy-coloured beige shirt, a wide tie diagonally striped with coffee and cream. On his feet he still wore filthy sneakers, ripped at the toes, gray knit socks let loose and tumbled to his ankles. Doris had begged, pleaded, "Some clean socks, Alek, for the sweet love of Jesus. People'll talk." But, no. He had shaken his head until the dab of grease gave up, and his hair hung once again in his stye-riddled eyes. Doris had to look away, focus herself on the good Reverend's green velour chair.

"No need to confess today, Clive," Alek called out to his brother standing at the front of the church. Alek's front teeth were rotten, black in his head, although his breath blew sweet like a baby's. He pushed back against the pew as Clive came close, wearing the black suit from his father's funeral. But he only nudged Alek hard with his elbow and said, "No b'y," a wink and a nod. "Not today. No b'y."

Arva was adorned in off-white, a simple sheath with crocheted lace around the hem and at the wrists. She wore no veil, hair out like a mink's pelt, in her shaky hand a bouquet of artificial blue carnations pierced with wire. Though she felt calm within, her hands seemed to know she was either on the verge of something miraculous or else courting certain disaster.

Before the service got underway, Arva and Lolly went to wait in the icy room just left of the pulpit, and closed the door.

"Have a wee sip," Lolly said as she held up the decanter of

communion wine. "It'll calm yer nerves right down."

"No thanks, Lolly."

"Jesus," she whispered though the room was empty. "I wonders is this where they keeps the bodies to?"

Arva's dress had belonged to Peggy Crane, and Old Man Crane suggested she borrow it when she told him her news. "Yer the spit of Peggy when we was married," he had said, cloudy eyes cruising from head to toe. "Not the look, of course, that's a given. But the shape's right close. No wonder I loves havin' ye 'round."

Doris Mercer had come down the hill that very afternoon, helped Arva dig the gown out of the attic, and try it. It fit well, but had yellowed in its hiding place, so Doris brought it home to clean. Hard as she tried, she had told Arva, the fabric was stubborn, the colour in it would not let go.

Reverend Parsons shuffled through the ceremony, his voice lingering to begin with, and nearing a full stop by the end. Only Arva and Clive took communion, and the crowd waited patiently while the Reverend sipped away at remaining wine in the bulky goblet. Even with his leisurely nip, the service itself was straightforward and to the point, much to the delight of Aunt Helen.

"Me rump is near gone dead sittin' on this old wood," she whispered to Doris. "Ye'd think with all the dollars we's givin' the church, someone'd have the decency to put a cushion in."

Doris stood immediately, leaving Aunt Helen with her mouth still open, next phrase dangling on the end of her tongue. She tugged her suit jacket down firmly, the pleats disguising a protruding lazy belly, and stepped straight up to the Reverend, new bride, and groom. "Reverend, ye'll be comin' back to the house for a little somethin' to wet your whistle, of course. A bite of lunch."

"On such a festive occasion, I normally would," he replied, breath saccharine. "But I's powerful tired, and I's goin' to take a short spell in the rectory."

"Please yerself, Reverend," she said. "Yer welcome to it, if ye change yer mind." Then, turning to Clive and Arva, she held out her pink clothed hand to the married couple. "Congratulations, me son. Congratulations, Arva. Ye can call me Mother now, me dear."

"Oh my, Mrs. Mercer," Arva responded. "I wouldn't feel right about that."

"Well. Doris, then. None of this Mrs. Mercer business, mind ye. Makin' me sound like Tom's mother, rest her soul."

"Doris, then."

"Now, Clive," Doris said, Arva and Clive still standing at the front of the church, crowd behind them waiting to pump hands and plant kisses. "Ye've made yer livin' arrangements, I'd imagine. Because ye knows there's not a bit of room with me. Not one bit, me son."

"Yes, maid," he said, catching Arva's hand. "Ye needn't worry 'bout that. Me lovely wife has taken care of everythin'. I'll be movin' in with Skipper for the time bein'. Never could've fathomed it, me movin' in with Old Man himself. But there ye got it."

When Arva had told Old Man Crane she would be married, he asked if Clive would move in, and they could take the bedroom opposite his, the one that had belonged to Alice.

"No flies on ye now, is there maid?" he said. "But onto the business at hand. Ye've got Alice's room to think on. Then there's Doris Mercer's house with Alek, and I wouldn't offer that to me dead dog, God rest him. Not that she's not a wunerful woman. Real sweetheart, that Doris. But if ye stay on here, ye can have a bit of a life, and I won't got to have Ethel Drover here collectin' gossip 'bout the state of me lungs or the state of me potty for all the cove to hear."

"If it won't be too much trouble. God knows I'd do my best at Mrs. Mercer's, but I have a feeling it wouldn't be starting out on the right foot."

"Me love, I don't reckon Clive Mercer come attached with nar right foot. I knows he got a bit of charm. Peggy near snatched him when he was in diapers. Though now he got a streak of somethin' else in him. Since Tom died, it seems. His father loved him like ye wouldn't believe, never shut up 'bout him. Though he was some hard on the boy, so I doubts Clive ever felt an ounce of it. But, he's yer pick, me dear, and I won't utter another word 'bout him. Ye'll stay on here then," he said. "And there'll be no more discussion."

"You're too kind, Mr. Crane. A real godsend," Arva replied. "But, we'll have to let Alice know, of course."

"To hell with Alice," he said. "Like she got a right knowin' what goes on here. Drove me mad havin' her comin' up for the weekends like that, goin' through my drawers, holdin' up me underwear there like me corpse is already ice in the bed, thinkin' she's doin' me a favour cookin' bread I wouldn't throw at a rooster. Probably kill him when he tried to pass it. No doubt what she had in mind for me. This is me house and I can do what I likes here."

"At least we can give her a call, Mr. Crane. It doesn't feel right if we don't."

"Go on down to Ralph Drover's, then, if it'll keep ye quiet. Into his post office, and send her a pink message. Nothin' more. I's not wastin' me last cent on a telephone call."

"May God bless ye both, and may yer life together be long and fruitful," Aunt Helen said, care taken with her pronunciation. She lifted her thimble of blueberry wine to her lips, wetted them, but never took a sip.

"That's right. Yes, indeed," Junior Lynch said, tumbler held high.

"All the best, Clive. And ye too, Arva," Rose Young said.

"She's a real doozy, Clive," Alf Jones slurred, flower missing from his lapel. "A good thing I didn't meet her first, me son, or we'd be down the road a ways, havin' the lunch to Aunt Dot's." He took a hearty drink of his whiskey. "And, listen up, now. If anyone sees me nice silk rose 'long the laneway, ye knows who owns it. Don't be stompin' it into the mud," he continued, finger pointing around the rooms, bloodshot eyes slit. "Bring it here. 'Tis a nice touch I likes to have."

Doris stepped up behind Alf, took her hard-soled slipper from her foot, and clapped him loudly on the back of his scalp.

"Jesus, Doris," he said, hand jumping to the spot. "Watch where yer stepping."

"Shut yer mouth, Alfie," Junior Lynch said. "And drink up. We're here for a time, b'y, not to be listenin' to yer yammerin'."

"Thanks Junior," Doris said. "I don't want to be hearin' no garbage out of the load of ye. This is me son's weddin'."

When the group had spilled in through Doris's back porch door, great bottles of whiskey, rum, and Junior Lynch's homemade blueberry wine were opened. A dribble of each in the corner for the unseen spirits, and then substantial drinks were offered around.

In a flicker, a cloth was laid down, starched crisp white, corners colourfully needle-stitched with the phrase 'Our Daily Bread.' The table was overloaded with cuts of chicken, creamy cubed potato salad, thick slices of crusty white bread, a bowl of wilted leaf lettuce saved from Lorna Lynch's garden, pickled hard boiled eggs, and sliced beets.

In the very center of the burdened table, Doris gently placed a round dark fruitcake, their wedding cake, coated with a generous layer of white fluffy icing. Alongside, there was light fruitcake, molasses cookies with raisins, walnut slices, and caramel squares all layered on the best platters, both owned and borrowed. Aunt Helen's husband, Harry Mercer, owned a camera and took several snapshots of people, chins up, looking their best, and lined against the living room wall.

"That's some spread," Junior Lynch said to Doris as he heaped several eggs, slices of chicken, and potato salad onto a plate, licked a stout finger.

"Yes," Clive said, his arm loosely around Doris's shoulder. "She got herself outdone and then some. If she put herself out anymore, I 'llows she'd be right out to the backyard."

"Oh, Clive," Doris said, moving to smooth the tablecloth, a faint flush to her cheeks. "'Twasn't all me, ye knows."

Lorna buttered a tender slice of fresh bread. "Watch yerself on those eggs, Junior," she said. "Ye knows what they do's to ye and I got to be livin' with ye after the weddin's over."

Junior knocked one of the eggs from his plate back onto the platter.

"The men'll be down to the Lodge tonight, fixin' to buy ye a drink, Clive," Arthur Drover said, his fork spearing wide rounds of sweet purple beets.

"I knows now, Art, Clive'll be headin' to the Lodge on his weddin' night," Dot Jones said.

"That's right. They's goin' to be disappointed this evening, Art. I won't be leavin' me new bride that fast," Clive said. "Nar chance of it." Ladies wrinkled their lips, nibbled at squares, men winked, swallowed great mouthfuls of whiskey, throaty laughs rumbling from down near their bowels.

"Let's have a go at this cake here," said Clive.

"It's really lovely, Doris," Arva said. "I've never made a fruitcake."

"Now, that's a sorry thing for a married woman to be sayin'," Doris replied, her tone light, friendly. "When Christmas comes 'round, come up to the house here, me dear, and I'll put that to rights. Always good to have somethin' on hand, and a decent fruitcake can last for months."

Clive's hand guiding Arva's, together they used a thin bread knife to saw through the wedding cake. It was so dense with fruit and molasses, not a crumb escaped. Once the bride and groom finished extracting the first piece, Dot Jones lifted it away, brought it to the coffee table in the living room to slice for the guests. Doris filled the kettle for tea, and stayed close by the stove, listening for the metal whirr that came just before boiling. She eyed the table. The mountains of her food, made mostly on her own effort in the wee hours of last night, had been leveled into a few scattered foothills.

"How's 'bout a bit of music, Clive? Now that the food is cleared away," Junior Lynch said. "I knows Tommie had a gargeous squeezebox, got to be 'round here somewheres."

An expression that looked close to pride fanned across Doris's face. "Yes, his accordion is on the floor of the closet, next to his shoes. Go and fetch it now, Junior."

To applause, Junior Lynch brought the accordion into the kitchen, dusted the shiny red instrument with a cup-towel, and unsnapped the shiny clasp. Accordion balanced on his knee, it pressed into his bulging gut as he tugged and tweaked, wheezing air going in, foot-stomping melody streaming out. Alf Jones hauled a pair of spoons out of a drawer, one thigh elevated, almost smacking the backs together in time. Rose Young clapped a dry clap, Arthur Drover whistled though his dentures.

"God, Junior," Dot Jones said, slightly winded. "Ye always did have a way with a squeezebox, me son."

Everyone, sitting or standing, was moving something. Even Aunt Helen's foot slid back and forth across the linoleum, more of a scrape, not quite a tap. Alf Jones put down his spoons and tried to pull Lolly up from the rocker for a spin around the hot kitchen, but she could not be budged. Lolly, "best girl," was sleeping soundly, mouth wide open, smile fallen to the side, tongue and teeth stained violet from blueberry wine.

"Someone'll have to carry her home tonight," said Rose. "I can't manage on me own."

"I'll lend ye a hand, maid," Alf Jones said as he knocked into the counter. Doris's pillbox hat was thrown to the floor, and Alf with his left dancing foot, squashed it flat.

"Can't have nothin'," Doris said, sickle mouth, arms like bands across her stomach.

Aunt Helen blew a warm stream of air through her flared nostrils, gentle curve at the corners of her mouth barely perceptible.

Clive took Arva in his arms, brushed her hair from her shoulder, then a firm grip between the shoulder blades. The others moved off to the sides of the kitchen, and Junior Lynch slowed the pace of his squeezing, a gentler tap of his foot. To a soft clap, the new couple danced together for the first time.

"Yer right lovely," he said in her ear, drawing her perfume with a breath. He turned her around the kitchen, she nearly matching his height. Doris had lit the wall candles, reflectors angled to the center of the room, casting the pair in tender radiance.

If she stayed like this, Clive thought, her sturdy backbone, her olive skin, her ribbon of hair, then he could be happy. She was satisfied with life, just being alive, content with what she had, where she was. Maybe, with her by his side, he would begin to feel the same, lose that grating itch always crawling under his skin.

Clive gazed over at his mother standing next to Alek, her eyes locked on Arva. As he watched her, her mouth, thin like a cut, thawed into a genuine smile.

Arva rose up from the bed at Old Man Crane's house and took a seat next to her trunk. Her hands smoothed their wedding gift, a quilt, mauve semi-circle bands of material interlocking, overlapping. Sections of a velvety white baby sleeper belonging to Clive were woven into the pattern. Doris, Lorna, Rose, old Clarice, and even Ethel worked most evenings around different kitchen tables to painstakingly bind the pieces together. There was something there, Arva felt it, something in the fabric. A burgeoning admiration, she thought, or maybe not, perhaps a trace of respectful acceptance. And that was more than she had expected, for now.

She lifted the lid of the trunk, a melancholy creak, her childhood tucked inside. Underneath her knitted sweaters, a pale yellow child's dress in tissue paper, a handful of Christmas ornaments crocheted from thread, a faded photo of her mother and father, her hand gleaned the edge of the shop ledger. It was pastel green, solid black writing on the cover, the sort a general store might use for accounting. Several knotted brown laces, wrapped around its body, laced into a simple bow. She smoothed her hands over the roughed-up edges and slipped her finger into a loop of shoelace. Just one quick tug, tempting.

Her mother had offered her the ledger in the middle of the night when she was seventeen. They were renting a room from Jacky Morgan on Wharf Road at the time, her eccentric mother claiming to be a writer. And as of late, that was exactly what she had been doing with a delirious, fevered pace. She had stopped taking in sewing a while back, and was instead spending the last few dollars she kept in a thick black sock, strand of fraying elastic tied around its neck.

She woke Arva wearing her best flowered smock, lipstick pale but definitely there, decent slippers on.

Arva already grasped what would happen by sunrise, though not accepted it. She had been walking through the high grass on the hill overlooking Conception Bay that afternoon and noticed her mother standing on the bleached wharf at the end of the road. She was casting morsels of crusted bread out onto the ocean, her palm opening slowly to the sky over and over again. Crying seagulls circling above did not notice the bobbing tidbits cresting on the waves, but instead dipped down in search of other treasures. A fierce wind that had been whipping Arva's dress against her thin body and lifting her hair like inky squid's legs never touched that unearthly woman on the wharf. She was radiant. Blithe. Her mother's forerunner.

"Here is the grime from my spirit. I've washed it clean," her mother said that night, sitting on the edge of Arva's bed. Handing the ledger to Arva seemed to take considerable effort, her mother breathing heavily, wheezing almost.

Arva reached for the bow, but her mother held tight to the curious hand. "In this ledger," she continued, "I have it all for you. The truth as best as I remember it. I have kept to myself these past years, knowing if I took a friend my truth would flood out, no way to stop it. Then I would lose you."

Arva once again reached to untie the bow, peer inside, see the words her mother had laboured over, wept over, vomited in the slop bucket over, but her hand was stopped again.

"Not yet, Arva," she said. "It's not time. You remember fragments, I am sure, but they come to you through a child's eye, an innocent eye, an unknowing eye. Only when you are so far in love that a man has swallowed your soul and consumes you completely will you understand. When you will give all, ask or want or need for nothing, that is love, Arva. Before that." She let go of Arva's hand. "Before that you will judge me."

Her mother stood up suddenly, and went to the window. "I need to see the ocean," she said. "Wherever I go, I need the water. Can't rest without the wind. Can't rest without the tide. I hope there's a seaside with Jesus."

She paused, forehead lying against the cold glass, lips void of blood, her hands up to her neck. "Oh God, Arva, he was my undoing. Our undoing." She turned. "Then again, there was never much to undo."

Arva remembered her mother's smell that night, unusual spices and lavender powder. The room overflowed, her presence more potent than it had been in years. "Arva, my love," she added, leaning down, holding her daughter's chin in her hand, grip strong. "Never think me placid. For if you do, everything I have done in my life will come to nothing."

Her mother freed one of Arva's hands from the ledger and placed something on her palm. Then, she folded Arva's hand within her own, paper on rock.

The sun started to rise, the black sky dragging up a deep redness on the edge of morning light, sailors take warning. Her mother walked from the room, a hauntingly slow pace, and held the doorknob in the turned position so the door would close with only a soft click. Arva opened her hand, her mother's silver dragonfly, delicate double-looped wings, tiny ruby eyes scratched away. She sat on the very edge of the bed until daybreak, willing the door-knob to turn back, the soft click to unsound, but it never did.

Jacky Morgan fished her out of the harbour in early dawn, her dress floated up around her waist, short curls drowned, slippers lost, a sea snail tucked into her apron pocket.

"I don't know what could've been in her head, wandering around here at night," Jacky said. "With any kind of dew, this wharf's as slick as an icy pond."

"I knew that woman was tormented first time I lay eyes on her," Ruth, Jacky's wife said, her arm wrapped tightly around Arva's shoulder. "A tormented soul. Lord have mercy."

Arva was still holding the green ledger tightly against her hollow chest, lungs like her mother's, no longer wanting air, left fist pushed into her gaping mouth.

"Don't you worry, my love," Ruth had said. "Jacky's got a cousin in Holyrood with three young boys, another on the way. She could use a bit of help, no doubt about that. I bet she'll take you in until you find somewhere permanent to go."

Arva looked over at Clive, his socked feet jutting from underneath their wedding quilt, lips slightly parted, breath seeping whiskey into the room. His arms were out from under the covers, folded hands resting lightly on his groin. She lifted the sweaters, the dress, ornaments, photo, and slid the cold ledger softly back into place. "Not just yet, Mother," she whispered, hearing her own quiet voice in her ear. "Not just yet."

"Put down the Skipper," Clive called out as he burst through Old Man Crane's bedroom door. "I's got somethin' come for ye."

Arva was just helping Old Man Crane out from the blue plastic chair, his tired bowels complaining with a mild case of runs.

"For the holy love of Christ, Clive," he roared, skeleton hands gripping the metal supports. "Can't a dead man have nar speck of privacy with his nurse? She was mine before she was yers, ye know."

"Oh jeez, Skipper," Clive said, head bowed. "Pardon me. I didn't realize. Take yer time. Take yer time. Arva, when yer ready, there's somethin' for ye on the kitchen counter."

Arva helped Old Man Crane into his bed, brought the bucket through the kitchen, her husband there smiling like a stray cat when the caplin roll. Out into the yard, she rinsed the bucket and threw it down the outhouse hole. Then back to the kitchen to find Clive leaned over a brown package secured with beige post office twine, return address 'Eaton's.'

"Go ahead, open it." He nudged the parcel towards her.

She slipped a finger underneath a fold and began to rip away the paper. Clive was on his toes, a child at Christmas, excited hand reaching over to tear the wrap from someone else's gift.

"A snowsuit," he said, box still sealed, an open grin showing most of his teeth. "I saw ye don't got nar one, don't know how ye've been gettin' through these winters without one. I ordered it up from the catalogue."

Arva put her palm on the powder pink two-piece snowsuit in the box, tags sticking out around the collar. Her hand expected to find the suit already warm, the pink colour actually generating its own comfortable heat. She scratched her nails on the fabric, a music of sorts.

"Go ahead then, try it." He grabbed the snowsuit from the box, held it up against her. "Go on. Give 'er a try," he said. "Timin' couldn't be better." He nodded his head towards the window, snow was falling, the first real snowfall of the season, a display of impressive fat flakes hovering in a windless sky. "We'll do the walk up the mountain."

Arva slipped into the suit, pulled the belt in as tight as possible. There was still plenty of room, even though her body was already bloated, swelling.

"I can tell I'm expanding already," she said, her voice sounding somewhat apologetic.

"Like ye should, Arva, me love," Clive said, his hand circling her powder pink belly. "Like ye should. I got a couple of sizes bigger so ye could wear it this season. That's usin' me old noggin." He tapped his temples with his index finger.

It was a comfortable fit, but for some reason the image of Lolly wearing the suit ruffled up and settled on her mind. Lolly seemed a pink person, while Arva considered herself a green, the colour of living, the colour of life. Lolly would love this suit, she would prance in this suit, catching the eye of both man and sheep alike. She envisioned Lolly, a pink bunny hopping up a hill, Frank Smith, or the like, in a dark blue bunny suit hopping up behind her. Arva smiled to herself.

Clive watched her changing expression. "Ye likes it then?"

"Yes, really. Pink. It's lovely."

She pulled on her heavy boots, woolen cap and red mittens, and walked with Clive out into the wonder of the first storm. Down the lane a ways, they could make out the shape of Ethel Drover's head in her window, her presence there a local mainstay, an attentive mind no doubt wondering who was climbing the crag in this kind of weather. "She got her nose glued to that window no matter what's goin' on," Clive said. "She'd be right there, parked, if a sheep was droppin' a button on her lawn." He laughed, voice light, trying.

They trekked up the front of the mountain, Arva's feet sliding in old boots, treads worn smooth. The ground was coated in clean white, as if God had unfolded a newly starched bed sheet, lashed it hard, let it float down onto an earthy bed, mountainous pockets of air trapped.

Clive showed her John Cabot's Cave, which was not much more than a hole in the rock, drips of water echoing within, plummeting to an unknown depth. Clive climbed in, dissolved into the damp darkness, and did not emerge until Arva, panicked hands cold and sweaty inside her mittens, had called down the hole in a high-pitched voice.

Together they sat on the lip of the hole. Snowflakes, like huge shavings of ice, glazed his hat, crystals landing on his curling eyelashes. He reached into his pocket for his flask of whiskey. "Just a swally to keep the cold away." Arva took a drink too, its sharpness shocking the chill from fingers and toes.

Through the snowy blanket, she could barely make out the usually thick painter's stroke of blue that was the sea. Across the harbour, Bell Island had vanished, enveloped. Arva brought her face to the sky, eyelids shut, and felt the flakes, like a child's fingers, caressing her cheeks. She resisted the temptation to brush them away, alleviate the slight itch they produced when melting, and instead relished the minor annoyance. Something so plain, she thought, let her know she was still here, still grounded, and growing something with Clive. She pushed back against the side of the cave, glancing down occasionally to make certain that the ocean was still just a stone's throw away.

"Arva?"

"Yes."

"What's got ye thinkin'?"

"Oh," Arva answered, her face returned to the sky. "I'm just enjoying the snowfall, Clive. That's all."

"Why don't ye tell me? I's not bad t'all for lendin' an ear."

"Really Clive," she answered, catching a flake on her tongue, feeling like a girl. "I'm just enjoying being here."

Clive slid from the lip of John Cabot's Cave, and searched out his mother's house. The snow was almost blinding, but the bright green two-story biscuit box shone through for him.

They had been married for four weeks now, and Arva's vagueness was already beginning to wear a bit thin. He had always loved a puzzle, yes, no doubt, but where's the thrill if it was never going to be solved? He thought for sure that once they were married, once he did the right thing, she would let him in on it. Her riddle, her story, whatever that was. There was something there, he was sure of it, and so was everyone else. They were waiting to hear, he'd bet on that. He thought if he tried to love her, and he was giving it his best shot, swear to his mother, she would share. He'd be the only one in the cove who would know. Although he might tell Alfie he'd been told, but that's it, as Alfie was as smitten with her as he was. Though Alfie was smitten with any female on two legs.

And Jesus, pregnant already. He was proud, proud as a man could be. Able to make a baby, and that's something. And God, he loved that little thing, boy or girl, didn't matter, but a boy would be real nice. Yes, he was in for the long haul. She seemed happy, living her days, taking care of Old Man Crane like nobody else would. And he'd just gotten her a new snowsuit, hadn't he? Picked it out on his own, well, with just a bit of help from Lolly. God, maybe there was nothing to her, maybe she was just slow. Sometimes she seemed it, taking so long to answer an easy question. Maybe she was simple. Like Alek. No. Hell no. Then the joke would really be on him.

Clive looked up at Arva, her head toward heaven, strands of hair spilling out from under her hat, jolting against the pink, a swell, black as pitch.

He stood, began making his way down the mountain, feet

sideways, slipping on smoothed snow-covered stretches of rock. Arva lingered a moment longer then followed. When they arrived at the highroad, he headed left, towards Mercer's Lane.

"I's goin' to Mother's for a bite of lunch," he said. "Then I's headin' to the Lodge." She watched him get eaten up in the storm, a swirl of flakes making him melt so fast, she had to stare down at her new snowsuit to be sure he had actually been there at all.

With boots like broad skis, body all powder pink, Arva turned right, and carefully slid down over the hill. She was moving toward Old Man Crane's, his red bungalow like a glowing hearth. A quick glance, she saw Ethel Drover still at her perch, probably wondering why Arva Mercer was making her way over the highroad alone.

4

I despised every minute of it, as most women likely do. Living together in a drafty house, the constant meals and cleaning, listening to him drone on, me watching his stubble grow. There was no room for my skirt to just swish. Everything was confined, my entire life was strapped down. What a breath I exhaled when the entire world was taut with the promise of war, and Henry left for the factories in Ontario. There was no finer time for the working man or the married woman.

It was a Wednesday morning in mid-November, when Arva glimpsed Lolly's feet skitter in front of the kitchen window, heavy winter boots unlaced, a flannel nightdress, bare legs. Arva had been stirring tapioca on the stove for Old Man Crane. "I hates eatin' fish eyes," she knew he would say, but it would give him strength.

Then black boots caught her eye, a hinge groan, bitter draft.

"For God's sake, Lolly," Arva called out as soon as the back door scraped open. "Come in out of the cold."

She rushed in, winter air still panting around her nightdress, and plopped down hard on the daybed. Lolly's face was swollen from sobbing, her eyes closing like a tapped clam, body bloated, a dead fish knocking at the shore.

"My dear Lord," Arva said as she poured the glutinous cream into a deep glass dish. "What's the matter?"

"Ye got to help me, Arva." Lolly spoke through pastry lips. "I don't know what else to do. I can't even go into the school. If I misses another day, I'll be canned for sure."

Arva sat down next to Lolly on the daybed and took her icy hand in hers.

"Yes, of course, Lolly. Anything I can do."

"Oh God," she said, words beginning to tumble out. "I had to tell Mother. I couldn't hide it no more, not with the way I's been feelin'. Then she starts into talkin' all kinds of talk 'bout food. Me bein' in a pickle, in a jam. Got meself in a fine stew now. I says, Mother, if ye don't quit talkin' to me 'bout food, I's goin' to throw up all over ye, and then ye'll be right sorry. Ain't got a kind word in her head to say to me. Not a kind word. Stompin' 'round the house with a mouth on her like a cat's ass." Tears welled up and held steady at the edge of Lolly's puffed lids. "And he won't marry me. There's no way. He's already got a wife, can't take on another, he says, though he'd love to." She snickers. "Dirty bastard. I tells Mother Alfie would take me hand, but she says she'd go down in her grave before she allows the likes of that." Lolly wipes her nose in the sleeve of her nightdress. "Now, there's a temptin' thought."

"God Lolly, what are you saying?"

"I met him the night of the dance, Arva. Same night ye met Clive," she said, chewing at cracked nails, flecks of cherry-coloured polish sticking to her baby-sized teeth. "He came down from Bay Roberts. Handsome as the devil. Should've given he a wide berth." Her lips shake. "Well, I knows now. I admits me mistake."

"Oh, I'm so sorry," she said, Lolly's dilemma finally finding a form in Arva's mind. Her own curdling wave of nausea pushed up, she stood, needing to busy her hands. "A cup of tea to warm you, then. A slice of toast with Ethel's partridgeberry jam." She reached for the wire toast racks on a hook next to the woodstove.

"No, Arva, I don't got no taste for nothin'," Lolly said, her mouth like a connor. "I told Mother all 'bout yer mother, bein' a midwife and all before ye was born. Mother says to me, if she knowed how to deliver 'em, then she knowed how to get rid of 'em. And Mother says she likely taught ye." She rubbed her lap with damp hands, nightdress jerking. "She took herself down to Lorna Lynch's just now, tellin' she I's wunerful sick, and tellin' me I'd better be comin' 'round by the time she climbs the hill. She won't have it in the house, she says. Like ice to me. Like ice."

"I'm not sure what you want me to do, Lolly."

"For Christ's sake, I's askin' ye to help me. Tell me yer mother told ye what to be at in these –" her eyes shifted, "– delicate circumstances."

Arva's mother had been a midwife when she was a young woman, having learned the art of delivering babies from her own mother, a midwife until she died. Most often during the darkest and longest nights of December and January, the women helped babies drop down towards light and into soft waiting hands. "People fall in love again during the springtime," her mother had told Arva. "Getting their babies underway for the cold season. That way, it saves on wood. A woman with child generates enough warmth to heat the whole house during the snow."

Arva began to rifle through the cupboards, pulling out jars, laying them on the countertop. "I suppose she did, Lolly. I suppose she taught me."

In fact, Arva remembered the very night that her mother had shown her the knitted bag. She had been twelve when a haggard woman had arrived at their door, with her fourteen-year-old daughter, vice grip on her arm, and a bright white wedding dress slung over her shoulder.

"Look what she gone and done to the family," the woman uttered, shoving the girl towards the center of the room, girth near her waist, but limbs of twigs. "I needs this dress hemmed for next week, and if ye can pull enough fabric 'round the center to give it a puff or a pleat, or somethin' to cover her, ye'd be a real saviour." Voice choked, mouth suddenly distorted, an apologetic wave of a weakened hand and they were gone.

When the woman and girl had left, Arva's mother looked hard into her daughter's eyes and said, "Never wear white for that. Never. Some men set out with that in mind, thinking they've got a good catch, best reel her in fast. Or they like the look of the father's boat or the mother's cow, you never know. But don't let that make up your mind for you. The kitchen is a woman's place, and she should know the uses of everything there."

Then her mother went to the knitted purse and pulled out various containers, showing each to Arva. Liquid ginger, peppermint oil, dried catnip, ground black pepper, cinnamon, parsley, marjoram, juniper berries from ground juniper found on the floor of most woods. Powerful spices and leaves in her hand-made sack. She never put her seasonings onto a shelf in any house, that would mean moving in, settling down, fashioning a home. After the last container was returned to bag, she said, "In high doses, these will bring on the curse. Get it early though, before its heels are dug in too deep."

"How can ye think 'bout cookin', Arva," Lolly said, standing up in her father's boots, puddle of water at her feet, "when I's in this state."

"I'm not cooking, I'm seeing what we have in the cupboard." She wiped her hands in a damp cup-towel, wanted though to swipe it across her forehead, cool her skin. "How far along are you?"

"Not far, enough to know is all."

Arva opened a jar and sniffed, no strong smell, the potency evaporated. "There's not much here by the looks of it. I can't see that Mr. Crane has bought a single spice since his wife died. Give me a minute to check on him, and we'll head over to your house. We can't do this here."

Lolly fell back to the daybed, splattering the water with her loose boots, bottom of her nightdress sodden. Arva brushed past her, stepping over the mess, on her way to Old Man Crane's bedroom.

"Mr. Crane, I've got to go with Lolly for a couple of hours. She's ill."

"Self-inflicted, by the sounds of her," he said, eyebrows tunneled together. "Nothin' wrong with me earholes, ye knows."

"Will you be okay on your own, then? For an hour or two?"

He pointed his finger to a shelf on the opposite wall. "Get me me Bible from up there. Might smooth the way if I gives up the ghost with the good book clasped in me hand." A thin smile, but when Arva's eyebrows furrowed, he said, "Go on with ye Arva. I'll be fine."

"What kind of ol' muck is that?" Lolly asked, mug of hot brown syrup in her hand.

"Drink it all. It will help you along."

She put her nose to the mug. "I can't manage it, I'll be sick."

"Well, it's your choice. Manage this or manage that," Arva said with a loop of her hand towards Lolly's abdomen. "If you don't feel right about it Lolly, throw it down the sink. No one's forcing you."

"Yes, no one, for sure. Ye've never been alone with me mother."
Lolly pinched her nose, tipped back her head, and gulped the vis-
cous stimulant down.

"Now drink this."

Arva handed her a tall glass of water, and Lolly sucked down
every drop.

"Twasn't that bad," she said, pawing at the corners of her
mouth with the back of her hand. "Sort of peppy taste in me
mouth. Game of cards?"

"I don't think we'll have time for that," Arva said, leaning her
back against the speckled countertop.

Even though Old Man Crane's and the Young house were
identical in structure, the two homes felt completely different.
Rocks outside the kitchen window sloped lower at the Young's,
so there was more light, but the Crane house felt warmer, as if
more tenderness and compassion were living inside the walls.
The Young's was somewhat stark, wallpaper yellowing, nothing
hanging on the kitchen walls except of a faded print of the
Lord's Prayer. "I can't fathom why," Lolly had once said to Arva,
"if the Lord Jesus hisself was s'posed to of been a carpenter, why
whenever I sees his hands they looks like he never touched a nail
nor a board. Smooth as a baby's rear end. Must've been some
type of supervisor, or somethin'."

The walls in the Crane house were filled beyond comfortable capacity. Peggy Crane had loved to cross-stitch, and over
the years her kitchen became smattered with framed flowers,
pieces of fruit, a God Bless This Home. Near her stove, she had
hung nearly a dozen colourful spoon rests, gradually collected
from Mercer's shop. Above the table, an enormous wooden
spoon and fork, a gift from Alice, adorned the wall.

"Oh God, Arva. Tell me it ain't goin' to hurt. Tell me that. I
thinks I been through enough."

"From my understanding, you're about to have the worst
bout of diarrhea you've ever encountered, but it won't last long."

"Anythin', I guess, is better than the alternative. This stomach. Having the likes of Alfie take me hand."

Lolly took a seat at the metal table, re-dealt the cards already
lying there, and set out a game of solitaire. She was placing a

black jack over a red queen when she scraped back her chair, bent over. She was cut in half, arms gripping her waist like a blow was struck, wind gone. "Good Jesus, Arva. Somethin's overtake me. Help me to the bucket."

In the corner of Lolly's room was a white enamel slop bucket used instead of the outhouse during frosty winter nights. Lolly crouched down, holding her nightdress up over her sweaty back. Her face was waxen, nose running, violent splashes and gurgling audible throughout the room. The smell was a peculiar jumble of human surplus and festive seasoning.

"Lord, Arva," Lolly cried out. "Mother's Christmas spice. She'll have me head on a platter." She began to whinny like a frightened horse. "Jesus, what have ye got done to me," she moaned. "Leave me be, for the love of Christ, leave me be. I's on fire." Arva retreated into the hall. "Oh God, Arva, don't leave me, for the love of God, don't leave me."

"I have to, Lolly. I need to make the bath." Lolly's grunts and whimpers leaked out into the hall.

Arva hauled the round galvanized tub into the middle of the kitchen. She lifted Rose's hot-water pot off the back of the stove, full kettle too, and filled the washing tub. Heat swarmed her face, steam uncovering forgotten handprints on the window. She refilled the pots from the water barrel in the porch, laid them back onto the woodstove to heat.

Lolly emerged from her room, crooked at her side, slop bucket in pale hand. "I got to clean this meself, own up for t'all. The stink's somethin' wicked," she said on her way through the porch door, boots still on.

Lolly returned to find Arva standing over the tub, stirring water with her long arm, sleeve rolled way up. When she brought her arm up, the skin was reddened. "Get in, Lolly," she said. "This heat will bring on the cramps."

"Bring 'em on? Ye've got to be jokin' me. I already got a knot in me belly that's as welcome as a rock cod," Lolly said, her words faded.

Nevertheless, Lolly listened, slipped out of her nightdress without a hint of shyness, underwear already gone. "I hopes to Jesus no one comes to the door."

Her body barely fit. "Keep down," Arva said. "As best you can."

Curled in the tub, she looked like a fat newborn with massive breasts, crisscrossed in dark blue veins. They reminded Arva of her own breasts, already preparing to fuel a milk supply. Lolly's skin was flour white, cheeks turning scarlet, berry wine stains on a tablecloth.

"Oh the heat, 'tis terrible. I feels like 'tis bringin' on a fever," Lolly said. "I feels me heart beatin' up in me head." The side of her face was floating in the tub, her blond hair darkened, knees bent up, water sloshing. Lolly moaned, "I's never goin' near that bastard..." She could not finish, the cramps intensified, eyelids lowering.

Arva squat down next to the side of the tub, keeping a firm hand on Lolly's shoulder. That was what her mother had always done when she was ill, kept a hand on, and Arva would draw her strength out through it. She peered up at *Our Lord's Prayer*, Jesus' hands open, palms up, leaving his strength out in the open for just anyone to seize. Then, she looked down at Lolly, and noticed her eyes had been fixated on the same image, not that there was much to stare at in this kitchen. Arva saw a thin stream of slimy blood ooze out from underneath Lolly's rump, snaking its way through the water, and she knew Lolly's body was empty.

"Okay," Arva said, her hand touching Lolly's damp hair. She helped her from the tub, into a fresh nightdress, gave her a wad of cotton shaped into a pad. "It'll be fine, now. I'll go collect your mother at Lorna's. She can tend to you. Are you going to be okay for a few minutes on your own?"

No response. Arva began to leave, Lolly deep under a heavy quilt, her back towards Arva. Lolly somehow seemed smaller now, shrunken, no longer glowing from housing a doubled-up quotient of souls. Just one soul now, weary, spent.

Then, "Mother says I should be more like Arva, less like me." Quiet.

"She's nothin' but a whore," Clive fumed when Arva told him about Lolly. He shoved his chair back from the table, scratching the linoleum, piece of unchewed cod still in his cheek.

"It was a mistake, Clive. She was in love."

"Love?" Clive retorted, swallowing hard. His eyebrows were lifted, face hot. "Jesus Christ, ye dumb broad. Only person Lolly

Young ever loved was herself."

Arva pushed the salted fish and boiled potatoes across her plate, stomach sour. She had only done what Lolly had wanted, what Rose had wanted. Lolly had asked, begged, for her help. A woman's body and its workings were nothing a man would ever understand. She should not have told him. A woman must always keep some things to herself. She was learning.

"Ye can't go 'round doing shit like that, Arva. People'll think yer some kind of witch. Is that what ye wants? Where'd ye find out the likes of that to anyways? Probably from yer mother. And we all knows what happened to her. Word gets 'round, Arva, ye needn't think it don't." He pulled his red and black lumber jacket from the coat hook in the porch, fist to the screen. November air stole in and swirled around Arva's legs. "Don't let me catch you near ...." His words were sliced as the door slammed.

Arva brought her plate to the garbage and scraped its contents into the bin. Her mouth tasted of metal, the unpleasant flavour of someone walking out. Just then, she felt a faint flutter deep in her stomach, a small bubble rising from the pot bottom as it neared boiling. There. Again. A nascent butterfly was unfolding its wings for the first time, the quickening. That awareness brought on a hunger that overwhelmed her, and she sat down in Clive's chair and ate every bite of his tepid meal.

Shortly after supper, there was a soft tap at the back door, knuckles shaped inside soft mittened hands. He had returned early, sorry for the harshness, wanting to be close. The back door creaked opened tentatively. No, it was Rose Young peering in from the porch, dull eyes blinking rapidly in the darkened storage area.

"I seen Clive leavin', and just came 'round to tell ye Lolly's fine. She's feeling right fine. I don't know what ye did, but it seems to of worked."

"I'm glad she's doing okay," Arva said.

"And Arva," Rose said, her feet cloaked in the very same black boots as Lolly wore earlier, shuffling against the linoleum. "It goes without sayin', right, that I could use, would appreciate yer..." She thought for a moment, scratched at her neck. "Discretion. Yes, discretion." Then, she was on her way out the door, turned her head, an afterthought. "And ye needn't be concerned 'bout me bit of Christmas spice. I'll pick up some more at Mercer's in time for the fruitcake."

That night Arva dreamed of a wooden spin-top, turning, turning on a rusted lathe. Dusty hands pressed a chisel into the softwood, creating faint lines, a manly ornament. Completed, those weathered hands held it open to two young boys, eyes fresh like dawn in summer. They both tried to clutch the wooden gem, pudgy fingers undulating like jellyfish drawing in water. But there was only one spin top, when two were badly needed.

Arva woke with the pressure, her bladder the size of a pinhead. Clive was asleep next to her, lying on his back, his snore a drone of swarming bees, his right hand warming a cheek. He had a right to have been angry. What had she been thinking? He looked peaceful enough now, though, she thought. Still a boy really. Married at twenty-two, baby already well under way.

The night was too pleasant to resist. Arva wrapped a shawl around her shoulders and stepped out onto the front step. Concrete, painted white, hardly bore a shoeprint, only a stranger would call using the front door, and there were few strangers here. The night was clear, wind a cold damp jet, ever salty on her lips. Snow was huddled up against walls, tucked in tight around rocks, concealed behind the wooden lattice decorating the step.

She looked out over the water, it mirrored the moon, not a whitecap in sight. Lights were on in the few homes on Bell Island, twinkling like diamonds on a white sheet, though Arva had never seen a diamond to be sure. Who could be up at this hour, she wondered, other than a pregnant woman? A woman who was trying to dig down, find fresh water beneath the stability of soil, nourish a seed, and reclaim a soul.

Clive did not stay angry for long, and Lolly was there on the eve of Christ's birth, dressed head to toe in passion red.

The Christmas season announced itself with a wicked snowstorm. Old Man Crane said he felt it in his brittle bones several hours before the sky opened up and the entire fluffy contents poured down. "That's a good sign," he had said. "Startin' fresh, not a bit of old dirt in sight."

Arva bathed him in the late afternoon as best she could with a soft cloth and bucket of soapy water. No matter how often she washed him, just to get him clean or because he had soiled himself, she blushed when she came to his groin, deflated, lifeless. He would always notice her colour, and twitter, "I's too old to be ashamed of meself. Keep on scrubbin', maid. 'Tis not sparklin' yet."

She shaved the scattered colourless bristles sticking out from his chin, and combed his hair up and over from the back, smoothed it with a daub of cream, helped him into fresh pajamas. Clive walked him to the rocker in the kitchen, next to the woodstove, his body an outline, shoulders stooped, a woolen blanket draped across his pinpoint knees.

"God, Arva," Old Man Crane said. "Ye've got some shockin' good job done on the tree."

Clive had chopped down a soft-needled fir, nailed a wooden cross into the bottom, dragged it into the kitchen. From her trunk, Arva has gotten out her white crocheted Christmas ornaments her mother had made, snowflakes, tiny stars, a winged angel for the crowning glory. Peggy Crane had a box of ornaments packed away in the attic, silver balls that came to an elongated twist at the base, each one individually wrapped in tissue paper.

"Ain't laid eyes on those balls in years. To be truthful, I ain't laid eyes on a tree in years. Alice was always wantin' me to come down for Christmas, but I got no interest in tryin' to get out over those roads in the winter. She gets rocks in her head this time of year, always did, fumes off the new catalogues makin' her right cracked." Old Man Crane snapped his gums. "A drop of whiskey, b'y," he said. "For a bit of cheer."

"Not too much, Clive," Arva said. "It's not good on his stomach."

"And who's problem'll that be?" he said to Arva, lips parting to a smile and a wink. "At least a finger or two up the glass, Clive. Come on, b'y. 'Tis Christmas."

Clive brought a generous serving to Old Man Crane and helped himself to a mug. Arva began to lay a few things out onto the table, Peggy's Christmas tablecloth hanging down, white with edges of green and red lace. There were plates of short-bread cookies topped with candied cherries, dense dark fruitcake, fresh bread, slices of corned beef from a can. She ran a damp towel over a bottle of bakeapple wine, a coveted treasure tucked away in the shadiest corner of a bottom cupboard.

Doris came into the porch on a snow-smothered gust, a dish of date squares in her gloved hand. She rushed into the heat of the kitchen, handed her sandy corduroy coat to Clive, and sat to put on her pink felt slippers with rubber soles. Then a second lick of wind curled in on the heels of the first.

"Pull the door to," Old Man Crane called out from his rocker. "For the love of Jesus. What do ye think I's at here? Tryin' to heat the damn harbour?"

The shiny smiling faces of Lolly and Rose appeared in the door, older version and younger side-by-side. Lolly shook her coat down from her shoulders, revealing a low cut red dress, snug across her chest, one, maybe two, sizes too small. Against a white door, she looked like a skinned seal belly-up on the ice.

"I knows," Rose said shaking her head at Doris. "A bit much for a drop of tea on Christmas Eve. She reckons the Queen might be droppin' by, I s'pose." Her eyes rolled, eyebrows up.

"Not me fault I looks good in city clothes," Lolly said, hands moving down the hot fabric. "This is the very thing they's wearin' in St. John's. The very thing. If I don't blend into this friggin' bay, then to hell with it."

"Watch yer lip, Lolly," Rose said. "Or we'll hove ye right back out into a snow drift. Heat comin' off that dress might knock the good out of the storm."

"What do ye think, Arva?" Lolly said. "I ordered it up from the catalogue."

"It's lovely, really," Arva said, trying to keep her eyes to the black window, flakes batting up against it, wanting to come in, not realizing that warmth would be their end.

Lolly was curvy, there was no hiding it, but she made every effort to accentuate it. Arva figured it was all to do with Lolly's father. Having grown up without Lyle in her life, living under the wide and rigid thumb of Rose, Lolly secured her attention from whatever sources were available. Then again, Arva thought, she grew up without her father, or very little of him. Though she did recall a few things when she cared to concentrate. His smell was similar to newsprint, stale, sterile, like he had not washed, but never had a need to. His eyes were light brown, with little yellow strings that curved out from the pupil, the whites often blood-shot. Missing from his mouth were two back left molars, she had seen the bumpy span of healed pink gum when he hooked open his cheek with a bent finger. "See what yer mother did to me?" he said. "Forgive her, she's not well in the head." Ah, yes, Arva remembered, her fairy book, the frying pan.

"'Tis awful out. Awful," Doris said with more zest than nec-essary, all eyes unpasted from Lolly's dress. "Hope this lets up, or I won't be gettin' back up the hill."

"Oh, I'll make sure ye do," Clive chimed in, a laugh though no joke. "Or, I'll carry ye up meself."

"Now, then. That'll be somethin' to see." Doris said. "But ye can put that right out of yer mind and get me a glass of yer syrup, Clive. Raspberry, if ye got it."

Clive was just lifting the jug to tip water into his mother's syrup when there was loud banging on the back door. He might have dropped the glass in the metal sink, but a mug of Irish whiskey, the good stuff, had steadied him. Arva made an obvious start when they knocked, even though she had been expecting it. Mouths pressed up to the door, drunk voices muffled. "Any jannies allowed in?" They were straining high.

Arva had only seen jannies before at a distance, between the crack in the curtains and the window frame; she had watched them slipping in the streets, intoxicated giggles. But in Upper Island Cove, no home was missed, no doorknob left unrattled. It was Christmas tradition, the jannies would descend upon homes, willing or otherwise, dressed in whatever bawdy clothes they could find to disguise themselves. The motley gang danced, sang, ate whatever they were given and sometimes what they were not, took a hefty drink, and then ran back out the same way they came, skipping on in search of another nip, optimism springing forth with the next lighted house.

The party boomed through the door, seemed to explode out of the porch and into the kitchen. One almost tumbled right into Old Man Crane, and would have if Clive had not hooked him around the slender belly and jostled him to the center of the floor. They were a whiskey-scented blur of old women's dresses, black ski masks, a disheveled curly wig, dripping black boots needing a dry mop. Music erupted from nowhere in particular, feet clacking the linoleum, warm hands smacking, a soft whistle, lyrical voice, mouth organ.

"Good to see ye, Skipper Jo," one of the jannies called out.

"Jesus, that one must be Junior Lynch," Old Man Crane says, pointing with a single finger unwrapped from his tumbler. "Gut on he like the side of a barn."

One danced by Clive, elbows out, head jutting back and forth like a pecking chicken, one foot lifted from the floor, then the other. He tried to grab Doris, but she predicted the advance, dropped her glass on the table, and held tight to her seat with both whitened hands. His pink polka-dotted smock was turned inside out, an old apron had the pockets facing inwards, even the hat was on wrong, white label protruding into the air.

"That there's got to be Alek," Clive called out, leaning down to nudge Old Man Crane. "Sure as there's shit in a cat." He took a wide mouthful of his whiskey, glass resting on his teeth, lips missed. "Don't let the fairies get ye, b'y."

Rose tipped her head towards one and whispered to Doris, "I knows who he be's. I's certain that's Alfie. 'Tis Dot's dress, the one she wears when she's haulin' caplin up off the beach. And look at the way he's onto Lolly. Lord help us. He's ol' enough to be her father. He'd better keep his distance or I'll go over there and rip the mask right off him."

Doris kept watch, her mouth a horizon. She picked up her glass when it was safe, and stole quick sips of the deliciously sweet red syrup.

As quickly as the jannies had flooded in, they withdrew, leaving the room in a state of stunned shock, the air a little spent, caved in. Whiskey had been spilt here and there, a piece of corned beef was in the corner, bite missing, and the dish of Doris's date squares was knocked askew, baked oats tumbled out onto the tablecloth.

"I hope that's the last I sees of them this year," Doris said, checking the bottom of her new slippers for wetness. "Knowin' jannies is comin' 'round always makes me nervous. 'Tis a wonder one of 'em don't rob us blind, and we'd be the fools offerin' up a drop." She put her foot down firmly. "Get me a cloth, Arva, I cleans up the water."

At midnight, when even Lolly had left and Old Man Crane was snoring in his bed, Clive gave Arva a box that fit into her palm. A gift. It was a simple cross and fine chain to replace the shoddy silver dragonfly she always wore. "Who 'round here wears a bloody bug on their neck, anyways?" he had said, sharing with Arva the careful reasoning behind his selection.

Both items in the box were made of gold, and on the back of the pendant Clive had put in a special order to have their names engraved. 'Clive' going down the cross, 'Arva' imprinted along the width, both awkwardly sharing the 'v.'

"It's lovely, Clive," she said. "Very thoughtful." Her gaze rested on the cross for some time, until Clive wondered if she had suddenly fallen asleep with her eyes still open. Arva reached to touch the fly at the base of her neck, then slowly ran a finger along the smooth pendant in the box. "Lovely, yes," she repeated, and snapped the box closed with a soft smile.

"Wha? Yer sayin' ye've never been?" Alf Jones said, his slender form seated at Old Man Crane's kitchen table. "How can ye call yerself a Newfoundlander if ye've never gone ice-fishing?"

"I guess I've never had the chance," Arva replied.

That was something Arva had never done, fished in any shape or form. She had never cast a line into the water or jigged crabs with a string and hook while dangling over the side of a wharf. She had never scooped up live caplin tumbling in with the tide, schools so dense the waves were more solid tail and fin than liquid. She had never cut a hole through ice, peered into a dim sludgy pond, and felt excitement when a trout nibbled at a stiff bit of salt pork, hook concealed inside. No. Never fished. Never.

"Well, ye'll get yer chance today, me love," he said, "if I got any say. Isn't that right, Clive."

"That's right, Alfie," Clive said, standing behind Alf, hands firmly gripping his shoulders. "We'll make a Newf out of her yet, b'y."

"We'll take ye 'round to Three Puddles," Alf said, lowering his voice. "That's me secret spot."

Alf began fastening line to branches, adding silver hooks to the ends, selected by cautious fingertips reaching into the corner of a small brown paper bag. Clive got up from the table, went to the pantry and pulled a blackened apple juice can from the nail for a boil-up, and then started cutting a slab of salt pork into fish-bite cubes. Arva prepared a lunch, loose tea, some leftover canned meat, caramel squares, hard tack. She made several sandwiches, a well-loved combination of white bread, molasses, and butter (margarine, really, though it was always called butter).

"Don't go to no bother for me, missus," Alf said. "But if yer goin' anyways, I likes mine with molasses on first, then butter on over top. Tastes right queer other way 'round."

Clive slid the gear behind the seat, and boosted Arva up into the cab of the truck. Alf stepped up and in next to her, windows instantly steaming from hot breath. When Clive was behind the wheel, engine chuckling, Alf said with a snort, "Do ye thinks we should blindfold her? If she lets Old Man Crane in on Three Puddles, he'll pass it off to Ethel Drover for nothin' more than a taste of her blueberry jam. She'll let her lips go, pass me spot right 'round the harbour, then we'll be fished out, for sure."

"You've got my word, Alf," Arva said, leaning in on him. "Your secret is safe with me."

"Ye knows, Arva," Alf said with a long wink. "I believes it is."

"Let's get movin'," Clive said as he revved the engine. "Or the ice'll be thawed 'fore we even gets there."

The truck crunched over the snow as it backed up, and Clive drove down Main Road and up onto the highway. He turned once, then again, and finally turned onto a dirt road, where he continued until the passage became so narrow snow-laden branches and twigs screeched at the windows. The rolling truck stopped, and with some effort, Alf forced the door open and helped Arva out of the cab. They began to trek down a bumpy slope, Alf trudging through the dry snow, Clive and Arva both stepping into Alf's mammoth footprints.

"God Arva," Alf said. "I's not lovin' that pink suit, me dear. Someone's liable to catch sight of us from the highway, me spot'll be given away. Should've gotten green, a bit of camouflage for yerself."

"Oh, but I think the pink is lovely," she told Alf, a quick glance at Clive, his head turned away. "And if anyone strains that hard to see us from the highway, then they deserve your spot and all the fish in it."

"Come to think of it, the fish are apt to heed ye right through the ice. Don't go whinin' if ye get neither b'..." He stopped short. Alf's eyes had caught a shine. With boyish face opened, glossy lips parted, he looked as though he had just felt his first wave of puppy love. "Ah," he said in a church-service tone. "There she is."

Three Puddles was not quite three puddles, but two puddles and a pond. Actually, just a pond, as the two puddles had dried up years ago. A solid blanket of snow cleverly disguised Alf's favoured fishing hole, and someone hiking by might think the area was only an insignificant valley surrounded by forest and mountain. They would scarcely consider, according to Alf, that in the very middle, underneath the snow and thick ice, hid a sizeable stash of fat trout starving for a wee cut of salt pork.

Alf cleared an area of snow with the shovel, and Clive used his father's sharp axe to hack through the ice, frosty splinters flying up in his face and onto the sleeves of his jacket while he worked. In no time, fishing strings were unraveled, hooks were baited, and trout were being pulled up through the holes, slapped onto the ice, flip-flopping, blood oozing from ripped jaws.

"We got some whack of fish," Alf yelled to Clive. "Arva's a real trooper. Never thought someone so pink could fish like that."

"Yes, a real trooper," Clive answered, his full back to Alf.

"I reckon she's hauled up a dozen or more. Not afraid to yank the hook out neither. Got to coddle most women. Coddle them. Not yer Arva, though."

"What would ye know 'bout most women?" Clive said, a quiet laugh. "Ye been takin' yer Ol' Aunt Dot out to the ice lately?"

"What was that, Clive?" Alf called back. "What's that 'bout Dot?"

"Nothin'," he answered. "I's goin' to take me lunch, if anyone minds to join me. Arva?"

"Just one minute, Clive. I'll be there."

Clive ground at his back molars as he began to light a small fire by the side of the pond. He dipped the apple juice can through a widened hole and collected pond water for tea. Then, he tore into one of the sandwiches, gone crusty, bread spotted and sticky on the outside, black crystallized molasses leaking through. He had bitten into Alf's.

He could hear Alf explaining the rights of fishing to Arva.

He told how he peered down into the hole, used the reflection of his eyes as lure, watched the trout skulking in, a little tug or two on the line, get them interested in the taste of salt pork, and there, one of them hooked on in no time. "Yes," Clive heard Arva say to Alf. "I can see why the trout like your eyes, they're like big green marbles." Alf described the size of the trout in Gilly's Gut, twice what you would find here on any given day, gorgeous spotted pelts on them, would love a coat of it, he said, if he could only catch enough.

"Only man in Upper Island Cove with a genuine trout skin coat," Alf said. "Now that would cause some talk. Yes, b'y."

"Yes, I suppose it would," Arva answered. "Definitely would turn a head or two."

"Like that suit, I reckons," Alf said, laughing.

Though he tried hard to focus on the fire, get the tea boiling, Clive could not take his eyes off the two ice-fishers. She was hovering, yes, hovering over him. Seeing what he was hauling up out of his hole, her hole ignored, she could have a fish on for Christ's sake. Alf there with his dirty brown knitted hat perched on top of his head like an idiot, not even pulled down for a bit of warmth. Clive could see the icicle forming on the end of his padded nose from where he stood, snot frozen right up.

"Jesus, Clive," Alf yelled. "I's tryin' to get over for a bite of lunch, but me ass is stuck to the ice." Then to Arva, "Pardon me, me love. Shouldn't be usin' that kind of language in front of a lady." Then to Clive, "Ye might have to bring that axe over here and cut me out of it."

Ass stuck to the ice. Clive could take the axe over there, cut Alf down before he'd cut him out. Jesus, she had her hand on his shoulder, nudging him, trying to help him up. She barely touched Clive, never had a single streak of wildness in her, not like... Well, he'd been trying not to think about that.

"Come on, Arva, Alf." Clive's voice erupted, jaw tired from grinding. He threw steamy water from the juice can onto the smoldering fire, and stomped out the rest with his boot. "Let's get on out of it. Me throat is right raw, me feet are froze off me, and the dark is comin' on."

Alf freed himself from his spot, tape tearing away from paper. "Okay, then," he said. "We'll pack her in."

5

Night and day I could not stop moving. My hands twitched, my feet tapped, and I would wake at ungodly hours to find my fingers smoothing the bedsheet in a distinctly female rhythm.

"Women who aren't given children," Bette Mackay told me, "will never truly rest."

It was then that I decided to go and find you.

"What in the name of Jesus was that?" said Old Man Crane, his voice a rag torn from a rotted towel.

Arva gripped the edge of the countertop, knuckles pale. "It looked like a bear," she called. "A giant gray bear. All hunched up."

Standing at the kitchen window, she had been watching a cluster of young boys playing coppers, a hole dug in softened dirt where the snow had let go, precious pennies expertly tossed in the air. Then suddenly they scattered, feet slipping on the pebbles, pennies abandoned, as a scratch, thud, scrape, crunch filled their ears. Something was bowling down the mountain with fantastic natural tempo. The interior of the Crane bungalow shuddered with a quake that tested the foundation.

"Jesus Christ. Almost knocked me teeth out."

Arva leaned in over the sink as far as her girth would allow. She heard voices, hasty syllables, strident tones.

"Just missed us. Think it hit the Young's house," she said, face still to the window.

"Jesus. Sweet Jesus. Well what are ye waitin' for? I can hear the hens cluckin' already. Go and grab a look for yerself."

Arva went out the porch and up across the back of the house. She walked as fast as she could, swaying side to side with her bulky weight. Her body, grown broad in just a few short months, was now reminiscent of her mother's, not her own. It was mid-April, and there were subtle signs of spring everywhere, snow softening, slickers of ice along the path lifting away from the rock, a pledge with every drop from the rooftop.

Next door, there was already a horde of onlookers, well-established, places taken.

A rock had freed itself from the mountain's grip and chose a straight path downwards. It crossed the high road without looking and just missed the boys crouched in the laneway. Gaining speed, it plowed an easy hole through the Young's back picket fence, struck the house with full force just left of the kitchen window, made two grand turns, and came to rest permanently in Rose's vegetable patch. Upon impact, the window had burst. Bits of glass were strewn everywhere. Rose, her back to the mountain, had been shoved to the floor, prostrate, right hand reaching toward the hallway where bedroom doors were firmly closed. She was stunned, shaken, but not hurt.

There was close to twenty-five people in and out of Rose's house and garden by the time Arva stepped next door. Rose was seated, a chair centered in the room, surrounded by neighbours, like fish around a feed. They were in the kitchen, crowding the porch, and spilling out into the lane. Her back door was permanently ajar with friends coming and going, mothers pacing with babes-in-arms, men wearing a stripe up and down the linoleum, anxious hands gesturing towards the mountain. Even with the main window missing and without a single pot on the stove, her kitchen retained the permanent smell of boiled cabbage, salt meat, and solidified grease.

Everyone was chatting, an incessant hum. Some were questioning, some concerned, some exhilarated, some disappointed.

"Jesus, Rose."

"I saw that comin'. Been sayin' it for years."

"Jesus."

"Ye can thank God ye wasn't squat flat."

"Good Jesus."

"Could've been the end of ye, Rose."

"Should've been a lot worse by the looks of that rock."

"Only a matter of time somethin' like this happened."

"Well, ye finally got that rock garden ye was after."

"Jesus. Jesus."

Two men began scraping shards of glass from the countertop into a bucket, their hands hidden inside plaid shirtsleeves. They remembered Lyle, God rest his soul, and were more than willing to lend a hand to help out his widow. It was no trouble. Alf Jones and James Young, Lyle's cousin, were already on their way to get a new sheet of glass to repair the damage.

"Arva, Clive's gone after Alf and Jimmy to help with the new pane," Dot Jones said. "Have a seat. Shouldn't be standin' in yer condition."

"Are ye sure ye trust Alfie with a pane of glass?" Junior Lynch asked. "I saw him comin' out the Lodge not more than an hour ago."

Rose rolled her eyes up to the heavens. "Good Lord above. If he brings me a pane in more than one piece, I ain't puttin' out a copper for it."

"We'll have her cleared in a minute, Rose," Johnny Adams said. "It'll be as good as new in here."

"Thank God Lolly's at her cousin's," Rose said to her cluster of women, voice lowered.

"Yes," Dot replied, clasping her hands together. "Thanks be to God."

"Me Patricia was at her cousin's once," Amanda Adams said in a hushed tone. The ladies shuffled their feet, inspected their shoes for bits of glass.

"I should've gone straight to me cousin's," Lorna Lynch said with a furtive chuckle, and a nod in her husband's direction. "Instead of marryin' the likes of Junior."

Amanda caught Lorna's hand and all the ladies snickered, like old worn pirates conceding to the loss of treasure. Lolly's mess seemed less important now. The rock had tumbled into their lives and offered its hardened perspective.

"Someone's goin' have to move that rock, Dot," Rose said. "I got potatoes to set next month. Or I won't make it through the winter."

Dot rubbed her hand up and down Rose's back. "Don't ye worry yerself 'bout it, Rose. I'll get some tea started."

"Not a budge from ye, maid," Amanda said, bringing the

sugar canister and tinned milk to the table. "Sit for a spell and catch yer breath."

Clive returned with Alf and James, they with a wide pane of glass wrapped in a blanket, he with two cases of cold beer. Nippy April winds gusted in through the open window, but no one seemed aware of it.

"God love ye," Rose said to Alf and James. "I don't know what I would've done."

"God love ye," Junior Lynch said to Clive. "I's right parched."

Tea was served to all the women, and the floor was clear enough for Dot to step out of her black rubber boots and pull on the good slippers she had been carrying under her arm. Rose told Lorna about a bit of dark fruitcake in a Christmas tin behind the pantry door. A few thin slices were served, heavy with cherries, raisins, and candied fruit, the hint of liquor from once being wrapped in the luxury of rum-soaked cheesecloth.

Beers were passed around, bottles opened, and the workers stopping for refreshment. But in less than two hours, the glass was gone, window replaced. Junior Lynch was kneeling on the countertop, an obvious strain. With brush and rusted bucket in hand, he touched up the scrapes along the window frame with a tin of old paint he had found in the basement. His belly was hanging so far out over the lip of his pants, Jimmy called out, "Hey Junior, what's keepin' yer trousers up?" He winked hard and said, "Don't be talking." Lorna blushed.

Then Arva heard her name from the hallway, a low growl that cut through the clatter. She glanced over her shoulder to see Lolly with a clown's head, full make-up and blond hair pin curled, poking out the last door on the left. Her hand scooped the air, bidding Arva to draw closer.

As soon as Arva passed through the door, Lolly quickly closed and locked it behind her. The room smelled stale, like unbrushed teeth, and was littered with books, catalogues, backs broken and face down. Make-up was strewn across the dresser top, an empty water glass attached to the wooden nightstand, pink log cabin quilt rumpled, threads picked away.

"Jesus Mary," Lolly said, as she wrapped her arm through Arva's, "yer bloody huge."

Arva looked at Lolly, a gentle swell underneath her father's shirt, slight but there, her face floured, lips exaggerated with deep red lipstick. She was too close, Arva felt a tickle at the back of her nose.

"And here I is," she continued, her hands spreading emphasis across her belly. "Mother's cross-eyed at me. Won't even look at me. What kind of bloody luck have I got, Arva? Tell me that. How is ye?"

"I'm getting along," Arva replied, her eyes working to locate the ocean beyond the bedroom window. "Getting along."

Water found, still there, she was able to glimpse back at Lolly. Arva blinked. Blinked again. No, the image had not melted away, it made Arva's eyes sore, she wanted to rub her knuckles into them. The weight, condensed around Lolly's waist, hips, and thighs, was still there. Her body was sheltering an unclaimed child.

Arva had not seen Lolly since the beginning of March, when she had told Arva, with a roll of her eyes, that she was going to her cousin's house in St. John's for a while, maybe take a secretarial course over the summer. "Mother's makin' me," she had said. "I ain't been to work since Christmas. She don't want me in the house doin' nothin'."

"What about your teaching, Lolly?" Arva had asked. "I thought you loved that."

"Yes, well. I took a leave," Lolly had said. "Can't hurt to know how to type, me love. Get a nice job in an office in the city. Meet a rich man for meself."

Lolly released Arva's arm, needing the motion of her hands to fully use her voice. "Jeez, ye looks great," she said.

"You too, Lolly," Arva managed.

"I don't know, maid, I just couldn't stay clear of him. That bloke from Bay Roberts. He's a real doll. Potent, too." Lolly emitted an instant laugh that lasted only moments. "Well, Mother said I should be more like Arva."

"God, Lolly," Arva said. "What are you going to do?"

"Mother's sendin' me to the city in another week. Some home for types like me, she says. They'll put this to rights, she says. Stay there until I haves it. Then come on back from me cousin's." Another wide-mouthed laugh stopped before the sentiment had a chance to solidify.

Lolly sat down on the bed, patted a spot next to her. Arva

remained standing, achy as her back had become.

"Mother says there's some kind of soul tryin' to come through me, and I best not stave it off no longer. Superstitious old bat." Lolly started taking the pins from her hair. "She got me locked up in this house. Should be illegal. Probably is. Won't even dry me few drawers on the line for fear someone'll recognize 'em. I's near gone mad with it all. Mother said as soon as I puts either pound on, in the house I goes until I heads to the city. Can't bring the shame down on us she says. Neither husband. Like I needs remindin'."

"What's going to happen to the baby?" Arva spoke, fingers to her mouth.

"I's keeping it, that's what. Mother says I ain't, but she got another thin' comin'. Nice baby girl is what I wants for meself. That's what I's goin' to get, I knows it too. Tie her hair up in little pink ribbons. I'll take Mother's wedding band when I goes, that's what, stay in the city, and tell the men I meets that I's a widow." She fingered the corners of her mouth where small balls of lipstick had gathered. "I thought this through, Arva. Not much else to do these days but think."

Lolly lifted a plastic handheld mirror to her face, smiled at herself, hair new-wig perfect.

"I was on the slop bucket when the rock hit," she said, eyes still evaluating her image, lip kiss for herself. "Mother came to me, told me not to budge an inch. Like I was goin' to keep me ass plunked there all afternoon. Was there much damage?"

"No, not to your house," Arva said. "Your mother's a bit dazed. The rock rolled off and landed in the vegetable patch. Alf and Clive don't think it can be moved. She seems more upset about that than anything."

"Like she would," Lolly said. "Her damn potatoes. Cares more about some bloody ol' rock than her own flesh and blood."

When Arva slipped out of Lolly's room, the crowd had already thinned. People wanted to move to their own homes and scrutinize the rock, to assess its impact on their lives. What would change? What would remain the same? What could have happened, what likely might have happened, what should have happened, all things considered. They would spend the evening in close quarters with family thanking God for the pleasure of a cup of warm milky tea, and contemplating the near-death of a good-hearted well-rooted local woman who gave what she could to the Church.

Alf Jones kept Rose Young company, shaken up as she was, until the last glug of beer had been swallowed. "Any Lolly of Mother's is a… Well, any friend Lolly's of a is …" he had said, tongue plump behind his teeth. "Now, Rose, you means what I knows." Then Alf left her, both feeling better, to wander up the lane, his shoes tied snugly on the wrong feet.

Two weeks later, Rose's mood was considerably brighter. The insignificant pumpkin glow that once radiated during the evenings from Lolly's bedroom window had recently been replaced by cold blackened glass.

It was mid-May, and even though the grass was still dipped in frost every morning, Arva, Rose, and Alek were working side-by-side to sow potatoes. Clive had just turned the pebbly soil, and its scent, a melancholy mix of tiredness and willingness, had seeped in through cracked windows. "I smells the mood of that soil," Old Man Crane had announced. "Best to plant now, I says, 'fore the willingness lets out."

James Young had brought down a burlap sack of seed potatoes yesterday afternoon, and this morning, all three carried bowls overloaded with starchy chunks, each piece baring a pointed pimply eye. Alek was helping Arva; the baby had dropped down into her pelvis, and her movements were sluggish.

"Sit on a rock," Alek had said to Arva, his voice a speedboat. "I can do this. I can do this." But Arva needed to keep busy, keep her hands moving, or her mind would start to wander behind into places Arva never wanted to go. Wherever they had been together, Arva and her mother would try to sow a few rows of a garden each spring. When the leafy stalks flowered, then began to wither and dry, white-fleshed potatoes hiding underneath, her mother would often watch the patch through the window, well beyond darkness.

"We've got no clue what kinds of people live around here," she had said one night during her vigil. "We're apt to wake in the morning, stalks uprooted, every potato gone. All we'll get out of it is the scent of a nice feed of hash frying in the neighbour's house, bit of corned beef, their leftover cabbage, and brand new potatoes, tasting all the sweeter because they were stolen."

On occasion, Arva had woken in the morning to find her mother sleeping, still dressed, backside in a wooden chair, head slumped against the window ledge.

The planters walked along the rows, gardens separated by low stone walls. Rose sowed as best she could around the boulder settled right in the middle of her plot. The sky was a washed out blue, strands of cotton stretched taut and low across the horizon. Dissolved salt, lifted up from the ocean and blown inland, settled on their clothes, in around their hair.

"Fine day for it," Rose said.

"Yes. Yes," Alek said. "Fine day. Fine day."

"Yer some man, Alek Mercer," Rose said. "Helpin' out a couple of women with their spuds."

"Some man. Some man," he said, patting himself on the head with his empty hand. He carried his bowl down to the other end of the garden to begin planting there.

"How's Lolly feeling? Any word?" Arva said in a low tone, bent over, her swollen stomach rubbing against her lap.

"Oh Lord help us, Arva," Rose muttered. She stood, lifted an arm across her eyes to block the sun, her flat nose flaring, broad bottom lip jutting out more than usual. "She's in some fine state. How could she do this to me? But, she's off to the city now, where anythin' goes these days. That's what Helen Mercer says. Anythin' goes."

"She's doing fine, then?"

"Yes, she's doin' fine, me dear. I bet she's goin' 'round actin' like she don't have a care in the world. I told her to stay away from that b'y, it would only bring on trouble. But, no. She couldn't listen. What do I know? An old woman like meself. Thinks I got no idea what it is to be likin' a man. She was out 'round only a week after that business the first time. I told her to be careful. But, no. She goes on and gets herself in the same state she had herself in before. I haven't even met the man. Not that I'd let he in out of the porch, mind ye. Terrible sin 'tis, terrible sin." Her voice faded, losing might. "Well, 'tis nothin' I ain't said before. Don't bear repeatin'." •

Arva stood to take a breath, her lungs crowded by jerking knees and stirring feet. Between the houses, down the hill, her eyes were drawn to a flash of orange. Orange gone. Then the orange stepped into her vision again. An attractive woman. She was clothed in a bright wrap-around dress, sewn from a fabric so vibrant, it seemed to pulsate. The wind picked up the garment with a delicate finger, fluttered it, laid it back down with some care. Alek lifted his head, and stared, potato pieces dropping from his tipped bowl.

On her feet she wore knee-high slick black galoshes, and stood with her legs apart, a tilled row of earth between them. She glanced up, waved a yellow rubber-gloved hand to Rose, and Rose lifted her arm from her eyes to wave back.

"Nora Parsons, the Reverend's sister," Rose said, answering the question Arva had not asked. "If ye can believe that. She was once Nora Best, married to Lew Best, brought him in from the city. Real handsome lookin', he was. But, his corpse weren't cold before she started callin' herself Parsons again."

Rose returned to the potatoes, pushing a chunk a few inches down in the mound, smoothing over the dirt with a practiced pat, stepping up the row on the balls of her feet.

"Lew was always down to The Lodge, loved a drink, he did. Made him real mean, though, not like most men, makes them a bit silly or a bit saucy, nothin' ye had to deal with. He'd go home, beat the livin' daylights out of her. Wouldn't see her 'round for a week. Then, when he died, thanks God he before her, she spent half of his money on catalogue orders, dresses, and fabrics, patterns, Vogue even, if ye fathom it. Said to Dot Jones, who told me, she never wanted to feel like a dog again. She hates dogs. Can't stand 'em. Kick one if it crosses her path. Now, she's dressin' like royalty everyday, no matter what she's doin'. But don't let the dress fool ye, she's tough as a gad. And look at her today. That get-up is speakin' five languages all at the same time, me dear. But no one faults her for it neither, hear me. Makin' the men drool, but she won't let one near her. Can't be blamed for that now, but she does own about a dozen cats, keeps them all barred up in her house. Feeds them bits of cooked fish, better than some of the people eats 'round here. But, now, that's all Nora's business and 'tis not me place to be discussin' it."

Rose stood, and raised her hand to Nora Parsons again. She thumped the rock with an open hand, mouthed a generous and toothy though silent laugh for Nora, so that she could appreciate the kind of conditions Rose was working under.

"The caplin will be rollin' soon," she continued, crouched again, bowl balanced on her thigh, left hand continuing the work. "We'll get Alf or Jimmy to haul us up a bucket each from the beach for fertilizer. Nothin' better, maid. We'll have potatoes for the winter, if the blight don't get 'em. And there's a good chance it might, with our luck. Oh, yes. Almost forgot. Don't cook a bite for supper tonight, Arva. Junior Lynch went out on the ice early this mornin' and clubbed hisself a seal. Brought up a whole flipper to me. A whole one. Don't know what come 'cross him, what's a widow supposed to do with a whole flipper? I got it cleaned up right nice, lovely bit of soft pastry ready to lay on top of it. Nothing more tasty than a drop of dark seal gravy. God it'll be right delicious." She sucked back the saliva rising up in her cheeks. "The meat's liable to be too rich for the Skipper, but Clive'll love it. Come to think of it, I don't know how Junior made it out onto the ice. How could a pan hold up the likes of he? I 'llows it was some size chunk. Got no idea what's flowin' down from the North this year. We'll likely have cold for the next week or two, at least. Not much chance for these potatoes to take hold. Better not rot with the rain before…"

Rose's voice was evaporating, fading, washing away. Arva had been squatting down near the ground, eyed-potato ready in her fist, when a dribble of salty water trickled down the inside of her leg. Then, when she shifted, dropped the seed in the shallow hole, there was a hot gush, warming her thighs, her calves, splashing in and out of her ankle-high rubber boots. She stood at once, looked out towards the sea, the wet soil blackened beneath her feet.

Alek noticed it before Rose. He dropped his bowl of potatoes and was over to Arva in a moment, kicking dirt up between the neat rows. Before Arva knew what was happening, Alek had her lifted from the ground, and was taking a sturdy step towards the house. Rose looked up, saw the dark earth, knew, and came towards Alek, grabbed at his arms.

"For the love of Jesus, Alek, put her down, put her down."

He laid her to the earth as lightly as he had lifted her. "Jesus," she said to Arva. "Ye don't know what that boy is thinkin', or what he knows. There's some kind of queer sensitivity 'bout him." Then to Alek, "She's havin' a baby, b'y, not a heart attack."

Alek stood there, wiggling on the balls of his feet, arms wrapped around his body. Rose took Arva by the elbow and began to walk her toward the house. Arva felt heat in her bowels, pressure on her bones, her toes squishing in her sodden boots.

Rose called to Alek over her shoulder, "Good God, Alek. Either yer goin' to pee yerself, or ye've got a powerful need to do somethin'. Go on up Lundrigan's Lane and tell Doreen Clive's baby is on the way. Don't forget, now, Alek. Little blue house on the left." Before she had finished, Alek had started in to run, Clive's freshly turned dirt flying in the air under the rush of torn gray sneakers.

Doreen Coombs, the local midwife, arrived in forty minutes, her hair tucked up under a lime green sheer scarf, pink pins and black rollers sticking out.

"Sorry for the wait, Arva, me dear," she said as she came in from the porch. "I was just settin' me hair."

Arva was seated in a wooden chair in the kitchen, towels sticking out from underneath her dress. Every few minutes, her head would lower, hands gripping the solid table, eyes turning off.

"Alek is headed to tell Doris, then to Ethel to get her to come 'round and check on the Skipper, then he's off to the school to tell Clive," Doreen continued. "Lord, that b'y's got some set of legs on him. Just hope his head can hold it all."

"How long do ye think for Arva?" Rose asked.

"From what I knows," Doreen said as they helped Arva into the bedroom, "babies take just about as long as they wants. Could be an hour, could be a day. But, by the looks of her, I'd say closer to the latter."

"Skipper, there's a baby coming," Rose called into Old Man Crane as they walked past him lying in bed, close to sleep. "So never ye mind the noise."

His lids popped up. "No matter about the noise, Rose. Peggy had Alice right here in this bed. Just let me know what it is. Me bet's on a b'y."

"Ethel's on her way to look in on ye, make ye a bite of lunch."

"Jesus. Ethel."

"Bite yer ol' tongue, Skipper," Rose said. "Ye should be thankful yer gettin' anythin' at yer age."

Arva lay down on the side of the bed. Rose pulled up a chair, and Doreen sat, placed her hands on Arva's mound, rising up and sinking as it hardened with each contraction. From her quilted purse, Doris retrieved an extended hollow wooden horn, the smooth handle darkened from years of use. She pressed the opening of the horn to the bulge, put her ear to the mouthpiece.

After a minute, Doreen eased her great weight back in the chair and said, "He got some heartbeat, honey. Like a grandfather clock. Me bet's on a b'y, same as Skipper's." Then to Rose, "Head to the kitchen now, then. Boil us up a bit of water. Cup of tea would be right proper. Boil a few cloths, pair of scissors, carry us in a bucket, case she wants to throw up." Rose was gone before Doreen finished.

"God the heat," Arva moaned, her hand at once tightening on Doreen's like a vice, then slowly relaxing. "Feels like my stomach is an oven door wide open."

"That's just the way 'tis s'posed to feel, honey," Doreen said.

"I don't know if I can do this."

"Of course ye can, there's not much choice in the matter. Yer doing some wunerful as it stands."

"Is it going to get much worse?"

"Never more than ye can handle, honey," Doreen said. "For some women, 'tis a real hard time. For others, not so bad. Me own mother told me that she was punchin' down raisin dough and shapin' bread into the pans just a half-hour before I came roarin' out. She said it..." Doreen was cut short, Arva's hands began to clench again, and she was no longer listening.

Time gradually changed its pace, slowed, sped up, Arva could not decipher. The contractions were growing stronger, waves rising, grand white caps, crashing onto the beach, receding effortlessly, the shore a little wearier with each progressive lash. Arva began to shake, salt water dripped down between her shoulders, into the crease of her backside. Her hair was tangled, in her eyes, she glanced out through black stringy seaweed. She managed a sip of watery tea from Rose, but heaved instantly, vomiting next to Doreen's foot.

"Where's the slop bucket?" Doreen said to Rose. "We got to get this cleaned before the smell soaks into the wood."

Arva opened her eyelids for a moment, Doris in the door-frame, afternoon sunlight on her severe face, opened her eyelids again, Doris on her knees washing sickness from the flooring, opened her eyes again, Doris sitting on the bed behind her, hair pulled from her eyes, someone tug tugging at the back of her head, a rapid plaiting.

"A perfect braid." Doris's voice. "I knew I should've had a daughter."

"Blessed because ye don't, I says." Rose's voice.

"Keep yer thoughts to yerselves. She got all she can handle. Don't need to hear ye's gettin' on with the likes of that." Doreen's voice.

And then the women were silent because they knew Doreen was right.

Something wrapped around Arva's waist, squeezing, squeezing, not letting go. The heat, a powerful heat, glowing downwards, pushing downwards. A guttural noise, her own, from deep within her frame, her ear caught another animal howl, Ethel's girl retriever down the lane, sounding empathy.

And when Arva could endure it no longer, her mind left the bed and brought her home, the waterside, her mother, her father. She walked up the rocky path, ocean bowing up at her back, a mass of blooming goldenballs swaying in the breeze. On the back step, her hands traced the two 'Z' shapes, wood nailed to the storm door, coat on coat of sea green paint drowning the splinters and smoothing the boards. Her treasures were lined along the ledge of the stoop, thornless sea-urchins, blue-lipped clam shell with iridescent insides, a near-round rock, full gull feathers weighted down by a pile of eroded glass. A red bucket, chipped plate over top, crushed egg shells, potato peelings, used tea leaves, good for the garden.

The heat carried her into the kitchen, the enamel wood-stove, a woven owl on the wall, wide-eyes staring, cold linoleum, dirty snowflake pattern, a chair covered in a knitted blanket, red, blue, red, blue. Her mother, dull sandy hair around her face, mossy eyes, humming to herself, shaping loaves, three fat buns to a blackened pan. Something bubbling on the woodstove, orange, yellow, bakeapple jam, sugar jumping out, sweetness burnt and smoking.

She drifted past her father on the narrow couch, deep red hair, ears of a rabbit, soft small hands, gentle puff of air through his pink lips, brown knit socks, heels darned with navy. Quiet, quiet, into her room, an antique dresser, no reflection in the mirror, under the quilt, gone crazy with the fabrics, damp and heavy on her bony chest.

Door click, candle coming. Shh, my baby, shh. Behind his back, a fairy book, princesses and their holed shoes, danced to pieces, an underground cavern, clever soldier, boats of wide leaves floating down an enchanted stream. A promise sealed for tomorrow night, another journey, another flight. Kiss on the forehead, wetness drying in the chilly room. Another blanket?

Sunlight, the heat through glass, cheeks warmed. Barefoot in the kitchen, mother, father. An accusation, her father, jaw open, saying the very idea, ill, sick, her mother, face on fire, saying vile, disgusting, where to go now. The heaviest frying pan, cast iron, specks of rust on the underside. Grayness flying through the air for a split second, a ghost howl, noise like no other, two shiny pearls awash in a sticky ocean, held out on his bloody palm for the child to see. Her princess book to light the stove, ward off the dampness. A soundless cry from twisted girlish lips.

"Keep yer jaw slack, honey. Relax it." Doreen. Arva was back.

"Push - it - out," Arva bellowed with every ounce of her being, her groaning voice giving advice to her own ear.

Fire around her bottom. Branded once. Twice. Then the first cry of a newly born infant, the first cry of a newly made mother. Both expressions sounding very much the same.

"A boy," Doreen announced, breath burdened as if the effort had just been hers.

"Clive's got his boy," Rose said, face flushed.

"Yes, Arva, ye've got yerself a son," Doris said, her hand resting on the top of her daughter-in-laws head. "Ye've got yerself a son, maid."

"God bless her," Old Man Crane said when Rose told him about the birth. "God bless her. She got herself a son."

Early evening, the sun still awake, Arva sat up in bed, child in her arms, to see the sky rinsed in what must be the colours of heaven, she thought.

Clive appeared, leaned hard against the doorframe, his eyes blistering with redness, hands held unnaturally as if he were aware of their position.

"So we got ourselves a son, Arva. That's somethin', now, ain't it?" he said, his words forming in a slow and careful fashion. "Alek came by, gave the girls a good laugh, runnin' into the classroom like the Devil hisself was bitin' at his ankles. Got on me way, I did. Had to stop to the Legion, of course, let the b'ys in on it. And, ye knows, they all wants to buy me a drink, see. Good will and all. But I's here now, better than ever. Let's take a gander at him."

Clive took a wavering step towards Arva, and Doris shot up from her chair, blocking his way. "To the kitchen table with ye, Clive. Ye won't be touchin' that b'y when ye can't even touch the nose on yer drunken face. And if I ever learns it, if I ever even thinks it, I'll be down here in a blink and ye'll wish yer cake dough, me son, ye'll wish yer cake dough."

6

He was waiting for me at Irene's general store, standing right between the jars of sugared mintleaf jelly candy and cherry ju-jubes. At first he tried to be coy, pretending not to know who I was or why I was staring at him. Silly, really. But still, I knew. He was the darkest man I ever saw, and he had come across the ocean for me.

Rifling through a worn dictionary, he tried his very best to appear lost.

"Strange ask," he murmured in a melodic tone. "Strange ask."
And my knees quivered at the mere thought of his question.

"There's nothin' lovelier than a drop of bull bird soup, me maid," Old Man Crane said to Arva as she rubbed the life back into his printless soles. "No bigger than a robin, like a baby turr." His tongue darted out over his thin lips. Then, in a hush, he said, "Be sure to bring me back a wee taste in a pot, if ye can manage to sneak it out. Nar chance of it if Junior Lynch is there, ye'll be lucky to get a lick yerself."

"I'm sure I can manage," she said, smiling. "I'll set it aside right when I get there. Ask the ladies to keep Junior clear of it."

"Soup supper to the Lodge," he said and smacked his wet gums together. "There's no finer time."

Earlier that morning Arva had seen Clive go to the woodpile and bring in a leftover piece of two-by-four. He took several coat hangers from the closet and, twisting back and forth, cracked the metal hooks from the tops. Kneeling on the kitchen floor, he fastened them to the wood near one end by hammering in nails and then bending their heads down over the hanger hooks. He fixed a decent length of string to the other end.

"Believe it or not, me love, this here's goin' to get me some bull birds," he had announced proudly, holding the contraption up for Arva to see. "If it works, ye'll be samplin' bull bird soup tonight for yerself." He tossed the board across the kitchen floor, drew it back hand over hand over hand, and glanced at her. "I sees yer mind turnin', and ye needn't worry. I'll bring me catch up to Mother. She knows ye ain't got neither clue about how to be handlin' a bull bird."

While walking back from Mercer's shop, Arva had seen the men dotting the shoreline, amidst fluttering tufts of feathers, mottled black and white. Clive was among them, cap atop his head, vest-liner of a jacket on over his short-sleeved shirt, heavy green rubbers covered his feet. Alongside him, Alf Jones and James Young were hauling in tiny catch after tiny catch as though fishing on the surface of the sea.

Arva finished rubbing Old Man Crane's feet and covered his slender legs with a woolen blanket. A cool June breeze was able to come through the window since Arva had sliced through the layers of white paint.

"I haven't tasted bull bird soup this three years," Old Man Crane continued, "Though when I was younger we had it every spring. I minds going down to the water with Reg Lynch, Junior's father. Me and Reg would heave up a load of them birds when we got a taste for the soup. They're dim on wit but grand on flavour, Reg used to say, and I found he was right."

Arva drew across the roller table and poured him a cup of tea. Then she took a damp cloth and began wiping over the nightstand, across the footboard of the bed, along the top of his shelf, grooving around books, a framed black and white of Peggy. Folding the cloth over, she moved to his wife's side of the bed, dusting the wooden panel, woman with wheat, and nudging the dense mattress with her thigh. Surely that must be painful, she thought while looking at Peggy's groove, to see this depression every day, certain reminder of an absence.

"I'm no expert on the makin' of it," Old Man Crane said after a slurp of his tea. "All I knows is Peggy made the best drop of bull bird soup on the shore. Ye can ask 'round 'bout that. She said it's because she browned the birds, but ye got me when it comes to that stuff. I knows how to drink it. Right down with a lovely slice of bread. That'll take me right up to heaven."

"Doris already asked Ethel if she would mind sitting with you," Arva said. "Seeing as I've never tasted bull bird soup."

"Lord Jesus. Not Ethel again. I believes Art is tryin' his best to be rid of her, puttin' her over on me."

"I can stay," Arva said, sitting on the edge of Peggy's hollow. "Honestly. I don't know how much I'll enjoy myself with Henry in my arms and all. As you know, he tends to be difficult in the evenings."

"Go on with ye, me dear," he said. "Get out and have a bit of a time for yerself. I'm only havin' fun. Ethel's not that bad. If she heard me, I allows she'd skin me. All she's after doin' for a crooked old geezer like meself. God love her, Ethel. Though it's too bad she don't ever try a hand of cards. Thinks cards is right sinful. Somethin' to do with the Devil. Makes her itch when I'm playin' me solitaire beside her. Cards is a real pleasure, I finds, so there might be somethin' to her thought after all."

"Yes, you never know," Arva said, standing. "Mr. Crane, I've got to look in on Henry, then see about your raisin bread. I don't want it rising over and I can smell sweet in the air already."

"I can't wait for a slice of that lassie bread," he said. "Long as it's Peggy's recipe. None of that old muck Ethel brings me. I hates caraway seeds, takes the taste off the bread, puts somethin' right wrong back on." He paused for a moment, blinked his eyes at Arva. "Now if only ye'd fry me up a feed of cod tongues, me love. I'd give me eyeteeth for a plate of them piled high, crisped right up, dribbled with vinegar. Would ye have the heart to do that for an old man?"

"I don't think you'd get much goodness out of a cod's tongue without a tooth in your head," she said, cupping his hand in hers for a moment. She poured more of the brew, brought his plate of lemon creams closer. On her way out through his bedroom door, she said, "You know, it seems like you're on the mend."

"I feels it," he answered. "God love ye, Arva." And then, "Yes, God love ye is right, maid, as long as ye don't forget me darlin' drop of bull bird soup."

The Lodge was crowded, full of noise, homemade music, cig-arette smoke, and the scent of something untamed. There were several rows of woodhorses lined across the floor, with smooth planks layered over top to create tables. Alongside, wooden benches had been dragged out from the walls for seating. Children were draped across them on their bellies, rocking the unleveled surfaces with their feet to see how far they could go without toppling them over.

Every few feet along the tabletop, there were dinner plates piled high with thick slices of white bread. In glass dessert bowls next to the bread, mounds of tempting creamy butter were found, broad knife jabbed in the center of each. Junior Lynch, belly touch-ing the table, was scraping knife-loads so generous, it was difficult to tell which layer in his hand was butter and which was bread.

"Julie Adams brought down a lovely bit of butter for the supper," Rose Young said to Arva. "She's the one owns the cow." Rose nodded towards Junior. "Look at he there. We're liable not to get a sniff of it if he keeps on." She walked up to Junior, took hold of his arm. "Come on with ye, me son. Put down yer bread and have a scuff."

Alf Jones was seated at a table, his section of the bench made invisible by a dozen children huddled in close. Alf had a bowl of ʼoup on the wood in front of him, but he was not taking a taste. Instead, he fished around in the dish with his fingers, withdrew two long skinny bones, and placed them up under his top lip. With the bones hung down like tusks on a miniature walrus, Alf had his wrists crossed, hands slapping, head bobbing. The chil-dren squealed like pups.

"Get on now," he said after pulling the tusks from his mouth. "Let me drink me drop of soup."

Clive strolled over to him and said, "Jesus, Alfie, ye was soundin' right like a seal in heat."

Alf kept his head close to his soup, not uttering a word.

Beyond him, a blur of people were carting steamy bowls secured in open palms, cigarettes nipped in lips, drips of broth spilled here and there, intermittent slurps, and on occasion, the prattle would part, making way for a boisterous declaration of

'Jesus, this is right tasty, missus.'

Clive glanced up, caught Arva watching him, her stare fixated, making his stomach gurgle, a gassy stone jammed down a tube. He pressed his fist into the tender spot, too much soup, perhaps, and waved a hand to her. "Come on, me dear. Let's get ye a try."

He motioned to her to sit with Doris and her friends. On the table Clive placed a deep white bowl, finish egg-shelled, roses and leaves intertwined around the chipped lip. A dark broth breathed as she stirred with her right arm, Henry nestled in the crook of her left. Cubes of carrot, parsnip, potato floated amongst threads of meat, a slender thighbone, brown slice of soaked goose-pimpled skin. The soup tasted hearty, down-to-earth, a hint of something feral. There was a sense that it was balanced, healthy, though she would never say she loved the flavour at all, or even found it pleasing. It was too wild.

"A bowl of soup like that'll bring down yer milk better than a glass of beer," Doris whispered. "The only time I stood a drink of beer was right after me boys was born. Though by the looks of him, I don't thinks ye need much of a hand." She reached over and smoothed Henry's silky cheek with the back of a bent finger. "Don't breathe a word of this to Clive, he'd have me hide if he knew I thought it, but Henry's just like Alek when he was a baby. Identical. When he stopped his bawlin', and that weren't very often, mind ye, he was the most beautiful thing ye ever seen."

Clive came up behind Arva, dipped his pinky finger into her soup, and tried to push a taste into the baby's closed mouth. "Drop of this'll turn him right into a man."

Doris smacked his hand away and said, "Leave him be, for the love of God, Clive. Can't ye see he's havin' a rest, givin' Arva here a chance to have her supper."

He lifted the baby up from Arva's arms, cradled him gently and began introducing him to anyone who was interested. "Ladies," he said. "This is me son, Henry Clive." Emphasis on the 'Clive,' 'Henry,' after Arva's late father, muffled.

Seated a few paces up from Arva was an aged woman, face a dishcloth crumpled and dried, hair so thin her scalp shone through. Her back had bowed under the weight of a vast chest, and her eyes, tucked inside her turtle head, were permanently fixed on the ground. Someone had carried down a soft chair, two benches pulled apart, woolen blanket warming sloped shoulders. With trembling fist, she gripped the handle of a soup spoon, bent in, slurped at her supper.

"That's Aunt Bertie," Doris said, between mouthfuls. "Older than the Skipper, she is, but still sharp as a filletin' blade. Nothin' got to her lungs yet, I reckon. Not like the Skipper."

"Madonna brought Aunt Bertie up to the house this afternoon," Lorna Lynch said from across the table. "Aunt Bertie wanted to give a hand with the soup, she says to me. Can you fathom it? Peeled up the carrots. And I'm tellin' the truth. I hopes I got half her strength when I'm that age."

As they were watching, Alf Jones edged up towards her, leaned over and took her two frail hands in his. Her head tilted up just slightly, eyes raised, eyebrows lifted so she could see who had hold of her. Alf was trying to cajole her up out of her chair and onto the floor, his grin wide, feet moving swiftly like a performer before her.

"For the love of the Lord," Dot Jones said, seated next to Lorna. "Will ye look at Alfie? Tormentin' Aunt Bertie to death."

"P'raps he's after a dance," Doris said.

"That's the last thing he's after, me dear," Dot muttered. "Alfie's just over there to bug the bejesus out of her. He'd torment the Saviour if He took upon Himself to come down to the soup supper."

"And see him now," Doris said. "Never got nowhere with Bertie, and this minute he's onto Annie."

"He won't be onto her long if Eldred spies him," Lorna said. "I allow he'd take a crack at Alf, right between see and smell if he saw him gettin' with the likes of that."

Alf had slid in next to a woman no larger than an older child, rounded blushing cheeks, hair ablaze, chin missing in a gullet of jiggling fat, and an unfiltered cigarette burnt down to stained fingers.

"That's Annie Barrett, me dear," Amanda Adams, sitting just up from Doris, said to Arva. "She's one of them war brides. Now if that ain't romance, I don't know what is."

"Yes," Lorna said. "Met Eldred over in Ireland at a dance. Fell right for her, he did. Over backwards and right back round again."

"Oh, she talks with the loveliest lilt," Rose Young said, seated next to Amanda. "Like the rollin' hills of Ireland themselves.

I could listen to she all day long."

"Likes ye knows all about the rollin' hills," Dot said. "Never havin' been farther than Harbour Grace. They's got some lovely rollin' hills there, I allow."

"But those two, Eldred and Annie, seems right funny together," Lorna said. "He with a bit of height to him, she barely to his belt."

"Well, that's somethin'," Rose twittered, "I often wonders how they - ye knows."

"Bite yer tongue," Doris snapped. "Gettin' on with that garbage."

"Now then, Rose," Lorna said, elbows on the table. "I allows ye do wonder. All these years with neither man."

"The likes of ye two," Doris said. "That's all I wants to be picturin' when I'm tryin' to have a swally of me bull bird soup."

"I've done fine for meself with neither man," Dot said, nodding together with Doris. "They're not all they're cracked up to be, I can tell ye that right here."

"Not that ye won't snap at one if he came within any distance, Dot," Rose said.

"And here's the pot callin' the kettle black," Dot said.

A laugh sputtered out from Lorna, and she caught her false teeth with one hand while she reached for a slice of bread with the other. When her teeth were back at home, she cleared her throat and said, "Lovely batch of bread. Must be Madonna's."

"Speakin' of the war, take a gander over there." Amanda jutted her chin in the direction of a stout man, his hair a smooth nut brown with a brilliant silvery skid above both temples. He wore a bright red flannel shirt buttoned to the neck, even though the evening air was comfortably warm.

"It's not hard to recognize Pepper Reid with a pelt on he like that," Rose said. "Good to see him out."

"Patty told me just the other day that his son's goin' 'round sayin' he got those skunk stripes from the battlefield," Lorna said. "Standin' in line there, all ready for the good fight, and the two alongside he dropped dead. He scored a strip for either from the shock of it, I allow."

"What men won't do," Doris said.

"Yes," Dot said. "Ye'd never see a line of us out there in the mud. We women got more sense."

"More sense, maybe," Doris added. "Or else we'd never find

the time for it after makin' the lunches and the suppers."

"I heard his dog died," Amanda said.

"That he did," Dot said. "February. Saw Pepper out back of his house with a pick-axe in hand, wickedest kind of weather. His face, now, was likely 'bout as red as his shirt. I sent Alfie out to see what his trouble was, and Alfie was back in a minute, told me about the dog, and askin' for a bottle. 'Give Pepper a nip,' Alfie says, 'the man couldn't even get a word out.' Beside himself with the grief. Pepper just don't seem right without Salty yappin' at his heels."

"Junior told me he was more worked up over his dog than losin' his wife to that salesman in St. John's," Lorna said. "He could let she pass without a sniff." She lifted her spoon to take her last mouthful of soup, but pushed the bowl away and said, "Gone cold." Then she reached for another piece of bread, hand to the butter knife. "Loves the taste of fresh butter, I do. 'Tis a real treat."

Amanda twisted her neck around and said to Lorna, "There's goes yer husband again, me dear. I sees he's up for another bowl."

Lorna took a hard bite of her slice, replied between chews, "I'm half ashamed, I is. I believes he's after drinkin' a whole pot by hisself."

"No doubtin' he got some appetite on him," Dot said.

"Appetite?" Lorna replied, shaking her head. "Me love. Keep yer tongue in yer head. Couldn't get clear of him when I was makin' the broth, even. If ye took a look inside he, I allow ye'd come across two or three bull birds down there not even picked clean."

"Arva," Doris said, all eyes shifting away from Junior. "Ye must fancy that soup, maid. There's not been a word pass out through yer lips."

Though every last dram of the bull bird soup was tucked away in satiated bellies, Henry gleaned the most attention by far. Arva barely held him in her arms once Clive went to show him around. Most women took a turn with the baby, while the ones waiting crowded in close, grabbing at a foot, worming a finger into his clenched fist, smoothing the top of his head, his hair like eider down.

"A real angel. Cheeks on he like little loaves."

"Get a load of the pudge on him, will ye. He's a fat dumplin'. Gargeous."

"Let me get a gander. Give him over. God, I could eat the face right off him."

Since Henry had been born, Arva often had the same notion, that she could eat him, devour him, wash him down with a mouthful of warm tea. She imagined there was something that joined love for a child to the stomach's appetite. Maybe it was a need to protect, or nourish, and what better place than inside the mother's own body. Safe, warm, dependable. When she stared at Henry, especially with his eyes sealed in sleep, her mouth began to water, her throat tighten. She felt a phantom hunger. Sometimes she would cradle the child and bring his silky hand to her mouth, a temptation to tear off just a little bite nagging in her teeth. She would catch a smell in the crook of his neck, or behind his toes when her nose worked to uncurl them. Inhaling to the very bottom of her lungs, her senses responded as if her son were a savory dinner, served at perfect doneness. An all-consuming adoration.

But now, baby Henry had deserted his nine-month nest, and was being subjected to pinches and sniffs, prods and wet kisses from a horde of well-meaning grandmothers.

"God love him, Arva," Dot Jones said when Henry was passed into her ample arms, his lips curved into a gassy smile. "He's got yer skin colour. Apt to get a bit of a tan in summer, not like most 'round here, gets red like a boiled lobster. Alek's eyes, don't tell Clive I says so, but yer skin. Ye got some strong blood in ye."

That night Arva awoke for no reason in particular. She had taken to sleeping on the daybed in the kitchen where it was warmer and Henry's nighttime fussiness was less likely to wake Old Man Crane or Clive. Her hand passed over the lined dresser drawer where Henry slept, his tongue and lips working milk from a dreamed nipple. A gentle breath told her hand all was okay, and she nestled into the thin mattress, pulling the woolen blanket up over her shoulder.

But sleep would not drift down to her. And a moment later,

she understood why.

There was no scratch on the linoleum or flicker of candle-light, no strong sour smell or sudden frost to the air in the kitchen to let her know. Arva was just aware, simply perceptive, and had been that way since her father died. Some things she knew, never questioned, accepted as her reality, different as it was from others.' When sleep continued to elude her with no rationale, she realized it had a reason. Someone else was in the room, watching her, willing her body to turn and look.

Arva twisted in the bed and her eyes traveled instantly to the doorway leading to the hall. There Old Man Crane stood, straight-backed, his legs taking an effortless step into the kitchen. She had grown accustomed to seeing him tucked in, body bent, shoulders hunched. It came as a surprise just how tall he was, towering nearly six feet two. His bony feet were usually bare and stiff. Often she would heat a beach rock in the oven of the woodstove, wrap it in a blanket, use it to warm his soles. Tonight though, his feet were shoed and shined. At the end of long emaciated arms, his hands dangled inside the sleeves of his one Sunday suit. A tie, needing the touch of a woman, was slightly awry at the base of his loose-skinned neck.

Moonlight, flooding through the window, reflected nothing in his dull pallor. His mouth gaped as though he wanted to speak, but no words came forth. He opened his hands, palms out, and a hand-ful of brown-gray sea sand poured from them, falling down over the sides of his shoes, producing small mounds on the linoleum. She looked into his eyes, they were luminous, peaceful. Arva believed the expression stemmed from a reunion with his lifelong love.

Arva swung her legs around at once and planted her feet firmly on the icy floor. She began to stand, but sat back as the old man turned with ease and left the room, his hard-soled shoes silent on the linoleum. Across the kitchen floor, there was not a grain of sand to be seen.

Old Man Crane was dead. Arva knew it without ever going to check, without feeling his cheek with the back of her hand, cold death having skulked in and stolen that last bit of warmth. The forerunner told her everything. His time to pass had come.

She noticed Henry's head, knocking from side to side, his mouth searching for something to soothe his hunger pang. Her breast's tingled and she felt that moment of utter joy that descended upon her just before her milk let down. Arva lifted Henry from the drawer and began to nurse. She could smell his butterscotch sweetness, put her hand to his delicate hair, and felt it growing moist from dripping tears.

As she wept quietly, Henry balanced in her forearms, she scratched relentlessly at the palm of her left hand until it reddened. A mighty itch had settled there.

Drizzle fell steadily. Dampness slunk in around an open neck, down the back of a shirt, in around the laces of a shoe. Fog crawled in off the water, clutched at the ground, thick like pea soup. Women held their scarves tightly under their chin, men kept their arms folded, heads bowed, mothers lifted young children into their arms as much for warmth as comfort. It was a day fit for a funeral.

Arva held sleeping Henry, wrapped in a small quilted blanket, and stood next to Doris and Alek. Clive was a pallbearer along with Alf Jones, James Young, and Junior Lynch, their faces solemn, expressions grave. "It won't be the same 'round here," Junior Lynch had whispered to Clive as they carried the pricey coffin down the front steps of the church. "Old Man Crane was the bread in this cove, we bein' the butter, of course."

Always bloody food with Junior, Clive thought.

"Let's hope Alf kept his nose out of the sauce this mornin'," Doris muttered to anyone listening. "All we needs now is for he to slip, bring the whole works down on top of hisself." The whole works being the corpse and coffin. Doris had told Arva she thought it was a delightful looking box and wouldn't it be a shame if Alf brought a dent to it.

Alice stood next to Arva, having arrived earlier without her sons, without her husband. "Can't stay long," she had said when she pulled up to her father's house. "But I arranged a lovely service, ordered a lovely casket. He'd be right pleased." She had meant to visit, she said to Arva, had meant to every weekend, just she had been busy, so, so busy, the boys and all, the house, Ron. Arva could surely understand.

As she stood there watching the men stride over the grass to the fresh hole, Arva wondered how little Alice really knew of her father, if she thought he would be contented with a flashy coffin. This was a man who never threw a single thing out, would pick up anything he found on the road or beach, and when he was younger, would take the occasional trip into the dump looking for treasures. "People hove out good stuff all the time," he often told Arva. "Ye wouldn't believe it. Take a look through me basement one of these days, ye might be real surprised, me maid. Don't let Alice come in here, toss everything out. Give me yer word on that. Ye go through it with a fine-toothed comb and take whatever ye needs or wants or whatever ye can put to use." Old Man Crane would have likely preferred a box made of planks, leftover wood, nailed together by Junior Lynch. Maybe a coat of white paint, but probably not.

As the body was lowered, Alek cried the loudest, his wails interrupted by gulping sounds, his body needing to suck in breath before the next wail clutched his lungs. His head rested on Doris's shoulder and she patted his back saying, "Now, now, b'y. Pipe down, will ye. Come. Pipe down, Alek." But her tone was soft, tender. Then Doris leaned over to Arva and whispered, "He never could grasp death. Never could. Not that none of us can, mind ye."

Back at Old Man Crane's house, entire countertops and tables were covered with dishes, bowls, jars, bottles, each filled to overflowing with food and drink. There was barely room to move with all the mourners in the porch, kitchen, and hallway leading to the bedrooms. Clive lit in the fire, even though summer had nearly arrived, it was necessary to cut through the dampness. Whiskey was opened, most people having a finger or two to stave off a cold, fill some of grief's hollow from the heart.

Doris began to hand lunch plates to the ladies, most from Old Man Crane's cupboard, but others she had carried down the hill by herself. No one had come to the house with an empty hand, instead with a plate of sweet squares, whole roasted chicken with stuffing, egg and bread pudding, dense gingerbread, bottles of pickles or preserves, a green jelly mold filled with a salad that refused to release onto a platter. There was enough food to feed the group, and a few could take home a bite for their suppers if they wanted it. Several women, wearing their colourless funeral outfits, began dishing spoonfuls of this and that onto the lunch plates and handing them around the room.

"Ye did a real job with him, Arva," Rose Young said more to the group than to Arva. "I never seen him happier than this past year. Since Peggy left him, that is."

Alice shifted in her seat near the entrance, pulled at the hem of her dark gray skirt, and took a generous swallow of the whiskey, lips punched, shiver moving through her.

"Yes, that's right. He was somethin', the Old Skipper," Junior Lynch announced. "Don't know how we'll get on without him."

Ethel Mercer began to speak, but her voice was a bird's squawk, tears sprung to her eyes. Alf Jones had to hand her his hanky, freshly ironed that morning by his beloved Aunt Dot. She had raised him like a son, Alf had said to Arva more than once, though she was getting on in years.

"Skipper was good to the lot of us," Clive said. "Even brought me Arva 'round."

"Can't say a bad word about him," Alf Jones said. "Though he did take a crack at me once." The room quieted down to hear Alf's account of Old Man Crane. "I minds once when he was into the moonshine down there in his basement. I was skippin' school and trippin' along the high road, right above Skipper's house. I recalls somethin' caught me eye, and next thing I knows I'm through Skipper's garden, couldn't help meself, and I got me face pressed hard up against his basement window. I was right curious, wondering what sort of stuff he had down there, I'd heard all kinds of stories goin' 'round. Well, who's face do I finds starin' right back at me? The Skipper's. And he's up out of the basement in a blink, comin' at me, shotgun in hand. Took a clip at me too, had it loaded with salt. Hit the rock right next to me." Alf laughed easily, a mouthful from his glass. "I suppose he wasn't really tryin' for me. Do ye think?"

"Proper thing if he was," Dot Jones said. "There's no need to be tellin' stories like that, now Alfie. Ye never knows who's listening."

"Now, hear this one," Junior Lynch said, scratching at his stomach where his bellybutton might be. "I recalls when we was just kids and Skipper was goin' 'round with Father. God, it must've been the winter when I was eight or nine. Father'd been havin' a turn of bad luck, didn't have a cent to his name. I remembers hearing them talk about the Christmas, what was they goin' to do for the kids."

"Yes," Doris chimed in. "I knows that year. Me Tom and Jo Crane had their share of hardship and then some."

"Well," Junior continued. "On that Christmas Eve, fat snowflakes outside the window, we had a knock to the front door. 'Who in the name of Jesus is that this time of night,' Father hollers. 'And comin' to the front door.' The lot of us runs out to see this six-foot tall stick of a Saint Nick standin' on the front stoop, sack in hand. God, he had lovely things for Mary and Margie, little knit dolls, candy. He gave Morrisey a wooden truck, painted up some nice. I remembers 'cause I eyed it real good, hopin' he'd have one for me in that bag. No sir. He hauls out a book on magic, tricks I can learn, somethin' I can practice at. I still got it on the shelf in me room. 'A book is a gift for the mind,' he said to me in a hush. 'And it's the mind that makes the man.' I thought to meself, what a strange thing for Santa to be sayin' to a wee lad. But, I was right proud, proud as proud could be. Then, when he left and I opened me book to have a gander, up in the corner of the inside cover was a name scribbled out 'Joseph Crane.' Well, I never said a word to the others, but I knew, and I knew he knew I knew. So, this is the first I spoke of it. I never forgot it." Junior coughed a few times, wiped his cheek with the back of his hand, sniffed hard.

"Yes," Doris said. "And ye've done all ye could to help him these past few years. God knows it, and so does we."

"Yes," Alfie added, tongue swelling from the whiskey. "And we used to call him tight as a frog's arse." A hiccup. "Pardon me, missus." He nodded his apology toward Doris. "Tight? No b'y. Not t'all. Not when it counted, least."

"Knowing he, Junior, I imagine ye'd find that red shirt poked away in his basement somewhere," Rose Young said.

Then Johnny Adams took a great drag off his cigarette, cleared hack from his throat, and began to wind his way through another tale about the colourful, generally well-loved Skipper, that was Old Man Crane.

There was no sign that the crowd was clearing, and Alice had to be getting back to her children. Perhaps her husband was home and waiting. She pulled Arva aside and said, "Of course, yer welcome to stay on here. In fact, that would work out best. I'll be tryin' to sell the house, mind ye, but it's easier to sell if someone's livin' in it. Though I doubts anyone'll want to buy if they gets a gander at that boulder to Rose's. And if they talks to anyone, that'll be the first thing they hears. That's a bit off-putting, I'd imagine. The chance that a chunk of the mountain will plow through your kitchen, knock your dinner right off yer plate."

Arva told her yes, they would stay on, both she and Clive appreciated the offer. As Alice continued to talk, Arva's eyes moved through a break in the crowd to the cluttered counter-top and fixed on something shiny. How had she missed it, not gotten around to cleaning it out these past couple of days? There, pushed back behind a plate of cut chicken, a near-empty bottle of whiskey, and a shallow dish of hard ribbon candy, was a tiny metal pot, filled to the brim with ice cold bull bird soup.

7

As he wanted, I allowed him into my kitchen, and I cooked for him.

After months on the water, he was sick to death of gruel and bland fish, and needed food handled by a skilled woman.

He ate and smiled, his black eyes twinkling like a gentle horse fed on sweet clover. And when he finally spoke, his words rippled over my body, flickered through my hair. Brazen, yes. But I was coming apart at an extraordinary pace.

Flattening his hands against his chest, he said, "Horacio."

I did the same with my hands and said, "Ruby."

"Ruby?" His very lips transformed my name into a babbling brook. Finally, he recognized me.

He held out his hand. Inside, the most delicate dragonfly, a weighty pendant. I said, yes, accepted it, but after I scratched out those tiny raging eyes that stared without a blink, taunting me because it saw everything.

The house was different, though not in the way Clive had anticipated it would be. There was no sense of release in the air or feeling that death had arrived, identified what it sought, and then moved on. The home's mood was not jovial after been freed from Old Man Crane's ancient tongue, his hawkish screech at every single lunch hour. There was no rejoicing that now, within its walls, there was only just livings, no longer half-deads.

Instead the home seemed to have let go, slackened, boards shifted and groaned. Drafts had multiplied, and their wheeze was frosty, even during the hottest days of summer. Clive felt unwelcome, and decided to do something about it.

"Of course we'll move over to Skipper's room," he said to Arva early one July morning, his feet planted extra-wide on the linoleum.

"I don't feel right about it, is all," she replied.

"What's that? Don't feel right." Clive made a sucking noise between his two front teeth, eyes on the floor. And then, the salesman, "It's bigger than Alice's room, and it's got a lovely light in the mornin', let alone a nice set of drawers. Ye could put a few things up on his shelf, clear out his closet, settle in a bit. No one'll be buyin' this house when we tells them 'bout their chances of bein' squat right flat."

"He's only been left such a short while, Clive, it's still got his air in there, his smell." She had thought to say his spirit, but did not, for she knew that was long gone. Absence of his spirit was more shocking for her by far.

"Yer gettin' on with ol' foolishness," Clive muttered. "We'll crack his window up a few inches. It'll be freshened out in no time."

She tried to form an argument, but Clive had already started in again.

"Stay on the daybed if ye likes, me dear. Old Man Crane's bloody stench or not, tonight I'll be sleepin' in a bit of comfort."

"Fine," she said. "Please yourself. But you're going to haul that mattress out of there, bring Alice's in."

"Yes, perhaps yer right about that. Don't want to be puttin' me head in the hollow of a dead man's."

But that's not what Arva had meant at all, though it really never mattered if Clive understood her. She did not want his body slipping so easily into Old Man Crane's well worn groove, her own bones, so weary lately, collapsing next to him in Peggy's. Sleeping there, calmed, dreaming. They were too young, edges too rough, and did not deserve to rest in the smooth comfort of indentations that took years of love to create.

"I'll get at it right now so ye can make up a clean bed," he said on his way down the hallway. "And while yer standin' there, doin' nothin', fry me up a few slices of bologna and a cut of that raisin bread. If ye was Mother, I wouldn't have to be askin'."

Doris soaked the softness back into several lengths of salted cod that were as stiff and yellowed as a chalky toenail. When her hands prodded at the fish, her jaw tightened only slightly as the salt burnt at her skin. She cast off the briny water, poured in fresh, and wrung her hands through the cup-towel looped over the snuggly tied belt of her apron. The soft fabric snagged, hitched at her chapped skin, though her movements remained swift, expert. Doris had lived her life with her hands in or around the sea, the permanent scaly ruddiness an ugly but unavoidable proof. She saw that Arva's young hands, cutting fat pork for crispy scruncheons, had already acquired the telltale spidery web of a housewife's soreness.

Using one of the duller knives, Alek peeled potatoes at the kitchen table, a heavy canvas flowered cloth draped over top. Doris went to his side, selected a curl of peel, held it for a closer look, then dropped it back to the compost heap that was rapidly growing.

"Thinner, me son," she said to Alek, her hand resting lightly on his longish chestnut hair. "If ye keeps on cuttin' into them like that, we won't have neither decent spud to boil with the salt fish."

With his tongue protruding off to the side, Alek clutched his next potato, fingers like a clumsy child working back the soiled skin.

Clive, who was sitting at the opposite end of the table, following the knife's movements with his eyes and said to his mother, "I knows if I was destroyin' them potatoes like Alek's doin', ye'd have some clap on the back of the head for me." He brought his tumbler to his lips, dragged whiskey into his mouth through his front teeth.

"I allows if I ever sees ye peelin' a spud," Doris replied, hands cutting into her hips, slippered foot tapping, "I wouldn't have a word in me head with the shock of it all, let alone a clap in me hand." Then to Alek, "Look, don't heed he. Yer doin' the best kind of job."

The screen door heckled from the porch, snapped to, and Alf Jones's red leathery face appeared in the kitchen door.

"Come in, me son," Clive said. "Have a seat for yerself and tell me how ye is. Rest for me ears, I'm worn listenin' to these three women. Well, two. Arva hasn't opened her trap."

"Hello Arva. Missus," Alf nodded to Doris and handed her a paper bag, top twisted and clammy around a bottleneck. "Lovely night out."

"Right nice," said Clive. "If this keeps up, they'll be comin' off the Mainland in droves."

"Yes, lovely," said Doris. "Though I doubts it'll last for long, if we goes on 'bout it. Someone up stairs'll put the rights to it in short order." Doris hauled out a chair, "Take a seat, Alfie. Yer makin' me nervous with all yer standin'."

"Get him a tumbler, Mother. Drop of sauce for the man. And while yer at it, get Alek a nip, he's not ten no more, ye knows."

Doris seemed not to hear Clive, but opened the cupboard to get two short glasses. "Alf, how's Aunt Dot these days? Haven't seen her to a service lately." Doris poured several fingers for Alf, coated the bottom of Alek's glass.

"No missus," Alf replied, a thirsty swallow, back of his hand drawn up to his puckered lips. "She been drivin' over to Bay Roberts to a service there with May Barrett." Alf tipped his glass back, it contents filling a spacious mouth until all that was left was a drip and the shine.

Before Alf's glass came to rest on the table, Clive said, "Bring the bottle, Mother. Leave it be, so ye don't have to trouble yerself goin' back and forth."

Again, Doris seemed not to hear Clive, but followed his instructions, as though bringing the bottle had been her thought.

"Ye didn't hear it from me," Alf said. "But, I believes she got some kind of man on the hook. Tore to pieces over him. She now, nearin' seventy. I never heard the likes."

"Last I saw of her was to the funeral," Doris said. "And I rightly minds she didn't mention it then."

"Yes, well, things have come 'round, me dear." Alf's hand, steady as a nun's, poured another generous serving. "I believes he's one of them Catholics, a McCarthy, likely. I recalls seein' him in the spring goin' 'round with the smudge on his forehead."

"Now that's a queer thing," Doris said. "She now, takin' up with a Catholic."

Alek opened his mouth, ready to speak, his eyes still on the potato in hand. Clive knew immediately what sentence was balancing on the tip of his tongue, that infuriating confession business. He wound his fist in the air near his ear and said, "Don't start with it, Alek. Or I'll come 'cross the table and make ye wish ye hadn't."

"Keep a civil tongue in yer head, Clive. Or ye'll feel this," Doris said, twisting water from a sopping dishrag. "Carry on, Alf, with what ye was sayin'."

"Yes, missus," Alf continued as if without interruption. "She's got me near drove. Worse than a teenager. One minute she got me hoistin' windows open, talkin' 'bout freshness in the air, like she never breathed it before in her life. Next, she come to her senses, got me stokin' the stove for a drop of tea. I thinks it's somethin' to do with that Catholic. All I can figure." Alf rotated his glass on the table, rosy adoration swelling into his cheeks. "And she's burnin' up all her stockin's. Goin' round the house with a bare set of legs on her. At that age – what's she got to be worried 'bout her legs for? Tell me that. On second thought, I'd rather not even think about it. If I hears tell of either child comin' from the two of them, I'll be out the door before she can haul the pins from her rollers." He cleared his throat. "Though time I got me own place, I reckon. Go on up and see her, maid, for the love of God. Somethin's got to be done with her."

"Lord Alfie," Doris said. "Sounds like she's gone off in her workin's. Must be. Though ye never knows what the Almighty got in store for us. Maybe it was her time to meet someone, is all. And a Catholic, no less."

"Listen to ye," Clive said, guided hand reaching for the bottle. "Nothing but silly talk."

"Silly, ye say?" Doris said as she stood by the stove, salt fish sliding into warmed water. "And what if I were to hook up? I'm not over the hill yet, me son."

"Yes, now. Yer so far over the hill that yer rollin' down the other side." Clive coughed out a garbled laugh, brought the slender body of a fresh cigarette to his flared nostrils. "I'm sure ye'd snare a decent catch if ye set yer mind to it. How's about callin' on Pepper Reid? Nar woman, nar dog. He might take ye on."

Doris lifted pot lid and stabbed the fish with her fork, frowned. "If yer father was here, ye wouldn't be at me with that kind of lip."

"No, I don't believe I would," Clive said as he watched his lit cigarette release a sultry figure up from between his fingers. He thought the curling smoke looked like a willowy woman, one he might like to meet late night up behind the shed. She'd be right off a slick page of the Eaton's catalogue, head to toe in wispy gray, a ladies hat hiding a gorgeous face. He shook his cigarette, erasing her image. Then, to his mother, "Ye likely wouldn't be talkin' 'bout hookin' into another man if he was."

"So what if I is," she said, her lips whitened, now closed for further conversation on the subject.

"Now, then," Alf said. "Shouldn't of mentioned it t'all. That's Aunt Dot's business. But, other than that, missus, she's wunerful grand, wunerful grand. Thanks for askin'."

"Alf," Doris said. "Don't go fillin' up on whiskey. We got a real scoff under way."

Alf jumped up to the stove, peered over Doris's shoulder, drink locked in reliable grip.

Alf Jones, Doris had told Arva, could tumble down a full flight of stairs on his backside, whiskey in hand, and never come close to losing a drop.

"Those got to be the loveliest scruncheons I ever seen," he said. "They's perfect little squares."

A muffled giggle from a woman leaning on the corner of the countertop, her voice such an unfamiliar sound in the room that Clive's ears climbed slightly on his scalp. He looked up, saw hips still bulky from pregnancy, mane of a black horse, a dark mole he had never noticed before on the back of her left arm. His wife. He wondered about her voice, its recent range of sounds limited to coos for the baby, so very few words for him. And now, such a sweet little laugh for Alf. Clive wondered, could she be that brazen right in front of his face?

The glass of his tumbler had warmed from his hand, and he filled it again.

"Did ye get a load of Junior Lynch's new boat," Alf said, back in his seat. "She's a real beaut."

"I did," Clive said, as Doris placed a plate of fish, boiled potatoes, and crispy scruncheons before him. "Robert Reid built her, right? Or was it Johnny Reid. One of Pepper's brothers."

"It's Robert," Alf said. "Johnny's off to St. John's this past year."

"I seen them heftin' her up onto a trailer," Clive said, "bringin' her down to the water. Junior'll be going full tilt in no time."

"Some colour on her," Alf said.

"That there is," Clive said. "Brightest red I ever seen. Real shine to her."

"They had her on the wharf when I hauled in me catch," Alf said, pushing fish around his plate, feeding whiskey to his thirsty lips. "Junior was down there with a little girly brush in his hand, paintin' on her name."

"Never caught that, what'd he call her," said Clive.

"The queerest thing," said Alf.

"Come on with her then," said Doris. "We're not waitin' all night to hear."

"I asks him what he's drawin' on her," said Alf. "And he says to me he's callin' her 'Lorna's Fate.'"

"Well, where on earth did he get the likes of that?" said Doris.

"I says the same thing to him," Alf said. "And he goes, ''Tis a bit of joke for Lorna.' Lettin' her know she made a good catch gettin' herself a fine man like hisself who can afford a decent rig."

"That's some kind of big name for a dory, though," said Clive. "He must be thinkin' he's a townie."

"I allows he read that in a book," said Doris. "Sounds a bit off to me. Though it's his boat, and he can name her what he likes."

"Well, that ain't the best of it," Alf said. "I took a gander after he had her done, and he got the 'e' on 'Fate' right ruined. So now it looks like she's named, 'Lorna's Fat' – plus a big white smudge of paint."

"Good Lord," said Doris, and a tinny twitter leaked out from her lips.

"That's a testament if I ever heard one," said Clive.

"Poor Lorna," said Arva, stopping all chuckles, except for Alek's. "She's likely to be embarrassed over that."

"Lorna's fat. Lorna's fat." Alek laughed, his mouth jam-packed with cod, hands to his face in a fingery jail.

"Now, now, Alek," Doris said. "Arva's right. If Junior catches us pokin' fun, he'll have his back out of joint with us for sure."

"I thinks he never had her built for Lorna t'all, but for Frank Smith," Alf said. "That's what they was sayin' to the Legion, anyways. Frank's been goin' 'round with Patty, and Junior's thinkin' he'll be slippin' her the question, and he wants somethin' to offer the boy, keep the two of them in the cove. I says to Junior this afternoon he should've called her Frankie's Fate, but that boy's slender as a reed, so 'tis a good thing, because it would've looked right dumb."

"Well, broad as it's long, whatever he names her," Clive said. "I hears Frank's goin' on to the city. Joey got somethin' set up for him."

"Joey?" said Arva, glancing up from her plate.

"Yes, me dear," Clive said. "Smallwood hisself. Bringin' them into the towns, settin' them up with decent jobs at fish plants. It's a real boom he got organized. Trawlers out in the harbour, bringin' in loads like ye never seen, freezin' the fish rock solid at the plants, and then shippin' it off to the United States themselves. I allows they never tasted nothin' like it."

"But, what about the fishermen here?" Arva asked. "What about their catches?"

"Time to make way for the future, Arva," Clive said. "There's neither dollar to be made here livin' like that."

"Joey says it's all about industry," Alf said. "But ye won't see me headin' to the city. No, sir. I don't care how poor I gets. I likes me fish split, salted, tails clipped onto Dot's clothesline. There's no finer sight in this world for me."

"Yer a dying breed then, Alfie," Clive said. "Give it ten years and ye won't see a dory in the harbour, it'll be the big trawlers. People won't never have to touch a raw fish again. Just fry it up and gobble it down." He rubbed his belly.

"Nothin' wrong with a raw fish, me son," Alf said. "Ye wouldn't be here but for the sake of a raw fish."

"I allows I would've found me way," Clive said. "Joey knows what he's at, is all I'm sayin'. He's a common man, hisself. Got a feel of what it's like to work from his pig-farmin' days. Not out of touch with us like most of them friggin' politicians."

"I doubts he's caught either whiff of a pig farm these days," Doris said. "I reckons he forgot the reek of pig the very day he went on to St. John's."

"Never ye mind 'bout it," Clive said. "If I had either bit of sense left in me, I'd be over to the city meself, settin' it all up with him. Nice desk for meself. Organizing a few papers. That's the good life."

"I minds ye could, too," Doris said. "Ye got more than enough tongue for it."

"Now then, Mother," Clive said. "Yer right smart, me dear. So why don't ye make yerself useful, and slide me down the bottle."

Doris closed her mouth firmly, and slid the bottle down. Then, once she had cleared the table, she laid a plate of her date squares in the very center, where an arm would have to make an extra effort in reaching. Clive poured another generous helping of whiskey for Alf, and filled his own glass with a deliberately slow trickle, his glossy eyes on his wife.

A few months shy of a year married, he thought, and most often he felt like he was living alone at Old Man Crane's house. That baby was always in Arva's arms, and she talked to him in some sort of annoying hush whenever he was awake. Then she would snicker, the two of them sharing some kind of secret, likely about Clive himself, he figured. He would prick his ears, listen as best he could, but she could've been speaking German for all he knew, and he wouldn't have been at all surprised if she was.

He thought that women loved to talk, never shut up. To the legion, men complained their wives talked so much they would walk down for a whiskey, and when they returned home, the wife wouldn't have budged an inch, muscled mouth still exercising, the news not yet drained out. Once when Clive was at Arthur Drover's, he was cooking up an enormous cow's tongue. When he hauled it out of the pot, dark pink, bubbly skin sloughing off, Arthur said, "'Tis a terrible thing, I knows, but I believes this tough ol' tongue here don't hold a candle to me Ethel. But, I'm blessed, ye see. Ye never got a load of her mother."

Instead, Clive found himself doing all the talking for he and Arva, likely just to hear something other than his food digesting. Most evenings, after she washed up the dishes, she would just sit in the wooden rocker near the woodstove, knitting, knitting, knitting. Soon, she would run out of wool and he'd be damned before he put out a penny for another strand of it. Not like she was knitting a sweater for him or a decent pair of mitts for herself or booties for the baby. No. It was just row after tedious row, creeping out from under her elbows, tumbling down over her knees, and collecting on the linoleum near her feet.

Jesus. What the hell had he been thinking?

He slurped at the whiskey, his gut increasingly sour, rot reaching from the back of his throat right down to the very bottom of his flipside.

Doris sighed as she slowly brought herself down into the

rocker. "The two of ye," she said, one finger pointed towards Clive, one finger for Alf. "Right soused. Three sheets to the wind. Go on out and walk it off." She used her head and neck to begin moving the chair. "And Clive, take yer brother with ye. I imagine the last thing he wants to be doin' is stayin' in on a Saturday night with his ol' Mother." Doris bent over and lifted Henry out of the breadbox, his head lolling back, body sedated with milk. "Ye go on too Arva. The boy can stay on here. He's nar bit of trouble."

"Not much odds if he is," Alf said, leaning hard against the doorframe. He pulled his baseball cap from the handle, white mesh on the backside, 'We don't tan, we RUST' written across the squarish front. "If he makes a ruckus, missus, cast he aside. Clive and Arva'll have a grand time makin' another."

On the way down the lane, Arva kicked at a flattened pebble with the nose of her shoe. She followed its path, adjusted her direction accordingly, and aligned her steps perfectly for the next strike. Her pregnancy had taught her how to stroll leisurely, enjoying each step, watching out for the things a speeding eye might miss. She noticed busy bee flowers blooming in the gutters, she found a lost muddied letter for Doreen Coombs from her son in Toronto, and once, after a moment of lazy rummaging in a field, she plucked a perfect four-leafed clover. It was now pressed into Old Man Crane's Bible, a green wafer-thin leaf of luck saved for a blustery day.

Clive and Alf were arm in arm, four feet making great timed strides to the left then to the right. Their loud voices were singing about pig's feet, cat's meat, dumplings boiled in a sheet. Arva could make out little more with the soggy-mouthed slurring. Alek walked on the very edge of the lane, taking rapid steps in his gray sneakers, placing one foot tightly in front of the other and counting 'one, two, three, one, two, three' in constant repetition.

"Jesus. I loves ye, Clive," Alf called out for anyone with window open or closed to hear.

"Yes now," Clive yelled back. "And I loves ye too, Alf. Yer a real time, me son." He twisted his body behind Alf's, jumped onto his back and wrapped his legs around his waist. Alf carried

Clive for a few steps in a wobbly piggyback. Clive pressed his face in so close it looked as though Alf was lugging a turtle shell, not a grown man. Then Alf toppled backwards, landing on his drunken casing, and the two screamed with tremendous peals of laughter. "Yer the best, me son. Yer right on!"

Alf had the notion to go and jump into Junior Lynch's boat. "I wants to feel me arse on some fresh painted planks. The ones on me own are near worn through. If I likes her, I'll have to be a mite nicer to Patty Lynch, see if I can snag meself a few runs out with Junior."

They came to the wharf, songs announcing their destination, and found Patty Lynch, in navy rolled-up jeans and home-knit sweater, seated atop a mound of sun-dried netting. Frank Smith, with similar jeans and matching sweater, was in front of her balancing on a painted orange cork buoy, falling back to the wharf, jumping forward, and balancing again.

"Now, then. What do we have here?" Alf said, a deep bow from his waist. "Hello Miss Patty."

"Evenin', Clive, Arva," Patty said, not even a glance to Alf.

"Lovely night," Frank said.

"Yes, lovely," Arva said.

"Now if it would only stay like this all year round," Patty said as she climbed down the mound, her heels hooking into toughened knots of rope.

"We're take to down a gander at yer father's new boat, me lovey," Alf said, straightening his back. "Take her out for a run of a bit."

"I 'llows ye is," Patty said. "I'd like to see ye try goin' anywhere in yer state."

"That I can, now then," Alf said. "Me whistles as clean as me mind. A minds as clear as me crystal."

"Why don't you and Clive go into the Legion for a glass of something," Arva said. "Alek and I can walk back to Doris's. Leave Frank and Patty to get on with their evening."

"That I won't," Alf said. "Came here to have a gander at Junior's boat, and Junior's boat is goin' to have a gander, if it's the does thing I last."

Alf dropped onto his belly, and using his hands and knees, crawled backwards on the wharf, then down into Junior Lynch's dory. Bent at his trim waist, his legs dangled near the stem, his fingers pushed in between two rough boards of the wharf. The ocean lifted, brought the boat higher, the tip catching Alf's feet, unsetting his delicate inebriated balance. Then a crack, flesh on wood, followed by the sound of a flat stone gulped down by hungry water, a hollow belch, no glorified splash. Alf's head had disappeared from the edge of the wharf, his body gone under, an empty white cap bobbing on a black wave.

"Jesus," Frank Smith yelled out. "He slipped right in."

"I can't make him out," Patty said, her heels lifted from the wharf. "I just knowed he shouldn't of gone near Father's boat."

All eyes scanned the waves, Alf's shirt and dark pants indiscernible among the boats, ribbons of slimy kelp, murky black water. No one spoke. They were waiting for a head to pop up out of the darkness, a hand to wave 'hi,' to see certain strokes of Alf's thin but strong arms bring him into shore. But there was nothing that would allow their lungs to breathe normally, their pounding hearts to slow.

Then, an abandoned splash. Alek had jumped in, his arms and legs dog-paddling like a fearless Newfoundland dog. He was moving steadily towards a faceless floating mass several yards out. Alek's head was held high, his eyes and mouth drawn inward with each lick from the playful sea. Arva saw white skin, a foot kicked up from behind, drenched sock holding onto clenched toes. Biting her bottom lip, she turned to look away, thinking Alek's sneakers had drowned. A moment of relief, two dirty gray runners were neatly placed side by side near the lobster pots. Another moment of relief, the dog had reached the drowning.

As Clive stood motionless, Alek swam back towards them, a committed stroke full of such force his fingers might well have been webbed. Clamped in a vice grip of Alek's brown teeth was the red plaid of Alf's shirt, the collar made all the stronger from a double layer of interfacing Aunt Dot had sewn in. When Alek reached the wharf, Frank reached over and dragged up Alf's flimsy remains, water soaking into the wood surrounding the body, a string of blood from his head. Alek monkeyed up over the side, and bounded onto Alf, straddling his waist, pumping Alf's chest with his forearms. Mouthful after mouthful of salty water, strands of hack, and flakes of white fish all whiskey-scented gurgled up and slid down his cheek into his ear, his sopping hair. A sputter, motor starting, another sputter, a glorious first breath, Alf Jones, the near drowned, re-born.

"He's hangin' on by the skin of his teeth, b'y's," Frank Smith said, face nearing explosion from leaning over so hard. "But he's hangin' on. Now, then."

Clive hoisted his brother off, and Alek grabbed immediately for his dry sneakers, held them securely against his trembling chest. At the same time, Alf's back arched with a cough so fierce it looked as though a demon exited through a crack in his sternum. Face pallid, his lips were lost, his hair like sucking leeches framing pockmarked cheeks and narrow forehead. They stared at Alf, mouths still open, and the only sound to be heard was water lapped at Junior's flame-red dory, 'Lorna's Fat - big smudge,' as it knocked against the wharf with another shameless invitation.

Alf blinked, managed himself to a sitting position, hand cupping the back of his skull, and said, "Jesus b'y, gargeous swim for a night." He shook his head, leeches lifted and morphed into a wet cat-fur hairdo. "Some crack I got," he said with pride, his hand showing watery blood from the cut hidden on his scalp.

Someone helped him to his feet, clothes stuck to his body making him look even more like a malnourished drunk. He jumped once or twice, water spewing forth from his shoes, drops from pointy tips of his collar.

When everyone was safe, Arva's mind surrendered to the memories that were saturating her like an aggressive rainstorm. For three beats, her heart decided to stop pumping and languid blood pooled inside her feet. Images before her eyes began to curl inward, a fetal positioning, colours melding into a hot white star in the center of her eyeballs. As her body crumbled down onto the wharf, a night blanket swallowing her, Arva's final thought was that if she were younger and her mother were here, Alf Jones would never have woken up.

8

Men know nothing of a woman's body. They are daft in that sense, and have every right to be.

Nine months later, you were born on a stony beach under a pale sickle moon. Tidal waves brought you forth. And there you were. Arva. My living seashore.

I carried you home. Henry was waiting.

After you arrived, his fatherly joy wheedled him into quitting the factory. For a few cycles, our little life was simple. My world stopped talking while you cried, and often I wished you would cry on forever. But you were far too genial for that.

The night before it happened, Arva thought she heard an engine humming. It was not the wheezy start-up of a distant boat or the rumble of a souped-up car chugging down the lane. It was a city taxi, with its smooth motor, wheels unaccustomed to gravel roads. At first she noticed the purr, approaching, a rusted hinge, quiet feet. Then, after a moment, a resigned crushing of rock, the complaint of a strained steering wheel, and the hum shrinking back into night. Arva listened, a stream of muffled words, no conversation, just one long-winded opinion. Somewhere a door closed with controlled frustration. And after that, there was nothing but typical nighttime noise, a cricket with its incessant chafing music, an irritated shingle, loose but stubborn, chiding the roof with each gust of summer wind.

Sunlight pestered Clive's tender eyelids, tormented them until they opened, squinted with the brightness. It had been two weeks since Alf Jones nearly drowned in the sea, two weeks since his wife had collapsed on the wharf, and two weeks since Upper Island Cove had seen any sign of the sun. Great sheets of cold summer rain had fallen for days on end, and when the rain was gracious enough to let up, dense fog had settled in. It was as though an immense bag of flour had been dropped on the bay, billowy clouds suspended, pressing against the windows, forming a near-dough that wrapped every dory, fisherman, and cod in the nets. Clive took the dampness worst in his shoulders, had them continually hunched as if he were trying to stop leaky valves from wasting warmth. But now, the sun had won a battle against cloud cover, and was hollering 'Get outta bed, me son. Dare roll yerself over, and I'll be gone.'

Since that night on the wharf, Clive treated things different-ly. He was not harsh with himself that he stood immobile, feet locked in ice, as Alek swam out to Alf. It was a mystery how his brother had even seen Alf, not to mention where he had ever learned how to swim. And Clive was also not upset over the fact that it had been his brother and not he who had lifted Arva from the wharf, carrying her back to their mother's home on the hill. Sure, he could have stepped in, taken her into his own arms, but the night was now a fuzzy memory, no point in re-hashing it all.

That very evening, blurry as it was, Clive had gained a fresh perspective on his wife, a new awareness. And so had the rest of the cove, when word got around. People now understood Arva to have a delicate constitution. She was a sensitive sort, faint of heart. Anyone who was able to do so should lend a hand, help her with the boy for an afternoon, bring up a loaf of fresh bread or a pot of fish stew.

Clive never considered she would need extra care or the like, but he was expecting to field occasional questions on her well-being. He had no doubt he would garner some additional respect from the men, for every man knew the difficulty of look-ing after a weak woman. Most of the women in the bay, once they got used to the routine of being a salt-water wife, were as strong as oxen, just in need of direction. But now he knew that

Arva would have to be handled differently. He was not sure how, but he was ready for the questions, and had both his response and expression prepared.

'How's yer wife? Heard she's not good,' Junior Lynch might say.

'Oh, we's gettin' on, gettin' on,' Clive would reply. His mouth would be grim and he'd shake his head side to side just slightly in the manner of someone slugging it out, doing the best he could with the cards God gave him.

'Yer a fine man, me son,' Junior would finish. 'I knows 'tis not easy. Best to ye both.'

And with all the talk, the questions, the offers of help, the bay would gradually spin its net around his wife and make her part of its home.

"Come on, now," Clive said to himself, trying to lure his body out of bed. When his feet were solid on the floor, he called to his wife, waited for the moment until she appeared in the door. "Fix me a cup of tea, maid. Warm up a raisin bun, split it, a spoon of patridgeberry jam in the middle. Ye knows how I likes it. Course ye do. Then, get yerself and the boy ready. We're goin' to Bay Roberts for a run."

He took a deep breath as Arva left the doorframe, lifted his face towards the sweet morning sun. The dark green curtains were wide open, as they almost always were. Since they had moved into Old Man Crane's room, Arva and Clive rarely found occasion to close them.

Clive jerked the wheel. They were thrust off the smooth highroad onto the wide gravel shoulder. Dust spewed up from underneath the wheels, blasted into the cab, temporarily blinding driver and passenger in a fine cloud of clay. Arva whipped a blanket over Henry's face, then braced her hand on the black dashboard, hot and tacky from pelting sunshine. Clive held tight to the steering wheel as the truck lurched to its final stop. With his right hand, he grabbed the brand new Brownie Bulls-Eye, a black and silver model, before it crashed to the floor.

"Here we is," he said, camera tossed into his other hand, prompt twist of the key. "Birch Hills. Let's hop out."

They made their way down the steep embankment, across a

boggy stretch of low-lying marsh, and over a downtrodden barbed-wire fence. Before them was a vast hill covered in wild grasses that were waving gently in the breeze. Where the hill began to dip, there was a dozen wild black horses galloping one after the other, their muscles rippling in the sunlight as they left zigzagging trails through the yellowed meadow. At the very top, a cluster of birch trees formed a leafy crown anchored to the swaying earth by silver-barked legs.

As they approached the circular mini-woods, the extensive carvings were noticeable several yards away. Over the years, teenagers needing to profess their undying love had stolen over the fallen fence under the secure cover of darkness. With a desire to immortalize their emotion, they carried kitchen blades or pocketknives in hand, post-office markers in back jeans pockets. Great strips of the papery bark had been cut away, tossed aside, and then names engraved. There were hearts encircling initials, Julia over Johnny like a personal fraction, the letters 't.l.a.' in monogram style, and coats of red and black ink applied for temporary emphasis. Some had returned months, perhaps years later, revulsion having replaced love, and cut great gashes from the trunks, removing all traces of the union that had once driven them to destroy a beautiful property.

"Seat yerself here, love," Clive said.

He had led her to an untouched side of the birch circle, and stomped down a patch in the meadow. When she sat, she was instantly blinded to the outside world. She could only see the grass, the blue sky, her husband standing before her, and several tree branches if she strained her neck. Her muscles tensed, and she felt her mouth fill with saliva. Arva swallowed hard. She had the sense she was being swept over, engulfed, and it stuck in her craw like a dry crust of bread. She tried to put the discomfort away and focused on the photo her husband was preparing to snap at that very instant.

Arva placed the baby onto her chest. Henry's mouth found his plump fist, and he chewed with toothless gums. She smiled at the box hiding most of Clive's face. The wind lifted strands of her black hair, made them dance, as if strings were attached, a maestro puppeteer tugging upwards.

"We'll do this sort of thing every couple months," Clive said.

"Have a record of the boy. I got no clue what yer feedin' him, but he's growin' like a weed."

"That's a lovely idea, Clive," Arva said as she stood, breathing again, her eyes once again seeing the names cut in, the names cut out. "Something for us to look back on."

He held her hand as they strolled back down through the grass, a firm grip, a decided grip. His disposition was light, he felt like a real husband, a good father. But, moments later, when the truck failed to start with its usual rattling cough, failed even to clear its throat, Clive's mood rapidly went black. He cursed his luck, his life, dropped down from the cab, slammed the door, and drew up his foot to strike the dusty tire. Henry began to cry, and the sound brought an instant sweat to Clive's lip, and he booted the tire again.

"Dumb piece of garbage."

Along the distant highway, he saw a gray slug inching its way up the road. By the time it neared the broken-down truck, the slug had grown into a dirty white van, 'Arn Chaytor's Best Dry Goods' written in indigo paint strokes on the side. Clive jumped, irritated the air above him with flailing arms, and the slug slowed, eased off the road, settled nose to nose with the mustard-yellow Chev.

As Arva read the name on the van, her hands became instantly clammy. She remembered Chaytor's living close by when she was a child, a family with lots of kids, a fat, smiling mother. Of course, they were a foggy memory, an image floating far out to sea, only a faint glimpse that something was there with each swivel of the lighthouse signal. Arva wiped her hands in Henry's blanket over and over again, but the sweat was mulish, replenishing itself, until a palm-sized patch of the tiny quilt was damp and wrinkled by her grip.

The driver stepped down from the van and ambled over to Clive. Reed thin in navy blue jeans, he had a faded square worn around the thick wallet in a deep front pocket, a dangling metal chain grabbing onto a belt loop. He wore a brown plaid shirt with sharp creases across the sleeves and chest as though it had been folded then weighted by a hefty slab of slate. On the back of his scalp, there was no more than a handful of coarse drab hair, combed up and over, a peppery-skinned octopus had been dropped from above and left to dry. Behind the safety of the bug-splattered windshield, Arva noticed that the skin of his face was so shiny, he could have pulled off the road moments earlier and shaved in a brook.

"Hey, b'y. Got some trouble here, do ye?" he said, reaching into his shirt pocket. He hauled out a pale blue plastic box, retrieved a home-rolled, and lit a second cigarette from the fuming butt of one already clamped in his teeth.

"She got nar bit of juice. Don't know if I left the cab light on or what I done. She gone completely flat on me."

"Me old van got no shortage of juice, that's for sure. Takes me all over the province, best dry goods outside St. John's. I never had a single trouble with her. 'Tis a boost yer after, I reckon."

Under the seat in his van, the man extracted black and red cording. The coppery clippers banged against the leg of his jeans as he positioned himself between the two vehicles. He popped his lid, then popped the truck's lid and in two shakes had them joined, one feeding strength into the other. As the van chugged on, the driver took deep drags from his cigarette, spit on the ground, and wiped the spot in the gravel with a dazzling white sneaker.

"Where ye headed?" he asked Clive.

"We was on our way back to Island Cove, until this here clunker died," Clive said, lighting up his own cigarette.

"Yeah, that's where I's going meself. With all the goods in me baby here. To the general store. Mercer's, if I recalls correctly."

"Well, now. I's a Mercer meself."

"Yer shop?"

"No relation. Well, not in recent years, that is. I fathoms there's some connection. Everyone in the cove is likely related if ye goes back a ways." Clive held out his hand, cigarette nipped in his lips, eyes slitted from the smoke. "Clive Mercer's the name."

The man clasped Clive's hand, then nodded towards the van and said, "That's me. Arn Chaytor. Arnold, really, but Arn seems catchier. Don't ye think?" He never waited for a response. "Dry goods. Got whatever ye needs, b'y, and then some."

"There's no shortage of need 'round the bay. No shortage of want neither. Sounds like a respectable business. Whatd'ye got back there?"

"Oh, clothes and stuff. Like I says, whatever ye needs.

Dresses, baby sleepers, nice pair of trousers for a man like yerself. I sees yer missus there in the cab with the little one. Why don't ye get her to take a gander while we get yer truck fixed up?"

Clive scooped the air toward Arva with his hand, but she pretended not to see him. When he double-scooped the air, she laid Henry in the fold of the seat, reluctantly climbed down from the cab, and followed her husband.

At the back of the van, Arn Chaytor released the doors by flipping up the substantial metal hook that was pinning them together. Inside was a packed mass of suspended outfits with dusty shoulders, boxes piled upon boxes, ripped opened, tipped over. There were lifeless housedresses on metal hangers, folded checked cotton shirts, boxes of children's striped clothes, piles of lisle stockings, hose, undershirts and underwear, bolts of corduroy, assorted cup-towels, a peachy set of bed sheets wrapped in hard plastic. Though there was little room, Clive took Arva by the elbow and helped her up into the van.

The two men stepped away, and Arva shuffled through the flowered smocks, plucked up a pair of children's underwear, and held them at arms length. Oh, how tiny, she thought. A smell was released when she disturbed more of the garments, and it was so stale, her eyes began to mist. She stepped back towards the doors, balanced on the grimy edge of the opening, and tried not to consider what lurked at the back of the van. Something in the darkness seemed to shift, and she could not decide whether fabrics were being worn at that moment, or if her eyes were playing tricks. She did not want to look. Instead, Arva stared down at the wooden boards lining the floor, and strained to hear the men's conversation while the idling van continued to rasp and wheeze.

"Anything she wants, b'y, I'll give ye a deal."

"Oh, yer helpin' us out enough already. We're not expectin' no kinds of deals."

Clive always hated the fact that his mother was constantly seeking out bargains, trying to scam a dollar here a dollar there, always putting up the poor mouth, when she likely had sewn into her mattress a sock full of bills that could choke a horse. He, on the other hand, paid what was due, never lowered himself to beg for a couple of cents. If he didn't have the money for something, he wouldn't even go looking. No one needed to know what was burning in his wallet or what was not. "Now, then. Chaytor," Clive continued. "That's a name I never heard. Not from 'round here, that's for sure."

Arva could have told Clive the name's origin the instant she saw the van pull up. Catalina, Trinity Bay. That was where Arva had been born. Right on a beach, three weeks early, having just dropped out. That was what her mother had told her anyway, whenever she had been upset as a little girl. "I had to scoop you right off the rocks before the tide got to you," her mother would say, then she would lift Arva in the air, clasp her close, as if the floor itself had become an immediate danger. "You were baptized right there with a drop of salty spray the size of my thumb. A born water baby." Arva always thought that was just a story made up to make her smile, but when it came to her mother, she never could have known for sure.

"Port Union," she heard Arn Chaytor say. "That's in Trinity Bay."

"Now that's some kind of coincidence. Me wife's from Catalina."

"Ye got to be jokin' me. People are movin' all over these days. She don't look it, though. Wouldn't of guessed it. What's her family name?"

"House."

"Yeah, that's a Trinity Bay name if I ever heard one. There was plenty of House's. What's her father's name? Ye never knows."

"Her father was Henry. Son there in the cab named after him."

"Henry House? B'y, ye got to be tuggin' at me leg. Well, now isn't that somethin'." Arn Chaytor drew another cigarette out from the plastic container, lit his third in a row. "Me uncle's good friend's brother was a friend of a Henry House's. Don't believe there was too many of them 'round. So, it's likely the same fellow we're talkin' 'bout. I tells ye, as long as I's been travellin' 'round the province, whoever I meets, I can find someone who knows 'em." He seemed to breathe through his cigarette, burning it down as he spoke. "That man me uncle knew used to work in the factories with Henry House up in Toronto. For a time, me uncle did too. Poor bastard, though. Sorry way to go."

"Who? Your uncle?"

"No. Henry House I was talkin' 'bout. That's likely why I remembers him. A real embarrassment for the beggar." He lowered his tone. "Washin' up on the shore without even a pair of drawers on. Must have been drinkin' a shitload of moonshine to get hisself into that state." A hearty laugh. "Right pissed. I figures he got up at night, after a bit of a time with his missus, and must've fallen in when he was takin' a squirt in the sea."

"Jesus," Clive said. "I never knew."

"Don't s'pose she'd be spreadin' that far and wide." He cocked his head towards the back of his van. "Ye say that's House's daughter?"

"Yes sir, like I tells ye, son in the cab there's named after him."

"Well, that's a queer thing. That man's hair was 'bout red as a robin's breast." He rolled the 'r' just slightly, holding the sound on his tongue longer than necessary. A thin smile tweaked his lips, stained teeth narrow like his frame. "Although, 'tis comin' back to me now. Yeah, Rita or Ruby or somethin' like that. I recalls hearin' 'bout his wife. She'd be a hard one to forget. Now, b'y, if 'tis the one I's thinkin' 'bout, she was another sort altogether. Me uncle used to go on 'bout her. Oh, yeah. I remembers now. Wish I'd a met her meself."

Then Arn Chaytor snickered in a way that made sun cloud over and Clive shiver in the sudden shade. He bit hard into his cigarette. "Now what do ye mean by that?"

"Oh, Lordie. I don't want to be gettin' into that here with yer missus in earshot. P'raps over a whiskey sometime. And if that don't happen, go to Catalina yerself, down to Mifflin's near the wharf and ask anyone. Rita or Ruby. Ah, just say Henry's wife. They'll tell ye all ye wants to know."

Arva had stepped down from the back of the truck.

Arn Chaytor sized her up and down leisurely and said, "Yeah, I sees it now. Henry's girl. Right, now. I knows." He chortled some more, like a choked-up starter, hock catching in his throat. He spat a licorice-streaked glob onto the pavement, and reached for another cigarette. "Yeah, it weren't all talk. I sees it now."

"Get back in the truck, Arva."

For a moment, she could not move.

"BACK TO THE TRUCK ARVA. Now. We don't need to be listenin' to this kind of bullshit."

Her feet carried her past the two men. She felt jammed in a nightmare, her mind telling her childhood body to run and hide, her legs swimming slow-motion in air like gooey sludge. Inside the van, she took Henry back up into her arms, a black-haired angel, and his baby body made her feel innocent. But still, the names hovered in the air, and she wished the discussion of her parents could be erased, forgotten, tucked neatly away outside of living memory.

Clive tossed his cigarette to the ground, left it to smolder. He tore the clippers from his engine, slammed the lid shut, jumped into the cab. Slamming his foot in on the clutch, he dropped the hacking engine into first gear, the truck coughed gently, then a contagious bark, and the relief of success. Arva turned back as they drove off and saw Arn Chaytor shaking his head in satisfied disbelief while a gust of wind lifted the octopus legs off his shiny head. Beside him, booster cable clips dangled from his open-mouthed van like pegged lobster claws. As she watched him shrink down, she felt something hard in her hand. She was pushing a translucent red button into her palm, strands of rotted red thread in all four of its holes. It had come from the summer dress she had clutched while the dry goods salesman mocked her dead mother with his revealing laughter.

Late that night, something nudged at Arva's shoulder, drawing her to the surface, out of the blackness of her dreamless sleep.

"Arva!" Warm breath across her face.

Her legs woke first, ready to dash. Then she opened her eyes.

Leaning over her was a female silhouette, cloaked in the spotty decay of darkness. Slowly her vision adjusted, as her eyes captured nighttime light streaming in through the open window. Doris's face emerged, eyebrows knitted together in one long strip, hair like fine mixed strands of silver and flax flattened on one side.

She was whispering to Arva trying not to wake Clive, though Doris could have exploded above the bed, and her son would not have budged. An evening at the Legion took good care of that. He had walked there right after Arva had served him his Jigg's dinner, a plate of boiled cabbage, turnip, carrots, and stringy deep pink salt meat. He shoveled food into his mouth, left half in his plate, the fatty meat likely still in his cheek as he had hurried down the lane moving away from his wife and towards the salvation of the Legion.

"Come on, me dear," Doris whispered. "Lolly wants ye."

"Lolly?"

"Yes, Lolly," Doris said. "Don't be askin', me dear. Ye'll find out soon enough."

Arva dressed quickly and followed her mother-in-law through the kitchen, out the porch, and up over the rocky ledge, the weathered surface softened with summer moss. There was a hint of sadness in the night air, a detached coolness pinching away at the warmth, a chill leisurely riding in on the edge of each windy breeze. That very day, Arva had noticed the silence at daybreak, the absence of crows squawking, robins chirping, chickadees dee-deeing. The birds felt it first, autumn's jaw opening slowly, biting at the bit. Only those that could not fly were mad enough to try and love a Newfoundland winter.

In Rose Young's kitchen, the moonlight was dreamlike in its brightness. Caught in the rays streaming through the vast window, the skin on Doris's face looked like worn plastic, an enormous old doll with eyelids flipped up, her jointed legs moving with swiftness across stained linoleum. In the sink, a pot covered with chunky yellow-green leftovers and charred at the base sat unwashed, ignored. Windowless air in the kitchen was weighted with the sharp smell of burnt pea soup. The sound of crying came from the bedroom, a child maybe, or else a grown woman completely lost.

"She came back," Doris whispered to Arva, moonlight holding them in the dream. "Rose was up to the house tonight, beside herself. Lolly, back from the woman's home to the city. Couldn't take it another day, she told her mother. Nice young ladies there, in the family way, havin' their wee babies, and not even 'llowed to take a peep at 'em, adopted out before they even knowed if 'twas a Jane or a John. But, that's the way it is. Lolly knew that goin' in."

Rose floated into the kitchen, the night light enveloping her, beckoning her to join the conversation.

"What a mess she got made of it all," Rose said to Arva, her two eyes sore and swollen like boils from a burn. "Never even had time to call Doreen. She in there now, child on the way. Said to me if I don't send for ye, she'd go over there and get ye herself. Thinks ye'd offer a bit of support to her, I s'pose. Ye don't question a labourin' woman."

Arva walked past Doris and Rose and into Lolly's childhood bedroom. The massive naked body on the bed seemed to have more than outgrown the elfin pink flowery wallpaper, the little girl's quilt, the great book of nursery rhymes on the shelf. Lolly was bigger than Arva ever could have imagined. Her feet were colossal tree trunks about to split seams from pressure, her face and neck blotchy mounds of over-risen dough, breasts like snow-coated mountains, peaks melted, an immense tiger-striped boulder hidden beneath them. Lolly's jagged mouth looked as though a spoonful of rancid cod-liver oil had just been forced upon it, and her once buttercup-coloured hair was now brittle and brassy, a solid inch of mousiness near the roots. Next to Lolly on the bed, easy enough for the roaming eye to miss, was a tiny knitted pink wool sleeper and matching hat.

"She now," Rose said, as she came into the room, "not a stitch on. Can barely even stand to look at her."

Doris kept her eyes averted.

"I don't know what they's teachin' in the city these days," Rose continued, "but this ain't the way she was brought up. No, me lovey."

"No one thinks it is, Rose," Doris said. "Ye did the best ye could. A woman like yerself on her own."

"Did I tell ye she stole me weddin' band? Right out of me top drawer. Some widow nonsense brewed up in her head. I don't know where it all come from."

Lolly was crying hard, her rolls heaving and shaking. Mucus ran from her reddened nose, her wet tongue darting out to catch it. Then she would catch hold of her breath, and the low howl of an aching animal would emanate from her chest and throb through the air. Lolly's little girl room was like a hollow cave, walls of damp pink stone.

"For the love of Jesus, Lolly, pipe down. Pipe down. Ye got yerself into this mess. Yer bed is made, now. Lord our Saviour, a fine stew. Do ye want to be rousin' the whole harbour with yer complainin'?"

Lolly motioned to Arva.

"Yes, Lolly. I'm here. So is your mom and Doris."

"I's so sorry, Arva," Lolly said. "So sorry."

"You have nothing to be sorry about, Lolly. Just concentrate on getting that baby out."

"No, Arva," she said again. "Yer right nice to me all the times."

"Yes, and I will be. The baby doesn't make that any different. Everything will be fine."

Arva sat on the bed behind Lolly. She put her hands on Lolly's shoulders, willing strength to pour out from them. Henry's birth such a short time ago, Arva knew well the kind of energy that was needed to bring forth a new life, one person separating into two, yolk from white.

"Ah, God," Lolly said, her sweaty body glittering in the candlelight. "I needs a nice little girl. That's all I wants. Please Lord, let me do this right."

Lolly got onto all fours, praying to God and Jesus and Mary and to anyone else who might be listening. She grunted and moaned, in the heat of passion, her baby moving lower and lower in her pelvis. Her mother was at her bottom, hot cloth pressed over her backside, Doris beside her holding up a light. With a scream of utter honesty, the head slid forth, a boar's snorting grunt brought out the shoulders, and an ecstatic sigh released the skinny body right down between Lolly's bent and bloodied knees.

Doris' thin lips parted, a slight gasp escaped, and she whispered, "I's never seen that before."

"'Tis got the veil over its head," Rose said in a low hush. "Good sign for the father, he'll never drown. Not that'd I care too much right now if he did."

Arva could see the baby's swollen eyes peering up through the murky membrane still covering its crown, a mass of wet dark hair pressed against the sack. The last child her mother had attended as a midwife had been born in the caul. It arrived two months early, a messy birth, her mother had said, and the child wrapped in its womb blanket. But it was a stillborn, her mother's first though she had helped with many babies. And touching the corpse, willing its birdlike fingers to open, clasp, tangled her mother's stomach into a bitter knot. "Something dead shouldn't have that kind of heat to it," she had said to Arva. "So

I took up sewing. Fabric doesn't need to breathe."

Rose pinched the membrane with her thumb and forefinger of each hand and gently tugged. Clear water gurgled up from the natural spring, trickled over her hands and down onto the newsprint layered under Lolly's knees. The baby kicked, clenched its fist, and Arva exhaled, not realizing she had been holding her breath.

Rose looked the baby over. "Well now, Lolly," she said. "Ye got what ye got."

Lolly's voice was a little girl's, spent after a tantrum, depleted with emotion, no longer able to kick the walls or pull at her own hair, "Mom, what is it? Tell me. Mom. Is she okay?"

A sigh from Rose. "Cough, me dear. Give me a good cough. Let's get that afterbirth out."

Lolly gave a weak cough, and the placenta slid forth, a warm mound of liver, two bright fleshy lobes around a sinewy cord. It was shaped like a perfect heart.

"Please God Mom, let me see her. Please Jesus. Me baby girl."

Veil removed, the baby never made a sound, as if it knew somehow its birth was not the most important event happening in the room at that moment.

"Yer little girl," Rose said to her daughter, "is without a doubt very much a little b'y."

With that announcement, Lolly laid down on her barren belly, rump still stuck out, her arms reaching up towards the headboard where Arva was sitting. Her moans were like a wounded animal, abandoning the notion of life, and hunting out a place to die. Could she possibly do anything else to ruin her life? And now a son. The very last thing she wanted, a boy. She would have rather given birth to a dog than any kind of man. To have it grow up and use her, hate her. A girl would have loved her, she would have made it love her. Lolly kicked out her left leg, the pink sleeper and hat thrown to the dusty floor.

But the crying did not last for long, and in a few moments a serious calm settled over her. She had to think swiftly, and the thoughts were coming, not failing her. Lolly had never felt quite this way before, and it scared her a little, but she could not stop. Her mind was moving forward at lightening speed, two years, five years, ten years, she could see there was no child by her side, a man, yes, but no little boy. Her wits about her, clear as a stream, she knew what to do.

Lolly was up, kneeling on the bed, crinkling soiled paper, pulling a sheet over her rounded shoulders. Then she began uttering words, seemingly random, at an idiot's pace. Her mind, in a chess game nearing checkmate, was calculating her next step, evaluating a future for the son she did not want.

"'Tis Clive's," Lolly said, her statement spoken with tremendous ease.

Arva searched the doorframe, expecting to see her husband standing there, or a reflection of his face in the window, at least a knock on the door. But no. Lolly, her friendly neighbour, continued with a second confirmation blow. "'Tis his son."

Doris leaned over, took one hard stare at the infant through her good eye, and said, "Good Jesus. She's right."

Rose followed suit with her inspection, and said, "Well, there's nar worry 'bout the father drownin'. We won't be findin' he out on the water any time soon."

Arva stood up and walked around to the foot of the bed to see Lolly's child. The baby fixed his hazy eyes on Arva, blinking, blinking.

"I's sorry, Arva," Lolly said. "Sorry to of done it. I couldn't help meself."

At once, Arva thought of swallowing something vile so that her body would feel as sick as her soul. A cry wanted to escape like steam from the potato pot, but she forbade its release, hoping it would dissipate. She could feel the child eyeing her, seeming to recognize her, willing her to accept him. Yes, it was so. With the impatient intent of an infant, a desire for sweet milk and folded arms, he followed her with his dark eyes, all pupil, his gaze an unmistakable match to that of her husband's.

Then Arva found herself in the Young's kitchen, her legs having carried her there, palms flat against the countertop, soothed by the chill moving up through her arms. Rose appeared in the room as if by magic, baby swaddled in a clean sheet, traces of stubborn cream still stuck in his hair, around his ears.

Doris drifted in next, her lips indistinct from her ashen face, words barely audible, spoken inside of a breath. "Who could of known? If Tom was alive. Somethin' got to be done."

"Somethin'," Rose said. "Oh, somethin'."

"A Mercer," Doris said. "At the likes of that. I never heard tell."

"Not much for a Young."

Doris clicked her tongue.

"Why, for the love of God didn't she stay to the home?" Rose said, voice cracking. "Answer me that. Just answer me that."

Doris went to Rose and rubbed between her shoulder blades. "Lolly was never much for thinkin' ahead now, Rose," she said. "Ye knows that."

"Yes, now," Rose replied. "Like yer Clive got the corner market on it."

"Never mind with that," Doris said. "This is no time for bickerin'. We got a baby here. He done nothin' wrong, and that's the truth of it."

"Yer right, me dear," Rose said, gazing down into the folded sheet. "He never done a thing. We got to do right by him."

There was a physical silence pushing in at Arva, asking her to act. She wished she could think of something to fill the space, ease away the whitened knuckles that had eased in through her ribs and were tempering her heartbeat. But her lungs were taking only enough air to support the legs, not considering the mind.

"I'll take him," Arva said, her mouth acting on its own accord, space neatly filled.

Rose bit at her bottom lip, chewed at the peeling skin. "Yes, now. That might be somethin'." She bounced the child slightly as he started to stir, her eyes towards the mountain. "When ye thinks 'bout it, he's as much yers as he is me Lolly's. And she's not fit for much, let alone a baby. That's as sure as can be."

Doris agreed with Rose. "They won't be able to stay 'round here, mind ye. But Arva might be the best one for the boy."

"We's too old to take care of a child," Rose said to Doris. "That's a given. Let alone the kind of talk we'd have to put up with."

"And we knows how wonderful she is with Henry," Doris said.

"Yes, that she is."

"Right wonderful."

"And when ye gets right down to it, what's one more?"

"Yes, what's one more? It's been done before."

"I 'llows it has."

"And then some."

"Yes, and then some."

"There ye got it."

"Now, then."

And so, the child's fate was sealed with the banter of two grandmothers in a kitchen stinking of burnt green pea soup. Rose passed the child into an accepting embrace. Then, once he perceived the new hold was real, permanent, the boy let out his first wail, arms and legs straining against the sheet, startled by newborn freedom, soles and palms facing heaven.

With the child pressed against her chest, Arva began to steal away. She paused outside Lolly's room, and saw a rounded lump rising and falling underneath the quilt. It was either a contented slumber, or soundless waves of mourning. Arva could not tell, and she never went to check. Stepping out the front door, down over the cement steps, her soft-soled slippers clung to the paint that was never scuffed dry by visitors. "That's bad luck if I ever seen it," Arva heard Doris say as the screen door clicked. "Goin' out a different way than she come in."

Down the lane she walked, not knowing where she was going, not caring, because she needed only change and change was everywhere. Around her neck, she could feel the wind, and was happy for it. Her mind would have come apart if the night air were still. She continued up and over the stony path, along the trail by the roaring sea, the newborn boy, buoyant in her arms.

As a child, Arva often wandered alone. She would scale cliffs by the seaside, jump rusted fences, and without a thought, approach a mongrel that had nearly bitten through its rope leash. She was not fearful when she became disoriented in a patch of fir trees or when an aggressive wave would wrap around her calves and threaten her footing. Somehow, whenever there was trouble, her mother appeared.

Skipping beside a layered shale wall when she was seven, Arva came across a group of schoolboys. They were loafing away the afternoon, scabby legs sticking out from woolen shorts, fishermen hats cocked on their shaved heads. While seeking a target to alleviate their boredom, luck had brought them Arva. Whistling and hissing at the unfamiliar girl, they became infected by the thrill of all against one. A fat kid in snug clothes marched up and down the wall crying, "Darkie, darkie, get yer dirty arse home." His lanky counterpart yelled, "What's that hum, b'ys? 'Tis stinkin' trash."

When she did not pick up her pace, they jumped down from their perch and ran at her. Feet hopping like baseball pitchers, the boys fired round after round of overripe damsons in her direction. The moldy fruit pelted her head and torso, and her thin yellow dress was instantly blotched with rotten juice and specks of reddish-brown disintegrating flesh. Handfuls of blueberries showered her hair, and a smooth beach pebble caught her shoulder with a hornet's sting.

Like an eagle, her mother descended upon the boys. They scattered, paper doll knees splaying on the dry dirt. The fat one dawdled. She caught him by the waist of his shorts; there was a yelp from strained threads as he squirmed away. Releasing her catch, she tapped him in the backside with a dusty slipper, with just enough force to knock him down and shame him.

"I's tellin' Mudder, ye crazy ol' witch," he called back at her as he clutched scraps of grass, his jumbo crab legs scrambling away from her.

Her mother had taken Arva by the elbow, and begun her characteristic rapid stride. "Saucy as a crackie, that child. If he was mine, I'd knock him right into next week."

As long as she could remember, Arva had never felt alone. Somehow her mother was always watching over her. Though this very night, she must have turned her eyes away. How could any mother stand to witness her child drowning without jumping in to save her?

When Arva reached the pair of rocks where she and Clive had talked the evening Henry was made, she came upon a middle-aged man, stout around the middle, warm red shirt buttoned to his neck. Immediately she recognized the silver streaks, luminous from having captured star shine that circulated in the night sky. Pepper Reid turned his head towards her, nodded slightly, then brought his face back to the ocean, his desolate eyes searching for something, anything in the low-hanging mist.

Arva sat next to him on her child-rock. She rubbed a cadenced hand over the baby's bony mounds. Beneath her feet, every blade of swaying grass had been brought to life by a near hypnotic moon. Though she did not notice. Instead she was contemplating that without the comfort of Pepper Reid, silent as a dead general beside her, she might never have stopped walking.

Arva returned home as the red sun poked up its head, a bloody gash across the graying horizon.

She found Clive in the kitchen with his mother, Henry asleep in Doris's arms. Clive scratched at his stubble, then rubbed the hair on the back of his head.

"We's goin' to start again, Arva," he muttered. "Mother's arrangin' everythin', and we's goin' to start again."

9

You were bald. The skin on your head was so smooth, I prayed to Mary for your rapid recovery. She must have been listening intently because after your third birthday, black hair flowed as though ink was spouting from your skull. In days, it reached your waist, and you whined with the weight of it. I trimmed it, chopped at it, threw lengths of it into the wood-stove, but it kept growing until it completely covered your back in a glistening pelt. And after that, much to my disbelief, Henry began to concentrate on you in a queer way.

Doris Mercer was remarkably strong-minded, but she was limited in her actions by her sense of the boundaries surrounding all women. Well, the women in Island Cove, anyway, because she knew from Aunt Helen that most things could pass in the city. In the isolated bay where Doris had lived her life, women knew their place and did what they were told. They may have talked amongst themselves, oh yes, that was a given, but rarely would a woman cross a man. And if a man crossed a woman? Likely, she would just wait it out, praying his number came up before hers so that once he was gone, she could stop holding her breath.

This time, though, Doris stepped across that boundary. She called her brother-in-law in Boston, and never asked, but told him the arrangements that were necessary for her elder son. Doris had imagined Harry's help one day with Alek, but never Clive. How could he have been so careless, coming so close to sullying the good Mercer name? He'd acted no different than some stray dog in heat. If Tom were here, he'd have knocked some sense into him.

Clive and his family would move into his uncle's house on King's Bridge Road in St. John's. It was a duplex, sharing a bricked wall with a Memorial University professor and his wife. Harry Mercer had retired, finally giving into Aunt Helen's insistence. She had said it was time they see the world, travel a bit, and enjoy the short years of living together they had left until she went onto her stint as a widow. The couple began their lengthy trip in Boston, where Aunt Helen's favourite cousins resided in grand homes with front wrought iron gates. "Each house has a parlour, wall-papered in roses or pansies. And an ivory-keyed piano in the very center, of course," she had said to Doris. "They drink their tea iced, me dear. In the afternoons on their front porches. And the wind is set to cool ye, not to clip ye. That's civilized livin', as I sees it."

Aunt Helen told her husband she could not care less if they ever returned to that godforsaken island. But Harry put his foot down to her when she wanted to sell the house in the city. And he put his foot down even harder when she suggested they sell the house out around the Bay. "I don't see no point to it," he had said. "We needs to have a base somewhere."

"I don't see any point," Helen corrected. "You can't go startin' in with that kind of Bay talk in Boston. That'd be the heights of embarrassment."

The Mercer home was beautiful, if a little cold, but Arva would certainly never complain. It was built around the turn of the century and was set back from the main road, a strong leafy oak well-rooted in the front yard. A gnarly iron fence surrounded the entire property, the black paint had lifted in a smatter of blisters, and there were signs of rust taking hold in the crevices. Both sides of the clapboard duplex were painted a calculating steely blue, both doors a seductive but demure scarlet. The shady lawn was awash in waxy groundcover like a lush green tablecloth, periwinkle flowers dotting the area in a sprinkled pattern.

Arva walked from room to room with Thomas in her arms. Most of the walls inside were papered, except the kitchen, done in a burnt orange, and the biggest bedroom, painted in storm cloud gray. Not a quilt to be seen in either bedroom or closet. Instead, crisp coverings like clean sheets wrapped the beds and were folded back with cutting precision. Everywhere, Helen's taste for antiques could be seen. Each room was adorned with dark wood furniture, thick-legged and glossy, stained walnut dressers with fronts shaped like a wave, a hard red velvety chaise-lounge. There was a hint of premeditated whimsy in the bright orange bubbled bowl overloaded with dusty chicken-bone candies sitting in the middle of the dining room table. Foot-wide white plaster mouldings decorated the ceiling edges, and a broad shiny black banister, sturdy enough to support even the most fatigued of legs, ascended to the second floor.

The wind had turned and was drilling down from the North.

"I'll get a fire goin'," Clive said.

"Please, not on my account," Arva said.

"We don't want the b'ys to be catchin' a chill," he replied, and disappeared outside to look for dry splits.

There was no woodstove, but an immaculately clean stone hearth. Beside it was an ornate metal container for logs filled with magazines and newspapers. Clive returned in moments with just an armload of kindling. He threw them onto the grate along with a June edition of Reader's Digest and a Friday Evening Telegram.

"We're goin' need to get some logs," he said. "Not more than a dozen or so there. I wonders where ye get logs to in the city."

Arva did not want the warmth, and she went to the back of the house. There she discovered a cramped porch, the painted hinges on the door showing no sign of rust, and little sign of wear. In one corner, a wringer washer stood next to a wicker basket and clothespins. A neat drying line could be seen through the glass of the screen door, sagging between the home and a second great oak tree in the backyard.

With a gentle slope, the backyard lost itself in a lush green of shrubs and ivies, so distinct from the wind whipped land of Upper Island Cove. There, tall natural grasses took root tenaciously, and a wild lilac was a rarity among the stunted bushes and tight rock coverings that bravely attempted settlement. Here, plant-life was so consumed with growing, so zealous with sending out shoots and sprouts, nature itself owned the backyard, and anyone strolling there would be merely a visitor.

On the back step, two white chairs, slatted bodies, wide armrests for warm coffee mugs, faced out to the city jungle. She sat down on the one nearest the lattice divider. Beside her, a square box, white paint flaking, was laden with clusters of spicy red and pink flowers, rounded variegated leaves like a child's hand. Arva knew with one look they were too beautiful to be wild. Helen, with her considerable gardening talent, had grown them.

The door opened on the other side of the divider, feet stepped out, and the scent of milky tea hung in the air.

"I haven't the faintest," a woman's voice said. "I would suspect it's some relation of Harry's."

"Yes, the woman is definitely no relation to Harry or Helen."

"That's plain enough."

"I wonder what her background is."

"That's not the sort of thing you can ask, Wally."

"Of course not, I never thought that."

"She's got an unusual colouring, though. Lovely, really. I wish I had a touch of it."

The man laughed. "Well, if the fog lifted for more than an hour or two, you'd have some chance, at least." A match was struck, pungent pipe tobacco wafted across. "I just hope he doesn't make a habit of stealing my few logs."

Gingerly, Arva stepped down the few steps and into the backyard. Along the side of the house, chuckly pear trees offered their bland useless fruit. She yanked a handful from the branches and threw them one by one into the bushes. From every angle of the home, she had tried, and still, she could not see the ocean. Even though it was just down the street, nearly overflowing out of the packed harbour, there was absolutely no hint of salt water in the air. Car exhaust and sweet city living had all but knocked it clear. Arva strode out through the gates to the top of a steep paved incline leading down to the harbour. There she caught a glimpse of blue, but there was no calmness to be found in the protected port, amid all the bustle of strangely foreign ships.

Henry adjusted instantly, never seeming to notice the change in location. He continued to coo in her arms, and to complain whenever he was lying on his belly. He was easily soothed by the words of promise Arva would whisper into his tiny conch-shaped ears.

Thomas, on the other hand, acted uncomfortable in his baby skin from the very first day. He always needed something, to be held or rocked, and his red-faced cry was angry, desperate, whenever he was abandoned for a moment. With an infantile grip, he would tug at Arva's sweater or cotton blouse, seeking out the warmth of soft skin. One morning, she went to their shared crib, and she saw Thomas sucking with confused desire at the pruned thumb of Henry. She wished she had the knack for singing, a lullaby to alleviate his distress, but her songs were shrill, tone jagged, and Thomas cried all the harder, arms and legs forever working the air. Arva had to hold him tightly, swaddled in a soft blanket, for fear if she laid him down, he might come apart in pieces.

Even Thomas's skin was sensitive. Rashes emerged when a dirtied diaper was left for only minutes. Around his eyes and nose, small red bumps would cluster, morph into tender scales, heal, and then re-appear. Often he would scratch at his own face, his stomach when he was bathed, and he would be left with sore welts even though Arva nibbled his fingernails to the quick. But, when he slept, when they both slept, they were the vision of cherubs. And it was during these rare moments of reprieve, when Arva had time for the luxury of reflection, that he believed she was meant for two sons.

Even with the continual uproar of children, Clive seemed content. For the first few months in the uncle's home, he took up whistling. Not a tinny whistle that was sharp on the ears, but dulcet tones of poignant Irish songs, whistled in the spirit of appreciation for his own newly found good fortune. Arva liked the sound, it warmed the strange house. She had lived in more homes than she could remember, but this particular one seemed to belong so much more to someone else than any other house she knew.

She had thought she was being a wife, a good wife. She cooked decent dinners, and even with Henry feeding every hour, her meals were on time. Her bread was tender and had a fine crumbed texture that Clive liked. His clothes were clean, folded, put into Old Man Crane's dresser drawers. Arva never bothered the man with her womanly opinions or thoughts, she kept those considerately to herself. And she offered her body, whenever she sensed he needed her, wriggling her bum over towards his side of the bed when her husband awoke from a talkative sweaty dream, his father wailing in his head, the young son sniveling.

But she knew something was missing. Her fondness had grown for Clive, but she would never allow herself to think she loved him. With two children to take care of, she could not consent to the vulnerability that love invariably entailed. Nor did she really want it. As much as the two boys needed her, she needed them, and their company filled her up. Their wants were simple, primal, with food, closeness, warmth, cleanliness at the top of their infant lists. There was something Clive required that she could not grasp, though in the beginning she had tried. She forgave him for Lolly, it was one time, he swore to that, and she trusted he was telling her the truth. She forgave him easily, even he seemed surprised at the lack of recoil. Though, to be sure, her mind never had the room to accommodate resentment or bitterness. With two babies, her thoughts had to focus on keeping grounded, stable, steady in a sleep-deprived haze.

When she had a moment to spare, Arva would watch the professor and his pretty wife from the glass-encased front sunroom. She had gone to the bookshelf and chose a novel to hide behind while she spied on them. With one pick, then another, she saw that every book had been inscribed with the name 'H. Noseworthy,' Aunt Helen's maiden name, as if each text belonged exclusively to her, nothing a Mercer could touch.

Behind the cover of Catcher in the Rye, Arva would survey the couple while she sucked away at a dusty chicken bone, the hot pink cinnamon melting down to a sweet warmed chocolate core. She was able to identify the components of a marriage, and what was missing in her and Clive's one-year relationship. Though, Arva went easy on herself with any form of criticism, she was twenty years old, two baby sons. Professor and Mrs. Mugford were childless, likely nearing forty.

In early Fall, face tucked down between unread pages, Arva saw Mrs. Mugford on the front lawn, pushing caramel-coloured peeling tulip bulbs into the cooling earth. She wore a vanilla shawl over her shoulders and a polka-dotted scarf around her head. Her husband, in tweed jacket and gentleman's hat with a sprightly feather, walked up the drive, and stopped where she worked. She looked up, a low sun shining through the golden leaves, and said something, made a wiggly gesture with her hips. He laughed, mouth significantly open, touched her shoulder. An old joke.

Another time, she watched Professor Mugford fashion a Christmas wreath on the bottom step of their front stairs. He worked piece after piece of spruce into a needled garland, wire twisting, a festive wreath shaping itself underneath his ungloved hands. Then, Mrs. Mugford was through the door, out into the still winter snowfall, steam curling up from somewhere. In her hands, she carried warm tea, maybe even a lemon slice floating for her husband. A nod of appreciation from him as she handed him the mug. She pulled a striped woolen hat from her side jacket pocket, tugged it down over his balding head with a playful yank. Another grin over his shoulder. 'Perfection' witnessed by Arva.

Then, with the boys asleep, she was reminded of her loneliness whenever the home was silent. She looked forward to when the children were grown into tiny people, when naps would be no longer, and she would never be alone. Unsettling as it was, she spent time remembering Lolly's visits to Old Man Crane's bungalow. Arva had the wretched notion that these days she would appreciate Lolly's distraction, would welcome seeing her stubby feet and broad calves skipping across the rocky ledge just beyond the kitchen window. But, the image of Clive on Lolly, constantly stewing in the back of Arva's mind, spat up to perish the thought.

Where was her husband now, Arva wondered. It was Saturday afternoon, riding on the heels of their second Christmas together. She pretended to forget for just an instant, but her mind would not be fooled. Oh, yes. He would be found at his usual post.

He had arrived, Clive thought. He knew it, and likely Arva did as well. He never could have dreamed that those evenings spent with Lolly could have led to such a gratifying reward. He deserved it though, after enduring her pig squeal in the cab of his truck, her endless whine about her mother even during the business, her guilt-inducing whimper after it was all done. Uncle Harry's house suited him just fine. It was a far cry from Old Man Crane's, and he felt as though he belonged there, enveloped in the comfort of St. John's most elite district. For Clive, this place was everything Upper Island Cove was not – refinement, culture, class. Not bad for a twenty-three year old.

When Clive had gone to Memorial some years earlier to get his teaching degree, he rarely had the opportunity to see the city. He had boarded on Merrymeeting Road with Mr. and Mrs. Ray Mullett, studied his butt off, and returned each weekend to his proud mother. Friday afternoons, at 4:30 p.m. sharp, he was on Fury's stinking bus to Carbonear, Junior Lynch or Arthur Drover waiting patiently to bring 'the near teacher' around.

So, the city had never been his. He had never explored, found his sweet spot, lost the cove coat and slid into the townie jacket. But now, his time had come. Clive was about as far away from jiggers and lines, nets and flakes as he could get and still live on the island. That racket was behind him.

Clive considered himself lucky that Arva never droned on about Lolly. He knew from talk at the Legion that most women would have, worked hard to make their man's life miserable, and for once Clive was pleased that Arva was always short on conversation. She did much of what a wife should, cooked and cleaned, took care of his boys. He noticed the snap of her jeans had returned when she walked, but he never walked with her very often, so her briskness never bothered him that much.

His Uncle Harry knew the principal at Bishop Field boy's school on Bonaventure Avenue, and Clive soon received a generous offer to teach Literature to the Grade 9, 10, and 11 class. He spent hours preparing class notes for those bright city minds, futures he could shape, students who might one day make a difference. He wore his best suit and tie everyday, well, his only suit, his funeral suit, but a decent one nevertheless. And, of course, a fresh shirt every few days, ironed to a crispness by his wife.

In the cool fall afternoons, Clive enjoyed strolling by himself along Water Street. When a shop window displayed fine imported goods, quaint homeknit sweaters, or volumes of the latest must-reads, Clive would always stop to regard them. He admired the ice-coloured dinner plates with the sailing ship motif in the window of Bowrings. After a paycheck or two, he would like to try a jacket from The London, something fit for lecturing those uniformed young men. After another paycheck, new cap-toe dress shoes from Parker and Monroe. He had already purchased an extraordinarily slick black umbrella from The Royal Stores so that his afternoon outings would not be hampered by drizzle.

On Harbour Drive, he would eye the hulking rusted liners, sailing from the world over, as they docked in the sheltered port. The names along the sides he could not have pronounced, though he tried under his breath. He saw the fishermen with scratchy beards, fouled faces, and overalls so encrusted and brittle, they would crack in a fight with the first fist to the ribs. And then he passed them on the streets. He could spot one at a distance, eyes tucked into wrinkled cups, skin like a rubber boot, fingernails filthy with a permanent stain of guts and grime that no soap could touch.

Those relaxed strolls made Clive deem himself all the more distinguished. One evening in early October, after seeing the new winter displays in store windows, he went to the closet in the front porch of his new residence, and pushed his red-and-black checked lumber jacket to the very, very back. His rubber boots with the leak in the left toe were thrown in the kitchen trash bin. Clive clipped his sideburns to a clean stripe, took a dry cloth to his shoes every morning.

Sure, there would be some lips flapping in the cove. He had just up and left without a proper send-off. That was almost unheard-of, not even a whiskey at the Legion. But, he had done right by Lolly, taken responsibility for the baby. Lolly would not have known which end of the child was up anyway, and if Arva had not of wanted the boy, Clive would have insisted, most likely. And everyone was happy. Arva's time was filled, his mother's name never had to be on the tongues of every woman in the harbour for what he had done, and Lolly was back teaching, probably had a new boyfriend already. The boy was well taken care of, fed, clothed, though he was a screamy little bastard, and thus the initial reason for Clive's extended walks after dinner and beyond.

But, beyond the tedious blaring on the homefront, Clive could not ask for more. His kissing lips wanted to whistle all the time. He thought he would try to build something, maybe a birdfeeder. That was an educated pastime, and he even priced a quality saw and hammer at Harris and Hiscock's. His life was pulsing ahead at full tilt, the sensation of success finally settling in. And it stayed that way, until one December day, standing near the cracked door of the staff room in the chilly hallway of Bishop Field, Clive overheard the science teacher talking with the math teacher.

"How he can teach English is beyond me," Mr. Barfitt said. "Someone must have pulled serious strings to get him in here."

"Yes," Mr. Duffy said. "I've heard some of the boys talking, they can't even understand him half the time. Thank Jesus they already know how to spell."

Mr. Barfitt brought his stained mug to his lips and smiled behind it. "Can you suppose," he said. "Mercer says 'spell 'apple,' Johnny.' Well, sir, it's h-a-p-p-l-e."

"Yes. Dropped the 'h' in 'olyrood, picked it up in H'avondale."

"His Shakespeare now, fresh out of the Bay. He's got one foot in the boat, still smelling like fish."

"Yar b'y," Mr. Duffy said, a sharp nod of his head and a wink to Mr. Barfitt. "Dat's roight h'on, me zun." He slapped at his chubby thigh with laughter, his voice sounding impressively close to Clive.

Clive turned away and his whistling lips forgot their tune. A distasteful blend of anger, humiliation, and indignation churned in his stomach making his lunch milk sour into cheese. He could suffer the comments on his teaching capabilities, he knew The Tempest, Romeo and Juliet, Twelfth Night inside and out, could recite dozens of sonnets. He was able to ignore the girlish amusement over his dialect, though he would work to eliminate it, and he was sure after some practice, no one would even notice it. But, what he could not abide was the suggestion that he smelled like fish. He washed everyday, had not touched a slimy cod since his father died. Clive took a deep whiff of his hands, thinking somehow the stench had worked into his blood, was oozing out through his pores. Son of a fisherman, when he was certain he should have been Harry's boy instead. Son of a banker sounded right in the ear. Clive wondered for a second if the fish might have stained him for life. No, that was foolishness. That kind of thing came off.

Still, Clive stopped going to the staff room, and ate outdoors from his brown paper bag even in the worst kind of weather. He stopped tying a fresh Windsor knot every morning, slipped a loosened one over his head, tightened until it cut into his throat, often raw from a dull-bladed shave. He stopped waiting for that cordial request to join some of the other teachers for a drink on Friday afternoons, as they called out 'see you here,' 'see you there' on their way out through the front door. And, when he realized he could not change where he was from, he stopped wanting to whistle.

After school and on the weekends, Clive began to spend less time strolling or admiring and more time in the place where money and a cast iron gut took precedence over brogue. At his new favourite place, smell was the least of anyone's worries. Badcock's pub was there for Clive like a lighted beacon comforting a dory gone adrift.

Strolling along George Street, he was first enticed by fiddler's music. When he stepped down the constricted concrete stairway, and through the solid wood door, the staleness and mustiness were a welcome signal, reminding Clive of the Legion. He straightened his back, licked his fingertips to smooth both sideburns, and walked squarely up to the bar, ordered a drink with St. John's confidence.

"I would like a whiskey for meself, sir, if you got... have it." He used his best townie drawl.

The bartender leaned his dry elbow onto the counter. A damp cloth, browning around the edges, was held loosely in his giant hand, a bear cub's paw. His hair was like bright orange squash, and this theme followed through in his freckles, his beard, and his more than ample ration of arm hair. Across the backs of eight stout fingers, he had tattooed in steel blue ink, T-R-U-E L-O-V-E.

But Clive never noticed the hands, the hair, or the tattoos. He had tuned into the ears. They were enormous and raggedly, as though the bartender's head itself was liquid, two huge stones were thrown in, and the ears formed from the uneven splashing. Even in the dim light of the bar, they appeared translucent.

Everything could pass. The mighty ears of a listener.

He said to Clive, "Now, I'm usually good at placin' accents. Not quite sure where that one comes from." And, over the course of several whiskeys, Clive was not quite sure himself. Not that it mattered though, after several more whiskeys, everyone began to sound the same.

Badcock's was a clean business, and Ernest Badcock could not care less where people came from, as long as they came. And they did, from all over. Jerry's Nose to Lushes Bight, Empty Basket to Nameless Cove. Everyone was welcome, if they were able to pay. Even that did not matter, if they were regulars, and if he knew where they lived. Ernest was not working for the money alone, though it came in handy. Instead, he was mostly working to soothe his heart.

Yes, there had been a true love. His knuckles, which he often laid out as question prompters, were not lying. But, as it went, that true love did not last long. He had married a Sweetapple from the West Coast, her name being Iris. 'Sweetapple, ye says?' his patrons would respond with near-timed accuracy. 'Did she know...?' Then, server and drinker would begin to weave a convoluted path of places and names until they discovered a mutual connection, however remote. Only then could they continue with united satisfaction.

Ernest's Iris had professed, or so he said, to love every freckle on his heavy-duty body. She said she felt safe cuddled in arms like muscled logs, and made him believe she would wait forever when he was employed as a deckhand on the lake boats in Ontario. And, yes, she had kept her word at the beginning, waiting patiently while he worked, taking care of their three skinny girls. But, anyone named Iris was not meant to be fixed, settled in a small rust-coloured house on a cliff by the sea. No, an Iris had to move, her mind and body needing to be constantly wrapped up in something, and that something just happened to be someone else. Ernest came home from the lake boats one day to find a damp house, knife still stuck in a jam bottle on the table, his coin collection that he kept in a lime green tobacco container swiped. No, he had not lost the girls, they were left down the street at his sister's. "A Badcock never should've married a Sweetapple," was all she said about the matter, and he was given back his three daughters. Ernest moved to St. John's, opened up a pub, told most of his patrons about his estranged wife Iris, and his heartache was lessened a little each time.

In turn, Ernest listened. Clive was like most of his customers, getting drunk and scraping off the scab of childhood. Ernest found most people never let their memories heal in peace. They held onto them like icebergs, pointy reminders above water, the bulk hidden below. Enough whiskeys under the belt, and they eventually dove down, chipped away, things seeming much starker when deliberated in a dark pub. But Ernest never grumbled or whined. Listening was part of his job, he did it well, and that was why Badcock's was always filled with unhappy men.

Clive was born in his mother's kitchen by the side of a roaring woodstove. At the onset of labour, Thomas Mercer stoked it full of mossy logs and dry splits, then disappeared for a few slow drinks of moonshine in Joseph Crane's back shed. The child wanted to come out rump first, so Doreen Coombs had to turn it by kneading Doris Mercer's belly in clockwise progressions. Doreen gave Doris the last full cup of whiskey, and she took it down with dry lips and gratitude. Her contractions weakened as she relaxed with the drink, and the infant did not fight against the tidal pressures reinforced by the flat of Doreen's hand. Though the head was smallish, the shoulders were like a bear's, and Doris lost consciousness on the daybed when she heard the snipping of her own skin. Doreen had to wrench the child out, her hands clamped under its chin, its neck stretched to a silly length. And when Doreen handed over the boy, still bloody but wrapped in a clean cloth, Doris felt nothing. There was no wave of adoration, no swelling from her heart. She felt shocked, shaken, and could not find an ounce of love for that wrinkled-faced baby who's searching mouth wanted to sap even more from her already drained body.

Doris tried to forget the birth, tuck it away some place where it would not bother her. And she did successfully, paving the way for love to breed and multiply. But her heart could only hold so much of the boy. He was not what she had expected in a baby. That was likely due to the fact she was certain through her entire pregnancy that she was growing a girl. But Thomas would not leave her be during the nine months as she had hoped he would, and that weekly production must have forced the issue in the wrong direction. When her son turned one year and she watched him take his first steps away from her, a fleeting trace of disappointment fluttered up around Doris and never went away.

When the boy was old enough to lean hard without tipping over, he was in the dory with his father. His first trip was when he was only five, and he was curious about everything, wanting to grow up to be a fisherman just like his daddy. After only an hour out, the child was bored. He lay on the bottom of the dory, his body lurching and writhing, pretending to be hooked and reeled in. Thomas gave him a hot clip to the back of his ear, told him to 'watch hisself,' he was there to learn the trade, not to horse around. But, when the net was coming in nearly empty, Thomas stopped explaining the glories of fishing to his young son. There was little room left for childish conversation between his rambling spew of curses.

Being a child, though, Clive persevered with incessant questioning that made Thomas grind at his teeth. "What kind of fish are we catchin'?" he kept asking, remembering the flatfish, sculpins, crabs and connors he jigged from the side of the wharf.

Thomas pawed at the vacant net, hand over hand over hand. He saw no dark parcels resisting, splashing water about in their last good but futile fight. "Just fish, b'y. Just friggin' fish." He gave Clive a second hot clip to the ear, a church bell sounding in the child's head. Thomas Mercer hated stupid questions.

Then the boy grabbed at a hook, wanting to help, and it pierced the fleshy part of his hand between the thumb and forefinger. The barb was lost beneath the skin. Thomas had to push the hook all the way in, his son sniffling so hard Thomas wanted to pitch the boy into the black sea. The barb burst through, Thomas cut it, and drew the hook back out through its original path with no time to waste. "Muck-h'up," was all he said to the blithering boy as he wrapped a dirty handkerchief around the bloody mess. "Just as well I 'ad Alek h'out 'ere wit' me."

Alek was never allowed in the dory. Each day during the season, Clive would be woken, and if he hesitated in his bed, Thomas would haul him out by the flannelette collar of his homemade pajamas. During the early mornings, when the living should rightfully be asleep, Clive would be standing with his father on the edge of a sharp cliff assessing the mood of the sea. The mood always seemed hostile to Clive, as he would watch the great heady curls of water colliding into one another. A dory seemed no more than a toothpick in its wet teeth. But, his father invariably gave the assenting nod. It was beside the point whether the ocean was like glass or whether the waves had the potential to rip homes from the shore, the fish were still there, waiting to be caught. Never mind the dreaded cold that was pressing in around him.

His body still slow with sleep, Clive would begin to shiver. His eyes would tear up, nose drip down to his boyish lip, and teeth clank together behind thin blue lips. Icy water would sneak up his sleeves. It would bead on his face and roll back to the sensitive skin under his hairline. It would splash up and over into his boots. His toes, shriveled from soggy wool socks, would slide around inside rubbers two sizes too big, bought that way to last a growing boy more than one season. Clive was never permitted gloves. "Ye needs t' learn t' feel yer way 'round," his father had said. "Can't do dat wit' gloves h'on. Real men don't wear gloves, me zun." At nine years old, Clive had no interest in being a real man. He would rather have been a real woman, a warm woman in a kitchen somewhere, sidled up to a wood stove, smell of bread dough in his nose. Though he never could have said that to his father because at the mention of it, he would surely have been thrust overboard.

When a run was good, Thomas would hum as he hauled in the fish, pat his son on the head and say, "Dat's me best b'y." They would bring fresh fillets home for Doris to cook, though the britches and tongues were the real delicacy. Doris would tenderly pat the cod's roe dry with a cuptowel, dredge it in flour, a sprinkling of salt, and fry them with cuts of salt pork. They looked like tiny pairs of beige pants sizzling in a black-bottomed pan on top of the wood stove. If the run were extraordinarily good, Thomas would save the crispiest cod tongues for Clive, letting the boy climb into his lap, eat right out of his own plate.

Alek would be in the rocker, feet tucked up in under him, pretending to knit a strand of wool with his fingers, and watching his brother's hand move teasingly from plate to mouth.

But, if the run were bad, which was more often than not, Thomas would lean into the wind and curse quietly, chain smoke, and chew at the shredded skin on the backs of his knobby knuckles all the way to the merchant.

The merchants were crooks, they had the fishermen cornered, and they could squeeze, squeeze, squeeze. And they did. Tightly. Fish was graded according to quality, and the merchants who decided the cull often did so on a whim. Hard-working men arrived with several quintals of fish in wooden boxes, and the hope of returning home with a dollar in their pockets. Times were tougher than tough, and every single penny meant survival. Most could not afford the basics. Frivolousness was unheard-of.

Morley Roberts was the merchant Thomas dealt with most often. He always wore a black bowler hat that made Thomas feel even smaller. Morley rarely touched a fish, and if it did happen, it was by accident. The merchant used his skinny checker to flick through the top few and decide the stingy rate. The conversation between Thomas and Morley almost always followed the same scripted lines.

"I'll give ye a dollar ninety-five a quintal for this. Not a cent more."

"Come h'on, b'y. Not h'even two? Two twenty-five?"

"Yer lucky to be gettin' that, Mercer. I'm doin' ye a favour."

"I got t' be gettin' a better price den dat. I got two young b'ys t' feed, h'annuder wee one h'on de way. Come h'on, now. Give 'er h'annuder go t'rou. 'Tis h'a lovely load o' fish, b'y."

"Lovely, me ass. Cull can't be any lower, me son." Then Morley said to the checker who was already unloading the fish, "Jesus, if Mercer here, the poor bastard, reached into a sack of gold, he'd draw out the one and only handful of shit." And the man snickered, his teeth like decaying stumps.

Clive's father took the few bills into his fist, shook his hand, it felt much lighter than it should be. Barely enough to pay for the gasoline to get back home, let alone enough to buy supplies. All that work for practically nothing, but what choice did he have? He thought of his brother Harry, moved on to St. John's, sitting in a square room somewhere with a hot water heater, a pile of papers before him, quill pen in his hand. Thomas would die there, he knew, the water was the only way for him. He tightened his fist around the paper money, his weary eyes murky, damp, a fishermen's knot constricting in his craw.

"What're ye gawkin' h'at?" he yelled, his voice like a girl's. Thomas had caught his son staring at him, the boy's gape reminding him of a dead rabbit stiff in a snare. "Ye wants me t' knock dose h'eyes t' de back o' yer friggin' 'ead, b'y? Ye good-fer-nothin' muck-h'up."

Clive was not sure if 'muck-up' was meant for him, or if his father was talking about himself. Though, he did not have to wonder for long. A black rubber boot rallied his backside, plunged him forward. His ribs struck the wharf first, then his hands, then his hairless chin. Clive would never forget the hoarse hoots of the men who lined the dock, their overalls stained with iridescent scales, black moist blood, and raw guts. While the windburn on his cheeks hid his blush, he sensed something bitter like undiluted loathing rinsing the back of his throat. It was his first taste of hatred for his father. He gulped it down, and his stomach ached instantly.

"Not h'annuder word, Muck-h'up," his father said through clenched teeth as Clive skittered back to his feet. "Christ. What'd I do t' deserve dis? Two zuns. One friggin' retard h'an one useless muck-h'up."

When Thomas brought Clive home, cut gleaming on the boy's chin, he met Doreen Coombs as she walked out the porch door. "She passed the baby," Doreen said to Thomas in a half whisper. "Never would've made it - 'twas that tiny. A girl, though. She would've had her girl."

When Doreen was out of earshot, Thomas let out the lion's roar that was spooling inside his gut. Its release never eased his pain. And that afternoon marked the first time he beat his first-born son with closed fists. He didn't know what else to do.

"'ow's 'bout h'annuder whiskey fer h'ole Muck-h'up 'ere," Clive said to Ernest.

When Clive was sober, Ernest could understand him without a problem. But, when the Island Cove man was thoroughly pickled, it was another story altogether. His accent was overriding like a mudslide, whole syllables ingested, others skidding and toppling on top of one another, rolling with horrendous swiftness straight out from a congested throat, often bypassing any tongue. Ernest caught the word that was most important, though. 'Whiskey' came through with unquestionable clarity.

"Of course, Clive," Ernest said. "On the house, friend."

"H'on d'ouse, fer h'ole Muck-h'up," Clive said as his head fell towards the bar with a hollow thud.

Ernest knew from his own experience what Clive described about his father and his childhood was not so much mistreatment, but more likely one man's manner of loving. It was exactly the way he had been loved as a child. That was how he cared to think about it, anyway, whenever he was reminded. And, when all was said and done, Ernest looked around at his growing daughters, caught a glimpse of his knuckles, took a breath of his reputable establishment, and decided he was not much the worse for wear because of it.

So, for Ernest, Clive's whining recollections were neither terribly original nor terribly worthy of note. Ernest had lived it already, and continued to hear about it from drunken customers - the driven but downtrodden father who had an affinity for doling out the back of his hand, the willful son striving for something more, ashamed of his old man, and feeling guilty for it. It was a standard among his patrons, and Ernest was getting just a little bored with it. The only remarkable feature of Clive's tale was the retarded brother. And stolen by fairies as a newborn to boot. Now that was something new.

10

The fabric came from Mifflin's. It was the type of rich red velveteen that would flatter jewels or clothe the Queen. Perhaps too much for a child, likely, in fact, but I sewed you a Christmas smock nevertheless. Around the hem, I embroidered a string of tiny fish in silver thread, swimming tail to nose, tail to nose.

Wearing it, you were a vision of life. The ripest apple at the moment before plucking. I could have admired you for hours, but I noticed Henry's eyes. Then, as I watched him look you up and down, the plug was pulled and blood drained from my head. At once, I realized what I'd done.

Arva, I turned you into fire.

And already I had married the moth.

Barb Mugford clutched the tiny blue ball as it rolled towards her. "Is this yours?" she asked, holding it out to the small child. When he didn't step towards her, she set down her basket of tulips and carried the ball across the lawn. The child pulled himself up against his mother's leg, hid his face behind her pants. "Yes, it would seem that it is," she said.

"Thank you," the mother said. The boy accepted the ball, brought it to his mouth.

"You must have your hands full," Barb said, looking at the second boy in her arms.

"Yes, not much time for anything else." The young woman reached up and touched her hair.

"Twins?"

"No, they are some months apart."

"Then, not brothers?"

"Yes." She hesitated. "Well, like brothers. A cousin's child. She was ill."

"It's a lot to take on for a young woman."

"I'd never thought of it like that. There wasn't much choice, is all."

"Oh, my dear," Barb said, crouching on the lawn closer to the child. "Now there is always a choice. Not making a choice is choosing in itself, don't you think?"

"Yes. I guess so."

Barb smiled at her; the woman didn't understand her silly attempt at philosophy.

"Well, they certainly look like brothers. One fair and one dark. Opposites, but the same. Absolutely adorable." Barb reached down and the larger boy willingly came into her arms. Walking back towards the house, she had to turn to the woman and say, "Come. Come. A cup of tea."

Inside Barb gave each boy a butter cookie, and then she filled the kettle for tea.

"Your husband. Is he Harry's son?"

"No, nephew."

"Ah. Resembles him a little."

"Some."

"Nothing like Helen though. So that's where my theory broke down." She smiled.

"My husband's mother is quite different from Helen."

"Quite different in a good way, I should hope. Would hate to meet her otherwise." Barb's hand jumped to her mouth. "Pardon me. That just popped out."

"That's okay. I know Helen's not the warmest soul in the world."

"You can say that again, my dear. Only living here a couple of months, and I overheard her on the back stoop. She wasn't being very generous in her praise, to say the least."

"I heard her at my wedding, and she didn't have a kind word for me either."

"Well now. In only a few moments we've deduced that Helen Mercer is not a very giving individual, though her horn of plenty is well stocked, and that she's keen on neither of us. That's being productive, in my book." Barb smiled again, and the woman nodded.

Talking to her neighbour felt light and easy. She should have gone over during the winter months, waved when the woman was sitting in the sunroom reading her book. Up close, she didn't look like an Indian. That's what her husband thought, with the dark colouring, a shiny pelt of hair. But when the woman spoke, her accent was typical. How could Barb ask? Of course she couldn't.

The kettle whistled and shot out an angry spray. "Ooo," Barb said, motioning to the steam. "Maybe Helen is listening."

The woman giggled.

"Aren't I terrible?" Barb said.

She poured steaming water into her teepee teapot, and when she turned back to her neighbour, she found the woman on the floor picking up cookie crumbs around her children. "Leave it, leave it," Barb said, and waved her hand.

"But they've messed your clean floor."

"Look around. I could use a mess, and crumbs will do. I'll take what I can get." She carried the teapot to the table. "Now, my dear, what might your name be?"

"Arva."

"Hmm. That's unusual?"

"Sorry?"

"I've never heard your name before. It's not a common one."

"I don't believe my mother went in for common."

"Yes? Well. No matter," Barb said. And after a few minutes, she took the teapot by its totem pole handle; rich tea tumbled out over the chief's headdress spout. "Now, Arva," she continued. "Just what do you think of this weather?"

Henry turned one at the end of May. By his birthday, he had not yet taken his first steps and preferred the dizzying effect of continuous rolling to walking or even crawling. Everything was 'da-da-da' to him, even though Clive ignored the child. Arva imagined fathers lifting their sons, tossing them high in the air, and catching them in a flurry of baby giggles. Clive barely acknowledged Henry even when the child held onto the cuff of his trousers. But even without any fatherly attention, Henry continued to thrive, and with skin tight from fat, he had more than tripled his size.

His half-brother Thomas was not faring so well. At eight months, he remained a small skinny baby with a mop of blond curls. He was still extremely clingy, selecting Arva's hip as his preferred mode of locomotion. For him, everything was 'ma-ma,' as though he needed to remind himself who she was. Arva thought he was constantly suspicious. He wanted to see her at all times. When she disappeared for a quick trip to the washroom, Thomas was soon gagging on tears, his frantic cries choking him. So she began to balance him on her knee even as she peed.

While Henry looked older than his age, Thomas looked younger. Yes, they could be brothers, Arva thought. Then she corrected herself. They were brothers.

When the weather was fine, she pulled the boys in a red wagon the short distance to Bannerman Park. On soft grass she spread out a blanket and they sat with a few toys. Arva tossed bits of bread on the blanket. The boys grabbed up the crumbs with finger pincers, poked them into their mouths like hungry birds, and clapped the air above their heads. She sang 'itsy bitsy spider' and tickled their bellies. Releasing their feet out of hard leather shoes, she counted out 'this little piggy' on their grub-sized toes. From their faces, she stole their noses. Henry always banged on her hand to retrieve it, but Thomas never seemed to notice the theft, and sucked on his freed toes instead.

There were always other mothers and babies at the park sitting and playing. At first Arva said 'hello there' and 'lovely day,' thinking that with children she had an obvious connection. But, they turned away from her, pretending she had never spoken, and positioned their children so that their eyes would not see this dark-skinned woman with what must have looked like two children from two different men.

Arva soon stopped trying to talk to the woman at the park, and instead began slipping across to Barb Mugford's side of the house while the boys napped in the afternoons. Barb was much younger than Arva had imagined and much lonelier too. Each day, when Arva stepped through the back porch, Barb already had the kettle on, or the cards laid out, or a bag of flour set up on the countertop waiting to be mixed into dough. They drank rosehip tea together and ate coconut cherry squares warm from the pan. Arva taught Barb how to make a better loaf of bread, and Barb taught Arva how to simply chat about nothing.

One afternoon while the boys slept, Barb laid two tumblers on the table with a bottle of amber rum in the middle.

"For a bit of fun," she said, as she poured a few tablespoons into each glass. She clicked her tongue. "Does this mean I've become the consummate bored housewife?"

Both of them sipped the hard liquor and grimaced.

"To hell with it if it does," Barb said after her second sip, less of a wince this time. After a third sip, she asked, "Do you think that's scandalous? Me marrying my professor? Please tell me 'yes,' even if it's a lie."

"Somewhat, I guess," Arva said. "But no worse than marrying the first man that crosses your path."

"He was almost twice my age, you know. Though I'm catching up. A tad too fast, I might add."

"You can't do much about that."

"Thanks for your insight," Barb said, and pretended to frown. "Maybe I should have another drink."

"I didn't mean it like that. It came out wrong." Arva wondered why she was always so awkward, when it was the very last thing she wanted to be. "Please, tell me why you married."

"For the dream, I think. Wallace could paint a really pretty picture, and I wanted to step right onto his canvas. Every word that came out of his mouth, I bought it all hook, line, and sinker. And, to be boldly honest, I guess part of me wanted the scandal too." She laughed. "He told me we'd go all over the world. Could you imagine? A girl from Two Good Arm in Africa or South America digging up ruins or old bones or something?"

"That does sound like a picture."

"He's a wonderful talker, but he teaches sociology. I don't even think he's ever been on a dig. So I never got further than King's Bridge Road." Barb sipped again. "But I love him though. He's as sweet as shu-gah," she said with a drawl and fanned the air. "Now, moving on, why would a woman go and marry the first man she meets? That's the real mystery."

Arva picked up her drink and inhaled the rum smell. "I missed my mother." She spoke into her glass, so her words were mumbled.

"What was that?"

"I missed my mother," she said more clearly.

"Now that is scandalous. Marrying a man because of your mother. Which was it - some man or some mother?"

Arva rolled the bottom of her glass around and around. "After being married for nearly two years, I'd have to say 'some mother.'" She took a quick sip and said, "She drowned."

"Oh dear." Barb refilled her glass.

Arva sipped again, and a tingle radiated out from her stomach. "The world was too alive for her. She couldn't find a quiet place."

"Now that sounds intriguing."

"Once she found me with a boy."

Barb put her elbows onto the table. "Do tell, my dear. I'm all ears."

"Nothing like that. We were just talking."

"About?"

"Oh, I can't remember. Nothing much. We weren't talking for long. I was walking along the beach. He was sitting on a rock, and said 'hello.' So I stopped."

"Like you would."

"I was only there a few minutes when I saw my mother was on the cliff crying out to me. She was frantic, tripped on the rocks coming down over the hill, cut up her knees. The boy was already standing by the time she got to us."

"I would imagine."

"She hissed at him."

"Hissed?"

"Yes. Like you'd do to a cat if you found him with his head in the garbage. Hissed."

"Did he leave?"

"Fast as he could. And then she took my hand like I was a child, walked me back to the house. 'Didn't you know?' she said. 'That boy was trying to put a spell on you. I could read his lips.'"

"How exciting. Nothing like that has ever happened to me. But I bet I'd be easy to put under."

"Yes, well. He wasn't trying," Arva said, and she realized she was telling this story more for herself than for Barb. "I told my mother we were just talking about the weather. And she looked at me in this strange way. In her eyes I could see she was so hurt, I didn't understand her. She lived in a different world."

"That's so sad," Barb said. "What would she have thought of Clive?"

Arva smiled a little, and murmured, "I think she would've hissed."

"You think?"

"Yes. And hissed loud. Definitely."

"Kssssssss," said Barb.

Arva sighed. "There was more than enough of her to fill two people, you know. And I think she filled up me. Once she left, I was just empty. Everything turned silent." She could hear her own words as they hung in the air around her. "I guess that must sound pretty strange."

"Not at all," Barb said. "You were so young."

"Yes, seventeen."

"So naturally you were lost when she died?"

"Completely lost."

"Smack in the middle of the woods kind of lost?"

"Yes, smack in the middle of the woods."

"Then along comes Clive, the Big Bad Wolf," Barb said, and giggled.

"To gobble me down," Arva said, and they both burst into laughter.

"Were you wearing red, Miss Riding Hood?" Barb asked, between tipsy peals.

Arva's breath caught. Abruptly, she stood up.

"Oh, my goodness," Barb said. "What did I say?"

"Yes," Arva said, her face a bleached sheet. "A red dress. And I invited him in."

"Of course ye can get another," Melvin Buckle said to Clive. "That's his job. Servin' drinks. Isn't that right, Ern?"

"Whatever ye says, Constable Buckle," he replied.

"Thanks Ernie," Clive said, as the bear paw poured another drink. "Appreciate it."

"Listen to ye. 'Appreciate it,'" Melvin mocked. "Ye'd think the Queen herself just kissed yer hairy arse. And all ye got was a lick of whiskey."

"Still," Clive said, after a liberal slurp. "'Tis damn good stuff."

Clive had been going to Badcock's for six months before he met Melvin Buckle, but the two had hit it off instantly. The young constable strolled in, took a seat right next to Clive and ordered a double. His hair was buzzed, but his moustache, hovering over his top lip like a sparrow's stretched wing, measured a whole inch longer. When he first sat down, Clive thought he smelled official, black ink on stationary. But soon after he began talking that smell of formality was replaced by something putrid, and Clive didn't mind it at all.

Melvin was the newest addition to the downtown beat. Being the son of Chief Constable Norm Buckle, Melvin's route was never very long or never very trying. He only strolled along Harbour Drive, up onto Water Street, cutting back past George Street, and down onto Harbour Drive again. Melvin had requested nights, and his request was, of course, granted. His favorite part of the job was inspecting the alleyways between the stores. How often did he find a sailor with a local woman in behind a stack of boxes? He couldn't count. They were never very quiet; the consumption of too much rum feeding a delusion that darkness disguised all. But it was Melvin's uncanny awareness that led him to the right places, and he could glide into an alley silent as a mink. When the dollar was almost earned, but not quite, he would blast his flashlight, holler 'police' triumphantly, and startle the two merrymakers and anything else that was within earshot. It was the best fun he'd had in years. And the most amazing part was he got paid to do it, paid to watch.

Though every evening was not quite that lively. So often Melvin would make several rounds, then stop into Badcock's for a leisurely drink. After his first double, subsequent rounds would be increasingly speedy, his well deserved breaks increasingly prolonged. By the end of the night, he would dash down the side streets, steal hazy glances up the main roads, and tear back to Badcock's, breath almost missing, to order a shot before the last of the patrons were ousted.

"I got a real treat for ye tonight, Clive," Melvin said one

evening after Badcock's closed. "Last weekend I discovered me new favourite spot."

"Where's that?" Clive said.

"B'y, 'tis best to show ye," Melvin said, scratched at his crotch with a thumbnail. "A picture's worth a thousand groans."

Melvin led the way to a two-story corner home on Gower Street. The clapboard was painted a pastel pink, and the windows had a subtle glow. A passerby might think the residents were sleeping by the level of light, but the home exuded the sensation of something very much alive.

"'Twas the colour first caught me eye," Melvin said, as he shifted his navy trousers with his forearms. "Then I sees a couple of men comin' and goin'. I knew I was onto somethin' sweet."

Clive followed Melvin's excited steps. Budding branches just ready to burst lined the gravel path along the side of the house. When they walked in, Clive could make out the figures of two men seated on kitchen chairs. A woman in a flower dress stretched taut by fatness was leaning against the countertop. No one looked up as they entered, though one man stood hastily and swaggered out the door.

In the hallway, Melvin introduced Clive to an older woman, her head crowned with a mat of flaccid orange curls. She was not quite fat, but her sallow skin gave the impression she had been soaking somewhere for far too long.

"Clive, this is Kate. The lassie of yer dreams. She takes a sparkle to blokes from 'round the bay."

"Is that so," Clive said, shuffling his shoes on the linoleum.

"That it is, me son," Melvin said. He nudged Clive hard with his elbow, and Clive teetered. "Hold onto yer lugnuts," he continued, "yer in for a real ride."

Clive cleared his throat.

"Ye from 'round the bay, honey?" Kate said.

"That's right," Clive said, at once feeling lucky. "Born and bred."

"What're ye doin' in the big city? Out for the weekend?"

"I teaches."

She grinned and pulled a package of cigarettes from the pocket of her dress. After she had lit up, she said, "I teaches too," and grinned again.

"Oh really? What subject?"

She snickered in his ear, brushed past him, and walked down the hallway.

"Come on with ye, b'y," she said. "Get yer lead out."

Clive glanced over his shoulder, but Melvin had disappeared, so he followed the wispy trail of smoke, the white noise of a radio.

Kate led him to a room where the window was shut tight and the bed was crumpled. He found it difficult to take a deep breath of the foul air. It smelled as though lit matches were tossed on a worn tire and left to smolder.

"Lovely night," Clive said.

"Yes, lovely," she replied. "Hot enough."

Clive eyed her plunging neckline, the swollen loaves on her chest, glistening as though just fresh from the oven, hot crusts slicked with butter. "Yes," he said, swallowing hard. How delicious a heel of his mother's bread would taste right now. "If we's not complainin' 'bout the cold, we's complainin' 'bout the heat. A Newf is never satisfied."

"Ain't that the truth." She moved closer. Choking baby powder billowed from every crevice.

"Why don't I hoist up the window, then," Clive said. "A breath of fresh air."

"Don't. Too much noise."

"From the street?"

"No, silly." She smirked at him, and took a long drag from her cigarette.

Clive felt like an idiot. "Buckle is here. That should count for somethin'."

"And then there is those," she said. "Like yer Constable friend. They don't count for nothin', me son. Though keep yer trap shut 'bout me sayin' that, if ye knows what's good for ye."

Clive tapped his toes on the floor, squelched in air between his two front teeth. He reached over to touch her, but her hands were already busy, hauling up the dress, unclicking the tan stockings. When Clive looked down at her thighs, he was reminded of enormous sacks of cod's roe waiting to be floured and fried. His stomach growled.

"Hungry, are ye?"

"Not really," he lied.

"Well I knows how to take yer mind off that, b'y."

Clive should have felt awkward. He had never done this sort of thing before – paid for the services of a woman. In fact, he was never actually sure that sort of place even existed. He had seen the ladies along Gower Street, but figured they conducted their business in cars or alleys, never in a decent home. Some of the men from Upper Island Cove spoke about the city, how a man can get his hands on just about anything, but Clive only thought it was talk, big talk based on nothing. But here he was, living it.

Whiskey coursed through his veins, his belly ached, the loaves of bread were ready, and he dove right in.

Kate's new customer was reluctant, though she prodded him gently until he admitted what he really wanted. All men really wanted something, she knew, and with the right encouragement and enough liquor, they always let it slip. And it was men from around the bay who had the most interesting ideas, ones she found the most amusing. She would never forget the older gentleman who referred to everything in terms of fishing. He dropped his pants to the floor and asked, "Now missus, what'dya t'ink a' me tackle?" When he lay back on the bed, he said, "Go right after me snippet a' bait, woman, 'fore he gets away from ye." In the midst of it all, he cried out, "Ar, me bait. Take me bait. Me bait." It was all Kate could do not to faint from her stifled laughter. That was a story to keep for the girls.

Clive was not quite as creative, but still he offered her some new material. Who knows? It might find its way into a book some day. She was no stupid woman. It could be done.

In his timid way, he asked her to wear black rubber galoshes, the thick knee high kind with a pink rubbery band across the toe. When it was over, he made his second tentative request. Bending at the waist, he solicited a swift kick in the bare backside, and Kate was more than happy to oblige. She wasn't sure how hard he wanted it, so she struck him promptly with the side of her boot and he tumbled face forward onto the floor. Behind his back, she beamed. Though she didn't mind her job, it was perks like this that really made it worth her while.

When Clive came out of the room, he could not see the

Constable, though he could hear his voice, his snickers. Clive did not wait. He stumbled out into the street and made his way up to King's Bridge Road. Parts of him felt dirty, and parts of him felt deeply satisfied. It was all jumbled up on the inside, and he figured he couldn't do much about it. Right now, he had to answer to his stomach. Eggs, it wanted. Hard-boiled eggs.

The next night at Badcock's, Clive was certain Melvin would have heard about the rubbers. But his friend never said a word. Kate was discreet, and Clive made the decision to see her as often as his teacher salary would allow.

"Pretend it's a square. You fold in each corner and press tight. As you go along, you create a second square for yourself."
"Like this?"
"Sort of." Arva put her hands on the dough and began to push in deep with her heels, twist and push, twist and push. "More like this."
As she watched Arva knead, Barb said, "Of course you'll drop over to my 'must-do' tomorrow."
"Must-do?"
"A horde of professor's wives will descend. It's a must-do, Wally says. Got to build good relations. So, I'm supposed to be extra peppy, and cut all the crust off the sandwiches."
"Will you be using this bread?" Arva lifted the dough and turned it over.
"Absolutely."
"What a waste of perfectly good crusts."
"My thought exactly. But their old jaws are worn out from talking. Not all professors married young vibrant students like myself." Barb smirked, and clapped flour off her hands. "Though I'm sure they'd love to."
"I don't know," Arva said. "I don't think I'd blend in with professor's wives."
"Who does? I don't even blend in. Please?"
"Maybe. I'll see." She dimpled the dough with her knuckles.
Barb leaned back and sighed. "You've got bread-making hands, my dear," she said. "Big and strong. Not me. I can barely peel a

banana with these hands. No wonder my dough is always tough."

Arva had never considered the strength in her hands before, they just got the job done. "If you keep working at it, it'll come."

"I doubt it. I don't have the knack."

"It just takes time to get the texture is all. When it's ready, it feels just like skin."

"Really? Like skin?" Barb reached over, closed her eyes, and smoothed the dough with her palm. "I've never felt skin like that before. It's pretty cold."

"Well, more like dead skin."

"Now what could a girl like you possibly know about the feel of dead skin?"

Arva stammered, and redness rushed to her cheeks as though she had been slapped. Stroking the dough, she felt the cool softness of it underneath her fingertips. Definitely like dead skin. Dead damp skin.

"Sometimes you say the most amusing things, my dear," Barb said. "You're really priceless." She ran her hand over the dough once more, then patted it. "The ladies are going to love you tomorrow."

The following afternoon, Arva sat on a hard-backed chair and kept her legs crossed at the ankle. In her hand, she held a tall thin glass of lemonade, but she was afraid to take a sip. What if one of the woman asked her a question precisely when her mouth was full, and the lemonade just stayed in her throat, unwilling to be swallowed? She would have to fake muteness, or else reply and have the sticky liquid ooze out of her mouth, down over the front of her dress. Or, what if she did swallow and then gagged, coughed relentlessly, until she was forced to leave teary eyed, lemonade dripping from her nose. Either way, she would be an embarrassment to Barb. So, she simply gripped the slick glass, let the condensation bead up, and dribble onto the carpet.

Throughout the room, suited ladies roamed and nodded, exuding crushed scents with every gesture. They talked enthusi-astically of their husbands' research, the need for improved com-munication among departments, and how, as a collective, they could be instrumental in putting Memorial University, a fine edu-cational institution, on the proverbial map.

Arva noticed one of the wives approaching. With her massive chest jutting out to the same degree as her rump, she waddled with a 'z-shaped' torso. Appendages sticking out from her teal belted suit were greasy from a sweet summer sweat.

"You've got the right idea, my dear," she said to Arva as she plopped down into a nearby chair, the cushion releasing its air in one grand wheeze. "All this standing around takes its toll."

"Not much of a breeze today," Arva said, her mouth dry.

"You can say that again." She placed a damp glass against her jiggly gullet. "This heat certainly is oppressive."

"Quite," Arva said. "Yes, oppressive."

"And that's surprising for this part of the country." Her chest and head turned towards Arva like a fused block. "Are you one of us?"

"A professor's wife?"

"Yes. That."

"No, I'm not."

"Lucky you," she said. "We really are an unruly bunch." From underneath her skirt, liver-spotted knees projected at right angles, the tree trunks crammed into doll-sized black pumps. She brushed at the flecks of dandruff on her shoulders, and said, "So what do you do with your time?"

"I have two young boys. They keep me quite busy, thank-you."

"Where are they now?"

"Sleeping, next door."

"Now isn't that convenient," she said, and took a handkerchief from her purse, patted her brow, the sagging undersides of her arms. "But surely you must do something for your mind. Reading, perhaps. Tell me what a young lady might be reading these days."

"When I have a moment, I do read." Arva thought of her spying book. "Right now *Catcher in the Rye*."

"Salinger," she replied. "How wonderful. Though I did find the language a tad coarse. You?"

Arva remembered the gloss on the cover, the arid scent of the printed pages, but nothing about the contents. She had not read beyond the title. "I thought the very same," Arva said. "I wondered if it was necessary."

"Teenagers these days. That book's about as close as I want to get."

"It can be a difficult age."

Then the lady smiled at Arva and touched her arm. "Why you're not much more than one yourself." She studied Arva for a moment. "You have such an unusual look, my dear. Tell me about your parents."

It was the sort of nosy question that would have churned Arva's mother into a wild storm. Arva could easily picture it as they had fled so many times. Within moments her mother's escape route would be charted and her suitcase would be hoisted onto the bed, yawning, ready to be packed. She would rush to the wharves. With her jacket unbuttoned and flapping in the wind, she would hail fishermen to bring them across to the next cove for the cost of a few coins jingling in her pocket. Arva always had to run to keep pace. Her mother's speed seemed effortless. It was propelled by sheer panic.

But that afternoon, under the scrutiny of a professor's wife, Arva could not find it in her legs to stand and leave. She was not her mother. And something in her wanted to be polite, wanted to be appealing.

Barb stepped in. "Isn't that a touch personal, Elsie?"

"I was only asking," she said, her turkey jowl shaking. "She certainly doesn't need to answer."

"We all know about your inquisitive nature," Barb said. "Don't let it get away from you, is all."

"No, that's quite all right," Arva said. "I don't mind. If the truth were told, a woman found me on the floor of a dory when the men came in from their run. No one knew how I got to be there, jumbled up with the net and the cod. I was wrapped in a clean fisherman's sweater, and this very pendant I am wearing was tangled in the wool. To think I was almost pitched up on the wharf by a fishermen's fork."

"You poor dear," Elsie said as she rubbed Arva's forearm. "That is quite a story. Quite a story." She hoisted herself off the chair, and the cushion sighed with relief.

Within moments, Elsie was swerving through the well-dressed throng, her rows of excited curls waggling towards Arva.

"Good for you," Barb said, taking Elsie's seat. "Something for her to chew on. She's got plenty of space to fill."

Arva laid her dewy glass of lemonade onto a pedestal table

and felt ridiculous.

"I hear Thomas," she said, though neither cry drifted in through the open window. Arva stood to leave and tried to simply walk across the room. But something ached in the soles of her feet, a sensation urging her to jump and skip. She couldn't help herself. It was as though she were stepping barefoot along hot beach stones.

11

During the winter evenings, while I was waiting for Henry to turn in, I watched never-ending snow tumble from the black sky. Tiny flakes would blow in around the bedroom window frame on the bottom left-hand corner. Henry blocked the hole up with steel wool, but I plucked it out soon after.

As I dozed one night, I heard your door creak twice — once to open, once to close. Then a muffled cry. Yours. And I was awake in an instant. Could I have been dreaming?

A gust drove three snowflakes into my room. An odd number. My suspicions were right, and I bit a piece from my wedding quilt as fear gave way to fury.

For months I was down in a dark place, so I took it all to the water. After that, I could cut through the waves like a knife.

It was the first of September, nearly midnight, and Arva's hands were stained a deep red. She was in Aunt Helen's white kitchen cleaning up an enormous mess. While she scoured away a splash from the cupboard, liquid trickled down her forearms, and dripped from the tips of her elbows. There were streaks everywhere, but her fingertips were worst of all.

Leaning over the sink, she filled a plastic pail with warm sudsy water. Scrubbing was useless; the dye clung to the dryness in her skin. She tossed the nailbrush aside, dried her hands in her apron, and lifted a warm bottle so she could peer through.

The front door slammed.

"How's me girl?" A drunken rasp from the hallway.

Arva froze. A tingle rippled out from her spine, shocked her tongue, straightened her fingers. The bottle dropped to the floor and shattered. Her legs and apron were instantly marred by bloody looking spatter as though she had just bludgeoned a calf.

"Jesus Christ, woman. Yer some jumpity." Her husband's voice, hoarse from cigarettes. He came into the kitchen, stared at the floor. "What the hell have ye been at?"

"Barb gave us some beet."

"And that means ye got start right in this very night?"

Arva could barely see her husband's mouth, his words sneaking out from underneath his newly grown moustache.

"This ain't a hovel, ye knows. If that's what yer used to," he said.

She knelt down to pick up the larger fragments of the broken Mason jar.

"Ye got nothin' to say?" he continued. "I thought as much. Ye never does." He knocked a piece of glass towards her with his dusty shoe, then turned to leave the kitchen. "I don't want to see no dirt in the mornin'," he called over his shoulder. "Hear me? Not one friggin' speck."

Underneath the sink she found a pile of terrycloth rags, and began to sop up the juice off the linoleum. What had she been thinking? She should have kept the beets for morning. But she needed to do something. Since she had moved away from the cove, she was finding it harder and harder to sleep. Darkness was drawn like a tarry strip of taffy whenever she was alone.

Arva tossed the brilliant-coloured rags into an enamel bucket, filled it with water, and poured in half a cup of bleach.

"May I offer the boys a dish of berries?" Barb asked Arva the following afternoon.

Arva hesitated, but Thomas and Henry had already deciphered the word 'berries' and their fingers were twitching with anticipation. "Of course," she answered. "Go ahead."

As though thieves were perched on their shoulders, the boys hunched over the plastic bowls and shoved fistfuls of juicy brightness into their mouths. Thin red moustaches and triangular beards appeared within moments, and before Barb had stepped away, the bowls were empty.

"I have more," she said.

Arva glanced at her children, their hands like tiny crab pincers opening and closing. "Only if you have them to spare. Don't feel obliged."

"Not at all," Barb said, and she refilled the bowls with more berries from her garden.

Arva sighed as she watched her children savour them this time, plucking up each berry, examining it, then nibbling. Henry stuck them onto the end of his tongue, while Thomas peered down the tiny hole before popping them into his mouth.

Her mother would never have allowed her to take berries from a neighbour. Take anything from a neighbour, for that matter. People could offer, and often did, but the items were never consumed. A spare loaf of bread brought as a welcome would soon be tarnished with mounds of silvery mold. Treasured bottles of jam or sweet cucumber pickles would collect coats of dust on a shelf and be left behind when they inevitably moved on. Even fresh vegetables a farmer's wife would place on the back stoop were left to rot, turn to slush, and the rain would rinse them away.

One icy winter afternoon, when Arva was almost nine years old, she had stood with her mother on the stoop of a widow's home. The rapid thaw and subsequent deep freeze had wrapped the barren yard in a blinding glitter, and the chill compounded Arva's hunger. When a widow opened the door to her new tenants, a smell of buttery sweetness rushed out at Arva, wrapped around her waist, and invited her in. "Women who are undone will prepare more than a kitchen can handle," her mother had whispered. "Somehow, they bake themselves back together." It made no difference to Arva; her belly was pleading for a taste.

The widow barely showed them to their room before sharing unsavoury details about her husband's death. "Blood comin' out every hole," she said. "'Twas the appetite that was up and gone first. And then his insides start eatin' themselves up with a vengeance. Lord have mercy. If ye could've seen. Only thing he could get down was a mouthful of me baked rice custard. Loved it, he did. Right up until the day he passed on."

At the mention of custard, Arva's mouth began to salivate until she was sure the corners of her lips were glistening. She could practically taste its coolness, slipping down her throat, coating her grumbling stomach in a rich eggy cream.

As though the widow had read Arva's mind, she leaned in closer. "Best custard ye ever had, me ducky. I gets a rum bottle filled with milk every mornin', and I got meself into the habit of makin' up a batch right then." She pinched at the tender flesh at the underside of Arva's arm. "Ye looks like ye could use some fattenin'. Let's see what we can find."

Before Arva's mother could say anything, the woman was gone and returned with two delicate glass dishes heaped high with mounds of golden custard, morsels of white rice jutting out, fat juicy raisins. "Go on, me ducky," she said. "Somethin' to tide ye over."

"Really, we couldn't," her mother said.

"Don't be so foolish. Eat up, maid."

As soon as the widow stepped outside the room, Arva grabbed one of the silver spoons, scooped a generous portion, brought it to her lips. But she did not get to taste it. Her mother smacked the dish from her hand and the works clattered against the wall, tumbled to the braided rag rug on the floor.

"Have you got no sense?" she said. "It'll make you sick."

Flecks of curdled milk and sticky rice dotted the blue dory wallpaper like a hoard of tiny white maggots. The floor creaked just outside their door. Her mother drew a fresh handkerchief from her purse and began to wipe the mess away.

Clive hurried down George Street in the early evening darkness. His woolen scarf was tied into a hasty knot just underneath his chin. He was rushing, as always, dying for a drink of something hard. In the hustle, he knocked into a gentleman in a long gray overcoat. Clive glanced up to say 'Scuse me,' but when he saw the man's weathered face, the words collapsed at the back of his tongue and played dead. Immediately, he drew the coarse hairs of his moustache into his mouth with his chapped bottom lip and started sucking.

By the time he reached Badcock's, his hands were shaking.

"What's today Ernie?" he asked as he sat to the bar.

"Tuesday."

"No, the date." Clive began to wring his hands.

"Twenty-first. Start of Fall," Ernest said.

"Wouldn't guess it by the freeze outside," Melvin Buckle added. "Enough to freeze the balls off a brass monkey."

"'Tis goin' to be a long one this year. Tons of wasps over the summer. That's a sure sign," Ernest said.

"Nah," Melvin said. "Ye got that wrong. Other way 'round. When we don't see none of those little bastards, then we'll be haulin' out the long johns."

"Are ye certain?" Ernest asked as he laid a whiskey before Clive.

"Sure as me ass is white," Melvin replied.

Clive downed his drink in one swallow and slammed his glass on the bar. Slowly the magic radiated throughout his body, warmed and calmed it.

"What's got ye all snarled up?" Melvin said. "Ye looks like shit."

Clive tapped his knuckles on the bar for another round. "I just passed meself on the road," he said.

"Pissed yerself," Melvin said. "Jesus, don't get too close to me. I don't want to be catchin' the reek of ye."

"No, ye asshole," Clive said. "I walked right passed meself. I swears I just saw meself out on the road. 'Twas either me or me father, and I don't know what's worse."

"Well now," Melvin said. "Whatever ye had before ye came down here, I'd like a shot of it."

"I'm serious. Half-serious, anyways. He had me face. Gave me some start, it did. I turns around, almost tripped over me own feet, but he kept on goin'." Clive gulped a second whiskey.

"Lord," Ernest said. "Somethin' like that happened to me aunt. She saw herself wanderin' by the window when she was sittin' have a cup of tea. Mindin' her own business."

"What happened to her?" Clive asked.

"Ah, she's long gone."

"Christ," Clive said when he finished his third drink in as many minutes. "I knows it. I'm not long for this world."

"That's the biggest load of horse shit I've heard this week," Melvin said. "And believe ye me, I sees plenty of shit in any given week. Ye might see yerself, but ye never smacks into yerself, ye idiot."

"Still," Clive said. "I don't want to be seein' meself t'all."

"Don't mind me aunt," Ernest said to Clive. "She was 'round for some time after that, and sure, we all knew she was a bit soft in the head anyways."

Melvin nudged Clive. "Buck up, me son."

"You's might be right," Clive said, his fourth drink gripped in his steadied hand. "I says this for him, whoever he was, he was some handsome."

Melvin chuckles, then points his thin finger at Clive's glass. "Ern, fill him up. Get another couple of drinks in him and he could pass Mickey the friggin' Mouse on the street and he wouldn't bat an eye."

Shortly thereafter, when Melvin left to walk his beat, Clive said to Ernest, "B'ys from the city. They don't know a damn thing. Tell me how long yer Aunt lived."

Ernest swiped the counter with a rank cloth, the sour odour lost among the cigarette smoke. "Ye got no worries. It was some time."

"Some time?"

"Not a doubt," Ernest said. "Some time."

Clive guzzled his drink. "'Tis his birthday today."

"Who's?"

"Me father's."

"Now, then. Maybe 'twas him after all."

"Jesus, Ernie," Clive said as he tapped his knuckles for more whiskey. "I got to quit me drinkin'."

"On the house," Ernest said, filling the glass. He hated to hear such blasphemy from his most reliable customer.

Three hours later, Clive was thoroughly soused, and his concern over the man in the road had vanished. That foolishness no longer mattered, and instead, he was preoccupied with more scholarly endeavours. Tonight he was having tremendous difficulty touching his tongue off the tip of his nose. It had never been a problem before, and it took him a few tries to figure out why. Ah, the moustache. Tomorrow, he would shave it. First thing. Kate couldn't stand it anyway. And as for Arva? She never said a word about it. A tiger tail could've sprouted from his backside and she wouldn't have known the difference.

At the very moment Clive had stretched his tongue to the utmost limit, he was jostled from his stool and knocked to the floor. His teeth clamped down hard, and the taste of metal washed through his mouth. Jumping to his feet, he rammed straight into one of the grimy sailors, but when the barrel chest failed to budge, Clive slid back onto his stool and never spoke the words that were so bravely swirling in his head.

Off-duty Melvin snickered and said, "Watch yerself, Clive. Ye might break a nail."

A stubbier sailor leaned his substantial forearms on the bar and said, "Duh-reenks," in a rolling accent.

"Comin' up," Ernest said.

"Where are they from?" Clive mumbled to Melvin.

"Don't be a dumb ass. The boats, me son."

"No, I means from where."

"A few steps from Hell, by the reek. I should arrest 'em just for pollutin' the air."

Clive watched them from the corner of his eye. Normally he wouldn't have been so brash as to stare at strange men, but hours of heavy drinking diminished his inhibitions. And so what if he got cuffed? He wouldn't feel it anyway.

There was something disturbingly familiar about the sailors. Perhaps it was the tone of their skin, tanned into deep leathery hides. Or it could have been their eyes, suspicious black saucers darting left and right. Something snagged at Clive's mind, and as he gawked, a silent movie began to roll on the roof of his consciousness, director unknown.

A wafer-thin actress made her onscreen debut with her back to the audience. Clive recognized the profile of his wife even before she had fully turned around. Behind her, a dirty sailor lurked in a shadow. 'Action!' someone shouted. Shifting his head, the sailor's features melded with Arva's until the two were indistinguishable. The newly formed face smiled and unhinged its snake jaw. Spotlights shone down from overhead corners to illuminate the rows of rotten teeth, enamel swords.

Clive wanted to tear Arva away, but at the same time he wanted to pummel her, rip her to shreds.

"See, I told ye, now, didn't I? Nar question 'bout her." A booming voice echoed behind the wavy tongue. His father's voice.

The reel ended and he heard the sound of loose film flicking against the projector.

Then Clive realized his eyes had shut. He snapped them open.

Alongside him, a sailor tapped his empty glass against the bar.

The smell of festering fish flooded Clive's nostrils and constricted his passageways. Panic fluttered his heart and his lungs allowed only painful sips of air.

Lurching past the group of yammering sailors, Clive spilled out into the street. With his sweaty palm against the brick wall for support, he choked out bitter whiskey and bile all over the corner of Badcock's clean establishment. When he finished retching, he stood and wiped his mouth in the sleeve of his shirt, shot spit into the alley.

"Christ," he whispered. "I really got to quit me boozin'."

Clive stepped away from the vomit and leaned against the wall to regain his composure. Peering into the dim light of the alley, he saw a scrawny calico tabby sharpening its claws on a cardboard box. He knelt down on one knee and called 'puss, puss, puss,' until the cat came out of the darkness and rubbed its jaw against his pant leg. Clive scratched down its bony back. When it rose to his touch, he scooped it carefully around the waist, snuggled it inside his jacket, and carried it all the way home.

The next morning he awoke to find his hands roaming over his body scratching every inch. Hard pink bumps were swelling on his arms, around his ankles, beneath the hair on his groin. His right eye had puffed to such proportions he looked as though he had been punched. With persistent fingernails, he scraped the tops from the welts and drew daubs of blood. His first thought was of Kate. Likely contagious, she had given him more than he'd bargained for. As he was reflecting on his last interlude with his Gower Street flame, a black seed sprang towards him on the white sheet. It was not a rash at all. The bed was crawling with fleas.

Near the baseboard, the vagrant cat was curled into a dirty ball. With luxurious strokes, it was licking its paws and patting its whiskers. Then up onto its matted haunches, it gnawed and tugged at the dried gray pads of its feet. When it shifted, a shake of ground pepper landed on the spread, the specks coming instantly alive and bouncing towards Clive, a tested but plentiful source of blood.

He grabbed the cat by the scruff of its neck and marched to

the front door. Swinging its body furiously, the cat caught Clive's wrist with its sharpened sickle claws. Three jagged scores were left behind, blood beading.

"Christ," he roared, and the noise made his tender brain winch. Kicking the screen door wide open with his bare foot, he flung the cat into the yard, its back legs splaying on the gravel lane.

He found Arva on all fours in the children's room scouring the rug and pinching fleas between her thumbnails.

"Jesus, woman," he said, his hand slapped over the wounded wrist. "What's got into yer head? Bringin' a stray cat into the house like that. I'm near eat alive."

Two weeks later, the fever came.

"I can't eat a thing," Clive said. He leaned onto the tabletop with his elbows, pressed both thumbs into the bridge of his nose.

Arva stabbed the last cut of fried bread, and pulled it from the buttery pan. "But you love toutins," she said.

"I got no taste for it."

She placed the back of her hand on his cheek. "You're on fire," she said.

"Probably a flu," he said. "One of me students is always down with somethin'. I needs a bit of rest is all."

Arva had to help Clive from the table, he complained of weakness in his legs. In the bedroom, he bundled into blue flannel pajamas, a navy terrycloth bathrobe. He instructed his wife on which woolen blankets were the warmest. Within moments of settling into bed, he fell into a deep sleep, his mouth wide open, a snore vibrating at the back of his throat.

When Arva returned an hour later with a glass of cool water, Clive had not moved. His arm, bathrobe and pajama sleeve drawn upwards, lay above him on the pillow like dead weight. Arva took a closer look. His wrist was a great tree trunk, his hand a bursting glove. Running her fingers over the purplish scars from the cat scratches, she felt a hard knot just underneath the skin.

His eyes popped open, but he only managed a murmur. "Waddya starin' at?"

"Your arm," she said. "When did that come on?"

He craned his neck. "I must've knocked it," he whispered.

"No, it's more than that. Something from that cat."

"Ar."

"From those scratches. I'm sure of it."

"Do it matter?"

"I'll have to get the doctor."

"No doctor."

"For heaven's sake, Clive. Your body's better than a woodstove."

"No doctor." His voice was faint but firm. "Doctors don't do no good."

"We'll see how you are in the morning. If it gets any worse…"

"I'll get Father," he said. His gaze soared upwards and his lids began to lower so all Arva could see were slits of white.

"But, Clive." She stopped. It was clear he was already somewhere else, his eyes skittering back and forth, as though he were having some fantastic dream.

The room was black when she came in that night. She drew across the curtain and stared out into the yard, its lushness thinning right before her eyes. Gusts were so strong, she could feel the house shift, the walls buckling slightly inwards under the unremitting pressure. Trees bowed deeply, and red leaves were ripped away with each pass of the wind's whip. Summer had been driven out, and winter was wasting no time in taking hold.

"I needs a smoke."

Arva turned to see her husband straining to sit up. "How about a cup of tea," she said.

"No. A cigarette," he replied.

She lifted his pants from the bottom of the bed, drew his cigarettes out from a pocket, positioned one in his mouth. He pushed it out with his tongue, let it roll down over his cheek and onto the pillow.

"Light it."

"I couldn't," she stammered, though softly. "I've never smoked. You know that."

"Just start it," he croaked.

She sat on the hardback chair next to the bed and awkwardly took the cigarette into her mouth. Then she struck a match and lit it. When she drew in a puff of smoke, her lips burned on the heat, her eyes teared. It tasted like she had just licked clean the filthiest ashtray. Coughing, she whispered, "This is disgusting. I don't know how anybody enjoys this."

Pinching the cigarette between her thumb and forefinger, she held it to Clive's dry lips. He inhaled deeply, then sputtered out the smoke in one garbled breath.

"Jesus, tastes terrible," he said. He brought a shaky hand to his head. "I thinks I got a fever. Don't feel right t'all."

Arva stubbed out the cigarette in the saucer Clive kept on the nightstand. She took a gulp of the water herself, swished it in her mouth, wanted to spit, but swallowed.

"What about a cup of tea now? A cool cloth for your forehead?"

"Yes, me love," he said, as he drifted away again. "Tea. Cloth."

"I'll fix it for you now."

"Yer a good girl, Arva. And no more smokin' for ye."

Laughing lightly, she stood beside the bed and brushed his hair away from his forehead. In a kitchen jar, there were dried wild rosehips she had collected over the past summer. She would make Clive a full pot.

For three days, Clive ate nothing and drank only a few sips of cold tea. His fever had not broken, though it lowered each morning, and peaked again around dinnertime. The swelling in his wrist and arm was stubborn, the sponginess held on, and his real arm remained hidden somewhere inside.

"Shave me," he said when he awoke one evening. "Shave me face."

"You don't want to wait?"

"I can't wait," he said. "I needs me face cleaned."

"Very well," she said. "I'll shave you."

Arva poured steaming water from the kettle into an enamel bowl and brought it to his nightstand. She lathered the bristle brush, coated his stubble. After she unscrewed the handle of his Gillette, she adjusted the blade tension, and started to coast over his skin, feeling each prickle, rinsing the razor in the hot water.

As she scraped off long strokes of foam from underneath his chin, her fingers trembled and she nicked his flesh. A fat drop of blood oozed out and ran down to his hairline. Clive remained immobile; he was drifting in and out of sleep as she shaved. Arva picked up a soft white towel, and gently daubed away the excess foam. She trickled several drops of Old Spice into her palm and she patted his smooth skin.

Arva clicked off the light on the night table, and watched her husband while he dozed. She caressed his soft face, and bent down to rub her cheek against his. So close to him, she breathed in his smell, fresh like something exotic among a forest of pine trees. The aftershave masked the sickness riding out on each breath.

After she had cleared away the shaving supplies, Arva crawled into bed beside Clive, brought her back close to his fiery body. When she closed her eyes, she considered how easy it all was in the darkness, when she could barely see her husband's face. There were moments when a glimmer of love surfaced. But those moments were so few and far between, she didn't delude herself into believing the struggle was worth the reward.

That night, his fever reached its highest height, and Clive's tongue swelled to the size of a cow's. His anxious teeth chewed at the edges until they were ragged. Inside his head, white fish skittered like lightning zigzags. His pulse marched on - left, right, left, right. When it wanted to rest, the drill sergeant roared 'forward step.' Clive opened a single eye. He saw his father leaning against the doorframe, and Clive's pupil stretched wide to let the light in.

"Hello Daddy," he said.

"'ello, zun," the light said.

"What time is it, Daddy?"

"'Tis h'early, real h'early. Time fer restin'."

"Then no water today, Daddy?"

"No water t'day, me zun."

"No fish?"

"No fish."

"I'm still Daddy's b'y?"

"Yes, me zun. Yer still Daddy's b'y."

"I'm so cold, Daddy. I'm so cold."

"Come 'ere, zun, into me h'arms. I'll squeeze de cole' right h'out a' ye."

The light expanded, but Clive turned his face away. He knew his father would never use those words.

But, sure enough, a bead of sweat formed under his hairline, welled into a driblet, and trickled down his cheek. Hair along his spine settled back against his dampening skin. His fever broke, the shivers left him, and within minutes, the sheets were soaked and sticking to his body.

Clive threw back the bedcovers and stood up on thin rubbery legs. Almost good as new.

Arva instantly sat up in bed. "What are you doing?"

He never answered.

"Where are you going?" she asked.

Clive smoothed the front of his stale T-shirt.

"You can't go out dressed like that," she called out to him as he wobbled from the bedroom. "You'll catch your death. Come back to the bed. Clive?"

Down over the stairs he stumbled, and into the main hallway. He shoved his feet into dress shoes. He never stopped to undo the laces, and bent down the heels instead.

In only underwear and a wet T-shirt, Clive wandered down the lane. Moonlight glided across his shiny skin and he looked like a ghost moving through the night. The police were not a consideration. He knew his appearance was indecent, and if seen, he would be escorted back home. But that didn't matter. He needed to go.

On his way towards the harbour, he passed drunks and partygoers.

"Jesus," he heard one man say. "He's havin' some time of it."

"Escaped from the Waterford, if ye asks me," the lady friend answered.

Clive paid them no mind. He had to get to New Gower Street. Everything was suddenly clear to him, and he had to let Kate know.

Into the yard he hurried, his loose shoes clicking on the pavement as he took each step. He rushed around back of the house. Lavender blooms filled the air with heady perfume, something Clive had never appreciated before. He was more alive than ever.

When he opened the door to the bedroom, he saw her sitting on the bed. It was as though she had been waiting. She made no comment on his dress, or the stench of the sickness that was leaving his body. She only smiled at him in that demure way when Clive murmured their secret words:

"Put on yer rubbers, me dear."

After she had helped him to further sweat out the illness, he lay back on the bed, his head next to her black boots, crossed at the ankle.

"I loves ye," he whispered.

"Oh me Jesus," she said, and a thin laugh escaped her lips. Another one thinking she's his mother. "Merciful Father."

His waxen face flushed and his skin prickled like goose flesh. The sweat on his body had dried and now he was simply cold. Clive could hear the clicking of ice crystals against the window, and he wondered how he was going to make it home with only a pair of dank underwear and that soggy gray shirt balled up in the corner.

Kate must have heard his thoughts.

"I can lend ye a dress, me son," she said, and her jelly gut shook with laughter. "'Tis time ye was on yer way this evenin'."

When her husband climbed back into bed, Arva was able to make it out. Something had merged with the sickness on his body, an odour of used elastic bands stretched to the point of breaking. She blinked back the tears as they sprang to her eyes, pushed her face into the goose down pillow, pretended to sleep. And if, in the future, she was ever asked to pinpoint it, it was then that she changed her mind.

12

Caplin were rolling the night we did it. I saw them when I went down to the beach to gather salt water. In the moonlight the balled-up waves shimmered as they tumbled over the rocks, silvery skeins twitching everywhere. The ocean was drawing up the living, spitting out the dead.

Standing knee deep in the water, it took some effort to get a full bucket without gathering the fish. I think that year the caplin were a surprise. No one made mention of it to me. And with such big plans, someone should have.

A glitter storm had coated all of St. John's in a slick layer of ice. Power lines hung low with the weight, and swayed like silvery strands of Christmas tinsel ready to snap at any moment. The whining gusts of wind were perilous, urging cars and pedestrians alike to glide with abandon.

As Arva inched her way along the downtown streets, she had to hold on to stone walls and concrete window ledges. Even with gravel tossed in scattered patches, the sidewalk was like a rink; her laced black boots might just as well have been skates.

When she opened the stained wooden door to Petten's Collectibles, a friendly bell tinkled. Shuffling her feet slightly, Arva reacquainted herself with the comforting sensation of a solid floor.

"Afternoon, Miss," the broker said from his stool behind the dusty counter. "Some kind of weather. Yes?"

"The road is pure glass," Arva replied.

"Lovely though," he said. "When you're not trying to get around, that is. Our little port has been totally crystallized.

Frozen in time."

Arva turned to glance out through the window. The panes were gemstones, and the outside world was a sparkling smear.

"Yes, actually," she said. "It is lovely."

The man slid down from his stool and stepped out from behind the counter. He was barely five feet tall, and his stout face was partially hidden behind substantial black-rimmed spectacles. "Now, from your expression," he said. "I'm guessing you're not here to browse. Am I right?"

"You are," Arva said.

"I'm a good guesser, you see," he said, and smiled.

"I'd like to pawn a piece of jewelry." The word 'pawn' sounded somewhat fraudulent to Arva, but still she forced herself to use it. That was what she was doing, after all. She needed money.

"Very well, Miss," he said, and clicked the heels of his shiny black shoes together. "Let's see what you've got."

Arva fumbled in her jacket pocket. The store was so full there was hardly room to extend her elbows. Shelves were laden with silent timepieces and chipped china plates, beaded purses and clusters of white and rust painted ceramic dogs. There was a choking smell of attics, old dust, tapped out memories, but it was not offensive, and Arva took a moment to breathe it in. Then she handed him the velvet box from her pocket, and he cracked open the lid to reveal her plain gold cross.

Picking up the pendant in his stubby fingers, he said, "Yes, I could take this." But when he turned it over, he frowned. "Hmmm. Not worth much with this engraving on it. You'd be better off keeping it."

"It's worth nothing?"

"You might appreciate it when you're older, Miss. People get more sentimental as they age."

"So you won't take it?"

He must have sensed her desperation. "Err, I could," he said.

"How much?"

"Only a couple of dollars, I'm afraid. Not likely anyone'll want it. Then again, someone might like a piece of jewelry with a bit of history to it."

"There's no history," she said with a bitterness that surprised her. "It's never been worn."

"There's history all over, my dear. You needn't doubt it. Everything here's got something to say." He gestured to the full shelves. "Now take that piece you're wearing around your neck. I'd love to hear the story there. All the hands it's passed through. May I take a closer look?"

Arva reached beneath her hair, unclasped the silver chain, and offered him the dragonfly. The pawnbroker pulled his glasses to the tip of his nose, brought the gaudy insect to his eye.

"Filigree," he said. "Such delicate work. The looping wings." He rolled the pendant over in his chubby hand. "I've never seen anything quite like it. Exquisite. What happened to the eyes?"

"I don't know."

"Interesting," he said. "Scratched away like that. How'd you come into it?"

"My mother."

"Ah. An heirloom. She had connections abroad, then? Relatives?"

"Not that I know of."

"And there the story begins, my dear. Even the links in the chain are unusual. I don't imagine it was made anywhere around here. Likely someone sent it to her from Europe."

"Then it's worth something?"

"Yes, most definitely."

"Then take that too. It's only silver, but please give me what you can."

"Look, Miss. I'm going to do you a favour, seeing as it's almost the holidays and all. Your pendant's not silver. Most likely, it's white gold. No craftsman would spend the hours to make something so delicate from silver. I could give you a price for it, but it'd be nothing of what it's worth, and if you weren't so innocent looking, I'd have grabbed it up already. We'll do a deal on the gold cross, but you keep hold to the fly."

Arva accepted the few dollars he gave her and went straight to Ayre's. She bought a ten-pin bowling kit with two red balls, a grooved wooden block set, and a pair of plastic marbled-green army tanks.

As she carried the purchases to the register, she silently cursed her near-empty purse. How could a university-educated high school teacher possibly bring home so little money?

It was Boxing Day when Arva noticed the perfume.

She had been in the kitchen, pressing dough with her floured knuckles, her ears listening for the snapping sound that signaled enough kneading. Then a smell wafted down the hallway on an icy breeze, curled around her head, tweaked her nose with its sharpness. She stopped kneading instantly.

"Well, now. This is some kind of comeuppance." An unmistakable voice.

At once, Arva drew back her hand and struck the dough with a stinging smack. She briskly wiped her hands in the dishcloth, and stepped into the hallway. With her feet firmly planted, Arva managed to look.

"Bonjour, me dear, Ça va?"

Standing near the front door was a curvy blond in a stylish tan skirt and jacket, shiny black boots to her knee. Her lips were stained a violent red, as though she had just bitten and drained the life from the flattened furry animal that was draped around her neck. Lolly's right hand reached up and caught hold of the tail, her fingers lost in its fluff.

"Clive isn't here," Arva said, her voice flat.

"I weren't lookin' for he."

Well then, what? Arva was caught off guard. Ill will and cordiality blended into sludgy confusion, and she was not sure what to do. "You can come in," she said. "Leave your boots on."

"I just..." Lolly replied, standing still. Then scuffed her boots on the mat, clicked down the hallway, brushed past Arva, and took a seat at the kitchen table. The room immediately filled with the scent of crushed lilacs, orange blossoms, a body sweeter than it should be. "Ye ain't done too poorly for yerself, by the size of it."

"None of this is ours."

"Still, 'tis ye who's livin' here."

Arva turned her back to Lolly and put the kettle on the stove. "Is that why you came? To see how we're living?"

Lolly never responded to the question, but began to talk, her words flowing so fast, they careened into one another, her motor seizing just long enough for a sip of gas. "I finally met someone decent, Arva. I finally did. His name's Anton, can ye believe it?

Isn't that right romantic soundin'? Anton Parent. That's French, case ye was wonderin'." Lolly puckered her full lips and repeated the name. "He came by Mother's lookin' for antiques. He goes 'round the outports collectin' up the good stuff and bringin' it up to Quebec to sell. Interestin', wha? Well, he got a gargeous maple table from Mother. It'd belonged to Lyle's family. She sold it for a pittance, not a tenth of what 'twas worth, but I never said a word, 'cause I had me sights set higher when I sees neither ring on his finger. He might've been a bit older than I likes, and not much in the way of hair, but he got a bit of charm, a bit of sense. He stayed in the cove for a week, took a room at Junior Lynch's, and we's been goin' 'round together ever since.

"I's been to Montreal, Arva. Can ye fathom it? And jeez, 'tis right lovely. All the ladies is trim and dressed to the nines. They don't go ruinin' their shapes eatin' the likes of greasy ol' fried fish. Though 'tis the bread that kills me. Puffs me right out. And they loves their wine, so that's right up me alley. I never did go in much for gin and the like, give me a glass of wine any day over it. And I even tasted a slug. Or a snail. Drowned in real butter. Real butter, hear me. They thinks nothin' of it."

"We's down for another run now, seekin' out the bargains. I got a knack for it, if ye can imagine me havin' a knack for anythin'. Ye won't believe how cheap we can get the stuff for here. People is almost willin' to pay ye to take it off their hands. And 'n the mainland, they'll empty their pockets to have it. Don't know who's worse off, the one's gettin' rid of it, or the ones buyin' it up. Makes no difference, me Anton got it all figured out. I could've stayed to the city, in Montreal, but I decided to come down. Be his island connection, right? I says to him that 'tis a queer time to be travelin', roads slicks like they is, but he says this is when ye'll find a crowd that's real hard up. The hardest. And that's when ye gets the best deals. He's a real thinker, me Anton."

Lolly talked until her tea was ice cold, until her tongue was tired, and until she could bring herself to notice her son. "This he?" she asked, though she never needed to. She knew without question which child was hers, the blond hair, broad bottom lip.

"Yes," Arva said. "Thomas."

"A tiny little fellar, isn't he."

"He'll grow."

"What're those marks? Chicken pox?"

"No, flea bites."

"Oh me Lord." One of Lolly's hands began scratching the other.

Thomas was standing between Arva's legs; apron pulled over his head, a single eye peeking out. When he spied the dead animal decorating her suit jacket, he threw back the apron wrapping like a veil and climbed into Lolly's lap. He stood on her thighs, trying to pry open its sharp dirty teeth, press a raisin in between them.

Lolly stood up, the child attached to her well-padded hip, her suit jacket pushing up so that the fur tickled her ears. At the kitchen sink, she picked up a damp dishcloth, squeezed it.

"Don't," said Arva, but Lolly was already swiping it over Thomas's lips and nose. She cleaned away the dried-on carrot, but replaced it with streaks of moistened flour.

"I can't stand seein' kids with grimy faces," she said.

Thomas grimaced and then sneezed. From his nostril, a slimy black glob oozed, then dropped to the linoleum with a teeny plop. A raisin, lodged hours earlier by a creative finger, had simmered, swelled, and reemerged. Then it was Lolly's turn to grimace, and she leaned sideways to eliminate her hip's ledge and the boy slid down to the floor. Access to the pelt denied, Thomas went back to the refuge behind Arva's apron.

"Well then," she said, backing up a few steps. "Bon. Everythin's okay."

Lolly rushed down the hall, away from the child. At the door, she turned and said, "I knows yer wonderin'." Her fingers twitchy, she poked at the desiccated animal head, tapped her nails along its clenched jaw. "And I don't know. I don't know why I come over." She gripped the doorknob. "Do ye think 'twas better that I...?" she began, but with a wave of her hand she erased the air where her words lingered. And with a swift twist of her wrist, she was out into the bluster and gone.

Arva scooped up Thomas, rushed down the perfumed hallway, and locked the door.

"Lolly was here today," Arva said to Clive while they were eating a cold turkey supper. "She wanted to see him."

Thomas was hiding his face in the cloth. Then there was a

sound like milk spilling, dripping off the edges of the table, splatting into itself on a smooth surface.

Clive stuck his head under the table, and recoiled, throwing knife and fork into his plate and scraping back his chair in one great motion. Wood struck wall.

"Christ," he said. "Another friggin' mess. If she come for the boy, let her have him. He's nothin' but a piss pot in a pair of bloody trousers."

Clive waited until he and Arva were well inside Belinda's Best on Military Road before he announced his proposal. They sat together at a wobbly table, and he tore a strip from an empty matchbox, folded it into a square, pushed it under the troublesome leg. His hands worked the air between them, voice invigorated. Then after giving their orders to the owner, he gripped both sides with solid fingers, flashed a smirk, and wet his lips.

"I's thinkin' we can try for another baby," he said.

"You are?" Arva pushed her chair back several inches.

"That I is, missus," he said, nodded his head. "What do ye think?"

"Yes, maybe," Arva replied, though immediately she thought not.

"Bring us closer together."

"It would," she lied.

"A fresh start for us."

"The freshest."

"And Henry's growin' like a weed." He applauded as though the child's size were his own accomplishment. Then, rescinding, he said, "I got no idea what yer feedin' him, me dear, but he's really somethin'. The other one'll catch up. They always do, right?"

"Yes, always do."

Arva caught sight of a man in checkered brown pants standing beside her. He laid a cup of steamy tea before her, and a plate of deep-fried chips in front of Clive. She concentrated on her tea, the relaxing colour. When she lifted it, loose leaves drifted, but never entirely met the surface.

"Don't ye want a baby girl for yerself?"

"A girl would be wonderful, Clive," she said. If she gulped a mouthful, could she catch a leaf between her lips?

"I figured that," he said. "Every woman wants her girl." He

laughed lightly, picked up a chip, licked away the salt.

"Hmmm," she said. "What every woman wants."

With an impatient left hand, he tapped the side of his plate, continued to eat with his right. "I thought ye'd be more excited than this."

"I'm surprised, is all," she said, stirring figure-eights with a cheap spoon so thin-handled, the heat threatened to melt it.

"Well, act it, will ye? Instead of sittin' there glazed over. Face on ye long as a loaf of bread."

He watched her gaze shift from his chest to his head to the wallpapered wall behind him.

"Givin' me lip, are ye? Is that yer thing? If 'tis, it don't look good on ye, missus, that's for sure." Then to himself, he said, "Only woman I knows can give ye lip without mutterin' a friggin' word."

"I'm not, Clive. Honestly." Her black hair fell around her face like a shawl, a woman in mourning.

"Ye better not be." He felt pathetic for even suggesting the baby now. This is not how he'd imagined it. He thought she would lurch across the table at him, wrap her brown-arms-in-winter around his neck, make it a job to balance his chair on two slender legs. Again, he was a fool.

Underneath the table, his leg bounced, circular ripples surged over the surface of Arva's tea. Then the brown checkered pants were beside her again, crisply ironed, neat pleats.

She glanced up, smiled.

"Anythin' else for ye, me love?" the owner said as he placed a stout glass dispenser of malt vinegar in the center of the table.

"I'm fine, thank-you," Arva said.

"And yerself?" he said to Clive, but the owner's back was turned before Clive even had a chance to open his mouth.

He bit down hard on a chip, clenched his jaw.

"I saw that," he said. "Needn't think I didn't."

"Sorry?"

"Ye was smilin' at that man. Makin' eyes."

"Smiling. Yes," Arva said.

"Jesus," he said. "She even admits it." He picked up the malt vinegar, turned it over, but the metal lid was not screwed on properly and the vinegar splashed out onto his plate. "Christ almighty. Me chips are spoilt." He tasted one, spit half of it back, and shoved his plate to the side. For a moment he looked as though he might cry. Then he said, "And yer not even listenin' to me. We come all this way for nothin'."

"I am," she said. "I am listening."

"The hell ye are," he said. "Ye got no more goin' on up there –" he knocked hard on his skull with his index finger, tap, tap, tap, "– than a dumb ol' mutt."

Clive leaned toward her, sharp elbows testing the tabletop's durability. Dribbles of vinegar speckled his chin, and he wiped his mouth on his shirtsleeve. He simply had the type of mind that couldn't conceive of using a serviette. Arva accepted both her slight twinge of shame at the sight of him, and her rinse of relief when he stood and walked out.

He was good at that. Leaving.

On the sidewalk, Clive had to stop, park on a doorstep for a minute. That chip he'd eaten was sliding down his tube like a fistful of flour, and the bone-dry pain in his chest was nearly unbearable.

Hooking her finger over the edge of the white plate, Arva drew the chips towards her. Shiny with grease and salt, most of them lay flaccid in a puddle of reddish malt vinegar. She selected one, brought it to her nose. It stank like the ripest feet, moldiest socks. So she dropped it and chose one near the very edge, a good distance from the vinegar. Nibbling it, she thought it was delicious.

She ate another, again avoiding the vinegar. Then another.

Here she was. Eating chips alone in a diner, amidst the clatter and crowd. She opened her wallet to take out a handful of change and placed it on the table. Sliding each coin so that it was grouped, she counted out her bill.

There were rules for everything, she thought. Simple rules of living.

And after she tasted her final chip, Arva dabbed the grease from her lips with the cheapest papery serviette, folded it, and left it on her seat.

13

He willingly breathed it in, like I knew he would. If he were innocent, some center in his mind would have roused him, snapped his head out of the slop bucket, released him from his shoddy drunkenness long enough to save his life. But, no. He lay down, and took the salt water into his lungs. He let himself go. I swear. He did.

For an instant, you may think 'how could I?'

When you do what you are told, my love, there is no room for guilt.

Arva had not yet fallen into a deep slumber when she heard the men stumbling up the drive. Though she had been lying in bed for nearly three hours, she had been drifting in and out of a restless sleep while listening to the sounds of a borrowed house in a port city during springtime. Most homes creaked in comforting acceptance of their natural settling, but Uncle Harry's had a continual gripe, like an agonizing bellyache rumbling as a reminder of a skipped dinner. The windows were often unwilling to open, and when Arva managed to scrape them up, pleasant noises did not waft in. The city produced a constant quiet whirr, as if something was always happening, someone was always awake. Irritation was ever present in the air. Car horns blared at all hours, and rambling drunks muttered as they staggered home before sunrise.

The more Arva listened, the more she missed the wind that draped itself over Old Man Crane's home and protected the structure against anything trying to establish itself. There was never a cobweb in sight, not a dry leaf caught in a corner, not a torn piece of crackled newsprint brushing against a closed door. Even a horse fly could not land on the rough boards. A gale force wind would tug the papery wings from the fly's body, forcing it to take rapid flight. Arva found not only did the gusts protect, but they also played a captivating lullaby that tempted sleep upon her.

As she dozed, Arva had a dream. She was inside a beaver dam, surrounded by layer upon layer of sticks and mud and pebbles and leaves. Damp walls dripped, and logs with telltale tooth marks snagged her hair.

She did not panic. Arva understood her trap, and was resigned to it.

Then Alf Jones swam up through a watery black hole in the floor. He wore a shiny coat that dazzled her eyes. As she examined it further, colours emerged, gently blurred stripes of pink, freckles of green and blue, a soft silvery overlay, like skins of enormous trout seamlessly melded together.

Alf began to dance with a stiff awkwardness characteristic of the older and more sedentary. Two bags stuck out from his pockets, and Arva heard the crunch of plastic when he swayed his hips. As though she had directed him, Alf reached into his jacket, drew out the bulging bags of striped sugary peppermint knobs, and tossed them towards her. The sweetness she had craved since her son was born was flying in a great arc towards her, and her mouth watered.

Arva caught them, one in either hand. She laughed. Completely effortless, though she did not recognize her own voice. It was then that sounds began to draw her out of her light slumber. She resisted, clinging to the filmy fabric of her dream, willing herself a moment to taste the candy, offer one to Alf. But her worlds separated. And when she awoke abruptly to a woman's piercing cackle, an unsettling union of guilt and delight was lingering just beneath her skin.

"Arva," Clive hollered. "Get yerself down here. We got company."
Arva could hear what sounded like a thousand muddy clops

and one high-pitched clip moving along the hallway towards the kitchen. When she reached the top of the stairs, the stench of stale cigarettes and spilled whiskey wafted up to greet her. But there were other smells as well - a ripe barnyard, rancid fish oil. She lifted her white nightdress well above her ankles, and watched where she placed her bare foot.

Earlier today, Alf and Alek had arrived from Upper Island Cove to spend a night "butterin' up the ladies in the big city," as Alf had said. But by the sight of him now, Arva thought, he couldn't butter up a slice of bread, let alone a woman. He was seated next to Alek behind the kitchen table, his head drooping forward, a cabled toque scarcely balanced on the top of his head.

While Alf was sedate, Alek could not stop moving. Over and over again, he swiped the back of his hand across his mouth, smoothed his unkempt hair, and checked the buckle of his gray belt. "I is, I is," he said. "I is. I is."

"Ye is what, me son?" asked the source of the barnyard smell.

Arva knew this stout man was undoubtedly a farmer. He was dressed head to toe in plain browns, except for his red suspenders, which were hiked so high, his left and right sides were revealingly divided.

"Whatcha doin' standin' there like a retard?" Clive said to Arva. "Drinks. We all needs drinks." He nodded at the brown man and motioned to a chair. "Take a seat for yerself, Murph. We'll get ye fixed up in no time."

When Murph's sack-of-sawdust body dropped into a chair, the wooden legs instantly dented the linoleum.

"Jaysus," Murph said, and he sighed. "Me mouth is that dry ye'd think it was hung on the line."

"Kate," Clive said to a worn looking woman, "take a load off, me darlin'." Then, to Arva, "Whiskey. Get me the bottle."

At the mention of whiskey, Alf's head bobbed up, his eyes like shutters clicked open and his gaze settled on Arva.

"Ye's the lovely of vision," he slurred, blinking slowly. "Vision of lovely."

"Lovely? Don't be talkin', Alfie," Kate said, and began to snort. "With that granny-gown on, she looks half ghost, half tar baby."

"That's what she ain't," Murph said, licking as much of his face as his fat tongue would allow. "She's a dandy heifer, if ye asks me. Real dandy." With fingers like enormous grubs, he gripped at his knees, his torso and head circling, glugging down a drain.

One drink, Arva thought as she brought the bottle. One drink, and then they would be gone.

"She is what she is, now fellars," Clive said as he poured liquor into Aunt Helen's weighty crystal tumblers. "She is what she is." He took a quick sip and said, "A toast, fellars. To me brother, Alek. As he's sayin' – finally, he is. Tonight, he can call hisself a man. Not bad for someone stolen by the fairies."

Kate slid partly off the side of her chair towards Alek, patted his damp cheek with the back of her fingers. "Now then, honey," she crooned. "Isn't that right special?" Then she caressed her leopard-print earrings and said, "Flora'll take a little cricket like ye any evenin', me lover."

"Cricket, ye says?" Clive said and slapped his thigh. "What was he chirpin', was he? Or was he rubbin' his back legs together?"

"A bit of both, I 'llows," Kate said.

"Hey," Clive said. "I just thought of somethin'."

"Now, then," Murph said, belched, rubbed the lower quadrant of his belly. "That's right swell."

"Shut yer trap, ye stinky bastard," Clive snapped. "Followin' us home like a bloody stray mutt."

"Don't mind he," Kate said to Clive. "What's yer thought, me love?"

"If Alek stays up long enough," Clive said, flashed a smoke-stained smile, "he can head straight on to the Basilica. He needs to be confessin' left and right and up and down this mornin'."

Alek pressed his shoulder into Alf's. His breathing was rapid, like a cornered animal, and he quickly gulped his drink.

"Let up, Clive," Alf said, and glanced at Arva. "Not in front of the ladies."

"Yer right, me son, as always," Clive said with a slicing tone. "Words of wisdom from the blessed lips of Alfie Jones."

Murph downed his whiskey in one fell swoop and slammed the glass onto the table. The circumference of his dizzying circles was gradually increasing, and he said, "Me guts is right queer." Then, mid-loop, he slumped down between his open knees, and a powerful gush spewed from his surprised mouth to make a hot splatter on the floor. Once upright again, he shoved his fist up under his ribs and said, "Ar. Now I's wunerful grand."

"Ye poor thin'," said Kate. "Sick to yer stomach." Her hand rubbed the air just over the shoulder of his faded plaid shirt.

"Christ," Clive said. "Ye gone now and wasted yer drink." Then to Arva, "Bring me whatever else we got, will ye?" No one could ever say he was a stingy host.

Arva had been standing a whole two feet away from the puddle of vomit, and still what appeared to be chicken feed clung to the front of her nightdress. "I'm sorry," she said, shaking her head. "There'll be no more drinking here tonight."

Clive stuck his pinky deep into his ear, gutted whatever wax that had been distorting his hearing, and said, "Huh?"

"I said there'll be no more drinking here tonight."

There it was again. He had heard correctly.

In an instant, Clive leaped to his feet, nostrils like a bull's. "What the hell do ye mean?"

Arva's instinct told her to move back, though she never budged. "There are two children upstairs sleeping. This is no place for it."

"Who the hell do ye think ye is?" He spoke slowly, but whitish spittle still balled at the corners of his mouth. "Me friggin' mudder?"

"It's just that..." she began and started to turn away. Her words were cut short as her head snapped back.

Jolt jolt jab jab. Clive like lightnin' in the schoolyard.

Clive watched his hand, as though it were at the end of his father's wrist, grab her sturdy braid. He jerked with such force it should have been audible.

He was sorry before he did it, of course, but that did not stop his hand. It never even came close.

Arva took a deep step backwards to catch her balance, but her bare foot plunged into the slippery vomit, and her legs glided out from under her. As she fell, her jaw smacked the farmer's rounded knee. Immediately, the smell of rotted squid and ground-in dirt filled her nose. But blood soon rushed in to push it out.

When she struck the ground, Clive realized he still clutched her braid. He told his hand to open, it did, and the braid was released. Down into the sour pool of vomit it dropped, and it lay there like a gnarled stick.

While making a whine only a dog could hear, Alek shimmied off his seat, under the table, and climbed on all fours amidst a jungle of nervous legs. When he reached light, he bolted towards the door, out into the yard. Scuttling down the drive like a drunkard gone blind, his gray sneakers churned the crushed stone.

Suddenly sober, Alf banged his chair against the kitchen wall, nearly knocked Kate over as he rushed to Arva.

"Yer a real shithead, Clive Mercer," Alf said as he offered his bony hand to Arva. "I got half a mind to take the boots to ye meself."

Just moments before Alf helped Arva to her feet, Murph had been staring down at her between his wide-open legs with painful hunger lodged in his eyes. As his gaze moved across her white cotton gown, Arva was aware of every inch of her flesh, and understood how appealing it might be to a stomach that was entirely empty.

Arva used her silver kitchen scissors to slice through her ribbon of hair, and the crunch sounded exactly like laying down a weighty burden in old dry snow.

The next morning when Clive awoke, a pounding train was trying to find a set of tracks out from his ears. He left the drizzle-coloured bedroom, walked past a black-haired man in the living room, then down the hallway. Each step he took caused a crack of lightning behind his eyes, thunder inside his head. He put his hand on the back of the kitchen chair, lifted the legs just slightly off the linoleum and gently pulled it out. Something dark caught his eye. Curled neatly on his seat was a braided length of black rope. Arva's hair. Coiled like a snake, ready to strike.

As Clive nudged the spiral off his chair with the tip of his toe, he heard an unfamiliar sound. The telephone was ringing.

The hospital room smelled like sickness, paled by bleach, but still holding on. In the vinyl covered wingback chair, Doris's small frame was accentuated. Her twiggy arms stuck out of the short sleeves of a flowered dress, her legs in tan stockings crossed sharply at the knee. She rocked back and forth slightly, kept her sunken eyes on her son. In one arm she cuddled gray sneakers, her hand patting a melodic rhythm into the dingy soles.

She glanced up as Arva walked in. After Arva sat, Doris continued to stare at the door.

"The b'ys?" Doris asked.

"They're with Barb," Arva replied. "Our neighbour."

"And Clive ain't comin'?" Doris asked.

"No," Arva said. "He's not."

"Good thin' he ain't," Doris said, her hands balling into fists. "He'd rue the day if he come 'cross me path." She held up Alek's sneakers. "They thought to throw these out. Blood and all. But he'd be some livid if I stood by and let 'em do it."

Doris gulped air and hiccuped. Her nose was inflamed and looked ready to burst.

"Doctor Wells says they don't know if he'll ever wake up. Took a good bang to the head, he did. Legs are ruined besides, beyond repair." She shuddered as she inhaled, sounding like a baby who was too depleted to cry further.

"The constable told me how it happened, ye knows. I thought Alek never looked. Just run out. But, that weren't the case. The driver said he saw Alek, and Alek saw he. Stared him right in the eye. Then, soon as he was passin' by, Alek darted right out, like a deer or somethin'. What could've been in his mind to do the likes of that?" She sipped at the edges of her cafeteria tea. "I don't care what he says, Clive never took care of him. Alek may have the face of a man, me dear, but he's still a b'y. Not much more than a young'un in his head. Right innocent-like. Wouldn't even let me swat a fly dead, he'd work for an hour to catch it in cupped hands, and heave it out through the doors."

Doris was silent for a moment, leaned back in her chair. She took a deep breath and a calm settled in around her, a calm that comes to those who have gone astray and are finally on their way home.

"There was no fairies, ye knows. No fairies t'all."

"I don't say the folks 'round the bay thinks there was fairies, either, but they'd rather believe that than have to see the truth.

"Things changed when Clive was born. Or, I changed, I s'pose. Though it don't really matter now. Tom and I was havin' a nice life together. We was right in love, always touchin', dancin' in the kitchen to his hummin', and he had a sweet voice, me dear, like a choir b'y.

"Lord, how excited he got when Clive was on the way. I remembers the night like 'twas yesterday. How he went up to fetch Doreen. He filled the stove with all dry junks of wood, and kissed me on the tip of me very nose before he walked out through the door. Whistling, he was, like a man without a care in the world. A man lovin' his life. But the child came out all wrong, ruined some part of me, and I was never the same after.

"I never knowed a child could steal so much away from ye. Not that I minded the time or the energy he took, I'd expect that. No, I'm talkin' 'bout the goodness. Yer very essence. Diggin' right down to the source of yer spring, and blockin' it up with stones and mud. Clive nagged the soul right out of me. That child was born sour, a chip on his shoulder the size of tomorrow.

"After dealin' with Clive all day, I couldn't stand to have no one at me. Didn't want Tom so much as puttin' his eyes on me, let alone his hands. Though I don't fathom a man can live like that for long. I don't think they's meant to. So, one night after a bit too much drinkin', he came at me, and not one bit did I blame him for it. I put it out of me mind.

"I don't claim to know what makes a mother love one child more than the other, but sometimes it just happens that way. And it happened to me. Alek came out of me like a dream, not a twinge, not one sliver of pain. 'Twas the most excitin' few moments of me life.

"And after how Alek was fashioned? Ye'd think it would've been a rough ride. No, me dear. And to this day, I can't wrap me mind 'round it. Clive came from a scrap of love, and he was born bitter as a stalk of rhubarb. Alek, on the other hand, was made with a burst of anger, and he come out sweet as the pie.

"I thinks somehow he knowed how he was made, and that's why he never stopped his bawlin'. I never once cried 'bout it all meself. Not a once. Wouldn't let meself, or I thinks I'd never of been able to give it up. So the baby was doin' what I couldn't, ye sees? And I was so thankful for it, ye couldn't imagine. Tom knowed it too. I believes that. I does. He knowed why that child cried and cried. 'Cause there was no love left between us. Tom was a good man once, and that was gone.

"All that screamin' can do somethin' to a person. For me, it filled me up, kept me mind from movin' 'round, the noise was too much to let it wander far. But Tom couldn't handle it a t'all. He told me if I don't get that child to shut its gob, he'd heave it out to the bay. I didn't think he meant it at the time, but thinkin' back on it, he likely might of.

"I couldn't do it. Day after day after day he kept that bawlin' up. When he was exhausted, he would sleep, when he was hungry, he'd eat fast and furious so he could start his screechin' again. We rarely got a bit of sleep. Days went by. I don't even remember where Clive was to. If he was at home, or if he was in the garden. Someone was lookin' after him, 'cause he was in his bed at night.

"'Twas weeks of it. Tom could hardly even fish, and the money he was bringin' home couldn't buy enough supplies to feed a hen. We was some strapped. Worse than ever. And that's the kind of stuff that will drive a person mad, drive them to do a bad thin', a thin' they wouldn't ever fathom if they was in the right frame of mind. I knowed for me, I was startin' to see stuff. I'd be smackin' spiders on the countertop, when I'd lift me hand, there'd be nothin' there. Out of the corner of me eye, I'd catch some flames flickin' out of the woodstove, then when I goes over to it, I sees that the lid is pressed in tight.

"Tom started drinkin' more and more. Moonshine from Old Man Crane's. 'Twas the awfulest time I ever remembers seein' him. It looked like someone had dipped their fingers in ash and swiped it under his two eyes. Black, black, black. He was near gone, I knowed. And, no matter what I did, the cryin' didn't stop. And still I didn't mind it; the damage was already done.

"One afternoon I took the b'y out blueberry pickin' with me. I smoothed out a blanket and lay him down on it. He screeched on the blanket, his little fists tryin' to grab hold to the air. By now, I was used to the noise, and went 'bout me work. I picked through the bushes with me fingers, and I minds I started havin' a daydream. I don't know what 'twas 'bout, that being so long ago. 'Tis more that I remembers I was thinkin' 'bout somethin', and listenin' to the sounds of the berries plunk into me pot, an ol' crow cawing up in a tree. Then I recalls thinkin' how strange 'twas that I could hear me berries, that I would even notice a squawkin' bird, and the hair stood up on me arms.

"I turned 'round to the blanket, ye sees, and 'twas empty. There was a dip where Alek had been lyin' and when I put me hand to it, 'twas still warm. Well, darkness was startin' to drop all 'round, and me first thought was the fairies. I knowed that fairies come at dusk, and there I was, stupid as a bloody boot, out at worst kind of time.

"I dropped me pot, berries spilled right down into me boots, and I tore out of the woods screamin' out the fairies got me b'y. Then, when I was near home, up behind the shed, I shut me mouth right quick. For, ye sees, there was me Thomas, drunker than I ever seen him, hunched over the b'y. He had a flat rock held high in the air over the child's head, and the rock was shakin'. I was too 'fraid to speak, lest I startle him and he drops the rock on the b'y. And I was too 'fraid not to speak, so I whispered his name, 'Thomas.' And that rock stopped shakin', and he brought it down to his hips. He turned to me, and started bawlin' hisself like ye never seen a grown man bawl. 'Twas right pitiful. And the curious thing was, Alek stopped his cryin'. Sprawled out on that ol' cold rock, 'bout as close to death as I cares to ever see, he stared at his father, and made not a single peep.

"He never started talkin' till he was near five. So we knowed there was somethin' queer 'bout him right from the get go. Then, when he opened his mouth to utter his first words, he started in 'bout confession. I knowed he could remember. Some kids remembers their birth, ye knows. I don't think Alek knowed 'bout that, but I's sure as I's sittin' here, he knowed 'bout how he almost died. He knowed, maid, he knowed."

Moments after Arva left for the hospital, Clive heard a letter shoot in through the mail slot. When he retrieved it, he had to squint to see it was postmarked from Rosedale. In the upper left-hand corner, someone had placed a stamp with perfect precision, equal distances from either edge. At first glance, Clive thought the image on the stamp was of a woman's face and hair, but on closer inspection he saw the tiny white house, windows on either side of a centered front door darkened with orange, curling flames licking up in the background. Five cents was what it costs to deliver some news.

He tore it open, crumpled the envelope and tossed it in the kitchen sink. There was only a short note. Snobbish loops and slender letters suggested the penmanship of a patronizing woman, but it was clearly signed, 'Yours, Uncle Harry.'

Clive,

We have thoroughly enjoyed our adventure, but have decided to settle in the blooming community of Rosedale. Though our home has been sold in the bay, we will be keeping the residence where you are presently staying until we see fit as to sell it. We cannot guarantee a stretch of time, so do seek out alternative accommodations at your earliest convenience. Of course, we will be collecting my treasured antiques. Movers have been scheduled for the first Tuesday in June. Please do not assist in the packing. They will take everything except for the mattresses. Repeat – I do not want the mattresses.

Clive felt it first in his teeth. Not more than an hour had passed before a massive dirty van crunched up the drive and rattled everything in sight with its bunged rev. First a clang of the metal knocker, then two men unlocked the door and entered before Clive had a chance to answer or hide, he had not decided which. Both were wearing crisp white overalls, one with the name 'Top Dog' embroidered over his heart, the other with the name 'Workhorse.'

"Oh sorry, guy," Top Dog said. "We wasn't expecting nobody here." The mover automatically began to assess the amount of work. Not too much, though the house was a bloody mess. An empty whiskey bottle stuck to the entry way table, stubbed cigarettes spilled out of the sculpted green glass ashtray, clothes and dirty plates were scattered, a half-peeled banana was squished into the rug. He had seen worse. Top Dog whispered to his partner, "Jesus, ye never knows how they lives on the other side."

"Don't mind us," said Workhorse. "Ye won't even notice we're here."

"Guy, ye looks like shit," Top Dog said to the man who must be the teacher nephew. Clive's face was the colour of old sidewalk snow; a dingy mutt had lifted its leg to create the holes for eyes. "Can we get somethin' for ye?"

Clive moved to the lip of the chaise lounge. "Either one of ye's got a fag?"

"Here, take 'em all," said Top Dog, tossing him a pack. "Got a carton under me seat in the van." He slid open his box of Salty Dog matches and struck up a light for Clive. "There ye go."

"Ye knows," said Clive. "I hasn't seen neither rabbit since I been here."

"No?" replied Top Dog. "Ye likes to hunt?"

"Not a sheep neither. Hasn't seen a one. Or a goat."

"Ye likes sheep?"

"Where I growed up, they just used to wander 'round, goin' into anybody's yard, eatin' up what they liked. Ye'd find shiny black buttons all over the place."

"Isn't that somethin'."

"They was all branded, though. Owners' names stamped right on beneath all that maggoty wool. But they had the run of the place. Still do."

"Well Guy, that's some kind of lucky sheep."

"When we was kids we used to try and grab on. Get a ride out of it. Sometimes ye'd catch hold, then ye'd get the women after ye with their brooms. I minds I got more than one crack over the head for even havin' a go."

"That sounds like a hoot, not much of a time for the sheep though."

"Not a fence 'round to keep 'em in. The Walled City, 'twas called. I thinks Joey called it that."

"Joey?"

"Yeah. Smallwood hisself. Been meanin' to see him since I come to town."

"Ye knows him?"

"He's a real short fella. Those stone fences should never of been called walls."

"I guesses that's the way he saw it."

"Or maybe he was talkin' 'bout somethin' else. Maybe he had that place all figured out. Once yer in the cove, he saw 'twas hard to find yer way out. And once yer out, once yer really out, 'tis damn unlikely ye'll ever be let back in."

Workhorse stood by as Top Dog nodded, picked up the pack of cigarettes, and lit one. He was always acting like some big shot counselor; too bad his packing skills didn't compare. "Come on," he said to Top Dog. "We ain't got all day, b'y. Let's get a move on." Workhorse smiled. He liked saying that. It sounded witty.

After five hours work, they had the home taken apart. Every piece of solid wood furniture had been wrapped in quilted mover's blankets, stowed neatly in the van. Above the fireplace mantle, a square of vibrant wallpaper had replaced the sitting portrait of Helen Mercer's mother. Good dishes, candleholders, even the glass ashtray had been emptied, wiped with a damp cloth, and packed into a cardboard box. Clive moved from chaise lounge to paisley chair, from paisley chair to kitchen table, from kitchen table to braided rug, and finally to a corner in the empty living room.

"Good luck to ye, Guy," Top Dog said on his way out the door. "Better days ahead, me son. Better days ahead."

The men left behind pressboard furniture, cheap glasses and plastic plates, towels that could have been used for rags, sheets from the beds, and, following clear instruction, the mattresses. In the center of the dining room, they had forgotten the orange bubbled bowl that had once been filled with spicy chicken bones. Clive inched across the empty floor, sliding on his rear, his curled fingers dragging a whiskey bottle by its elegant neck. He wrapped his bare legs around the bowl, so that the cool glass was touching his thighs, an edge pressed into his groin. For a moment, he set the liquor aside and used his shaky hands for caressing the enormous candy dish, feeling the tiny mounds ripple underneath his fingertips. It was soothing for him, the predictability in the texture. So he stayed that way, body not budging, save for the exploring fingers, until darkness stretched across the front bay window and dissolved him.

"Me dear," Doris said to Arva, "do ye mind waitin' here 'til I goes to the toilet?"

"Go on," Arva replied. "Take your time."

As soon as Doris stepped out into the hallway, Arva opened up her purse. Reaching in, she found the folded paper. Inside was a leaf of the thinnest fabric, dried, yellow, and tough. "It's magical," her mother had said. "The caul can heal better than any medicine." So, that morning three years ago, when Rose had been digging the hole to bury the placenta, Arva had plucked up the gauzy membrane, brought it home, and left it to dry.

Arva placed the parchment-like hankie into Alek's hand. It would be thrown away by nurses in a few hours, but perhaps it would do some good.

Coincidence or not, six days later, he opened his eyes.

"A drink of warm milk," he said. "I's right parched for a taste of warm milk."

14

Ned discovered Henry on the beach — my husband's bare skin flickered with silvery fish. The scene was arresting, like a strikingly lewd portrait. Late night accident, they called it. That it was, my dear. That it was.

Shortly thereafter, the singing stopped. Or, maybe not. Perhaps the other noises simply drowned out my song.

I heard a hermit crab clamour when ousted from its pebbled crevice, and a jellyfish moan like a dying wolf as its edges withered on the sun-warmed shore. Once, I even made out a lost strand of kelp, pleading, pleading, as it was tossed about, piteously decimated into shreds.

There was absolutely nothing I could do. The cries were relentless. I thought I would lose my mind.

"Ye've made a friggin' mess a' yer life, me zun. A bloody friggin' mess."

It was his father's raspy voice bounding left and right between the stubborn panels Clive had constructed in his head. And since the night of the accident, the echo followed him everywhere.

Clive was fired from Bishop Field boys' school the day after his brother Alek returned home to Upper Island Cove. He did not fault the school board for his dismissal, would have done it himself, in fact, if he were in the position. To varying degrees, he had been drunk since the accident, sometimes pleasantly, sometimes sloppily, and sometimes aggressively. Principal Leonard was forgiving, he knew the power of drink, and simply told Clive to get himself cleaned up. But Clive did not submit, and when he broke a student's nose, Leonard canned him on the spot.

It was difficult for Clive to teach while sober, and additionally challenging while intoxicated. Focus was compromised, clarity was reduced, and any tenuous reins of control were entirely released. Mayhem often ensued. Clive had seen the boys in the hallway imitating his swagger, how he kept the back of his hand to the wall for security. They loved to mimic his accent, intensified as it had become, though they never could get it quite right.

Then in the classroom, when they stopped listening, Clive knew it had all come undone.

One afternoon, he was reciting John Keats, but he could only manage the first line - "When I have fears that I may cease to be." Hearing those words of despair, Clive's voice came apart like a stale biscuit dropped to the floor. He tried to persevere, but was quickly overwhelmed, and slumped by the chalkboard, plump tears coursing through his stubble, splashing onto his dusty shoes.

At the sight of his teacher bawling, Cecil O'Leary hollered, "Geez man, get a grip on yourself."

Clive never heard it. Instead, something entirely different rumbled through his mind. "Get yer lousy h'arse h'off de floor, ye friggin' muck-h'up." So he thought he was justified when he sprang to his feet, pounced on the lippy bastard, smashed his perfect pug nose into the open anthology gracing the boy's desktop.

Yes. On second thought, it was no wonder he was let go.

But getting fired was not enough to snap Clive out of his hazy funk. He continued to drink, partly because he felt bad, and partly because he wanted to feel better.

The following week, he never changed his clothing, shaved, or gave any reflection to the merit of a toothbrush. One night, he threw up mouthfuls of acidy fish and brewis in Aunt Helen's orange glass bubbled bowl, and when he awoke before dawn, his memory failed him so he called Melvin Buckle over to check the house for vagrants.

Each day, he guzzled more and more whiskey until he could barely see. When he sobered, he attempted food in hopes of weakening the racket vaulting between his temples. Arva would not cook for him, would barely even look at him, so he fried up great greasy omelets on his own. He mangled eggs with grubby fingers, tossed in hastily chopped onions, and corned beef, the formed meat not diced, but pinched off the sides of the can with a dirty-nailed thumb. Clive never took a plate down from the cupboard, but ate the stuck-on mash directly from the pan, and after a few morsels, he would throw the works into the kitchen sink, stomach duly turned.

During rare moments of lucidity, he reflected on his brother. Even though Alek was out of the hospital, Clive's guilt was well rooted. Whenever he thought of that night, his gut balled into a fist and he was forced to drink to loosen it. He blamed himself for the accident, and rightly so. He never should have brought Alek to Gower Street. It was like bringing a boy to a peep show, and creating in him a disturbing mixture of disgust and longing that was certain to hamper a pure sleep. To his credit, Clive had not seen Kate since.

Clive also took time to consider his wife. Thoughts of her he could grind his teeth on, and he did until his jaw was sore. Ever since they had married, she was missing, checked absent from his daily class. He found her numb, as though someone she trusted had shoved her out into a blustery storm, bolted the door, and ignored her frantic banging. He even tried to force a reaction once by calling her 'Lolly,' but it was a dumb, predictable prod, and she never even responded. Clive remembered that night on the mountain, dried grass in her hair, innocent eyes flashing. It was she who had proposed up there. Surely that meant something.

One afternoon, while Clive picked at his teeth with a piece torn from a book corner, he had a moment of insight that would have escaped him if his brain were sober, arrogant, and full of defense. The woman he married never honestly wanted him. She had wanted someone, that was for certain, and he was the first arsehole available. It was suddenly clear to him Arva was not his, and the harder he prodded at his mouth with the folded paper, the more certain he became that his wife belonged to another. As if on cue, the damp piece of cover jammed between his front teeth and drew blood from an under-nourished torn gum.

Then, as he rinsed the warm metal flavour away with liquor and looked out towards the shared lawn of the duplex, he saw the gesture. It was all there before him, and he felt like a stupid idiot for having missed it for so long.

The precise instant that it happened, Clive was in the front room with the windows cracked open all around. Bright sunlight filtered in through the dirty glass, swiped with grime on the outside, layer upon layer of children's fingerprints on the inside. He could see Barb and Wallace Mugford standing just a few feet from the oak tree. They were always there, heads tucked close together like sly-faced connivers appraising their next strategic move.

"There's talk of starting up an archaeology department. What do you think of that?"

Barb knew not to get too excited, as the University had been broaching this subject for years. "It sounds promising, Wally."

"Apparently they've got this young archaeologist on the string. He's got some new-fangled theory on the Beothuk extinction. Word is he's already completed a fair amount of substantial research."

"Really? Well, that sounds even more promising." And it did.

"Could you imagine it, darling? I'd love to get my trowel dirty. Of course you'd come along on any dig. Right by my side."

"That would be nice, Wally. But, in the meantime, how's about doing a little trowel-work here, and planting these petunias." Barb placed a small plant in Wallace's hand. She loved his rambling, but it could go on forever. He was a man who needed direction.

Clive leaned forward to watch Wallace get onto his hands and knees and do exactly what he was told. He forced a thin handheld shovel through the groundcover and into soft earth. Dropping the flower in, he patted soil around it, reached up for a second plant, and began to build a carpet of red between a mess of tulips.

At the sight of it, Clive blew air out his nostrils. Every one of Wallace's movements seemed educated, precise. Then Clive permitted himself to re-think, and decided instead there was nothing more feminine than a man gardening. He hated how every spring Wallace and Barb's side of the lawn looked like Holland, his side like Hell.

Next, Arva appeared at the side of the house. Clive still found it difficult to recognize her, black tufts of hair, neatly shorn like his mother's. Now she appeared untroubled some-how, more independent, even further away from him. These days she wouldn't even look him in the eye, saved any softness she could muster for those two damn children whose names reliably escaped him in the best of times.

The boys emerged from behind Arva and bounded across the grass. Thomas ran straight for Barb. "Bar-bar!" he cried. With a grunt, she lifted him, and he wrapped his legs around her waist. Henry began to tumble, rolling in scattered sprigs of grass, twisting left and right like a dog trying to scratch an impatient itch between its shoulder blades.

From the window, Clive watched their mouths move. He was surprised that he could see with such ease, and promptly poured another serving of whiskey to toast his youthful eye-sight. As he was dribbling the last drop, something caught his attention out of the corner of his bloodshot eye. It began when his wife sneezed - a simple sneeze that required 'Bless you,' and nothing more.

But Wallace went to her. He planted his arm around her slender shoulder, rubbed it up and down so that her chest jiggled slightly. Clive had to lay down his drink and rub his eyes. Arm around her shoulder. Yes, there it was. And then the gesture. Innocent enough to the average onlooker, but Clive prided him-self on being more astute. He watched Wallace reach into his shirt pocket, pull out a crisp hankie, and pass it to Arva. Clive zoned in on his wife's hands, as they teased the white fabric from Wallace's fingers, tugging the hankie ever so gently, ever so playfully from his grasp. And then Wallace had the audacity to resist, Clive was certain of it. So Arva had to caress his hand open, blow on his knuckles as though he were holding dice in a board game, until he reluctantly released, and the adoring con-nection was broken. Arva dabbed at her nose like a delicate flower, and still his arm was there, his vulture's head lunging dangerously close to hers. She probably smelled his sour Ph.D. breath on her tanned face.

Clive noticed his hand had picked up the whiskey again, and a vise grip on the glass threatened to crush it. He swallowed the remainder in one hard gulp, and laid the glass down carefully. It would be just his luck to cut himself, and who would hire him on as a teacher with visible parts sliced to smithereens, unable to write on a chalkboard. Clive knocked his knuckle on his skull. He was always thinking, even when he was sloshed.

Once he had safeguarded his future by way of protecting his hands, his next idea was to pound the professor into a pulp. The altercation he conjured up almost had a delicious flavour, and Clive's mouth salivated. After knocking Wallace down, eyeglasses splintered, Clive envisioned himself raising and dropping the heavy heel of a boot into Wallace's erudite nose. A bloody river would gush out from the hairy holes of both ears. Then Clive would grip the planting shovel, and with the metal edge, he would smash Wallace's teeth one by one until there was nothing left but razor-sharp shards of reddened enamel. Though perhaps the professor wore a bridge. Hmmm. His fantasy skipped a beat.

No. Time to re-focus. Clive Thomas Mercer was not a barbarian, and besides, he was far too wobbly on his feet to take on any man, even one with a drip-name like Wallace.

So he went to the bedroom he shared with his deceitful wife. He began to go through her things with no method. Simple speed was his goal. Out of plastic bins flew socks and stockings, underwear, clean white bras. He took a deep whiff of a pale green slip with a tempting bow, trying to smell an unfamiliar aftershave over the lye. No such luck. Jeans and sweaters were tossed from the closet, and an ironed pink blouse torn from its hanger. In a pile by the nightstand, he rummaged through letters neatly penned from his mother to his wife, "Dear Arva, I hope this letter finds you and the boys well." A quick scan. No query from Doris about her first son. Clive came across Henry's scribbling of a hundred-leg spider, Joseph Crane's bible. He threw them all across the floor, and stepped with his big boot on the sketch as he began to scour though Helen's books, needing to find evidence of something tucked away between the pages.

When he sat on Arva's trunk at the bottom of the bed, his eyes roamed around the ransacked room. Clive was nearing surrender when the perception of the cold trunk persuaded itself up through his rump, through his spinal cord, and into his thought processes. He stood at once. With a booted foot, he slammed the catch. Then again. The lock, never having been properly closed, fell away with the force and rattled to the floor with a muted clunk.

Clive was on his knees, hands and forearms diving in without restraint. He grabbed their wedding quilt and hurled the heavy mass onto the bed. There were old woolen sweaters in his way, a crocheted runner, a yellow dress so thin he poked his fingers right through the fabric. When he came upon a photo of a stern plump woman and a thin man, he stopped. The two were not touching, their captured images did not even overlap, and the man appeared to be stepping out of the photo just as it had been snapped.

The woman was holding a baby, though it was engulfed in such fleshy arms, pressed so tightly into her bountiful chest, the infant was barely visible. In fact, for all Clive knew, she could have been cradling a cabbage. On closer inspection, he identified some features that resembled his wife, the shape of her eyes, the hairline. But the man, with his foot treading backwards toward a latticed stoop, never offered a single trait. He was completely unrecognizable. Clive creased the photo, shoved it into the back pocket of his jeans.

And the hands continued to burrow.

Up in the air he threw dozens of lacy snowflake decorations and they descended like a sudden flurry. But beneath that last obstruction, he retrieved the reward for his efforts. A pale green accounting ledger, tied around with shoelaces, knots upon knots upon knots. He tugged, but the laces would not snap, and biting with his teeth only caused them to shrink with moisture, shut him out even more. Clive remembered his pocketknife. He yanked it from the black case on his belt, flipped it open, and sliced through the cording with three hard swipes. His blade was dull, though he had just sharpened it a week ago.

His fingers could not move fast enough. They skidded over the cover and into the first page of the ledger. There were no numbers, no calculations, no sign of any sort of accounting. On the top right of the first page was the name 'Ruby House,' the capital letters swooped and curled, a shaky line not quite underneath, but cutting through them all. It was difficult to focus. The sunlight was waning. He managed a line, but immediately clapped the ledger shut. Christ, he thought, this would need whiskey, and the house was bone dry.

Clive shoved the book up under his arm, kicked his way out

of the room, out of the house, and stumbled past his wife and children still standing on the lawn. He was heading down the street towards Badcock's. There he could read without being disturbed. He had a feeling what he held in his hand would unravel his wife down to a single strand of useless nubby wool.

Arva never noticed her husband storm out of the house. She only saw the ledger as it strode across the grass, moving swiftly, as though under neither arm at all. It was not unwilling, never kicked up any dust and dirt along the drive, and when it passed onto the sidewalk, it did so with a purposeful march. Coming upon a corner, the ledger took the turn sharply, decisively, but not before it abandoned its severed binding. The knotted brown lace drifted through space and fell into the thick layer of sludge coating a storm drain.

"What's he up to now?" Barb asked.

"In some kind of hurry to get somewhere, I'd say," Wallace replied.

"Too bad he didn't think to put on either shoe," Barb said. Then, to Arva, "I don't know how you got mixed up with the likes of that in the first place."

A strangled sob oozed from Arva's mouth, and her knees buckled.

"Oh my heavens," Barb said. "Let's go in." She reached to take Arva by the elbow. "A cup of tea."

"My ledger," Arva whispered, staring at the corner where Clive was last seen.

"Has he got something belonging to you?" Barb asked. "I can send Wally after him."

Arva put her hands flat across her diaphragm and felt her ribs swell as air expanded her lungs. "No, let him be," she said. "Let him be."

Arva collected the boys, fed them cereal for dinner, and put them into their bed. Then she returned to the kitchen, washed the bowls, placed them back into the barren cupboards. She ran her hand along the spotless countertop, rapped her knuckles on the edge of the sink until they were sore. The hollow sound resonated through the empty home.

Fill it up, she thought. And then she began to bake.

In a beige ceramic dish, she dumped cupfuls of flour, each mound holding its shape for just a moment until it buckled under gravity. Then she added the exact amount of salt, gauged in her knowledgeable palm, a daub of margarine, a whole egg. Dry yeast foamed in a glass-measuring cup filled with sweetened warm water. Mixing all the ingredients together, she gradually transformed the sticky mass into smooth elastic dough.

Moving on. She spun molasses through a heap of granulated sugar, eggs, flour, margarine, and created a batter at the end of her worn wooden spoon. Each drop cookie was released from a calculated height and they plopped to the greased sheets in desirable mounds.

With the heels of her hands, she flattened soda dough on a floured board, and cut perfect diamonds. Every piece, dappled with dozens of juicy raisins, was precisely placed on a pan.

She scalded fresh milk on the stove, heaped in porridge, cinnamon. When the first loaves finished baking, she would have a second batch ready to go in.

Using a dull blade, she scraped the last stick of butter from the dish in the fridge, and began cutting it through icing sugar, flour, and cornstarch to make shortbread. After rolling one-inch balls in her palms, she used the tines of a fork to squash them with a decorative crisscross.

By three o'clock in the morning, she had used up every last trace of the staples in Aunt Helen's kitchen. Every bowl, dish, and dented baking sheet left behind by the movers was dirtied and piled in the sink. Racks of the countertops were laden with baked goods, layers of sweets, slightly burnt loaves of bread. A film of flour cloaked every conceivable surface.

Arva leaned onto the countertop, put her hands to her mouth, took a deep breath. Something tickled her throat. Then a girlish giggle blossomed, and within moments she was laughing hysterically, her body bent from sharp pains knitting up her sides. As she laughed herself down to the linoleum, tears formed clean rivers through the dusting of flour on her cheeks. Laughing into a tight ball, she hid her head between her knees. She was unable to contain it. And with a great peal of laughter she unfurled like a fiddlehead, until she was lying flat on her back on the kitchen floor. Putting her arms above her head, she rolled over and over the hard surface. Spilled ingredients dredged her dress, her skin.

When she hit the stove, she lay motionless. Even though the laughter subsided, her mouth remained locked in a startling expression. Every tooth was visible, her gums besides.

Then there was a flicker. The electricity, with payment months in arrears, was finally severed. And in the sweet darkness, her mind high on the bakery smell, Arva thought she could hear a humming from her smile.

"Investigate? Ye must be cracked," Chief Constable Norm Buckle said to his son Melvin. Then, to himself, "How in the Hell did I produce such a horse's arse?" He flipped the ledger closed and shoved it across the table with a whoosh. "What ye got there is the works of a real nutcase. Nothin' more, nothin' less. And what woman don't dream 'bout poppin' off her husband at some time or another? Just go ask yer mother."

Melvin slipped the ledger into the front of his bomber jacket. His father didn't know his ass from his elbow when it came to a criminal mind. Melvin zipped and patted his chest. Maybe Lucky Power at *The Evening Telegram* would have a different opinion.

Late the next morning, as Arva prepared to leave, Clive came in and sat on the bed. His hair had fallen into his bloodshot eyes, and he smelled like someone's favourite ashtray. After catching only a few hours morning sleep while leaning against the side of the refrigerator, he was still drunk. Willing his tangled tongue to straighten, he pictured an iron, plenty of steam.

"Ye knows, we ain't had one decent talk since we got married? Not a one."

She never responded.

He patted the bedspread. "Sit. Tell me somethin' 'bout yerself I don't already know."

It was a weak attempt, he knew, but maybe she would bite.

No. No chance. Instead she continued to methodically fill the trunk, rolling her clothes into tidy sausages, placing them in, never cramming.

As he watched her, he suddenly felt a rush of love for her simplicity, how she moved through the house like an old reliable ghost. There was nothing wicked about her. She was not continually fraught with emotion like some girls, bursting into tears at imagined slights. And she never veered close to that irritating female mania whenever there was a joyful event. Arva was pleasantly dim, accepting, never inquisitive – appealing enough, but not so much as to attract another man's attention. In other words, the ideal woman.

"Now, then," he said. "Stop that packin' business. We'll get through this work." Damn his tongue.

Then Arva laughed. Not a bitter pill sort of snicker, but a whole-hearted chuckle of exhilaration and reward.

He had not expected that. Anger bubbled in a blink.

"Christ," he spat, his saliva acidic. "Ye got nar tongue in yer head, or wha?"

Bringing his hands to his mouth, he chewed at his knuckles. "Ah, I gives ye a week. Wait n' see. Ye'll be crawlin' back to me." He chewed off a piece of dried skin, shot it to the floor with a blast of air. "Ye don't know what ye got here."

Or maybe she did. A real muck-up. He chewed harder.

"Yer goin' nowhere without me," he continued. "Ye knows that, me dear, don't ye." It wasn't a question.

She calmly closed the lid of her trunk and stood to face him. His stomach soured as it always did when she looked at him directly. Then she reached down, took the trunk by both handles, and with considerable ease, lifted it right off the ground.

"It's a feather," she said with amazement. "Just like a feather."

Then she carried it down over the stairs without making a single grunt, and out into the yard where a sky the colour of dirty gulls was releasing its first snowflakes. There would be a spring storm. Strokes of white had already been painted between the petunias.

Clive could hear her singing, "I don't want your maggoty fish. That's no good for winter."

"Don't go thinkin' I don't know what's goin' on," he hollered after her. "I knows what yer all about, me lovey. I've known since day one."

With those words, a sickening sense of doubt washed over

him. He knew nothing. And had known nothing since the moment he drove past her on the road. The very day she ruined his life when she casually peered over the folded lip of a brown paper bag.

15

Knowing nothing, I waited for some sign.

And sure enough, everything was answered while I was sitting in the outhouse. An unusual place for enlightenment, yes, but mine was never to question.

I peered though the cutout moon to see Bette Mackay on our stoop. She had a lovely bottle of squashberry jelly in her hand, and the way she held it up to the sun, light dividing her face into a rosy gem, I was certain she knew all. After he tromped back the way she had come, I tore a glossy page of the catalogue and threw it down the dank hole. I could see the frothy waves crashing underneath. Then, as I watched, the wind grabbed my very page, and without a moment of consideration, sucked it out to sea.

There you have it, plain as day. It was time for us to leave.

In an early morning taxi, a fresh copy of the provincial newspaper traveled out to Upper Island Cove on the pleats of Mary Lynch's tartan skirt. No sooner had it reached Junior Lynch's kitchen table than Patty scooped it up and headed down to Mercer's shop where her husband, Frank Smith, was mending his net. Dot Jones tore it from Frank's fingers before he had finished reading aloud the second paragraph and carried it to Amanda Adams who put the kettle on before even taking a glimpse.

"Utter nonsense," Amanda said. "They don't got much to be reportin' these days."

"That poor girl," Dot said, shaking her head. "No wonder

she's always been a bit queer."

"With a mother like that," Amanda said. "Ye can imagine, now."

"Here, here. I haves a look." Dot pulled the paper closer. "Almighty Lord," she said, her finger smudging the print. "Just look what it says here. 'Evidence handed over to officials by her husband.'"

"If ye'd keep yer hands from messin' it right up, p'raps I can get a glimpse," Amanda said, wrenching the paper out from underneath Dot's finger. "Have mercy. That man ain't got his head screwed on all the way."

"Never did, me dear."

"Ye called that one, maid. And did ye know he saw Alek not once when he was to the General?"

"Well, that ain't the best of it." Dot leaned in and whispered, "Lorna told me, and she got it from Doreen who got it straight from Doris herself, that young Arva's face was a real mess. Lorna says Clive knocked her up side the head with a huge junk of wood."

"For the love of Jesus," Amanda said. "Ye got to be kiddin' me."

"No, me dear. That's the gospel truth." Dot glanced upwards. "Strike me down now if it ain't." She waited a moment, then nodded to Amanda. "There ye goes."

"I never heard the likes."

"A real lout, that one."

"That he is. A piece of work. Though I ain't surprised one bit."

The second taxi traveling to Upper Island Cove that day carried Arva and her two sons. Arva sat on the hump in the backseat, her purse gripped with two hands. In it, she carried a brass key, and more than once, she slipped her hand through the opening until her fingers met with metal, and she breathed a sigh of relief. She had two months, Alice had told her, just two months until she had to pay some kind of fee for use of what was without a doubt a desirable rental property.

With heads resting on folded elbows, Thomas and Henry slept in their snowsuits on the slushy floor mats. Each had a hand loosely wrapped around an ankle of Arva's boots. Near Henry's feet, a quarter-sized hole had rusted through, the carpeting disintegrated, and a continual icy wind whistled in.

When the taxi first groaned down the drive, Arva ignored

Clive as he leaned against the doorframe, mouth gaping, tongue retired. Instead, she focused on the driver's hat. A knitted salt and pepper, it offered covering to the matted sprigs poking out from underneath. Please Lord, she had thought, let him keep that cap on. As though to spite her, he cranked the heat and cast his hat aside. His full head of hair was glued down with grease. A stench like drying seal pelts filled the enclosed space, and Arva's stomach swelled. She positioned herself so that the thin stream of air was blowing right at her face. Concentrating on the blur of pavement as the roadway rushed by, she conceived God had constructed that hole for her.

As the road sloped towards Upper Island Cove, snow that had been enveloping the car let up and the sky cleared. The smattering of homes, the jagged rocks, the colourful dories turned bottom up were all disguised in clean generous curves. There was nothing so startling as layers of fresh snow in May.

Arva sighed, her heart brimming over with a foreign feeling she could only have attributed to familiarity. "Ease in, ease out," her mother always said when they fled a harbour. "Never look back. Never leave a trace." And here Arva was, moving through it, towards a well-known place, breaking every rule along the way.

She nudged the boys softly and they climbed onto the seat. When they turned onto Main Road, the car fishtailed, wheels skidded, Thomas and Henry held onto Arva and cried gleefully.

Henry knocked on the window and said, "Ah-yick."

Sure enough, Alek was riding in a wooden cart, the front wheel replaced with a ski from an old toboggan. Dangling out over, his lower legs were well-hidden inside dirty casts, gray woolen socks yanked on over the exposed toes. With Alf pushing, they cut lines through the snow, sliding left and right across the lane.

"Get a job, will ye?" the taxi driver mumbled as he leaned on the horn. "Get a friggin' job."

When Alf noticed Arva, he put down the cart, saluted, then bowed deeply at his waist. Alek vigorously waved both hands in the air, and the taxi cruised past, continued up the slushy gravel road.

Junior Lynch raised his mitt to Arva as her taxi drove by. A tiny blond-haired head popped up in the window and waved back.

"Why that looked some lot like Lyle Young," Junior said to his wife.

"Right ye is, Junior," Lorna replied. "And that's the last word ye'll be sayin' 'bout it." It was fine to know the truth, but it was another thing altogether to talk about it.

Inside Old Man Crane's home, there were far too many drafts to allow for staleness. Instead, the home smelled fresh and clean, like saltwater air, although a fine layer of dust had settled on the countertop and table. Berated by a relentless brackish mist, the windows in the front room had crystallized, obscuring the ocean view.

"Tummy," Henry said.

"One minute," Arva replied. She stared up at the ceiling. There was not a bite of food in the house. She tapped the boys on their backsides and said, "Go. Poke around."

A gentle tap on the back door, the hinges squeaking, and Nora Parsons appeared in the porch wearing a tangerine-coloured zippered sweat suit, a matching hat and sweater knit from the softest-looking wool.

"Saw yer taxi," she said. "Thought I'd bring ye up a loaf of me bread."

"Come in, come in," Arva said.

"Alright, me dear."

As Arva drew out a chair for Nora, she realized she was still wearing her long winter coat. After she hung it on a nail in the pantry, she said to Nora, "I'm sorry, but I haven't a thing to offer you."

"Then that's perfect," Nora said, smiling. "There ain't a thing I needs."

Henry was in the hallway doorframe. "Tummy," he repeated.

"Here, love," Nora said to Arva, handing over a warm package wrapped in a cuptowel. "Give him a bite of this."

Arva sliced two thick cuts of bread and gave one to each of the boys. Henry held up his empty left hand for a second piece, and Arva said, "Eyes bigger than stomach again, I see."

"Take a spell for yerself, maid," Nora said, as she sat down at the table. "'Tis a long run from the city on a wintry day."

"Yes," Arva said. "It is."

"Can ye believe this weather?" Nora said, lighting a cigarette. "Just startin' to get comfortable with thoughts of Spring, and then the likes of this smacks ye right in the bloody face."

"I'd welcome some warm weather," Arva said.

"That and then some," Nora said. She opened her full lips, let the smoke waft out and ripple over her face. She looked up to the mountain, took a deep drag, and watched a group of children sliding down on canvas squares. "Just as well I be's the one to tell ye," she continued when Arva sat down next to her. "They all knows."

"Know?"

"'Twas in *The Telegram*. All 'bout it." Nora leaned in towards Arva and whispered. "That business with yer mother. Gone 'round like wildfire. No chance of keepin' somethin' under wraps in these parts, me dear." She puffed on her cigarette as though life itself was surging through it. "Sure I even knows when Junior Lynch is bound up. Lorna's on 'bout it to Dot Jones, what a time she's havin', he now, with all his gripin'."

As Arva listened to Nora, her face began to crinkle and she put her head in her hands. "I'm honestly not sure how I'm going to manage."

Nora got up from her chair, took a saucer down from the cupboard, stubbed out her cigarette. As she took her spot back at the table, she wagged her finger rapidly. "How ye won't manage is doin' what I done. Stayin' with a dirty good-for-nothin' bastard who thinks all ye wants to be doin' is takin' a gander at the back of his flyin' hand. No, maid. That ain't managin'. That's givin' up. Ye haves to get tough. Yer young, me dear, ye got that goin' for ye. Ye'll find yer way."

"I don't even know what I can do."

"Ye'll find somethin'. No worries 'bout that. Pick berries for a livin', if that's what gets ye through. Think, me dear. Think. How did yer Mother get by?"

"She was a seamstress. We made do with that. I could take in a little sewing, I guess."

"There ye go, now. And if ye likes, ye can have me Singer."

"Your machine? Don't you need it?

"Not no more," Nora said. "I'm done with sewin'. Over.

Finished. I's sewed enough for me lifetime, and likely someone else's lifetime as well." She glanced out the kitchen window, fixed her eyes on the rocky ledge. "'Tis a funny thing, ye knows, how ye can find yerself at the end of a bolt of bright orange velour."

"Yes. Well." Arva said.

"That's alright if ye don't get me, now. Some day ye will." She patted Arva's hand. "'Tis settled then. I'll get Junior or Alfie to bring me Singer 'round."

The porch door groaned open and snapped to. Alf was in the doorway.

"Speak of the Devil hisself," Nora said, "and He's right up in yer face."

"Afternoon Nora," Alf said. "Arva, stopped up to see what ye needs. I got a bundle of splits for ye."

"Come in, Alf," Arva said. "Where's Alek?"

"Ah, I got tired of haulin' him 'round, so I heaved him in a snow drift, left him."

"You what?"

"Just tuggin' yer leg, me dear. I dropped him on Kipper Hussey's doorstep. Alek's taken a shine to his lass, Jeanette. That bang to his head seemed to knock the queer right clear of him."

Arva smiled. "Alf, a cup of tea. I was just about to make some."

"That'd be right nice, missus," he said. "Let me cart in those splits, a few junks of wood. Not July yet, maid, so ye'll be after a fire to warm yerself." He knocked his knuckles on the wood-stove, smirked. "And how's ye goin' make me a drop of tea with an ice cold stove?"

He cocked his head, winked, and was back out the door.

"Ye knows," Nora whispered. "Alf hasn't taken a drink since Alek got runned over? And that's somethin' for Alf."

"Yes. It is. He did like to drink."

"Not always, me dear," Nora said, her voice lowered. "Not 'til after Margie died, and their baby girl. She was Junior's little sister. Margie Lynch. Well, Margie Jones, by the end of it. A thin girl, turn her sideways and ye'd be bound to miss her."

"Alf was married?"

"That he was. Lovelier couple ye'd be hard pressed to find. Died havin' their little one, she did. Lord, she was all baby, not one speck of fat on her. Took the good out of her, I s'pose. The baby made it through though, hung on for near a week. Doris had Alek at the time, so she was helpin' to feed Alf's. Not that Doris didn't have her hands full with Alek, mind ye, but ye do the best ye can, right?"

"I never knew," Arva said.

"'Twas then he took up the drink," Nora said. "But ask anyone, he's never missed a fit day out on the water. No, me dear."

"No."

"P'raps cause Alek was the same age as his wee one, he took a real likin' to the boy. Looks after him now so good, ye'd think he was his son."

Nora was cut short when Alf returned to the kitchen with an armload of splits and spruce logs. He began stoking the stove. "They's right sogged," he said. "I'll work me magic." And in a few moments, cracks and pops of damp wood burning, the smell of sizzling turpentine perfumed the air.

Doris and Rose arrived next, stomping their feet in the porch, removing wet boots, meandering into the kitchen.

"Saw yer run pullin' up," Rose said, as she laid a blackened pot on the woodstove. "Had a load of fish stew on, thought ye could use a bite of dinner. I's always cookin' way too much, what now with Lolly…" She stopped, and Doris stepped in.

"I bet ye got neither stain of jam in this house, but I sees ye got a bit of bread," she said, "And now, ye'll have a bit more." Doris laid a second fresh loaf on the countertop, took two bottles from her apron pockets. "They's from last years bakeapples, a wunerful batch. 'Twas."

When blond curls appeared near the bottom of the hall doorframe, Rose sucked in her breath and whispered, "Oh me Jesus." When Thomas's face appeared, she looked at Doris and said, "I don't know what we gone and done, maid. I don't know what we gone and done."

Rose knelt down on one knee, and said, "Come here, me son." Over her shoulder to Doris, "He's right like a doll, he is." Thomas walked across the kitchen towards Rose as though he recognized her. She compressed the boy into her ample folds, threatened to rob his air. Into his ear she said, "I's yer nanny, b'y, and don't let no one tell ye nothin' different." She sniffed.

"What's all this?" Junior Lynch called in from the porch. "She now, not back for more than an hour, already havin' a time." He came into the kitchen, lifted the lid on the stove, inhaled deeply and rubbed his belly. Then he said to the children, "B'ys, come feel in me coat pockets, see what I got for ye."

When the boys reached in and retrieved black licorice pipes, Junior said, "Pop them in yer gobs, fellars, I's goin' to learn ye how to smoke 'em."

Thomas began eating his, but Henry followed Junior's example and puffed away on the end. Then Junior lifted Henry up onto his lap, showed him how to wink, and Henry imitated, but closing both eyes at the same time. "Yer a real whippersnapper," Junior said. "A real whippersnapper, me son."

Doris fished a paper bag filled with tea out of her purse and dropped several spoonfuls into a teapot. Rose dusted out bowls from Old Man Crane's cupboard and ladled creamy fish stew, handed the bowls around. Nora sliced up the remainder of her loaf, layered it on a white plate, brought it to the table.

"Andy Mercer, down to the shop, said ye could get what ye needs on credit, Arva," Junior Lynch said between spoonfuls. Then, to Rose, "Jesus, maid, never knew a woman who could turn a fish head into somethin' so lovely. 'Tis some shockin' good."

"How in God's name did I know ye'd be here," Lorna Lynch said from the porch, the bitter wind swirling in around her. When she stepped into the crowded kitchen, she clicked her tongue, plucked up a slice of bread, took a substantial bite. "That's me Junior, for ye. Ar house with a bite of dinner on and an unlocked door is as good a house as any."

When the others had shuffled out, Alf lingered in the porch.

"I knowed ye'd be back, me dear," he said. "Right from the get-go."

"And how did you come to that?" Arva said, looking down. With her slippered foot, she pushed a rag through the puddle of melted snow.

"Easy. Ye sees, there was nar scrap at yer weddin'."

"Scrap?"

"Nar fight."

"And that was a good thing?"

"Not a chance. Here in Island Cove, maid, 'twas the worst kind of thin'. But ye wasn't goin' see meself throwin' the first punch." He tipped his ballcap that read in fuzzy white letters 'Newfie's Makes the Best Lovers,' and stepped out into blinding sunlight.

The night that Arva left, Clive never stayed home feeling sorry for himself. Instead he went to Badcock's pub for a drink. Why fret over things he couldn't change?

But after close to a full bottle, the coy 'what if' sneaked in, and Clive began to dwell on it. And at the same time as the dwelling, he tried to squeeze down through the slender neck of a second whiskey bottle.

"Pull yerself together, Clive," Ernest said at closing. "Can't be that bad."

"'Tis pure shit," Clive mumbled. "Everythin's shit. I's a real muck-up."

"Come on now," Ernest said. "It'll work itself out."

"Nah, she's gone."

"Who? The missus?"

"Yeah, the missus. And she's ain't comin' back."

"Ye never knows, Clive. She might be there when ye gets home."

"Nah, she won't come back. How can she?" Leaning his head back, he opened his mouth, drained his glass, and slammed it down on the bar. "She was never there to begin with, me son."

"Ye thinks? Didn't make enough to keep her? 'Twas the money she was after? B'y, lots of 'em are like that."

"Not the money. Somethin' else."

"If not the money, then what? From what I knows, women are always after the almighty buck. 'Cept for me girls, of course."

"Don't know, me son. Ye got me."

"'Tis got to be somethin'. Women always wants somethin'."

"Yer right 'bout that. But, still. Ye got me."

"Ye'll be all right, Clive. Ye'll meet someone else. Yer a fine catch if I ever knowed one."

"Ye thinks? Ye thinks I's a fine catch?"

Ernest reached his mitten of a hand over and clapped Clive on the shoulder. "Sure, I does," he said. Anything to persuade Clive, his last customer, to finish up.

Clive tilted back his glass again, trying to drain the last drop. The back of his plump tongue delved in and collected what whiskey it could. He laid the glass down softly this time, and then inched his hand across the bar, fingers moving like an exhausted crab on a sandy ocean floor. His hand crawled up onto Ernest's, settled and held fast. Clive gazed at the bartender, and though he could barely see him, he thought Ernest had a glow, a light about his neck and face. Among the fragmented thoughts that cut in and out of his mind was the notion that he wanted to exist closer to that light, and he buckled his ribs into the edge of the bar, his face leaning over.

Ernest snatched his hand back, grabbed the sour dishrag and began to wipe down the spot where he and Clive had touched.

"Yer that drunk, Clive," he said through tight lips, "ye best be gettin' yerself home."

"Annuder drink."

"No, another nothin'."

"Come on wit' ye. Annuder drink. I's dat parched, now. I needs somethin'. Ye can't be sendin' me out like dis."

"Yer more pissed than parched, me son, as I sees it." Ernest continued to wipe at the hand-sized spot. "What ye needs is a good kick in the arse, and ye'll be gettin' it too if ye don't find yer way out of here on yer own."

Clive slid off his stool and landed hard on his right ankle. Pain shot up the outside of his leg, but it was dull, and he never even flinched. Limping up the two stairs to the exit, he turned to Ernest, hoping to see something that would welcome him back, that holy glow, the loop of a come hither hand. But the glow was gone, and the hands were hidden away.

Ernest turned his back on Clive, and dropped two tumblers into a pail of soapy water. As he heard Clive pause on the stairs, Ernest prayed that a drunk in the darkness would never notice the blush heating up the jagged edges of his enormous ears.

Clive tripped on the top stair and crashed to the cement sidewalk, door slamming to behind him. Sharp fragments of gravel and sand cut into the heels of his hands, through his pant legs into his knees. He didn't feel a thing. Laughter charged through the air, and Clive came up swinging blindly. His fist met with nothing, and the force of his own thrust caught him off-balance. He was thrown to the sidewalk again.

With his head resting on the icy cement, he noticed the weighty smell of deep fat that had sunk down to the ground. Up and at 'em, he stumbled to a fish and chips shop, dug deep into his pockets and brought out every coin. He normally never spent his change, preferred to jingle it, let others know he was a man with money. But food had to come first, and he was hungrier now than he had ever been as a child.

Back to the alley besides Badcock's, he nestled down with his hot paper bag. Tearing it open, he gulped the steam as it billowed up into the chilly air. He ate every scrap of golden cod, fried potato wedges, and burnt bits of batter that had been recycled through the fat a dozen or so times. He licked the grease and salt from the bag, his nose and cheeks soon glistening with an oily shine.

"I'll go up and see Joey tomorrow," he muttered aloud to make certain he would hear it. "I got all kinds of background. All kinds. He'll take me on. Now, then."

His belly full, sleep thundered towards him like a bullet. He curled into a tight ball on his side, his nose between his knees, and in one lonesome blink, he dropped down into a dreamless slumber. A calico tabby that had been watching the familiar man and waiting from inside a cardboard box cautiously crept over and licked his face and fingers. Then, feeling heat seeping out from under a lifted arm, the cat turned round and round and round until it lay down and purred beside him.

It was the first day of summer when Arva put her spices on a shelf in Old Man Crane's cupboards.

Later that afternoon, she rummaged through the trunk until her hand found something sentimental, looped with threads, riddled with intentional holes. From the deepest crevice, she retrieved a crocheted table runner, its form lost from a decade of being rolled, the weave flaccid, design collapsed.

"A good soak in sugar water will harden this right up," she spoke aloud to herself, using the recent but comforting habit to lend noise whenever there was silence.

On the edge of the woodstove, she placed a sturdy saucepan,

and half-filled it with water from Peggy Crane's jug. Two cupfuls of sugar melted as the water warmed, her pinky dipped in to check the temperature, tepid liquid licked away. Arva had forgotten how to stiffen a doily, did she need to bring the syrup to a boil? Soak the table runner when the pot was warm? Let the syrup cool first? She decided to toss the runner into the sweetened water, stir it until all threads were coated, and cross her fingers.

Arva turned to collect the runner, arm reaching, and her flexed elbow caught the handle of the pot. A quick back-turn, she had meant to grab the handle and with a swift shove, push it further back on the stove. But instead the pot was knocked clean, as if by its own doing. Warm syrup sloshed out, sticking onto the side of the stove, water evaporating, sugar instantly burning. Bottom-side-up onto the floor near the back wall, warm tacky splatter from the heavy pot mottled the spoon rests, dove out at her bare feet.

Arva reached at once for a wet cloth, fell to her knees to swipe the floor, but the syrup rapidly disappeared, lured downwards, finding its way through cracks and crevices in the linoleum, around the baseboards, dripping down into the cellar of the house.

At the back of the kitchen closet, she located the narrow set of raw wooden stairs descended into a damp darkness. The walls were dappled with hooks that held dusty frying pans she had never used, an orange pot with bottom blackened, a hanging clump of some dried herb bundled round the base with gray wool. In the shadowy corners, long-legged spiders had crafted lacey homes, their fat bodies hunched over round pearly eggs. Smells of honest earth and age rose up from the basement on cool air that seemed burdened with moistness. Arva could hear the rhythmic dripping of the syrup from the low ceiling onto a packed dirt floor.

Holding onto the walls, she bent at the waist and made her way down the rickety stairs. Arva thought that Old Man Crane, with his considerable height, would have had to accordion himself in order to make his way. When she reached the underground room, Arva could barely stand tall, wooden joists catching at her short hair. Old Man Crane must have been in a continued state of hunching when he spent his hours hidden away down here, engaged in illicit but well-loved activities.

A sliver of light seeped in through a muddied rectangular window near the back of the cellar, so Arva was only blinded by darkness until her eyes adjusted. The window reminded Arva of the story Alf had told during the lunch after Old Man Crane's funeral. Alf, brave with a teenaged truant spirit, had pressed his face against the glass, with high aspirations of discovering the secrets of moonshine production.

There were shelves nailed into the walls and several tables knocked together with slabs of wood and long log legs. Every available surface was covered with piles, containers, cardboard boxes reddened with mold, once wilted under the humidity, now hardened against the cold. Rusty nuts and bolts, a miniature engine in pieces, a cracked face watch, an old corroded clock with arms long gone, a green tartan necktie already set for wearing, rows of dark brown glass bottles with finger-sized handles, a small pile of books, pages fusty, dog-eared, rippled. These were Old Man Crane's collections, his treasures, and being so near to them made Arva's tear ducts constrict and her throat catch.

She located the dripping, the syrup soaking through the floorboards, fat drops collecting dust, sliding off the main support beam, dribbling down to the dirt and leaving a rich stain. Hordes of energized black ants had already identified the novel sugar source and were calling out for reinforcements. When Arva stepped up to the edge of the stain, the dripping stopped, the valve exhausted.

With a nearby spade, she struck at the earth under the ants, then tried to dig away at the rock-solid soil, but the mass climbed onto the shovel, skipped up the handle and won urgent pinching battles on her hands and wrists. Arva searched the room for a solution. She reached for a wooden barrel, cut down to size, a twisted rope handle knotted on either side. It was filled halfway up with sea-sand the colour of a pigeon's feather. Arva grasped the handles, the coiled rotten rope making her palms itch, and she dragged the barrel to the ant-infested mound.

As she poured the sand, drowning the ants in escapable grains, and sealing in the syrupy mess, a shudder traveled up through the soles of her feet, into her spine, and tickled the back of her thin neck. Arva glanced behind her into the empty cellar.

A peculiar sweet taste delighted her tongue, she would almost guess molasses, but that was impossible. "Sugar must be floating in the air down here," she said. Her words falling flat, not offering the echo she expected.

Then, something caught her eye, a flicker of paper, a tight roll. Anticipation washed through her, and she suddenly felt dizzy, faint. The bucket laid flat, she identified more papers, more tight rolls, each one secured with layered rounds of hardened catgut. She watched her hand as it reached into the sea sand. Her eyes locked on as her closed fist withdrew one of the spools. It felt substantial then in her open palm. She scooped up others. The weight was significant. And there were more – dozens upon dozens of firmly bound, thoroughly sodden, but still undoubtedly useable, twenty-dollar bills.

She heard him clearly, as though he had instructed her only moments before.

"Don't let Alice come in here, toss everything out," Old Man Crane had said to Arva days before he died. "Give me yer word on that. Ye go through it with a fine-toothed comb and take whatever ye needs or wants or whatever ye can put to use."

After bundling the rolls into her apron, she carried them upstairs and placed them neatly in the darkest corner of a cupboard.

Arva held the last of Junior Lynch's snared rabbits by the hind legs as Doris worked away the fur, peeling it back like a strip of stubborn adhesive. She pushed her face into her sleeve as the sickeningly sweet smell of freshly killed meat climbed into her nose, but Doris never hesitated, she plugged on, her broad tongue protruding out over her bottom lip.

With a practiced hand, Doris severed the confused head, leaving it hidden inside a snug turtleneck. Several flicks of her blade and the still-furry paws were lopped off and the belly scored. With a scoop of her hand, Doris tore out the dark ripe innards, lungs and heart, the intestines housing pre-formed buttons. She rinsed the cavity, sliced the meaty parts, and Arva pushed them into sterile pint-sized bottles along with a length of salt pork, pinch of salt.

"Last batch," Doris said as she tipped water from the jug into a wash basin. "This'll do us the winter. God love Junior."

Arva folded the newsprint over the black streaks and strands, encasing the stench and pile of guts in a neat package. Sweat beaded on her upper lip.

"I nearly forgot," Doris said, wiping her cleaned hands in her apron. "This come for ye today. Seems from right 'round the bay by way of St. John's." She handed a letter to Arva. "Not that I was sizin' it up or nothin'."

Arva sat down in the rocker by the woodstove and slid her thumb under a fold in the envelope. She read:

Dear Arva House,

First let me say that I am sorry to have waited such a time to do what was right. The Evening Telegram takes its sweet time making it to the outports, and often a few household share the news. So, as you are likely aware, it can sometimes be quite a spell before the news gets around.

That being said, I recently read the sorry report about your parents. I saw the photo and my heart leapt so far up my throat, I had to clear it to catch a breath. All those years ago, I knowed something bad was going to come of it, and there it was staring me right in the face.

I knowed your parents for several years as I lived down the road from Henry and Ruby. Henry was off in the factories a lot, but he was a fine man whenever he came home. An honest, fine man. He and my Bill would often get together and enjoy the times spent.

Please believe that it gives me no pleasure to write this, but I feel I must. I'm not sure how I can manage this with either bit of tact, so I'll just go ahead and say it. Ruby, your mother, was not a wife like most men would want. Oh, she was a hard worker, the hardest, a fine midwife. She helped with the birth of my first son Gerald, and I couldn't of asked for any more. Not one thing. And she was a fine seamstress. Could sew a lovely dress just by looking at a picture in the catalogue.

There was something in her that was different from the rest of us women living in the bay at the time. This may not mean much to someone living in the city, but for we women, it caused quite a stir. When Henry started working to the factories, she changed. A lot of the men was working up in Ontario during those years, so it was hard and times was lonely. Most of the women enjoyed the company of each other, playing cards or making a quilt, but Ruby never went in for that kind of thing. I'm sorry to say that she got quite the name for herself on the wharves. Most of us would give the boats from Portugal a wide berth for fear of talk, but not Ruby.

When you was born, I recalls you was bald as could be. We was all praying you'd grow some fine red curls, but your black hair started coming and didn't stop. Like someone had turned on a tap. There was no mistaking it. We all knew where you come from, but no one ever spoke a word about it.

That said, still Henry loved you like his own. He stopped with the factories and got a local job culling fish. When you was old enough, he'd carry you all over the streets on his shoulders like you was a prize or something. And Ruby cleaned up her act. I don't believe she set foot on the wharves after the day you came along, in fact she never came out around much at all.

What happened after that was surely an accident. There was never any question about it. Not even from Elias Dalton – he was the one who checked into those sorts of things, not that they happened much, mind you, but you never knows. Your father, Henry that is, liked the drink. And the stuff going round at the time would burn a hole right down through you, not that I ever tasted it, mind you, a whiff of it was enough. But never mind that. Henry liked a drop, and on more than one occasion he might have had a drop too much. I knows 'cause he fell fast asleep on my kitchen table once and I had to get Frank Dalton, Elias' son, to carry him down the lane. Once I even remembers him getting into a fight and some man from across the harbour knocked out a couple of his teeth. He had a streak, but most of the other men did too.

That night he drowned, they was playing cards and enjoying themselves more than they should of been. No doubt about that. Henry wandered down to the water and must of slipped in. That's what the men was saying anyways. There was nothing fishy about it. Nothing at all.

The very notion that Ruby had something to do with it is just about the saddest thing I ever heard. Ruining what's left of the memory of a poor woman who had more than her share of troubles. Everyone did during those years. We was lucky if we had food enough to feed ourselves, let alone be thinking about how to do away with our husbands. I don't know what's going on in the city, but it seems to me, they're always looking for a bit of smut these days, and

what's fit to print is not always the truth. Not even close.
It's my hope this letter finds you and helps to put your mind to rest.
A friend of your mother's,
Elizabeth Mackay

Arva stood, laid the letter on the countertop and said, "I think I'll just go for a short walk."

"But 'tis near midnight, me dear," Doris said.

"A breath of fresh air will clear my mind."

"Please yerself then, maid. 'Tis a lovely night out and the boys is fine."

"It's a lot to bear is all."

"I knows, Arva. But he never gives us more than we can handle."

"Is that what you think?"

"I does." Doris nodded, taking a swift glance at Alek's gray sneakers. "I honestly does."

Outdoors was painfully serene, and Arva slipped into the darkness without causing a ripple. The winter sky appeared pregnant, ready to burst, and everything under it was bathed in the glorious hue of pink newborn skin. Near a back corner of the shed, a wood-horse slept underneath a voluptuous white mound and naked wild lilac branches were coated in ice, silvery fingers pointing the way. A chill pressed in around Arva, persuading her to clench up, keep herself together.

As she crunched down the laneway, snow began to drift calmly to the ground, coating the yard in a crisp clean sheet. "'Tis a good sign," she remembered Old Man Crane saying. "Startin' fresh."

When she came to the bottom of the lane, she saw a set of footprints in the snow leading up the trail along the cliff. She followed, treading into each print, her boot marks virtually undetectable.

Pepper Reid was perched on his rock, tufts of silver licking out from underneath his cable knit hat, his hollow cheeks ruddy from the cold. She moved in next to him, hunched over and drew her arms sharply across her chest, mittened hands tucked inwards.

Before them, the sparkling ocean was unusually calm.

"Everyone's got 'em," Pepper said suddenly. Arva had never heard him speak before and his voice was a jolt in the darkness.

"Sorry?" she said.

"Mem'ries, maid. Followin' ye 'round like a pack of hungry ol' dogs." He patted his silver streaks, his shiny reminders of the war. "Wherever ye goes, they's right there, starin' ye down, droolin'."

"Yes. Well." She paused. "Yes."

Pepper wiped his nose with a stiff glove and nodded. "Some days'll never leave ye, maid," he said. "But I thinks dead men shouldn't press on."

"Press on?" Arva asked.

"Keep movin', maid," he said.

"I don't understand."

"When their time here comes to a halt," he replied. "And they stops then, for the most part. They don't move 'round ye no more. That's simple enough. But, sure as I be's sittin' here, they keeps movin' through ye. And there's the part that gives the trouble."

Gazing out over the glassy sea, Arva thought of her father's bare back, insanely pale in the moonlight, her mother grasping him by the armpits, and with goliath strength, lugging him to the water. She remembered the tide rollicking in, binding the body with its demanding tentacles, coursing into every crevice, shamelessly claiming the abandoned for its own. Her mother quietly washed his heels. Then she had lifted her head, eyes pure pupil, and said, "There. Not a grass stain in sight."

Arva glanced over at Pepper Reid, his eyelashes glistening like icy ferns on a winter window.

"Yes," she said. "They shouldn't. Press on, that is."

Steam billowed out from his nose and mouth. "I knows ye knows what I means, me dear," he said. He shook his head, puffed air like a horse trying to drive off hornets during summer. "Truth be told, maid, there's only the odd bird out there who don't."

In the distance Arva heard the hasty crack of an axe as it ate into wood. Then came the split, the promise of warmth. Who could be chopping logs at this hour? A pair of busy, busy hands.